Apocalypse Grit

An Apocalyptic LitRPG series

By

Tao Wong & Craig Hamilton

Copyright

This is a work of fiction. Names, characters, businesses, places, events, and incidents are either the products of the author's imagination or used in a fictitious manner. Any resemblance to actual persons, living or dead, or actual events is purely coincidental.

No part of this publication may be reproduced, distributed, or transmitted in any form or by any means, including photocopying, recording, or other electronic or mechanical methods, without the prior written permission of the publisher, except in the case of brief quotations embodied in critical reviews and certain other non-commercial uses permitted by copyright law.

Apocalypse Grit

Published by Starlit Publishing
PO Box 30035
High Park PO
Toronto, ON
M6P 3K0
Canada

www.starlitpublishing.com

Ebook ISBN: 9781778551451
Paperback ISBN: 9781778551444
Hardcover ISBN: 9781778551468

Books in the System Apocalypse Universe

Main Storyline

Life in the North

Redeemer of the Dead

The Cost of Survival

Cities in Chains

Coast on Fire

World Unbound

Stars Awoken

Rebel Star

Stars Asunder

Broken Council

Forbidden Zone

System Finale

System Apocalypse – Relentless

A Fist Full of Credits

Dungeon World Drifters

Apocalypse Grit

System Apocalypse: Australia

Town Under

Flat Out

Bloody Oath

Anthologies & Shorts

System Apocalypse Short Story Anthology Volume 1

System Apocalypse Short Story Anthology Volume 2

Valentines in an Apocalypse

A New Script

Daily Jobs, Coffee and an Awfully Big Adventure

Adventures in Clothing

Questing for Titles

Blue Screens of Death

My Grandmother's Tea Club

The Great Black Sea

Growing Up – Apocalypse Style

A Game of Koopash (Newsletter exclusive)

Lana's story (Newsletter exclusive)

Debts and Dances (Newsletter exclusive)

A Tense Meeting (Newsletter exclusive)

Comic Series

The System Apocalypse Comics (7 Issues)

Table of Contents

What Happened Before

Nearly two years ago, the System arrived on Earth, bringing with it the glowing blue boxes of notifications and status screens that heralded the new way of life. Classes and Skills offered humans a chance to survive as all electronics failed and society collapsed, but the boons of Levels and magic were no match for the dangers that followed. Spawning monsters and bloodthirsty aliens killed off nearly 90% of humanity within the first year.

Medically discharged Marine and former bail bondsman Hal Mason has come a long way from the gunfight in a meth lab on the first day of the System's arrival on Earth. After Hal was hired by Pharyleri to clear the monster-infested ruins of the Pittsburgh International Airport, the industrious gnomes turned the complex into the world's first starport. The success of being paid for his efforts encouraged Hal to register as a member of the Bounty Hunter Guild, before pitting two other alien groups against each other as they vied for control of downtown Pittsburgh.

Steering clear of the city in the aftermath, Hal ended up searching for bounties in more rural communities, which brought him to the attention of the Truinnar Countess Dayena Baluisa. Fleeing an arranged marriage on her homeworld, the dark elf maneuvered Hal into accepting a contract where he was obligated to serve as her guide and escort on the Dungeon World.

The pair spent several months working bounties before signing on as hired guns for a gnomish expedition to establish a rail line that crossed the new wildlands of the American Midwest. While the train reached Denver successfully, the return journey turned into a bloody skirmish as a string of mercenary groups assaulted the train in pursuit of a priceless artifact smuggled aboard the transport. Hal uncovered the smuggler and used the artifact to draw the attackers away from the train, but ended up possessed by the sentient relic in a battle that left the bounty hunter a hair's breadth from death. Despite Hal's efforts, and the return of the relic to its rightful owner, a significant number of passengers and crew were slain before the train returned to Pittsburgh.

Chapter 1

"Bounty hunting is a complicated profession."

So the adage went, according to a popular pre-System sci-fi show, and "complicated" certainly described my current circumstance. The frigid night wind that descended from the nearby Rocky Mountains tugged at my poncho and sent its edges lashing about as I zipped up the side of a Galactic building in one of suburban Denver's ritziest neighborhoods.

The twelve-story townhome rose sharply above the surrounding multimillion-dollar mansions, the tower's construction of alien metals and reinforced glass overshadowing the comparatively mundane estates in the middle of Highlands Ranch. Amongst the fancy homes of the formerly wealthy, the towering building was a bold statement on the way that the Binary Eclipse Sect lorded their power over the human inhabitants of the city.

I intended to blunt the impact of their object lesson tonight.

It had been several months since the Binary Eclipse Sect betrayed their diplomatic overtures with the Pharyleri clans. They had nearly disrupted the inaugural journey of the only secure transit route across the Midwest of the former United States, a rail line forged by the gnomes. The attempted hijacking of the train left a number of Pharyleri crew and their multi-species passengers dead.

The Sect hadn't been alone in the attack. It turned out there were three separate parties involved and only the lack of any coordination between our foes allowed us to survive the assaults. The second group consisted of Krym'parke who hit the train in the final stretch back to Pittsburgh. The brutal aliens, known for their savage practices of devouring the young of other species, were hired and led by Dayena's cousins to assist in returning the wayward Countess to her family.

The third and final group were the Zabotkermanne, who played the largest role in assaulting the train through a series of raids, but the reptilian mercenaries had hurried to sue for peace with the Pharyleri in the aftermath of the incident. The kobold losses in the course of their offensive had been considerable, largely in part to the efforts of myself and my team, so the lizards were willing to pay a significant sum in order to placate the gnomes and avoid retribution.

If there was anything that drove the Pharyleri trading clans, it was the language of Credits. I wholeheartedly subscribe to that motivation, which is one of the reasons I'd accepted this current bounty assignment and now dangled stories above the carefully architected landscaping below.

I wasn't one to leave Credits on the table once they were offered, but truth be told, I'd have taken the job on the cheap.

None of the gnomes on that train had deserved their untimely fates, but I'd considered at least a couple of those gnomes friends. Or at least as close as I got in this monster-infested world. I shook off the memories of Wrefen's bloody corpse on the floor of the train's workshop and the bodies lying across the aisles of the passenger cars, focusing back on the task at hand.

Normally, the sconces that illuminated the sides of the building from ground level would have been shining up at me, but the low-tech solution of wedging a tightly packed tumbleweed over the uplight kept my ascent in darkness. The simplicity of the "natural" sabotage also avoided triggering any of the building's automatic repair or alarm functions that the System-enhanced structure boasted.

The grappling system mounted to the forearm of my vambrace pulled me steadily upward to the overhanging balcony jutting out from the penthouse suite, the whining of the mechanism barely audible to my Keen

Senses over the biting wind that swirled around the building. The perpetual chill that permeated the city was courtesy of the dragon which had taken up residence in the Rockies to the west. Not nearly far enough away for comfort, in my and the city residents' opinion.

Not that the dragon was asking.

The reel finished its ascent, and I hung by one arm just under the lip of the glossy flooring of the underside of the balcony. After a short listen for any sign that the terrace above was occupied, I reached with my free hand and gripped one of the balusters that lined the railing above. Once I had a firm hold, I detached the grapple's fastening before pulling myself over the balcony's edge in a rapid burst of motion.

I landed lightly on my feet and slipped between several lounge chairs as I crossed to the wall beside the door that led into the penthouse suite. A palm-sized device materialized in my hand as I pulled the System tech from my Inventory and placed it over the door's lockplate. The Pharyleri lockcracker was designed to open mechanical and magical doors, and the device announced its success with a dim green light blinking a moment later.

The penthouse door slid open silently and a wave of heat swept out from the darkened room beyond the gaping portal. The humidity flowing through the door carried a pungent amphibian scent that contrasted sharply with the crisp cleanliness of the Denver chill outside. I braced for the changed environment and ducked through the opening, leading the way with a pistol drawn from my shoulder harness and a knife to replace the lockcracker.

Instead of the beam pistols I usually kept in the holsters of my shoulder rig, I'd substituted projectiles for this job. The dependable damage of energy rays and the rechargeable nature of their Mana batteries was great for fighting monsters, but handcrafted rounds fired from enchanted semi-automatic handguns were a more reliable method of combating sentient aliens. The long cylinder affixed to the end of the pistol barrel would also silence any shot completely, something only Hollywood fiction could accomplish before the System's arrival on Earth nearly two years ago.

Expensive upgrades but worth it when my life was on the line.

The balcony door closed behind me with a whisper, and I crouched in place, letting my eyes adjust to the dim space. The room I'd entered was the master bedroom and the humidity was no surprise, given my target. Especially since the majority of the chamber consisted of a pond rather than a traditional bedroom. Light from the open doorway on the far side of the room glinted from the ripples over the surface of the water, where large, lily pad-like alien plants bobbed.

I momentarily dismissed my dagger to summon another device from my Inventory, placing it on the floor just inside the doorway as I activated it. My target had already proven to have a teleportation or portal Skill of some kind. He'd disappeared from the train months prior, so the device I'd just triggered would lock down dimensional movement abilities within the building's penthouse suite.

Resummoning my knife, I stalked around the pool until I circled my way to the door leading further into the penthouse.

My caution paid off when I caught the sound of conversation deeper in the apartment.

"Of course we've scouted their forces, Manager Yimishi. The Pharyleri won't have the troops to hold their City Cores against us, once we've moved the bulk of our forces up from Colorado Springs. Except for those left maintaining the siege on the humans barricaded in the Air Force Academy, the rest of that element should be here within a week."

"Then keep to the schedule. Once we hold Denver, we'll double back to overwhelm the human defenders with our full might. We need to solidify control of the region before the humans stir up more trouble like they are out west. Useless Zarrie. The damn humans are using funds from settlements along the coast to fund the Hakarta's elite Sixty-Third Division and set practically the whole coast on fire. They even somehow managed to kill two of their Master Classers."

I'd paid little mind when I'd heard rumors that a portion of the military still fought the good fight across the west coast to free human settlements from Galactic control. With at least three different factions claiming to represent the true United States government, the effectiveness of any coordinated response would be limited. Still, if the conflict was gaining traction out on the coast, that news would be worth something. The fact that the Galactic groups were bringing in, and losing, Master Class combatants would also be good information to pass along, on top of the fact that the Sect were planning their own offensive against the Pharyleri.

Splurging on a few extra language packs from the Shop was paying off. Though I didn't know much about the manager, the first voice was one I recognized, and I confirmed the presence of my target with a gentle probe from Greater Observation.

Jer'myeh Anura (Sect Assistant to the Regional Manager Level 41) (B)

[Binary Eclipse Sect]

HP: 410/410

MP: 650/650

Status: None

My upgrades to the Class Skill, courtesy of a Shop-purchased Skill Point, now showed the Class tier of my target and any status effects along with any System-registered affiliation. The improved ability didn't detect anyone or anything else in the room beyond, which meant that the second voice came from a communicator of some kind.

If only my other recently purchased points had increased their respective ability as usefully. Seventy and eighty thousand Credits each for two points in On the Hunt and the ability that allowed me to disguise various portions of my Status still couldn't hide that damned Knight Errant of Demarcia title.

"The humans are advancing fast enough to face Master Class combatants?" Jer'myeh asked, fear and uncertainty tinging the alien's voice.

"They sacrificed some of their highest Leveled troops and even a few Hakarta mercenaries in exchange. I'm not overly concerned with a bunch of primitive natives four hundred leagues away. Just take the Pharyleri cores like I've instructed."

"I'll take care of it, boss," Jer'myeh said.

"See that you do, I'll be there soon."

An electronic snap, like an old TV turning off, followed the response and Jer'myeh sighed. "Micromanaging svaratya. I bet he's already on his way here."

Though I didn't have a clue what a svaratya was, the tone indicated it was nothing positive. The audible disparagement of his superior also marked that the communication had ended and it was time for me to finish this bounty.

Swapping my knife for another silenced pistol, I stepped through the open door and into the room with both weapons pointed at my target.

Knowing Jer'myeh's location within the room from my Skills made the ambush almost trivially easy.

The humanoid bullfrog stood with his back to me, and I triggered a flurry of shots before the alien noticed my presence. The first handful of rounds splashed against a rippling shield that sprung into existence between us, and Jer'myeh jumped in surprise at the shimmering blue bubble that had appeared to protect him.

By the time Jer'myeh turned, the projectiles from my shots were already digging deep into the emergency shield. On top of the bonuses bestowed by the hand-crafted nature of the rounds, my own Class Skill, Expose, stacked increasing damage with each subsequent attack on defenses.

The wide-eyed Sect administrator flinched when he saw me attacking from the doorway and squeezed his eyes closed, presumably to activate the escape Skill. The alien flinched and opened his eyes in shock when the Skill failed to activate. I knew the device I'd planted wouldn't last long against repeated attempts, so I needed to wrap this up quickly.

The emergency shield flared out, failing as suddenly as it had appeared. My following shots bored into the center of the flat forehead, between the alien's wide-set eyes, before punching into his brain as my first pistol ran dry.

I launched myself forward and swapped the emptied pistol for my knife once again as I ran my second pistol empty. Jer'myeh dropped like a pithed frog and I pulled up short only a step away from following up with a melee strike, a flurry of notifications announcing my kill with a rush of experience.

Bounty Completed!

You have successfully eliminated the subject of an assassination bounty. This bounty request does not require the return of the subject as proof of death.
10,000 Credits and 10,000 XP Awarded

Title Advancement!

You have successfully cleared enough bounties to be promoted to the Bronze rank within the Galactic Bounty Hunter Guild. You are now eligible to pursue bounties at the Bronze tier and below. Title updated to Galactic Bronze Bounty Hunter.
1,000 Credits and 5,000 XP Awarded

Level Up!

You have reached Level 45 as a Relentless Huntsman. Stat Points automatically distributed. You have 2 Free Attributes and 11 Class Skill Points to distribute.

In this case, the high payouts were due to the target's connections and not the difficulty of the elimination. The payout for advancing my bounty hunter tier came as a surprise, given that I'd had to pay Credits to acquire the initial certification. I wasn't going to complain, not when it pushed me over the edge of my next Level.

Less than a Level left now separating me from the final tier of Class Skills that unlocked at 46. Then onward to grinding out the final stretch to Master Class.

"You better be close to finishing, Hal. Sect elites have arrived, and they appear to be escorting a VIP." Dayena's voice over the party chat provided by her Diplomatic Contacts Class Skill spurred me back into action. No doubt Sect Regional Manager Yimishi had shown up early, just as the late Jer'myeh suspected.

"Target eliminated. Proceeding with extraction," I replied as I hurried to loot what little I could from the alien. Then I withdrew two S-shaped meat hooks from my Inventory and stabbed them into the dead alien's back. Hooking the bottom of each blade under one of the amphibian's shoulder blades, I pulled the body behind me. A trail of blood and other fluids streaked the floor beneath the corpse the entire way through both rooms as I retraced my footsteps back out to the balcony, but I wasn't worried about covering my tracks. The entire point of this job was to send a message, and the Sect would soon have bigger problems than me.

I paused long enough at the door to scoop the dimensional lockdown device back into my Inventory before hauling the dead alien outside. With a grunt, I hefted the dead alien up onto the railing and set the hooks in place as I slid him over the side to hang.

Completely visible from the ground below if anyone looked up.

The sudden jerk as the body came to rest caused the alien's mouth to fall open and its lengthy tongue unfurled out of its wide mouth. I took a moment to nod in satisfaction at the display before climbing up to stand on the railing next to the carcass.

Then I launched myself outward and away as I jumped off the ledge.

Chapter 2

Air rushed past me as I fell, but I was already triggering another piece of my kit via my Neural Link. I stretched my arms out wide as shimmering blue energy appeared between my limbs and along my sides. The modified Elysian Drop Harness, which normally just served as my shoulder rig for holstering an additional pair of pistols, now generated a forcefield that created an instant wingsuit. My freefall turned into a glide as I angled myself away from the building.

Flying a wingsuit was like piloting a plane and required precise control of one's own body in order to manipulate the air currents over the suit's airfoil. With the System's improvements to my attributes over the last forty-five Levels, that precision was trivial.

I soared over the trees that lined the golf course and out above the overgrown rough in the center of the fairway. Flaring out with my arms, I pulled up until it felt like I was almost standing upright. The maneuver transitioned much of my vertical fall into horizontal momentum, which left me flying nearly fifty miles-per-hour through the air.

Cutting out the wingsuit's energy field, I rolled as I hit the ground and popped up to a crouch while skidding a dozen yards through the frost covered grass of the open field. Finally coming to a stop, I checked my backtrail but saw nothing to indicate any immediate pursuit.

To earn a bonus for the already completed bounty, I summoned an imaging device from my Inventory and focused the cell phone-sized device back on the balcony I'd just departed. It only took a moment to snap several holographic still shots of the displayed body hanging from the railing before I stowed the device.

"I'm clear," I signaled to the rest of my team, only now taking the time to swap out the magazines on my pistols for full ones.

"Confirmed. Meet you at the rendezvous," Dayena replied.

For a moment, I debated whether we should circle back to hit the elites and their charge, but the manager lacked an outstanding bounty, and I wasn't going to modify our current plans without sufficient Credits for justification. Instead, I jogged north across the field at the heart of the park. My two elven squadmates would have no trouble sneaking out of their overwatch positions at the front of the building. The Countess was a near prodigy in subterfuge, and that was before the bonuses offered by the Advanced Class she'd taken against the wishes of her parents.

Class Skills and spells only took you so far. After that, training constantly was the key to improving outside of the numbers dictated in an individual's Status Screen. And there were plenty of training opportunities on a Dungeon World. Monsters spawned constantly in the wilds beyond the bastions of settlement Safe Zones.

The lessons on combat and stealth that Dayena drilled into our party in the wilderness helped significantly now that we had returned to civilization, where we accepted missions that required subtlety. That experience was badly needed by the Alliance. With the City Cores of Denver split between the two factions, more than half the area of the city held by the Binary Eclipse Sect stood in an uneasy standoff with the Pharyleri Steamspanner Clan.

With any luck, the bounty I just finished would be the first step in reducing the Sect's control of the city.

Hurrying across Lone Tree Parkway, I left the empty street behind as I slipped between a row of expensive houses. The homes appeared mostly abandoned. With only those who toadied up to the Sect really wanting to be anywhere near their territory, the Sect's backyard neighborhood had seen better days.

I only tripped a single alarm on my way through the district. A motion-activated light triggered as I hopped a fence and an automated turret immediately fired an energy ray. The simplistic tracking of the cheap defense unit was designed for a much slower monster, and I dodged several shots that left burnt streaks of grass behind. One final shot trailed over my shoulder as I leapt the next dividing barrier, and the whining turret cut out like a dog that had reached the edge of its invisible perimeter.

I was already two more yards away before the backdoor of the alerted house creaked open. The owner had little chance of spotting me now that I was well beyond the reach of the floodlight's illumination. The angry old man began shouting at the unseen monsters to stay off his lawn, but I just shook my head and continued onward.

Some things, it seemed, hadn't changed even in the apocalypse.

The rest of my trek remained uneventful, and I soon reached the mostly empty shopping center near the intersection of 470 and 25. The plaza showed little signs of life in the middle of the night, besides a former Starbucks renovated by a group of System-enhanced baristas. The new proprietors hadn't even bothered taking down the iconic sign. The coffee shop was brightly lit, despite the midnight hour, and stood out from the other frost-covered buildings that surrounded the plaza.

The white layer coating the structures here had nothing on the frozen northern outskirts of Commerce City, where the buildings remained solidly encased in ice. Even with the months that had passed since my last visit to the city, the ice there showed no signs of abating. At this point, it seemed that even if some high-Leveled party took out the dragon in the Rockies, its impact on the local climate would likely be permanent. Nobody local wanted to mess with the creature though, certainly not after the last time a group of Adventurers pissed off the massive monster.

The frost-covered structures around me showed the results of the dragon's rage but I didn't mind the cold permeating the area. Something about my Ice Affinity, low ranked as it may be, allowed me to shrug off the effects of the dangerously low temperatures when combined with the natural resilience offered by my high Constitution attribute.

"You made it," Dayena said, stepping out from the shadows surrounding one of many abandoned businesses along Park Meadows Drive. I wasn't surprised that she'd beaten me to the rally point with the roundabout path I'd taken, but I still scanned her Status out of habit.

Countess Dayena Baluisa (Agent Provocateur Level 45) (A)
Sultana of the Whispering Strings, Mistress of Shadows
HP: 1460/1460
MP: 1520/1520
Status: Active Camouflage, Shadow Shroud

A little sense of satisfaction shot through me as I picked up more than just empty question marks from my primary employer's status. The change indicated that my abilities were advancing to the point that, hopefully, I'd be less outclassed by the enemies I made from being her contracted guide and bodyguard.

The dark elf's onyx-skinned face stood out in the moonlight that shone down on the dilapidated suburban business strip. Her silvery-white hair glinted on top of her head, and the lengthy strands transitioned into tightly wound braids of blue and red. Though the Countess normally kept her hair down, those braids were pulled back into a bun to keep it out of the way in the course of this evening's conflicts. That promised violence had also encouraged the Countess to trade her typical black armored suit for one more adaptable to the range of environments in the city. Despite the active camouflage of the Truinnar's armored jumpsuit attempting to shunt the eye away as it shifted between shades of white, gray, and pale blue in a cross between arctic and urban patterns, I could recognize the lithe dark elf as a stunning and dangerous figure.

While I could read the Truinnar's status, the same couldn't be said of her heirloom luitsalin. The Relic resting behind the dark elf's shoulder was a violin-like instrument that barely registered to Greater Observation or my mundane senses. On top of boosting Dayena's stealth abilities, the luitsalin somehow had the unique capability to fade from memory when not in view and it slipped from my mind as our final party member approached.

A second female form materialized out of the gloom, though the pale-skinned Movana's face blended more seamlessly with her camouflage outfit and her standout feature was the combat rifle cradled in her arms. "Can we get out of here now or at least get some hot coffee? This place is freezing."

Lyrra Valjyn (Combat Medicae Level 49) (B)

HP: 820/820

MP: 860/860

Status: Active Camouflage

Despite the historical enmity between the Truinnar and Movana, including a bit of initial tension after I'd rescued Lyrra from an Alpha monster den, the pair now seemed to get along like a house on fire. The medic had proved herself a reliable member of our party in the intervening months, with her Class providing a solid mix of active combat healing and marksmanship for ranged fire support.

Only a few wisps of Lyrra's golden hair slipped out from beneath the brow of her combat helmet but their healthy sheen glowed in the light reflecting from the targeting optics built into the armor's visor. It felt good to see that, since her hair now was far fuller and healthier than the scraggly, matted clumps I'd cut free from the webs that imprisoned her on our first meeting.

I'd made it clear to Lyrra that she didn't owe me for the rescue as I'd have cut just about anyone short of a Krym'parke free from those webs. Still, I appreciated the loyalty she showed by sticking around. The Credits that Dayena offered as employment probably didn't hurt either.

I nodded in response to Lyrra's question. "A cup of coffee sounds like a nice way to finish off the night."

I pulled open the door to the coffee shop and held it for the ladies. The baristas inside focused intently on my more exotic squadmates when the elves entered. It only took a moment before the woman behind the counter began blushing and breathing heavily as Dayena launched into her complicated order that included extra cream, extra flavor, and an added shot of espresso.

When Dayena finished her order, the barista kept glancing over at the Truinnar even while Lyrra ordered.

"Iced cold brew. Black," I repeated myself for the second time. I shared a look with Lyrra and rolled my eyes at the effect of the dark elf's Charisma, but she was too busy looking disgusted at the fact that I was drinking iced coffee in the middle of winter.

Fortunately, the other barista seemed less affected and managed to pull together our order. After we finally received our drinks, I took a long pull of the chilled beverage. Good coffee was hard to find after the apocalypse, though Galactic substitutes like kipatchya weren't uncommon. The bold and rich flavor boosted my alertness and provided a minor buff to my Mana regeneration as the drink filled my stomach.

Cups in hand, we filed out of the shop, and stood enjoying our drinks for a few minutes in the silence of the night.

"Back to base?" Lyrra asked, pitching her empty cup in a wastebin outside the shop.

Dayena agreed, wheeling out her hoverbike from where she'd stashed it behind the building. She climbed on and offered Lyrra a hand, while I summoned my Outrider and activated its anti-grav conversion. My refurbished ride bore no signs of the damage that left it almost inoperable after the conflict with the Zabotkermanne. A few thousand Credits in repairs and now I was hovering with a gentle hum a couple feet above the icy surface of the streets. A nice way to ignore any concerns over traction.

We were still well behind Sect lines to the south of the city, which meant that we had two options for our return to friendly territory. The first choice was to slip through the Binary Eclipse-held districts, much in the same way that we'd infiltrated the area on our approach. Conversely, we could swing wide around the city to the east, which would take longer but reduced the chances of encountering any Sect forces to almost nothing. I sent across the waypoints for both routes.

"Let's take the scenic route. Maybe we'll find a few monsters once we're outside the Safe Zone," Lyrra said, looking over Dayena's shoulder at the nav display on the Truinnar's bike.

The dark elf nodded and I throttled up, leading the way out of the parking lot and onto the highway. We followed the empty lanes of 470 east until the former toll road left the Sect territories and we left the Safe Zone. Monsters appeared on my minimap at distant intervals, but it wasn't until we turned north that I found foes worthy of a stop.

I drifted my bike to the berm and eased to the ground alongside the road just beyond the curving highway, then sent the results of my scan over to the elves, who pulled up beside me.

Jackalope (Level 43)
_HP: 622/622_
_MP: 597/597_

A small herd, consisting of a half dozen rabbit-bodied creatures that were each the size of a Shetland pony, meandered through the tall grasses and overgrowth rising up from the snowy fields. The razor-sharp antelope horns that sprouted from the heads of each monster flashed in the moonlight.

Dayena reviewed the scan and nodded before providing her thoughts through party chat. _"A bit low Leveled, but they should still give a bit of experience and some crafting materials if we keep the kills clean."_

"Sounds good," I agreed.

After dismounting from my bike and stowing the vehicle in my Inventory, I drew a pair of beam pistols. Once the elves were also prepared, we opened up on the herd simultaneously. We dropped two monsters between the initial volley and the follow-up shots, before the monsters figured out they were under fire and charged in our direction. Two more creatures fell as they sprinted across the field and the final pair went down just before they reached us.

"A bigger herd would have made more of a challenge," Lyrra said as we looted the slain monsters.

"Also higher Levels or an Alpha," Dayena commented.

I shook my head. _"I'm not going to complain."_

We finished up and got back on the road, though it took longer to trudge out into the field and loot the carcasses there than it had to actually slay the monsters. We stopped twice more along the way for monster shoots, though none of the creatures proved a significant threat. Once we reached Interstate 70, we turned west and followed the highway as it arched to the north of the city. While we could have followed Colfax Avenue, the Sect still held the areas around City Park, so we avoided that direct route into downtown.

The monster population decreased, and the temperatures dropped further as we approached the edges of Commerce City. My companions grumbled about the cold, but the temperature didn't bother me much. Then again, I was the one drinking iced coffee in winter. I blamed it on my Ice Affinity.

Still, if the assassination tonight was any indication, things in Denver would soon be heating up.

Chapter 3

After passing through the eerie frozen district on the north side of Denver, it didn't take long to head south and reach the edges of the Pharyleri-held section of the city. A lightly defended checkpoint, manned by gnomish guards, cleared us through without issue after a quick scan. The gnomes were clad in the bronze-plated, steampunk-style power armor of the Steamspanner Clan, and the heavy armor reminded me that I needed to start considering upgrades of my own.

The hazy blue energy of a settlement shield rippled in the sky overhead, something the Sect hadn't bothered with in the larger area they controlled. The local Denverites seemed pretty happy with the new precaution though, since it indicated that the Pharyleri weren't just writing off the human population or purely looking to take advantage of them.

The area around Union Station also showed signs of the gnome's military buildup. A wall now surrounded the expanded complex that served as the Alliance headquarters, in addition to housing one of the two Pharyleri-held City Cores. Serving at the north gate for the base were a few more Steamspanner-armored guards reinforced by a squad of normal troops in the olive uniforms of the Pistongrinder Clan. The gate guards performed another, more thorough, check on our party and verified us against an access list before they opened the gate.

The fact that the gnomes had enough troops to guard their perimeter, gates, and various checkpoints throughout the city showed the rapid growth in combat forces of the combined clans over the last few months. Despite that increase, I wanted to warn Ismyna of the Sect's own buildup and the plans that I'd overheard during my completion of the bounty.

As the doors slid open, the sergeant in charge stepped over to me. "Adventurer Mason, the brass is requesting that you visit the command center, at your earliest convenience."

I thanked the gnome and confirmed I would head there first. As with any military organization, "earliest convenience" really meant right damned now.

"I'll go check in," I told my companions as we parked outside Union Station, then collapsed my bike into the nano garage module that fit into my Inventory.

"It's early, but they should be serving breakfast now," Lyrra said, glancing at Dayena.

The dark elf nodded. "We will be in the Great Hall cafeteria when you are finished."

The renovations to the historic building included replacing the wooden double doors with reinforced sliding portals that retracted into the walls on either side when we approached. A closed-off antechamber with the far end sealed like an airlock served as an additional checkpoint. The lack of windows combined with the murder holes in the ceiling to lend an ominous air to the small room, but the second set of doors opened within moments after the exterior entry shut behind us.

Inside the building proper, the Great Hall opened up into a three-story chamber that was lit from chandeliers that hung from the ceiling and sconces that lined the walls. Half the room was an open lounge, where small clusters of comfortable chairs provided space for small gatherings, while the remainder was dedicated to long tables that served as a mess hall for the Pharyleri forces. The Terminal Bar still served as a local watering hole for after-hours intoxication, but all the gift shops and a couple of the smaller dining options had been repurposed into kitchen spaces for the cafeteria.

The population heavily favored uniformed gnomes and Galactics serving under the Pharyleri banners. Though there were still a fair number of humans, my native species was in the minority.

The scents of bacon, eggs, and pancakes filled the air, and my companions hurried off toward the nearest breakfast serving stations, leaving me behind without a word as my stomach growled. Unsurprised, I headed in the opposite direction.

The front desk of the Crawford Hotel was still in place, though the doorway sported an upgraded security system and reinforced paneling. The clerks were also accompanied by one of the bronze-armored gnomes, but I recognized one of the attendants from my last visit.

"Morning, Cara. Glad to see you've managed to avoid any Sect troubles here."

One of the women at the desk blinked in surprise before the realization sank in. "Adventurer Mason! I'm very happy to have managed that as well. I thought I recognized your name on the list of incoming personnel to be assigned quarters for today, but it didn't click until just now. We have the rooms assigned to your team prepared if you're ready for them."

"You can send me the assignments, but I'm off to the command center first."

"Done. Please enjoy your stay, sir."

I smiled at the "sir" and thanked the clerks as my Neural Link pinged with the room information. The guard beyond the desk had already scanned me before I passed the desk and opened the door into the hotel, where signs directed me to the location where the Pharyleri had set up their military command center.

Yet more security stood outside the room, but the door slid open when I reached it. Inside, a quiet murmur filled the room as aides moved between communication relays and control consoles. At the center of the room, several gnomes stood on a raised platform with a table displaying a holographic image, but I couldn't get a good look from my position just inside the door. A better view was provided by a flat screen duplicate of the hologram that was projected onto the front wall.

The image showed a map of Denver, broken up into color-coded districts that each aligned with one of the City Cores. There were four districts tinted in red, indicating they were held by the Binary Eclipse Sect, and two shaded in green to show Pharyleri control. A grayed-out section to the north showed what would have been the seventh district, but the defunct area of Commerce City lay uninhabited under the dragon's curse.

Within each of the districts, tiny dots of varying colors shifted slowly along streets or clustered at strategic locations throughout the city as representations of forces both hostile and friendly moving about the city.

"Took your time getting back after completing your bounty, didn't you, Hal?"

Strips of bright green streaked through the gray hair of the older female gnome who turned away from the cluster of officers around the holotable. I hadn't realized the clan elder had made the trip from Pittsburgh at some point, but she'd picked up a Level along the way. No mean feat at the sheer amount of experience required to advance a Master Class.

Nesdyna Pistongrinder, Pharyleri Clan Elder (Logistics Coordinator Level 32) (M)

[Industrial Alliance]

_HP: 4830/4830_

MP: 5320/5320

Status: Portable Energy Shield, Clan Regard, Will of the Elders

"Congratulations on the new Level, Elder Pistongrinder. You're right, we circled around the outside of the city rather than make a straight line back here just in case we ran into any Sect forces on the way."

The older gnome nodded in acknowledgement before a second gnome stepped over beside her, more youthful with bright green hair and clad in the olive Pistongrinder uniform. The younger gnome grinned at me. "And how many hunting stops did you make to grind experience and loot on the way?"

Ismyna Pistongrinder (Stalwart Operator Level 33) (A)

[Industrial Alliance]

HP: 1020/1020

MP: 1400/1400

Status: Company Commander, Caffeine High

I grinned back before pulling the imager from my Inventory and tossing it to her as I approached. Ismyna managed the catch one-handed, while holding onto her mug of kipatchya.

"You got them?" the younger gnome asked, somehow still sounding hopeful while glaring at me for casually throwing the device.

I nodded.

"Great work! You definitely earned your bonus to go with that new Level, but I'm more thrilled that you got the raw images. This will play well in our propaganda campaign."

I held up a hand to stall her excitement. "Don't get too worked up just yet. I overheard Jer'myeh on the comm with his boss before I took him out. The Sect's got a bunch of human armed forces locked down in a siege at the Air Force Academy in Colorado Springs. Within a week, they're planning on shifting everything not needed to Denver in order to engage you."

Ismyna's face fell, and she glanced at her mother. The clan elder frowned. "I hoped to have more time."

"They're worried about taking too long to consolidate their hold on Denver. There's a human force taking back cities on the west coast and managing to kill a couple Master Class combatants in the process."

"We know about the humans and Hakarta fighting with the Zarrie, but nothing about losses on either side," Nesdyna said with a frown.

I shrugged. It had all been news to me, but I hadn't been paying much attention to anything across the larger expanse of the North American continent. Outside of local intel and general political updates at a high level, my interests stayed focused on the continued expansion of the Truinnar territories, as those would be the places to avoid while the Countess was slumming with me.

Ismyna considered her mother for a moment and then turned back to me. "Could you take out a Master Class?"

I shook my head. "Not by myself unless they just stood there and let me shoot them. Do you have a way to counter if the Sect brings in one?"

A stern expression crossed the gnome's face as she considered my question without answering, but the way her eyes darted to the non-combat Master Class standing beside her was an answer of its own.

I held up a hand and then pointed to the floating hologram of the city. "I'm not asking for details. I just want to know that you have a plan before you're fully committed to this fight with the Sect. War is an ugly business. You got a taste of that ugliness on the train, with the losses on the way back to Pittsburgh, but an urban conflict with Master Class opponents will be on an entirely different scale."

"I know," Ismyna replied. Her voice was quiet but confident.

"Alright then, just making sure. I'll be here as long as the Credits are."

I grinned with that last line and the gnome smacked my shoulder in mock offense, then she held up the imager that I'd thrown to her. "You'll get your Credits."

Smiling, I nodded to the map. "That's an impressive display table. Could I take a look at the map?"

Ismyna looked to the clan elder, but Nesdyna just beckoned for me to join them. Nesdyna began pointing out the primary locations when I reached the holotable, starting with a lake on the west side of the city.

"The Steamspanner Clan, which means the Industrial Alliance as a whole, controls the northern and central districts from the City Cores here and at the Central Library.

"The Lakewood district is the primary Binary Eclipse stronghold for the region. They purchased that tiny island in the middle of Kountze Lake, stuck a pre-manufactured tower on it, and have turned the place into a fortress. It holds the western City Core and the bulk of their elite forces.

"Southwest is the Core on the grounds of a university that closed down before the System arrived. Southeast is Tech Center, where the Sect has turned many of the office buildings into manufacturing and production locations. Finally, the last Sect Core is at the Wings Over the Rockies Museum, where they're using the old hangars to house skimmers and other vehicles their forces use to raid unaffiliated settlements surrounding the city."

"But they aren't hitting your holdings or suppliers?"

Nesdyna shook her head. "They did, until we built up our defenses and security forces. Now they leave our places alone in favor of easier prey."

"That could be an opportunity to whittle down their forces, if you can hit their raiding parties when they're exposed. It could be a way to make friends with those isolated settlements too."

The pair of gnomes looked thoughtful as they considered my ideas.

"Was there anything else you needed, since you asked for me to check in?"

"Don't go far. We've got drones out, and surveillance coverage over most of the city now, so we'll soon see the Sect response to their administrator's death. If they don't make any surprise moves, we'll initiate our offensive in a couple days when the next trainload of Alliance troops arrives from Pittsburgh."

"We might do a little more hunting but we'll be around. Before I go though, do you have a trade center for Adventurers selling off their loot and monster carcasses?"

"We do." Ismyna nodded and sent me a waypoint that added directions to the Alliance quartermaster's office.

"Thanks. I've got a haul to unload, then I'm heading for breakfast and sleep. Let me know if you have any missions for my team. We're always up for more Credits."

Ismyna rolled her eyes and waved me away before turning back to the central holographic map.

I turned for the door and stopped mid-stride as I locked eyes with a grizzled Pharyleri who'd been just beyond Nesdyna. Half of the gnome's skull flashed with cybernetics that had replaced one side of his face, including an eye that glowed crimson.

Drynac Blockwarder, Stoic Guardian (Executive Protection Specialist Level 12) (M)

[Industrial Alliance]

HP: 3430/3430

MP: 3380/3380

Status: Fade into the Background, Nick of Time, Hale and Hearty

That answered another part of the question about whether the Pharyleri could deal with Master Class combatants. The gnomes had at least one Master Class holding the line on defense here.

The good eye of the clan elder's bodyguard narrowed as I analyzed him and I got the sense that I shouldn't have even noticed his presence with those status effects in place. I nodded respectfully to the gnome, who said nothing in response, before continuing on my way.

I retraced my steps out of the command center and followed Ismyna's directions to an office adjacent to an exterior wall. The room had a narrow accessway in front of a counter set into a reinforced divider that separated the rest of the chamber from the secured storage space in the rear of the room. Through the barred window above the counter, I could see the shelves loaded with weapons, armor, and various pieces of gear. I also saw a sealed roll-up door in the exterior wall that looked like it led out to a loading dock.

"What do you want?"

A gnome scowled at me through the window, a shining bald spot reflecting the ceiling lights in the middle of a ring of jet-black hair.

Grylk Copperbit (Quartermaster Level 47) (B)

[Industrial Alliance]

HP: 470/470

MP: 510/510

"I was told that I could sell off monster carcasses here."

"This is an Alliance only office. Who told you that you could come here?"

The surly gnome's sneer disappeared when I mentioned Ismyna and he hurried to work through analyzing the Jackalope carcasses. Despite his attempt to turn on the charm, Grylk still tried to haggle from a low enough value that I questioned whether it had been worth it to even use my connections here to sell the goods. I eventually negotiated a decent sum of Credits in exchange, but not as much as I'd hoped.

Leaving the quartermaster's office behind, I headed back to the chow hall. Though I spotted my teammates seated at one of the long tables, my growling stomach demanded that I continue in favor of grabbing a tray, utensils, and a couple plates of food from one of the serving areas. Bacon, sausage links, and eggs filled one plate, while a stack of pancakes covered in butter and syrup rose six-high on the other. I added a scoop from a chafing dish half full of a Galactic take on hash browns, twisted into thick spirals like cavatappi noodles with the potatoes recognizable from the partial strips of skins that remained. To the mostly full tray, I added a glass of juice, which looked like OJ but probably was a beverage made from a local mutated fruit, and a cup of coffee. Hot this time.

With the stacked tray in hand, I finally found a seat next to my teammates, though their trays were already empty. "You two didn't waste any time."

"You didn't expect us to sit here and just smell the food, did you?" Lyrra rolled her eyes.

I looked at Dayena. "You know, I think your snark is rubbing off on her."

The dark elf glared at me as I dug into my breakfast. "What did Ismyna want?"

Between bites, I updated the elves on the conversation in the command center before sending them their shares of the Credits from my sale of the carcasses. They were silent as I finished, digesting the information while I scarfed down my breakfast.

"What does that mean for us?" Dayena asked as I mopped up a bit more syrup with the last of my pancakes.

I glanced around but nobody was sitting nearby. Enough noise from numerous conversations and the general clatter of silverware filled the Great Hall that I wasn't worried about being overheard. "Stay close, stay out of trouble, and be ready for the next job. It sounded like they're just waiting for the next train to arrive."

Dayena's eyebrow arched as she looked at me. "You think you can stay out of trouble?"

"Hey, it's me."

"Yes, Knight Errant of Demarcia, that is my point."

I took on a wounded expression. "Don't blame me for that. I didn't see you arguing with that Knight Commander at the time."

"Nobody argues with Master Classers," Lyrra chimed in.

"Thank you. That was my point," I said.

"Guess you will just have to live up to those high aspirations of chivalry," Dayena said, blinking innocently as Lyrra laughed.

I shook my head and sent the pair over the room assignments that the clerk had passed on to me earlier. "I'm too tired to put up with this. I haven't slept since we got back into Denver yesterday morning. I'm going to get some shut eye. Let me know if you decide to cause any more problems."

I left the table and the giggling elves, depositing my tray at the cleaning station, which whisked the evidence of my meal away into the service areas behind the kitchens. Then I headed for the waypoint saved as my own room in the hotel-turned-headquarters-and-barracks.

When I reached the room on the second floor, the door unlocked at my touch and I went inside to find a small suite. Directly inside the entrance was a small lounge with a couch, writing desk, and office chair, beyond which was the bedroom with a king-sized bed. A well-appointed bathroom with both a tub and shower finished off the space.

I stripped down and took full advantage of the shower to get clean, then dried off and flopped onto the bed to review the gains in my status after my latest bounty completion.

Advancing my rating to "Galactic Bronze" with the Bounty Hunter guild meant that I'd see a slight bump in the Credits earned for each successful bounty, as well as the ability to take on tougher targets for even higher payouts. Though the pay at the starter tier was certainly nothing to sneer at, I could make some serious money now that I'd proved my worth.

With the Pharyleri getting serious about holding onto the Denver end of their cross-country trade route, the funds the gnomes poured into their military expansion were significant. Even the pay for auxiliary support groups, mostly mercenaries and bounty hunters like my team, was well apportioned.

Credits were only one factor though. We needed experience if we were to continue growing, both the kind rewarded by the System and the kind that came from living through tough fights.

The idea that Master Class fighters were showing up in combat was concerning. I'd meant what I'd said to Ismyna: I didn't think I could take one out alone. Not if I wanted to survive the experience.

They wouldn't be cheaters like me who skipped a tier. They'd have all the supporting Skills and accumulated attributes from the Basic and Advanced tiers, not to mention the lessons learned over those years of building up their abilities and fighting techniques. Master-tier Skills would be beyond anything I'd faced yet from a sentient, though I imagined that they'd be on the level of some Alpha and Boss monster abilities.

And yet, I kept thinking of ways to turn those long odds in my favor.

It would take a team and a way to engage the opponent on our terms. Knowing the enemy's strengths and weaknesses beforehand would be critical. Finally, it would only be possible if the target was on the low end of the Master Class rank. Any Master Class above Level 20, after they'd unlocked the second of their three ability tiers within the Class, would likely be beyond us.

Without any intel yet on what the Binary Eclipse Sect was bringing in, there wasn't much sense in worrying too much for now and I turned my attention back to my own status. I still had two fresh Attribute Points awaiting assignment, in addition to my growing stockpile of Skill Points. One more Level, when I hit 46 and unlocked that final group of my abilities, then I'd spend that hoard.

For now though, Willpower lagged behind my other attributes and I assigned both points into the stat before confirming my selection. Then I brought up the full status for a review.

Status Screen			
Name:	Hal Mason*	Class:	Hunter*
Race:	Human (Male)	Level:	45
Titles			
Dungeon World Delver*, Galactic Bronze Bounty Hunter, Knight Errant of Demarcia, Sharp Eyed*, Slayer of Kobolds* (*Title hidden)			
Health:	1410	Stamina:	1410
Mana:	1010		
Status			
Normal*			
Attributes			
Strength	77	Agility	152
Constitution	141	Perception	92
Intelligence	101	Willpower	75
Charisma	100	Luck	24
Class Skills			
Efficient Trail	1	Expose	1
Greater Observation	3	Hinder	2
Implacable Endurance	1	Keen Senses	1

Meat Locker	3	On the Hunt	5
Quality Over Quantity	2	Rend	1
Resilient Nature	2	Right Tool For the Job	2
Non-Class Skills			
Blood Scent	1		
Perks			
Gut Instinct			
Combat Spells			
Earth Spike (II), Firespray (II), Frostbolt (VI), Frostnova (IV), Greater Healing (I), Greater Regeneration (I), Howling Blast (I), Ice Armor (I), Lesser Disguise (V), Minor Healing (IV), Minor Renew (II), Whiteout (I)			

Other than my usual discontent over my inability to hide the ridiculous Knight Errant of Demarcia title, everything else looked satisfactory on the screen. I dismissed the status window and stretched out on the bed. With no intention of throwing my armor back on, I remained bare-assed naked, but if I couldn't feel safe enough inside the headquarters of my gnomish friends, then there wasn't anywhere in this System-infested world where I could get away with it.

Luxuriating in the feel of the sheets beneath me, I drifted off within minutes.

Chapter 4

It was early afternoon when I rolled out of bed, enjoyed another hot shower to rouse myself, and then geared back up.

No mission updates from Ismyna waited when I checked in at the front desk and the party chat remained silent, indicating that my teammates were either sleeping or off doing their own thing. That left me to my own devices, and I decided a little hunting was in order. Though Ismyna had said to stay close, sticking around wouldn't earn Credits or experience.

None of the guards gave me any problems as I rolled out of the compound gates on my Outrider. Since I wanted to avoid the Sect areas to the south, I was soon cruising northwest though the outskirts of the city.

It took about twenty minutes to find a good spot on the northern shores of Standley Lake, where a massive colony of mutated prairie dogs burrowed through the snowfields around the defunct remains of several old wind turbines. My minimap lit up with a plethora of targets within the Level 40 to 60 range and I dismounted before stowing away my bike.

Remembering an encounter with a similar batch of monsters, where I'd been met by a rushing horde of groundhogs pouring out of their burrows, back near the beginning of the System's initiation on Earth, I sniped at targets of opportunity with my Banshee hybrid rifle from as far away as I could to draw out the bear-sized monsters. Once I'd pulled a lone prairie dog away from the colony, I closed in with beam weapons to finish off my target.

The strategy proved effective for a dozen or so kills as I worked my way around the north edge of the colony. A few higher-Leveled monsters prowled around the outer edges of Greater Observation's detection range, their dots fading in and out as the creatures prowled in their own hunting patterns. Only when the sun began to sink behind the mountains to the west, stretching long shadows out over the prairie, did the lurkers make their move. As I knelt over the carcass of my latest prey, a shrill howl echoed over the prairie from the west, announcing the presence of another hunter stalking the frozen lakeshore. An answering cry from the east and then a third, even closer, from behind me to the north, indicated that they had me surrounded.

A grin crossed my face and I charged up the incline of the rolling hill toward the nearest howler. Time to show the local monster population who was the real predator.

A shaggy, oversized quadruped loped over the hilltop and the canine monster paused, almost comically, at my rush to meet it. An aura of cold emanated from the monster, sapping at my strength and attempting to slow me, but I resisted the effect and the slight hesitation gave me a chance to scan the monster before I opened fire with my beam pistols.

Tundra Coyote (Level 61)
HP: 680/680
Status: Pack Bond, Frost Aura

The beast yipped as the first energy rays seared blackening lines across the mottled white and tawny fur of its chest and snout. The coyote launched itself into the air in a frenzied leap, but I slid to the side and out of the way as I raked more beam fire across its flank.

The monster spun around but I circled behind it, keeping up a steady barrage of fire that burned away its health pool. I kept part of my awareness watching my own back, but I was attempting to put the creature down quickly since there were at least two more hunters from the pack.

Sure enough, as I dropped the first coyote, another pair of monsters darted in from either side with a smaller third following behind. The adult monsters attacked, one high and one low. I kicked out at the coyote lunging for my legs, striking it in the front shoulder and hearing a snap as I twisted below the second creature lunging for my throat.

The leaping creature's claws raked across the shoulder of my vambrace but failed to find purchase. In turn, I emptied both energy pistols into the monster's underside as it passed by me. The coyote yowled in pain and stumbled on its landing. The juvenile nipped at my heels and a swift kick sent it tumbling away. That bought me enough time to swap out my spent pistols for a fully charged pair.

The coyote with the broken leg limped toward me, still attempting to snap at my calves, but was slowed enough by the injury that I easily avoided the attacks. The one I'd shot in the stomach remained fully mobile and came at me once more, the stink of burnt fur and scorched flesh the only indication of injury.

I darted around the hilltop, leading the monster away from the rest of its pack and keeping it under assault from a steady rain of beam fire. Soon its charred carcass keeled over, and I finished off the remaining pair without any further interruptions.

The sun had set completely by the time I finished stowing away the loot and then the entirety of the dead monsters into Meat Locker. The fields around the lake were empty of monsters now that it was fully dark, with the prairie dogs all retreating into their burrows.

An impact slammed into my back and sent blood spraying from my mouth as I found myself twisted sideways. Wind brushed my skin as a sudden surge lifted me off the ground. A pointed talon emerged from the side of my chest where it had punched through my rib cage and pierced a lung. A second set of talons wrapped around my waist, holding me in place as wings, each at least the size of a double-wide garage door, beat in eerie silence to raise the massive bird of prey into the air.

Great Horned Owl (Level 78)

HP: 2937/2937

Status: Night Sight, Silent Flight

The giant owl's beak twisted down as it prepared to rip me apart and there was no time to even summon a weapon from my Inventory. Instead I raised my right hand, triggering the flame projector set in the wrist of my vambrace. The tip of the owl's beak scraped across my vambrace, leaving behind a deep gouge as the creature hooted in startlement from the sudden bloom of fire.

The beak jerked away from the flames, but the owl still didn't let go of me. I gritted my teeth in pain with every jostling motion and each flap of the wings. The talon that impaled my chest ground broken ribs against one another and tore at my muscles as I rode through the turbulent flight.

The tips of the feathers over the bird's upper torso ignited and pungent smoke streamed away from the burning area. Since the flamer wasn't designed for continuous use, the propellant from the weapon ran out after about five seconds. Though I'd set the creature on fire, I hadn't done nearly enough damage to dissuade it from its dinner of Hal tartare.

With one of the owl's feet wrapped around my waist and my best pistols stuck in their holsters, I pulled out a set of spares and opened up on the burning section of the torso above me. The shots chipped away at the monster's health, but it wasn't enough.

The flames began to die out and I knew I was in trouble. Well, more trouble than coughing blood normally indicated.

Desperate, I flung out my left wrist toward the owl's wing and activated the grapple launcher on the wing's downbeat. The hook-like tip of the grapple punched into the leading edge of the wing and I hurriedly twisted the line around the talon sticking out of my chest before the next lift of the wing.

As the wing attempted to extend for another beat, the line snapped taut and wrenched the talon toward the restricted appendage. I was jolted along with the talon each time the bird frantically tried to flap harder, but the wing couldn't extend and the bird keeled over in midair.

The owl and I spun around as we plummeted, the world twisting viciously beneath me. I summoned a ridiculously expensive health and regeneration potion into my hand and punched the injector into my chest just before we hit.

This was going to hurt.

Badly.

The owl landed beneath me as we smashed down on the frozen surface of Standley Lake. Cartilage and bones snapped before the impact ripped the talon from my chest and sent me skidding across the ice-covered lake. I spread a trail of blood and other bodily fluids in a streak two dozen yards long, before I finally slid to a halt.

I couldn't breathe and I looked down to see my heart pounding amidst the shredded wreckage of my lungs within my open chest cavity. The entire left side of my ribcage was just completely gone.

If this had happened before the System, I'd already have been dead.

A detached portion of my mind registered that I was deep enough in shock that the pain had yet to fully register. That and Pain Resistance was keeping me sane-ish.

My natural regeneration kicked in, aided by the potion I'd used just before hitting the ground. Before my eyes, bronchi slowly sprouted like growing trees. New flesh wrapped around them as my lung rebuilt itself and my chest heaved with a bloody series of wracking coughs. Air flooded into the restored organ, offering much-needed relief. I threw my head to the side and spat out blood as the coughing subsided.

A shriek from the owl warned me that this wasn't over yet.

Cradling my left arm protectively around my still-healing chest, I hit myself with a round of healing spells before slowly sitting up and finding my way to my feet. When I was confident in my ability to walk steadily, I drew the master-crafted handcannon Ace from my right hip and leveled the massive pistol at the giant owl flopping around the ice twenty feet away.

Somehow my grapple line had remained in place. As I watched, the owl's beak snapped down on the tightly stretched line and snipped it apart. The wing dangled limp with the line's tension broken, evidence that the monster was in just as poor shape as me.

The owl's head rotated toward me, and it froze as we locked eyes. Then the beast went wild. It stood on its right leg, its left foot, with the blood-slicked talon that had been in my chest, twisted to the side from being wrenched by the grapple line. The bird's right wing extended fully as if unable to fold, a sharp bend showing where the wing had snapped in the landing.

Didn't stop it from hopping towards me.

The beast's wide amber eyes glared balefully and I fired Ace directly into its face. The left eye exploded in a splash of gore and the owl shrieked in pain. It didn't slow down in the slightest, so I backed away as I traced my successive shots across the monster's face and into its other eye.

Despite its blinding, the monster barreled recklessly toward me. It shifted its head to the side and continued straight for me, even after I angled my path away from it. With the owl's excellent hearing, it was tracking me by the sound of my footsteps on the ice.

My wounds were still healing but I needed to change up my tactics to end this. Still cradling my side with one arm and firing Ace with the other, I turned and ran in a circle around the owl. The injured bird struggled to keep up with my movements and I managed to get behind it.

I tightened my circle and jumped onto the extended wing that dragged along the ice as the creature tried to spin. The monster bobbed and jostled as I climbed up its side but the injuries it had sustained prevented it from bucking me off.

Reaching its head, I grabbed hold of one of the feathery tufts that gave the horned owl its name. Once my handhold was secure, the fight was all but over. Driving shot after shot down the auditory canal into the brain cavity stripped away the last of the owl's health and it keeled over before I emptied the hand cannon's magazine.

I looted the twitching carcass and dismounted, then stored the entire dead owl away in Meat Locker. I had to discard two of the smaller prairie dogs that I'd slain earlier, but any Artisans who harvested monster bits from carcasses would pay out even better for something this big.

With the monster removed from the ice, only streaks of blood, gore, and scattered feathers remained strewn across the icy surface of the frozen lake. It still took a few minutes to find where my backup pistols had fallen after I'd dropped them in the rough landing. Once I had reloaded the spent weapons and replaced the fuel canister for the flamer in my bracer, I changed out my shredded jumpsuit for a fresh one. There's a reason why I buy armored jumpsuits in batch lots.

Preparations complete, I pulled my bike from my Inventory and turned toward town.

After this little escapade, I needed a drink.

Chapter 5

After returning to the safety of the city's settlement shield, I paused long enough to ask one of the gnome guards for directions to a slaughterhouse. The guard laughed as he provided the quickest route and told me to "just follow my nose" when I got close.

Fortunately, the slaughterhouse was still open, despite the late hour. With a city the size of Denver, the Adventurer population was active pretty much around the clock and someone was always looking to sell off monster bits. While I could just sell everything at the Shop, local Artisans were usually desperate enough for raw materials that they'd pay premium rates and the slaughterhouses served as a sort of clearinghouse for those trades.

Adventurers could make a single stop to unload their Inventory or vehicles at once and got their Credits up front for their efforts. Then once the monsters were butchered down to their constituent parts, the crafters could buy the parts they needed. Bones and scales were usually purchased by armorsmiths, weaponsmiths went for teeth and claws, and alchemists generally focused on organs and blood.

Since the gnomes had emplaced a similar exchange at the starport outside Pittsburgh, I wasn't surprised to see them instituting the practice here. In this case, the location they'd set up was at the old puppy chow factory a short way east of the intersections between Interstates 70 and 25.

The guard had been correct about the smell. The stench of viscera, blood, and offal lingered in the air as I pulled up to the facility's clearly marked drive-through lane. Obviously, no one had bothered to purchase a System upgrade to keep the air clean. Once I unloaded, I took my time haggling with the Pharyleri manager, who wore a breathing mask that presumably filtered out the nauseating bouquet–providing the gnome an advantage in any negotiation that stretched out for any length of time.

Maybe the lack of an upgrade was an actual tactic and not just cheapness gone rogue.

My own penny-pinching nature refused to allow the gnome an easy victory, so I stuck through it. Still, I was more than glad to leave the slaughterhouse behind once we finished the exchange and my Credit balance climbed a bit higher. A cast of Cleanse cleared any lingering smell after I'd left the facility and I rode off in search of a local watering hole.

I found a promising location about halfway between the puppy chow slaughterhouse and the Pharyleri headquarters at Union Station. Neon signs for beer companies that no longer existed flickered in the narrow windows of the single-story building. The thin stone slabs of varying depths created an interesting texture for the exterior walls, while red light poured out from the single, diamond-shaped window at head height in the solid wooden door.

Pulling open the dark green painted door, I stepped inside. The mingled smells of stale beer, spilled drinks, and fried food accompanied the classic rock playing from a System-enabled jukebox at the back of the bar, announcing that I'd found exactly the ambiance I'd sought.

Ten or so locals, humans, and a smattering of Galactics stared at me from their tables and booths as I entered the bar, but a quick glance showed no signs of any immediate threat.

I slipped onto one of the stools that lined the bar and deftly performed a scan of the patrons while I waited for the bartender to take my order, keeping the probe light enough that no one should have been able to sense it. Nothing the Skill found set off any alarm bells, so I tapped my fingers idly on the bartop, which consisted of tiles featuring alternating red and black playing cards.

"What'll it be, stranger?"

I looked up from the bartop at the not-quite-hostile voice of the bartender. Black hair, going gray and pulled back into a ponytail, framed the middle-aged woman's leathery face and spoke of a lifetime spent outdoors, while hinting at the possibility of Native heritage.

"Whiskey, please. Straight up and make it a double. What do you have on draft?"

"Just local brews, mostly IPAs from Wynkoop." A spark of amusement lit in the woman's eyes as my expression turned sour at the mention of IPAs. "Ah, not a fan I see. We also have their Rail Yard red ale and Imperial Rye lager."

"I'll take a pint of the red to start."

She nodded and headed back down the bar, where she started to fill my order. It only took her a minute before she returned and rattled off the bill as she set two glasses in front of me, the full pint and the rocks tumbler with two fingers of whiskey.

I sent over the Credits along with a tip, then threw back the double without hesitation.

When I returned the glass to the bartop, the bartender considered me with a raised eyebrow. "Rough day?"

"Just the end of it." I slid the empty glass towards her and tapped the rim to indicate my interest in another pour.

I sipped the ale as the woman refilled the whiskey glass and I found the brew a pleasant chaser to the shot. After I paid for the second round, the bartender leaned onto the bar. "Want to talk about it?"

I shrugged. "Not much to talk about. A great horned owl thought that I'd make a good meal."

The bartender looked at me skeptically while I savored the second whiskey for a long moment. Then I knocked back the rest of the drink in a smooth motion. "I disagreed."

"Well, I'm glad you made it out in one piece," she said when I didn't elaborate further. "I'm Mattie. Let me know if you want another drink."

I slowed down after ordering another round of both drinks and the bartender returned to serving the other patrons. A murmur of conversation filled the bar and I spent a few minutes listening to the various exchanges.

In the middle of overhearing a Gimsar complain to a human coworker about their boss at a textiles factory, I felt the sensation of being watched. It wasn't the usual distant feeling of observation that sometimes occurred when I was in the middle of combat, but a more immediate scrutiny.

When I turned to the direction of the sensation, I caught the barest glimpse of a silver-haired Truinnar female, clad in a black form-fitting armored suit, before the door closed behind her. I shot off the barstool and was halfway to the door before my mind caught up to my instincts. I wasn't sure why I'd felt there was a threat, but I knew better than to ignore my gut and pushed my way out of the bar.

Outside, I stepped from the corner of the intersection and looked in all four directions, down both streets. It had only been a few seconds, but there was no sign of the dark elf. I turned slowly, studying for anything out of place.

I found nothing but the usual foot traffic and a few moving vehicles too distant to be the quarry I'd thought to pursue.

A woman walked along the sidewalk and I turned to her, gesturing to the bar behind me. "Excuse me, did you see a Truinnar come out of the bar here?"

The brunette looked at me in surprise and shook her head, continuing on her way without speaking. I checked with a couple other pedestrians, but no one else had seen anything else either.

After a few more failed inquiries, I shook my head and walked back to the bar, still troubled by the encounter but unable to put my finger on exactly why. I hadn't seen the Truinnar's face, only her profile from behind. She'd had a short, wavy bob cut, and I hadn't met any Truinnar with hair cut that short.

My return to the bar got a few looks from the patrons as I resumed my seat at the counter. While the strange occurrence had dampened my mood and left me feeling unsettled, I was at least going to finish my drinks before calling it a night.

"You ran out in a hurry. Everything alright?" Mattie asked.

"Thought I saw someone I knew," I replied, playing off my unease. "Do you get a lot of Truinnar through here?"

"We get a bit of everything. As long as they're not with the Sect and pay their tabs, we'll serve anyone."

"As it should be. I haven't been in town long, but don't think I've heard anyone say anything good about the Sect."

"You won't. They've been locking things down tighter and tighter. Makes it hard for the everyday folk to get by when they keep having to jump through more and more hoops just to get the basics."

"Desperate folks do desperate things."

Mattie sighed. "Hopefully, the gnomes will get their act together. Things wouldn't be so bad if they were running the city."

I nodded in agreement, unwilling to speak on that subject with my inside knowledge. Before my lack of further response became too obvious, a man wearing a cowboy hat approached the bar and Mattie stepped away to fulfill his order. Several new patrons entered shortly after that and the bar rapidly began filling up as the night progressed.

Feeling that it was time to move on, I finished my drink and sent the bartender a few extra Credits as a tip before sliding off my stool.

"Thank you, hun. Have a good night!" Mattie shouted after me as I walked away from the counter.

I waved in response, unwilling to shout a reply over the noise of the crowd. A burst of sound from the inside accompanied me out into the street, dropping away to faint vibrations pounding through the door after it swung closed.

I looked around once again for any sign of the dark elf from earlier, though I wasn't really expecting to find anything. If I hadn't turned at exactly the right moment, I wouldn't even have noticed the Truinnar slipping out.

Huh.

Taking my time since I wasn't in any hurry, I walked back toward Union Station from the north end of Larimer. The streets were hardly empty, though there remained far less traffic than there would have been any night at this time pre-System. Bicycles were still popular, though there was plenty of System tech in use. I even saw someone using what looked like rocket-propelled rollerblades.

I chuckled as a group of teenagers skated by while floating a few inches above the ground. At least we'd finally gotten *Back to the Future's* hoverboards.

The walk helped me wind down more than the drinks after the nearly disastrous hunting trip. By the time I returned to the headquarters complex, I was feeling pretty good about the day. Despite the close call with the owl, I'd raked in a decent number of Credits and climbed a bit higher on the mountain of experience needed to gain my next Level.

Unless I got a huge influx of quest and bounty experience, that Level would still take a while yet, but then, I was in the middle of a city about to explode in urban conflict. I wouldn't rule anything out.

Was it bad that I was kind of looking forward to it?

Chapter 6

"Hal! Where have you been?"

Looking up against the morning light streaming into Union Station's Great Hall and rubbing the sleep from my eyes, I searched for the source of the voice that greeted my entrance to the cafeteria. A gnome with neon blue hair and matching mutton chops pushed through the early breakfast crowd, which seemed busier than usual. The Pharyleri wore a grease-stained set of beige coveralls, despite the abundance of System-aided cleaning options.

Eldri Giltwrench (Repair Technician Level 43) (B)
[Industrial Alliance]
HP: 560/560
MP: 720/720

"Sleeping," I replied. It had been a late night and I was still up with the sun. Enhanced Constitution was great for many things, but lounging the day away in bed was not one of them.

The gnome hurried over to me and looked around before glancing up at me. "Ismyna was looking for you. There's a briefing for tonight's operation in the command center. If you hurry, you might be able to slip in before you miss too much."

I frowned at the gnome. "Kinda early for a briefing, but thanks for the heads up. I'll try not to cause a fuss."

The tech gave me a look that said he didn't quite believe my words, but I just grinned as I hurried off. After pausing long enough to grab a cup of hot coffee and a breakfast burrito to go, I headed to the command center as I scarfed them down.

An extra pair of guards stood outside the door and performed an extremely thorough check before I was permitted into the secure control room. The briefing was in full swing when I finally made it inside the crowded chamber.

Though the room was filled with uniformed gnomes, most with rank insignia of officers with command over smaller units, there were enough non-Pharyleri in the command center that my presence didn't stand out. I spotted Dayena and Lyrra on the far side of the room, but I knew better than to push my way through the assembly just yet.

Several humans stood in groups, along with several other clusters of various Galactic species. Most of those groups appeared to be wearing their own distinct sets of gear or uniforms, presumably making them independent contractors for the Alliance, like my own group. I just hoped the Pharyleri had vetted these mercenaries a little more thoroughly than the last pair I'd worked with.

Nesdyna stood on the central platform with the entire room focused on her. The clan leader gestured to the holographic map of the city, the image hovering overhead so that everyone throughout the chamber could get a glimpse. Different sections of the city lit up as she spoke, and it seemed that I was in time to catch the initial portion of the briefing. I definitely owed Eldri a favor for his timely notice.

"The Binary Eclipse Sect currently holds four of Denver's City Centers, giving them control over two thirds of the settlement. Right now, they're spread thin, but that will change with their reinforcements soon arriving from Colorado Springs. We have a narrow window to cripple their current forces and take three exposed City Cores."

Three of the red districts blinked at the gnome's words and she looked at three Pharyleri who all held some variation of officer Classes.

"Task Force Banewolf will be targeting the southwest district, where the Core is located on the grounds of the former Colorado Heights University. Task Force Chimera, you're heading southeast, for the Core at Tech Center. Finally, Task Force Gryphon, your assignment is the east Core at the Wings Over the Rockies Museum. The fourth, and last, of Denver's Cores is the Sect headquarters for the region. That location is the most defended, so it will be our final objective, and only once the others are under our control."

The Pharyleri scanned across the room, meeting the eyes of the various teams throughout the room. Her eyes narrowed slightly when she spotted me but moved on without any other hesitation.

"For the rest of you, each team leader has your assigned objectives for the evening, along with an additional listing for targets of opportunity. Even if your unit is not part of any Task Force, there are sizable payouts for successfully hitting your own targets."

A low murmur ran through the room as the mercenaries anticipated the prospect of Credits. I glanced over at Dayena, revealing the Truinnar watching me closely. Enough amusement lingered in her expression that I just knew Ismyna had given our assignment to the dark elf when she couldn't find me earlier. I lifted one shoulder in a half shrug to show my indifference to who had received the orders. As long as we got paid, I was good with it.

On the platform, Nesdyna cleared her throat and the buzz of conversation died off as a new image replaced the holographic map floating in the air. The wireframe schematic displayed a towering cannon that pointed towards the sky at a steep angle. "There is one more thing. The Sect has procured a number of Skyfire orbital defense cannons in an effort to deter a repeat of the incident with the Rocky Mountain Dragon. These cannons are also quite capable of anti-air fire and able to engage any flying vehicle or ship within their sightlines above the horizon. Keep your troops on the ground until the cannon network is taken out."

The briefing wrapped up quickly after that and the command center cleared out as the teams headed to their staging points. I worked against the tide of departing gnomish officers and various mercenaries until I met up with my teammates.

Dayena gave me a once-over and raised an eyebrow when she noticed the new scratches on my vambraces. "Good night last night?"

"A little eventful."

Lyrra folded her arms across her chest. "So after telling us to stick close, you went running off."

"A bit of hunting and a few drinks. You could've reached me through party chat if you'd wanted." I responded with my own accusation and her expression further soured as my words hit home. In my defense, Ismyna had said they were going to wait for a few days before starting their offensive, so something must have changed for the Alliance to move up their timetable.

Dayena sighed. "You should know by now, Hal has a bad habit of going off alone. What happened here?"

Her fingernail scraped over the gouges left in my vambrace by the owl's beak.

"I had a brush with a giant owl."

The dark elf closed her eyes and massaged her forehead as if pained by my actions. "I do not even want to ask. Not that we have time."

"Is that what our assignment says?" I asked.

She opened her eyes and got serious. "A Sect armory is located at the site of the Denver Museum of Nature and Science. We are to hit it, once the attack begins tonight. Our objective will be to destroy any weapons or munitions we are unable to secure."

"And how pissed is Ismyna that she couldn't find me earlier?"

Dayena's amethyst pupils glittered with amusement as she shrugged. I would find no answers there. Lyrra just shook her head when I looked at her; she wasn't going to help me out either.

"I'm not going to worry about it then. Let's get moving." As long as the gnomes were still paying, I'd live with a little annoyance on their part. I'd bled enough for the Pharyleri, on several occasions now, that I doubted they would turn me down when work was available—as Dayena getting the assignment for tonight's operation proved.

Leading the way, I joined up with the trailing end of the forces filing out of the command center.

"Excuse me, might you be interested in signing on with a larger group?"

The voice came from a freckle-faced young man, who couldn't be more than eighteen, with a mid-tier projectile rifle slung over his shoulder. Though I kept walking, the kid took my appraisal of him as permission to launch into his pitch. "I'm Ben Carson from the Wolverines mercenary unit. We're the fastest growing mercenary unit in Denver and hold full accreditation with the Mercenary Review Board."

The earnest pitch wasn't enough to sway me, but I almost chuckled at the unit name. "Sorry Ben, not joining anybody."

"Oh. Thank you for your time." The kid couldn't quite mask his disappointment as he slipped off to join a few others with similar-colored jumpsuits and matching pawprint shoulder patches.

"Wolverines?" Lyrra asked, having caught my amusement.

I shrugged. "It's either their high school mascot or a movie reference. I think they're too young for the movie reference though."

It didn't take long until we were outside the Union Station headquarters, finding a throng of idling vehicles waiting as the officers filtered out to where their troops were already loaded into various transports.

When I'd returned to the headquarters before the briefing, I'd come in through the north end of the building, so I'd missed seeing the assembled forces in the plaza outside. The only way for this many troops to gather would be to strip the checkpoints and perimeter security around the settlement nearly bare. I hoped the gamble would pay off for the gnomes.

Over two dozen Pharyleri transports made up the majority of the gathered vehicles. Hovering a few feet above the ground, the lengthy vehicles with a pointed prow looked like some kind of high-tech canoe that floated in the air. The front of the craft had small slit windows in the heavily reinforced armor that protected the cockpit and articulated side-bay doors that would pop out before raising up to allow the troops inside to drop out. Each of the transports looked like they could hold twenty or so people—and probably thirty of the smaller Pharyleri infantry would fit inside if they were in standard armor, without using their bulkier armored mech suits.

The remaining transports were far more varied. One group of humans had both a refurbished Abrams tank and a Bradley Fighting Vehicle. A second bunch loaded up into a dingy old van that looked like it should have the words "Free Candy" spray-painted on the side.

A Galactic group loaded up into a six-legged walker with a bulbous troop section that looked like a beetle shell. Another bunch of mercs, a combined Gimsar and Pharyleri squad, rode individual four-wheeled go-karts that sat so low that they looked like they'd bottom out on a speed bump.

When the elves and I found a clear space to pull out our bikes, I thought we were actually one of the more normal looking crews. Nobody paid us much attention, remaining focused on their own preparations, before the compound gates opened up and the transports began streaming out in a steady flow.

Lyrra climbed up behind the Countess on the Truinnar's sleek bike. I mounted my Outrider and waypoints appeared on my nav system as Dayena linked our objectives with our vehicles. While I waited for our turn to depart, I gave my gear a final once-over to ensure that my weapons were fully loaded and prepared for the combat that lay ahead throughout the night.

Our party was one of the last units to leave the plaza and I noticed that a full squad of heavily armed Steamspanner guards remained on alert at the entrance when we pulled out. At least there was more than a skeleton crew left behind, so the Pharyleri weren't gambling everything on this assault.

I throttled up outside the gate, only to immediately brake to a halt behind a stopped transport. I took a deep breath and sighed.

Even two years into the apocalypse, I couldn't get away from "hurry up and wait."

Chapter 7

Once clear of the transports, as they branched off in different directions to their individual assignments, we slipped through the streets until we reached our secondary staging area.

The Sect would have eyes on the headquarters and know that a large force had left. Waiting them out in secondary sites across the city would confuse the defenders. If they had been alerted when we left, then they would be on high alert all day, until the actual attack launched.

It took most of the day, but as the sun dropped behind the mountains to the west, we got back on the move. Steering onto the empty expanse of Interstate 25, Dayena and I split our attention between driving and keeping a wary eye out for any Sect forces. With Lyrra riding double, the Movana focused on a bracer-mounted datapad as she leaned into Dayena's back. The elf gave directions along our route, keeping her words concise even over party chat.

"Sect units are active across the city and fights are breaking out all over. The task forces are engaged short of all three primary objectives."

The gnome offensive targeted the Sect-owned City Cores that provided control over half of the municipal region, leaving small teams like ours free to cherry-pick less defended installations. Of course, there was another reason the unaffiliated groups were hitting the smaller targets. It was another way for the Pharyleri to ensure that their Alliance ended up taking the Cores. Since capturing a Core was finders keepers, the gnomes were eliminating the chance that a third party would dilute their control of the city.

"Any response on our target?" I asked as I leaned low over my bike's handlebars. The edges of my poncho fluttered and snapped behind me in the wind.

Lyrra hummed for a moment as she scanned data on the net. *"There's a Steamspanner drone in the air near the museum. The reports show the barracks emptied when the alert went out and the route looks clear now, but it looks like some of those enforcers stayed to set up a mortar battery in City Park."*

I made the call to continue regardless. *"We'll scope out the mortars first. If it's too well defended, we'll bypass it for the next site. If not, we'll hit the mortar section first and hopefully get another bonus for our contribution."*

Our target, the old Denver Museum of Nature and Science, was a large structure on the eastern edge of City Park. As one of the northernmost points held by the Sect, it served primarily as a staging area and armory for their forces. Since the majority of those forces were now tied up in reinforcing the City Centers, we'd thought to strip anything left in the armory with little resistance, but a firebase in the park with indirect fire capability wasn't something our intel had warned of before the conflict began.

"I like it," Dayena agreed.

"I pointed out the mortars to Alliance command. They're offering a 1k Credit bonus for any Basic Class kill and 5k for any Advanced Class we can eliminate, with an additional 5k for rendering the battery inoperable."

I grinned. *"Even better."*

Closing in on our destination, we veered off-road onto the gently rolling hills of the City Park Golf Course in order to have better cover for our approach. The grounds of the Denver Zoo lay across East 32nd Avenue to the south and west but the street and an old baseball field separated us from the museum grounds.

The three of us dismounted and stowed away our bikes in the shadows of the overgrown treeline that encircled the sports field as the thump of mortar rounds rung out in the night. The moon disappeared behind a large bank of clouds, leaving the fields around the museum shrouded in darkness.

We slipped through the shadows along the side street running between the overgrown baseball field and the zoo, using the abandoned vehicles and trees as cover. Dayena flanked me, off to the opposite side of the street, while Lyrra trailed a half dozen yards behind to provide overwatch and scan our backtrail.

Before we reached our destination, I caught a glimpse of movement from the corner of my eye. I held up a raised fist, freezing both elves in place as I searched for the source of the motion.

When I thought I saw the outline of a hidden sentry leaning against a tree, a gentle probe of the area with Greater Observation identified not just the one I'd spotted, but also a second Sect sentry just beyond.

Sect Thug (Level 41) (B)
[Binary Eclipse Sect]
HP: 480/480
MP: 400/400

Sect Sentry (Level 46) (B)
[Binary Eclipse Sect]
HP: 540/540
MP: 540/540

Neither foe amounted to any significant threat in and of themselves, but the danger of warning the rest of the Sect forces in the area was real. It would likely prevent us from succeeding with our mission and impede the payout for dealing with the threat of the mortars. We could sneak by the two guards but the added bounty for taking out Sect members tilted the scales against them.

I pointed out the pair of enemies over party chat and slowly worked toward the initial guard, leaving the rearmost enemy to Dayena. Once I reached striking range, only the body of a rusting Ford F-150 separated me from the Thug. I paused until Dayena closed with the higher Leveled Sentry from the far side, equipping my melee weapons for some close-in, dirty work.

"In position, Blackout ready," Dayena signaled, her communication-disabling Skill prepped to cut the sentries off from sending out any alert.

"From three. Three. Two. One. Go!"

I kept low, already moving as I started a mental countdown to the end of Dayena's ability. I rushed around the truck, swinging my axe into the throat of the startled guard before the man could do more than push himself upright from the tree he'd leaned against. He twisted with an instinct that turned the critical hit into a glancing blow, then I stabbed my knife into his chest. The blade pierced through a weak point between the segmented ballistic plates protecting his torso, but the guard recovered from his surprise and delivered a punishing blow to my stomach. The two of us exchanged strikes, my knife and axe against the Thug's powerful fists.

I was running out of time before Blackout would cut out and allow the guard to use Skills or tech to sound the alarm. Just as my mental timer expired, Dayena appeared behind the Thug and plunged both of her short swords into his back. His body sagged to the ground and the Countess spared me a disappointed glance.

"Targets eliminated," Dayena reported over party chat.

The lack of any overwatch fire from Lyrra meant we had escaped detection so far, but I crouched beside the body and listened for any sign of discovery. The steady crump of mortars continued unabated, easing my concerns.

I stashed away my blades, stuffed the guard's rifle and sidearms into my Inventory as free loot, and then gently heaved the body up into the bed of the truck to hide it from casual view.

Lyrra crept beside the truck, rifle at the ready as she repositioned to watch over us. Dayena and I darted one at a time across a Y-intersection beyond where the sentries had hidden. The high grass in between the forks provided us perfect cover as we edged into a tangle of unkempt trees that separated us from the museum grounds, finally gaining visibility of the target before us.

Chapter 8

Sitting within the copse, we had a view out over the gentle slope and a circular patio in the middle of the level field behind the museum. The trio of sect mortars were spread out in an arc within the grasses beyond the eastern edge of the patio. Runners scampered between the tubes and a stack of crates in the middle of the paved area.

Three sect members serviced each tube with a fourth couriering ammunition from the boxes to each mortar position. The courier would grab a mortar round from the central cache and carry it out to the firing line before handing it off to the ammunition bearer. The ammo bearer primed the round while a gunner fiddled with the control unit affixed to the side of the mortar tube. The final individual, the squad leader, then called out a command, once both gunner and bearer were ready, and the prepared round was dropped into the tube. At a closer range, the noise of the mortar launching as it hit the bottom of the tube sounded more like a heavy gunshot.

The process had been repeated several times at each station by the time Lyrra moved up to where Dayena and I peered through the frosty undergrowth.

The Movana bit her lip as she took in the scene. *"Can we take a dozen of them?"*

"What do you think, Hal?" Dayena's eyes twinkled as she raised an eyebrow.

I snorted quietly, confident that the sound would go unnoticed amidst the firing mortars. *"Don't look at the numbers or just the Levels. Look at their Classes."*

Already having noticed what I was pointing out to Lyrra, Dayena kept her focus on the Movana as the elf looked over the Sect forces more carefully.

"Auditor. Courier. Driver. Slaver. They're all Basic, and only a few are Combat Classes."

Half of the Sect members in front of us were human, but it was the Galactics who controlled all of the squad leader and gunner positions at the mortars while the human lackeys held the runner and ammo bearer roles.

I nodded. *"Getting shot by an Accountant with a rifle is still going to do damage but unless they've taken a second Class, they're not going to have the Class Skills to give them the edge they'd need to even out the playing field."*

"Unless one of them is hiding their Class, like you." Dayena grinned.

"If it happens, we'll deal with it. Improvise. Adapt. Overcome."

"The usual plan then?" Lyrra asked.

"If it ain't broke, don't fix it," I replied.

Lyrra and I waited as Dayena snuck away toward the lake in the center of the park, circling wide around the firing mortars to come at them from the opposite side. She would handle the farthest crew while Lyrra and I took on the nearest ones.

Once my minimap showed that she was halfway around, I cast Ice Armor on myself before beginning my own sneak. The spell created a set of armor that layered itself over my jumpsuit. The extra protection offered by the translucent barrier served as an additional defense that further buffed my overall health. While any determined assault would still penetrate, the spell helped prolong the useful life of my jumpsuits.

My chest and elbows scraped across the turf as I low-crawled forward in a slow creep. Each movement flowed with deliberate smoothness from one motion into the next. With my poncho breaking up my outline, the trick was to seem like another uneven patch of grass in the wide-open field. That meant keeping the motions natural enough to avoid any wandering eyes focusing on any sharp or sudden movements.

I was only two-thirds of the way across the field when the stealthy Truinnar reached her destination. Her marker on my map froze in place only a few yards from the oblivious mortar crew. Though the Countess kept silent over party chat, I could practically feel Dayena's annoyance that she now needed to wait for me—especially when she would likely clear her targets faster. Fortunately, it only took a few more minutes until I signaled that I was close enough to begin the assault. I summoned a portable shield generator out of my Inventory, placing it in front of me but not activating it yet.

Then I pulled out a grenade into each hand.

I confirmed my companions were prepared and started another countdown. I threw the grenades as I launched myself into motion, rising to a crouch and drawing my silenced pistols. The first grenade was a straight throw at the gunner on the left side of the mortar closest to me, while the second arced high overhead toward the centermost mortar position.

The gunner facing me lurched when the fist-sized explosive bounced off his chest and his expression was almost comical as he realized what had hit him, wide-eyed horror replacing surprise. A blue flash erupted from the grenade and the gunner disappeared as plasma enveloped the position. All three Sect members screamed as they burned, completely distracted by their own pain as I opened fire into the backs of the squad leader and ammo bearer.

The exploding grenades made any attempts at keeping quiet largely a moot point but using the silenced weapons would delay notice of my position. The longer it took for the Sect members to pinpoint me, the longer I'd be able to keep up my attacks unopposed.

The human ammo bearer dropped after only a couple shots and I shifted my left-hand weapon to also fire at the more durable squad leader, a hirsute Scrofalori. The alien turned to face me on instinct from the rounds digging into his back but was too busy slapping at the flames that engulfed the entirety of his hairy boar-like front to spot me.

The Scrofalori's head snapped back, followed by the sharp crack of a rifle shot from behind me.

"Good shot!" I complimented Lyrra as the alien keeled over. I snapped off two more shots at the human gunner, who writhed on the ground to put out the flaming plasma. The last member of the mortar crew's frantic stop-drop-and-rolling stopped abruptly with my second round, leaving another smoldering corpse on the field.

An impact smacked into the side of my waist, just above where Last Word sat holstered on my left hip. The bruising impact shifted me sideways but failed to penetrate my armor. A second shot grazed across the front of my chest before I pivoted to find myself facing the Sect courier who'd been carrying rounds from the central stockpile. The woman wore an expression of absolute terror and squeezed off her shots in a panic without really aiming. Her pistol wavered wildly in an unsupported one-handed grip and it was easy to dodge the ensuing attacks.

I sighed sadly and returned fire.

Three rounds to the chest staggered the woman and she dropped onto her backside with a significant chunk of her health missing, blood pumping out and removing even more slivers. The third shot made the slide lock back on my pistol. I kept my eyes on the courier as I slowly and deliberately released the spent magazine, swapping it for a full replacement from my Inventory.

The woman dropped her pistol and scrambled backward in a desperate crabwalk. Good. I didn't like killing non-combat Classers, at least when they were smart enough to run. It wasn't fair and the experience gain wasn't worth the Credits spent on the ammunition. I let her flee, turning my attention to the centermost mortar crew in time to see a flash from a very large-bore weapon pointed my way.

The projectile hit my arm just above my left bicep and tore a chunk of flesh out as the force spun me a full three-sixty. I slammed into the ground and bounced off the turf, instinctively rolling away from where I'd landed. My instincts had kicked in not a moment too soon, as a gout of soil erupted where I'd been only an instant before.

I'd lost both my weapons at some point, blood ran down my arm from the fist-sized chunk missing from my vambrace, and I couldn't feel my left hand. Rather than pull out a new weapon, I flipped over and dropped my hand down on the activation switch for the portable shield generator that I'd set before we launched the attack.

A slightly curved field of transparent blue energy snapped into place above the generator, extending from the ground to over six feet high and stretching nearly four feet wide. The field rippled as a projectile splashed against the middle of it, right above my head. The metallic slug was the size of a grapefruit and dropped to the ground on the other side of the shield.

I pushed myself up, tentatively squeezing my left hand as a throbbing ache announced the return of feeling in my injured arm. It felt like an animal had taken a bite out just below my shoulder. Without the combined defenses of my Ice Armor spell and the hardened carapace of my vambrace, I'd be regenerating a missing arm.

Again.

"Die, human!"

The shrill voice came from the Sect member marching toward me beyond the protection of the shield. The alien was a species that I'd encountered before, a hulking, rhino-like Ceratophimi.

Ro'khan'sat (Sect Slaver Level 49) (B)

[Binary Eclipse Sect]

HP: 700/700

MP 180/180

Status: Rock Hard, Enraged

From the similarity of name to Ro'khar'sar, I wouldn't be surprised if this Ceratophimi was related to the last Sect alien that I'd slain from the same species. Not that it really mattered much, since this one was definitely trying to kill me too.

Ro'khan'sat raised his heavy cylindrical weapon vertically as he pumped its slide and then leveled it my way once more. A gout of flame bloomed from the end of the slug-thrower and the projectile hit my shield an instant later. The energy field flickered at the impact, indicating it might hold up for one more attack.

Beyond the gray-skinned alien, flames still flickered amongst the remaining trio of the mortar's crew, but the fires were dying down and they would soon join the fray. Still not trusting the recovery of my left hand, I summoned my Banshee rifle out from my Inventory rather than try to draw the master-crafted pistols holstered at my waist.

Ro'khan'sat flinched as another rifle shot rang out from behind me. Lyrra's covering fire provided an opportunity, so I stepped out around the side of the shield with the hybrid rifle already spooling up to fire from my hip. My wounded arm wouldn't hold the rifle high enough for an aimed shot, but the alien stood close enough that precision was optional.

A glittering azure beam streaked out from the rifle, carrying with it a projectile that punched completely through one side of the alien's lower torso. Blood and chunks of entrails sprayed out, splashing onto the rest of the mortar crew behind him. The three were up now and stepping forward, even as Ro'khan'sat dropped to one knee.

Another sniper shot from Lyrra dropped one, but the other pair launched attacks at the visible attacker in front of them—me. The first's pistol released a crimson energy beam that seared along the armored vambrace protecting my right forearm but failed to burn through. The second held up a hand, casting a spell that projected a flaming ray of fire out from her palm to sweep across my lower legs.

I gritted my teeth against the intense heat and lined up a shot on the spellcaster. The moment that the swirling beam of the hybrid rifle lanced out, the woman's eyes went wide. Then her head disappeared as the projectile obliterated the upper half of her torso. The remaining part of the spellcaster's body, at least what was left from the waist down, collapsed as one arm shot off to knock the pistoleer off balance. The pistol carrier had a moment to acknowledge the horrific death of his companion before Lyrra dropped him.

The distraction of dealing with the other Sect members had allowed Ro'khan'sat to get back on his feet, despite missing a good chunk out of his side. The rhino charged toward me with his head lowered, covering the distance between us in two short strides.

I squeezed off one round from my rifle, but the alien batted the gun aside with his horn as he lunged. The shot punched through the charging rhino's bicep but failed to stop him. Ro'khan'sat drove forward like a linebacker making a tackle and wrapped his good arm around me as he lifted me up, only to slam me back down into the ground.

The impact drove the air from my lungs and my rifle clattered away across the turf. In one sense, I was fortunate that the alien had turned his horned head to the side to deflect my shot, since that meant said horn hadn't speared through the center of my chest. On the other hand, it would have been nice to have just blown away the damned alien.

I gasped for breath and pushed up against Ro'khan'sat as he struggled to free the arm trapped beneath my back. His injured arm flopped uselessly and I could see bone glinting beneath the gushing alien ichor that poured out from where two thirds of the hulking bicep was missing.

Instinctively falling back on my old training for ground-fighting techniques, I pulled up my legs and wrapped them around the alien's waist. Though he was above me and I was still struggling to breathe, the guard position afforded the opportunity to control my opponent's posture using my legs.

My hand slid over the pebbly flesh of the alien's bulging arm but the thick mass of flesh was too large for me to get any sort of grip, at least until I reached the exposed wound from my last shot. Hot blood poured over my hand as I grabbed onto what would have been a humerus in a human. Ro'khan'sat squealed in pain and thrashed against me as I dug my fingers in around the bone, but the combined hold of my feet locked behind his back and my grasp on the bone of his upper arm prevented him from pushing himself up or breaking my hold.

In one of the old pay-per-view Octagon fights, the stalemate between us would have lasted until either one of us made a positioning mistake or someone got free enough to land a real blow. With the System, I cheated.

Summoning my soulbound combat knife into my left hand with the blade pointed down, I plunged the dagger into the alien's back. Ro'khan'sat's health plummeted with each stab and I repeated the attack until the alien zeroed out. I pushed the limp body off to one side before wiping off the worst of the blood on the frosty turf and rolling to my feet.

A glance around showed the third mortar crew dealt with, though I saw no visible sign of my sneaky dark elf companion. My minimap placed her beyond the stack of ammo crates in the center of the patio, so I gathered up my dropped weapons and started reloading them.

"How's the ammo cache looking?" I asked as I slipped my Banshee rifle back in my Inventory.

"Barely touched. It is a significant stockpile," Dayena replied.

I grunted as an idea hit. *"I wonder how badly we messed up the mortars and if we could get them back online."*

"Mine should be fine. I did not throw explosives at it."

I rolled my eyes and headed for the first of the mortar sections. Sure enough, the two mortars that I'd grenaded were out of commission with the tubes warped. The third mortar sat untouched and undamaged in the middle of four evenly spaced bodies.

Shaking my head, I reached the ammo stockpile as Lyrra jogged up from her overwatch position. *"What's the plan, boss?"*

Looking over the stacks, I found that the crates were separated into three piles with different colored stripes on the lids. Boxes in the first stack were filled with mortar rounds that looked like normal shells used with any 60mm mortar in a pre-System Weapons Company but the second and third stacks were different.

The rounds in the second appeared more high-tech, with circuitry and external thrusters positioned evenly in a ring around the middle of the oblong projectile. My guess was that the floater rounds were designed to hover at the top of their firing arc and then to be called in by a forward observer for a precision barrage.

The final stack had the fewest crates. The rounds within those boxes glimmered with energy in runes etched across their shells.

Appearing behind me to look over my shoulder as I knelt over the open crate, Dayena whistled. *"Spell rounds. Very expensive."*

"We've got pallets of ammo but only one working tube. Once we secure the building, we'll call it in to Command and see if they want to take over this spot as a depot. If not, we'll take the spell rounds and blow the rest.

"Actually, we'll take the spell rounds now and split the Credits from selling them back to the Shop three ways."

Lyrra grinned and gave a thumbs up as she pulled out a communicator. Dayena smiled and patted me on the shoulder as I closed up the spell round crates and stowed them.

I nodded toward the building that loomed behind us. *"We still need to clear the museum itself and see if the Sect left behind any goodies in their haste to deploy."*

Before standing, I slipped a remote detonator into a crate in the middle of the pile for the standard rounds. Just in case. No sense taking any chances while we were occupied with the rest of our mission.

Chapter 9

A three-story wall of glass windows made up the central atrium at the rear of the old museum, though no one appeared inside as we approached. Off to the right-hand side of the atrium were three sets of double doors leading inside. Though the faded signs proclaimed the doors were for emergency exit only, none of them were secured and we entered the multi-leveled lobby with our weapons at the ready.

My nose wrinkled immediately in disgust as we pushed through the inner doors and into the atrium. Stale alcohol mingled with the faint but acrid stench of urine and vomit, the distinct aromas of really shitty dive bars.

Ignoring the stench, little remained inside to hint at the building's original purpose. A sparsely fitted weapons rack sat just inside the doorway, the low-quality blades and cheaply manufactured rifles a sharp contrast from the family friendly displays that I would have expected in a museum.

A staircase took up a good portion of the middle of the room and climbed up to the second level. Scattered around the rest of the floor were a variety of armchairs and circular tables that gave the floor the atmosphere of a quiet hotel lobby or coffee shop. The worn cornflower blue carpet had seen better days and the faded pastel blue-gray paint on the walls seemed like leftovers from the original museum, while neon pink and blue light strips ran along the walls of the dimly lit room. Whoever originally designed the museum must have had a thing for shades of blue.

Motion along the rear portion of the lobby drew my attention and I aimed my pistol automatically, only checking my shot at the last moment instead of blasting the head off a serving droid that was wiping down a bartop counter with a rag. I kept the weapon trained on the droid as it completed the task and returned to a motionless state.

Bartender (Level 31)

[Binary Eclipse Sect]
HP: 310/310

The robot had HP but no MP. It had a Level but no Class. It was a construct, following programmed instructions, with no sentience of its own.

"What. The. Hell?" I muttered, confused enough by the whole setup that I spoke out loud instead of using party chat. Still keeping an eye on the bartender, I glanced at Lyrra and Dayena, but the elven women just shrugged. They didn't have a clue either.

I'd expected an armory filled with weapons, not a lounge lizard den.

With no sign of any Sect members in the lobby, I weaved between the haphazardly placed tables and chairs as I crossed the open space to the bar at the back. When I reached the android bartender, its amber eyes lit up and it straightened upright before stepping up to the other side of the counter.

With two arms and two legs, the android's frame resembled a humanoid, but the proportions were different enough that it was clearly not based on anyone from Earth. A thin, clear shell surrounded the robot's form, offering a view of the wires and circuitry threaded around a metallic skeletal structure.

The bartender scanned me from head to toe and then gave off an audible harumph. "Humans may not be served without a full Sect member chaperone."

The robot server didn't have a nose to look down at me but it felt like it was. The nasal voice and posh accent reminded me of a golden droid from a pre-System movie series.

A glance to either side confirmed there were no Sect members in the lobby. "There are no Sect members here."

"Then you will not receive service."

"Can you tell me where I might find the nearest Sect member?" I asked.

The droid paused for a moment and tilted its head to the side as if in thought or communicating with some kind of internal network. "There are… three… Sect members in the primary armory but non-Sect personnel are not permitted to enter that portion of the base."

The bartender definitely had access to a network that updated it to the locations of personnel within the armory in real time and that meant it had to be eliminated before it could warn them of our presence.

"Oh, I think we'll be fine." My first shot echoed loudly through the atrium as it punched a crater into the android's head, shattering the clear shell over most of its cranium. Sparks shot out of the hole and the robot's entire body shuddered, though it remained standing as it staggered back against the rear counter of the bar. Liquor bottles rattled as the impact shook the racks but none of the glass containers fell over or shattered.

The android's amber eyes blinked out and then returned with a crimson glow. "Hostile actions detected. Engaging combat mode."

Not a good sign. I fired again, the shot glancing off the curved armor of its torso as both arms snapped out from the robot's sides until they were fully extended. Then the clear carapace of the arms split apart into upper and lower halves as the two arms became four. The hands stayed attached to each of the lower arms while long blades unfolded from the forearms of the upper limbs. Arcs of electricity rippled and sparked along one blade while the other glowed white hot.

"Hello there," Lyrra quipped.

"Really?" I asked. I doubted that she heard me over the noise of gunshots, but I still glanced at the Movana in annoyance as I backpedaled away from the bar. My companions went in opposite directions, spreading out through the lobby so that the murder bot couldn't easily reach us all at once.

The bartender hurdled the bar in a single leap but the armor over its central torso shattered from my sustained fire as it landed. An energy beam from Dayena's pistol raked across the exposed chassis, melting enough of the wires and circuitry within that they began smoking.

Despite the Truinnar's attacks, the android remained focused on me. The blades swept in wide arcs that sent me ducking and scrambling around the tables scattered throughout the atrium. The lower arms punched out in a furious flurry of fists.

Focused completely on dodging the barrage of attacks, I all but abandoned offense as I relied on my team to damage the rampaging robot. With no time to holster my pistols in my shoulder rig, I dismissed the weapons directly into my Inventory rather than drop them.

I deflected the next descending strike using the outer portion of the vambrace protecting my forearm. Electric current danced from the blade and along my arm. My muscles seized for an instant from the shock before my resistances overcame the status effect.

The moment of paralysis cost me as the bartender's second blade slashed through the armor over my midsection, melting through the outer layer of Ice Armor before it seared across my stomach. The lower arms followed up with the attack by pounding against my chest, but their damage was inconsequential compared to the pair of energized short swords.

I stepped closer to the murder bot, weathering the storm of fists to grab the bladed arms. My strength surpassed the android's by a slim margin. Not enough that I could rip the limbs free but I could prevent the blades from tearing into me.

Holding the robot in place also allowed Dayena and Lyrra free reign to blast away at the android's exposed back. Gunshots from Lyrra's rifle echoed painfully within the enclosed space of the atrium, far more than my pistols. Several of her shots grazed my flanks, but I felt the robot shudder with each impact as ricocheting bits of hot metal bounced off my exposed flesh. Dayena's fire was less precise and several of her energy beams burned across my armor while she tried to get in attacks of her own.

The struggling robot sagged against me a moment later, as the last of its health evaporated under the constant assault. Rather than trying to pull apart the robot for useful salvage, I dumped the whole thing into Meat Locker to deal with later.

Despite the pain of the wound to my stomach, my natural health regeneration was already dealing with the worst of the injury, and I drank a regeneration booster potion to accelerate my healing. Then I slapped a nanite patch onto the edge of my torn jumpsuit and watched the edges of the damaged portion pull toward each other.

I'll admit, I watched it for a little longer than I needed to. High-tech tomfoolery was still astounding to my 21st century brain at times.

My stomach wasn't fully healed but I didn't think we could wait around. Whoever controlled that murder bot would know that it had been disabled and that the lobby of the armory was breached. "We're on the clock. Let's find those three holdouts."

The elves were already prepared when I looked at them, having finished their own post-combat tasks while I was literally patching myself up.

"Just waiting on you," Dayena responded, her eyes glinting in amusement.

Lyrra charged the bolt of her rifle, having seated a fresh magazine. "You're the one dragging your feet.

I sighed and headed toward the hall that led out of the atrium, finding that someone helpful had taped a written sign to the wall that indexed the building's facilities by floor. The armory we were looking for was listed on the second floor, so we backtracked to the stairs in the center of the atrium and ascended to continue our hunt.

A massive metal door sat on the south side of the atrium's second floor. Wide strips of reinforcing metal banded the portal, and it probably would have been nearly impossible to pry open from the outside, except that the door was currently cracked open. The door opened outward, giving little hint to what lay beyond, but music blared out from within, loud enough that the occupants apparently hadn't heard the firefight in the lobby below.

At Dayena's questioning glance, I shook my head. The armory's heavy reinforcement shielded the interior from Greater Observation, showing only static on my minimap beyond the door.

The Truinnar slid against the door and Lyrra stacked up behind me as I posted against the wall. I nodded to the dark elf, and she heaved on the door, pulling it open enough that I could step through with pistols raised.

Piled just inside the doorway was another stack of standard mortar ammunition crates, this time on top of a hovering pallet jack. If this is where they kept their weapons, why the hell were these idiots keeping the ammunition here too? The Marines always kept ammo well separate from firearms, which was standard practice across the other service branches.

Thankfully, I knew better than to toss grenades sight unseen into an armory. In this case, the consequences of that kind of foolishness would have been explosive.

"Careful with your shots, they've got live ammo piled up in here," I cautioned over party chat as I stepped around the crates and finally got a good look at the armory beyond the stacked boxes.

The nature dioramas and reconstructed fossils from the museum days were long gone, removed by the Sect as they had converted the space into this storage depot. Now the room was filled with large bays of shelving, broken up into smaller units based on the items being stowed. Metal tables ran down the middle of the short and wider side of the L-shaped room, twenty yards straight ahead. The longer side was narrower but split in half by a row of cabinets.

Stepping around the mortar rounds also put me into the view of the Sect members in the room. I recognized a Gribbari goblin but not the other two species: one a purple tree-like alien with green leafy limbs and the other something like a white-furred polar bear standing ten-feet tall on its hind legs.

They saw me and froze in surprise at the sight of my weapons pointed at them. Then Lyrra swung around the other side of the crates with her rifle at her shoulder and all hell broke loose as the alien trio burst into motion.

Clawed gauntlets appeared on the polar bear alien, and he charged toward us. The plant creature backed away and began gesturing out a spell with its tree-branch limbs as the goblin rolled under a table out of sight.

"Brawler, spellcaster, sneak," I tagged each of the aliens in party chat, targeting the goblin first.

Lyrra opened fire on the bear with her rifle in fully automatic mode instead of her usual sniper configuration. Crimson splotches blossomed across the chest of the massive white alien.

I ducked down, snapping off a shot that managed to catch the back of the green-skinned alien's hamstring, hopefully slowing down the fast little bugger. I sent several more shots into the alien's backside, only stopping after I lost sight of the Gribbari behind another pile of crates beneath the counter. Rather than chase after the evasive goblin, I shifted to the bearlike brawler rushing at Lyrra. I opened fire with both pistols and activated Hinder to slow the alien's charge.

Both pistols emptied in seconds, and I dismissed them to Inventory as I pulled out my master-crafted handcannons. The heavy revolver-like weapons thundered in the enclosed space so loudly that the percussion seemed to stun the caster at the end of the chamber, but the spell form in the alien's gnarled hands flew outward.

Green energy swept across the armory as the magic rippled along the walls and floor. Thorny vines sprouted along every solid surface the energy touched, flowing across the room like a new carpet unrolling.

The tendrils twisted around Lyrra, pinning her in place, and then attempted the same with me but failed to find purchase. Unfortunately for the Sect members, the magically spawned brambles still counted as a terrain feature for the application of Efficient Trail. The Class Skill kept me moving freely as I waded through the writhing weeds.

Hinder had slowed the white-furred alien just enough that I cut in front of the charging brawler before he reached Lyrra. Shooting into the bear's chest at point-blank range, I continued around to the massive alien's side and drilled successive attacks into the space beneath its armpit. My attacks drew the creature's ire and distracted him to buy time for the trapped Movana to work herself free of the spell.

Only instead of freeing herself from the thorns, Lyrra trusted me to deal with the brawler and instead focused her fire on the spellcaster at the back of the armory. She continued shooting despite being tugged to her knees by the vines that constricted around her, damaging her health and holding her in place as an easy target.

Any of the polar bear's wild swings would have pasted me if they connected, but the Sect member's attributes clearly emphasized his Strength, and my high Agility and Perception allowed me to dance around the brawler's ponderous blows. Dodging around the alien's side, I poured shot after shot into his midsection as I turned him away from facing Lyrra to stay focused upon me.

Though the armory's shielding properties still interfered with Greater Observation and prevented me from getting a read on the brawler's stats, the sheer number of shots his bloody torso absorbed told me that he was an Advanced Class. The spellcaster holding up against Lyrra's concentrated fire likely was as well, along with the unseen goblin sneak.

A roaring wind swept through armory, carrying with it a whirling hailstorm of razor-sharp leaves. Tiny cuts opened up on the exposed skin of my hands, face, and neck, forcing me to blink rapidly to shield my eyes from the worst of the attack.

Of course, the magic avoided the Sect brawler and the distraction proved almost fatal.

The bear-like alien roared as he engaged an overdrive Skill and suddenly picked up an incredible burst of speed. A swipe from the gauntlet claws scraped deeply into the armor that protected my upper arm. It continued on, the blow tearing across my chest through my armored jumpsuit and into the flesh beneath, before spinning me around from the force of the hit.

Two more strikes gouged my back, dropping my health bar by a quarter. I staggered away and spun around to face the brawler again, the movement buying me a fraction of time. I activated Hinder once more, desperately casting a Frostbolt at the same time. The icy shard lanced into the bear's shoulder, checking an upraised claw before it could swipe down into my face, just long enough for me to angle out of the way.

The wind died off and the magical murder leaves disappeared abruptly, letting me know that one of my squadmates had dealt with the nature mage. The brawler bear didn't seem to care, intent on tearing me to shreds.

The alien spread its arms wide and lunged forward with a roar for a literal bearhug. I stepped back again and again and brought my arms together as I fired both pistols side-by-side into the approaching alien's open mouth. Focused as I was, the drip of blood and saliva from carnivore teeth and the smell of mint-and-flesh filled my senses, accompanied moments later by the ringing explosions of my handcannons.

The shots punched through the roof of the fanged maw and into the bear's brain, the damage finally overcoming the last of the alien's massive health pool. It dropped, sprawling at my feet, and lay still. With the arms of the corpse spread wide, it almost appeared like one of those giant bearskin rugs from a hunting lodge.

Now that the threat of the bearserker was eliminated, I scanned for my next target. At the back of the room, Dayena clashed with the goblin over the body of the bark-skinned spellcaster. The pair moved too quickly for me to risk a shot. Instead, I activated Hinder on the goblin, making good use of my Skill.

The Gribbari slowed and Dayena tore into him, deflecting his blades wide and plunging her short swords into his exposed torso. The goblin froze in place and the dark elf ripped her weapons free as she spun away. As he dropped his daggers, blood poured from the goblin's chest and mouth. Then Dayena slipped back into range and sliced the head from the alien's body before he could recover.

The fight had ended in seconds once Dayena held the advantage in speed.

Expensive enchanted weapons for the win.

Only the sound of our breathing filled the room. The last of the vines collapsed as the spell duration ran its course, the tendrils disintegrating into dust then nothing before ever hitting the ground.

I glanced back at Lyrra and the Movana nodded, confirming that she was fine. The elf had managed to avoid taking any significant damage besides the shallow cuts marring her face and hands from the leaf storm.

"Thank you for stepping in front of the brute," Lyrra said.

Dayena had a nasty slice open on her side from the goblin's counter-ambush, after she'd put down the spellcaster. Our surprise attacker got surprise-attacked herself. Something almost poetic in there. Beyond that, the dark elf suffered only a few minor injuries from the ensuing fight.

Of the three of us, I was the most injured. Blood seeped from the wounds on my chest and back. My jumpsuit quickly became uncomfortable with the warm, wet clinging that soaked down across my stomach and into the crack of my ass from my back before my regeneration sealed the slashes shut. I endured the tacky feeling while I looted the corpse of the bear, receiving a decent sum of Credits and stuffing the lightning claw gauntlets into my Inventory. The bare-chested bear hadn't worn much besides a utility belt, which I also looted, along with an ankle bracelet and the alien's boots, before absorbing the corpse into Meat Locker. Once my bleeding stopped, I burned the Mana for a casting of Cleanse to eliminate the discomfort and turned my attention to the state of the armory.

Already shuffling through one of the lockers at the end of the room, Dayena jerked her head toward the bare corpses of the goblin and tree alien when she caught my eye. The dead disappeared into Meat Locker and I turned to the next storage locker beside the Truinnar, only to find it secured with a cybernetic padlock.

I pulled out my gnomish lockcracker and the device whirred as it went to work. When it finally flashed green and the lock popped open, it had been quite a few seconds. It took longer to crack the security here than at the Sect administrator's penthouse balcony. Apparently, the Sect felt the need for higher security on its weapons than on its personnel.

The padlock twisted free, and I stored it away with the lockcracking device before swinging open the formerly locked door. My eyebrow raised as I saw the contents. "That's not a bad haul."

The vault contained racks of armored suits that ranged from thin coveralls to full plate. Nothing powered, but all rated in the upper tier III to tier II. Mass-produced, but high quality nonetheless, and certainly better than what most of the hired guns outside had worn.

Which begged the question of why those forces hadn't been equipped with the contents of this armory. Was this gear being held for yet more troops? My eavesdropped conversation with Jer'myeh had hinted at more forces converging on Denver. The stockpiled equipment made me wonder if even more troops were converging on the city from elsewhere.

Still, pristine gear hanging on racks in an armory beat stripping armor from leaking corpses. Whatever the reason, I wasn't going to pass up free loot. There was too much for us to carry, even with the three of us, and we spent a good twenty minutes sorting through the most worthwhile gear.

We ended up leaving behind the lowest tier equipment, piled in the middle of the vault with some of the explosives tied to the detonators outside. No sense in leaving anything for the Sect if we could help it.

After closing the vault and the armory doors, we moved back to the foyer. Lyrra checked in with Pharyleri command, who had no spare elements to take over the remains of a mortar battery.

No matter the species, everyone enjoyed a good explosion, so we gathered at the windows before I triggered the detonator. The munitions pile outside erupted into a small mushroom cloud that rose higher than the building as a slight rumble from behind us marked the destruction of the leftover equipment in the vault.

My only regret was that I lacked the room in my Inventory to steal even more gear from the Sect.

Chapter 10

No ambush waited for us as I pushed out of the reinforced doors of the former museum's main entrance. The pitch-dark sky outside showed that dawn remained several hours in the future.

I pushed my senses out with Greater Observation but found nothing unusual.

"Shall we make some more Credits?" Dayena asked as she summoned her ride.

Before I could respond, Lyrra jumped excitedly. "More experience!"

I raised an eyebrow at the Movana, who normally stayed fairly reserved.

The blonde elf met my expression with a smile, still bouncing on her toes. "I'm almost to my next Level after that fight inside. Advanced Class time!"

"Know what you'll pick?" I asked, summoning out my own bike.

Lyrra shrugged, still smiling as she climbed up behind Dayena. "Nope! I know what options the System usually offers at the next tier but I'm hoping maybe something rare will pop up. After all the trouble I've been getting into with you two, maybe I'll meet the obscure requirements for some unique Advanced Class."

"Don't get your hopes up too far, we're not that special."

Dayena frowned at my comment. "Rude."

Lyrra rolled her eyes. "Sure you're not special, Mr. Hunter who Levels at Advanced Class pace."

I glared at the Movana, though there was no real anger in my gaze. The last time I'd exposed my actual Class had been just before entering the contract with the Countess, so Lyrra had never seen what I kept hidden. Despite that, there were certain things I couldn't hide over a long enough period of time.

As Lyrra pointed out, my Levels grew more slowly than hers and were more on par with Dayena's advancement. Also, my resilience, afforded by my resistances and abnormally large Constitution, kept me on my feet after taking damage that would have demolished even a Basic Class tank.

"You're not wrong but drop it. Some things should not be said out loud." My shift to party chat emphasized my seriousness, but I waited until Lyrra nodded in understanding before I continued. "I'm happy you're close to ranking up and would be delighted to help with gaining more experience."

The elf clapped and I looked at Dayena with a shake of my head at the Movana's enthusiasm. I had to admit, I was a little jealous of the elf. It would be a while yet before I could achieve my next Class. I hadn't even made it to the final tier of my current Class to unlock the final rank of Class Skills at Level 46. I was really looking forward to that last batch of Skills, especially with the Skill Points that I'd been stockpiling.

The last unlocks for a Class were always the most powerful abilities and they were taunting me with how close I was to getting them. Less than a Level to go now, but even the Sect members I'd slain tonight only inched my experience bar up miniscule amounts.

The higher the Level, the harder it was to advance.

At least the new Skills would help me grind the rest of the way to Level 50, though that challenge remained off in the distant future. The present needed my full attention, and that meant continuing with our raid through the Sect holdings.

"Next target then?" Dayena asked.

I revved the engine on my bike but the communicator on my belt vibrated before I could throttle up to pull out of the museum drive. I grabbed the Pharyleri device and put it to my ear, where it stuck in place in a hands-free mode that didn't annoy me like pre-System wireless earbuds.

"Hal, I need your help," Ismyna chirped in my ear. The gnome who had captained the forging of the System-enabled railway that connected Denver and Pittsburgh now commanded the gnome's local military forces.

"I'm listening."

"I know you've got your eyes on all those Credit payouts from the target of opportunity list, but you're in position to intercept a few Sect members that are heading east. We've got a drone on them but it's almost out of juice. We don't know what they're doing but they don't look like they're running away from the conflict."

"What are you asking us to do?"

"Follow, observe, and, if the opportunity arises, eliminate the Sect cohort. And yes, before you ask, I'm prepared to release Credits for each of those tasks, so you won't be missing out on your payday. We had another merc unit lined up for this kind of thing, but the Wolverines got themselves ambushed and the survivors aren't in any shape to accept missions."

"Send the coordinates, we'll check it out."

"Thanks, Hal. I'll owe you one."

"Keep your one Credit. I'm looking for a whole lot more."

Ismyna chuckled and killed the connection. The communicator hummed a moment later and I punched the newly arrived coordinates into the nav system on my bike.

"Change of plans," I informed the elves using party chat. *"I'm sure you heard part of that. Some Sect members are acting suspicious and Ismyna wants us to check them out. Since she's willing to pay out for the ask, it's probably serious."*

"Hopefully, we'll get to take them out for their experience!" Lyrra was enjoying herself far too much.

I raised an eyebrow. *"Since when did you become so bloodthirsty?"*

"Level 50!"

In some ways, the siren call of higher Levels and new abilities was just as intoxicating as any drug. Though it would fade into the grind once she hit the next tier, Lyrra was riding that buzz now.

With a shake of my head, I gunned the throttle of my bike and sped away from the museum. I turned south onto Highway 2 as Dayena followed behind and I slowed just enough to allow the Truinnar to catch up.

Thick, white flurries of snow began drifting down out of the sky to swirl around us as we continued south. We stayed on the 2 until the waypoint guided me onto the offramp for 83 East. I slowed us not long after, as the coordinates relayed from the Pharyleri drone were just ahead.

I caught sight of a vehicle and eased to the side of the road, slowing further once I locked Greater Observation onto the target. The contraption was a two-part vehicle propelled by tank tracks in the rear with the cab of a truck at the front. A turret faced forward above the cab, while an armored compartment took up the truck bed to the rear.

As if it had waited for us to get caught up with the Sect members, the snow picked up from gently drifting flurries to a swirling snow squall. Visibility plummeted and, if I hadn't already locked onto the vehicle, we would have had to get dangerously close to follow. If we'd even found them in the snow since I doubted the drone could have stayed on track through the growing storm.

High tech met high magic and half the time, high tech lost.

Damn dragons.

Dayena pulled up tight on my flank to stay close enough to take visual cues on directions from me, but the half-track remained on course down Highway 83. I squeezed my eyes tight against the wind and the temperatures dropped further as we pursued the Sect vehicle. If the storm got much worse, I would need to pull a helmet from Inventory and I hated wearing helmets.

Though the cold didn't affect Dayena or me all that much with our Advanced Class resistances and higher Constitutions, Lyrra felt the effects enough for all of us. She nestled tight against Dayena's back to hunker out of the wind as much as possible.

The link to the drone was already disconnected. A check on my bike's nav system showed that either the drone was out of range or it had lost power in the storm. We'd caught up to our quarry just in time.

It was well below freezing by the time the ungainly vehicle pulled off the highway, turning down a divided road into Cherry Creek State Park. When the vehicle stopped, not far from the frozen edges of the reservoir at the center of the park, I signaled for my compatriots to dismount. We stowed our bikes and approached the rest of the way on foot, slinking through the darkness amidst the shadows of the trees that lined the road until we reached a gated encampment on the lakeshore.

The snow swirled around a watchtower standing above the gate, but the lone guard within seemed more intent on observing the inside of the compound than any threat from outside the walls. A few automated turrets surrounded the perimeter to deal with low tier monsters but were widely spaced enough that they wouldn't prove a deterrent to any serious external assault.

I hummed over party chat as I noticed another detail about the compound. *"The razorwire on top of the wall is angled inward like a prison fence. The Sect isn't worried about keeping anyone out of this base—they want to keep something inside."*

"I will see what we are dealing with," Dayena responded.

The Countess crouched low to the ground and slipped forward, disappearing in an instant. The dark elf was practically invisible in the snowfall as her active camouflage distorted her outline. Only the connection to her over party chat allowed me to track her progress.

If you ignored the presence of the Sect structures, sitting in the center of the snowstorm felt calm and peaceful after the violent activities of the night. For a few minutes, nothing disturbed the serenity of the falling snow.

When Dayena's voice resonated telepathically over party chat, I let out a long sigh at having the momentary lull in activity broken. *"There is a Dungeon portal at the edge of the reservoir leading under the water and several buildings for slaves."*

"An underwater Dungeon sounds nasty. Were you able to get close enough to check the Level rating on it?" I asked.

"Twenty to thirty."

"Kinda low, don't you think?" Lyrra asked.

"For a City Dungeon inside a Safe Zone, I think it is decent. Suitable enough for low-Level adventurers and civilians who are not focused on combat Classes," Dayena replied.

I couldn't see any way that crafters or civilians not associated with the Sect were getting through the compound defenses. *"The question is, who exactly is running the Dungeon with it walled off like this? Most of the Sect members we've been fighting are toward the upper end of Basic or somewhere in the Advanced Class range."*

Dayena snapped back. *"That would be the poor souls normally kept shackled up inside the primitive bunkhouse next to the Dungeon entrance."*

"Is the Sect running some kind of Dungeon sweatshop?" I asked.

The dark elf remained silent for a moment. *"Is that something like a sauna?"*

"It's a term for a factory paying absurdly low wages for long hours of manual labor. The System's arrival made most of the goods produced from them almost irrelevant, though I'm sure some assholes have managed to adapt to the times. Besides coffee and chocolate, you're not missing out on much."

Lyrra chuckled darkly. *"That term certainly describes more than a few Galactic corporations and their exploitation of Artisans under their employ."*

"I haven't had the pleasure of interacting with many corporations yet here on Earth." I shrugged with a glance over at her.

The elf shook her head. *"Soulless, monolithic, and willing to do anything to squeeze out an extra Credit for their shareholders."*

"Sounds like the System didn't change anything there besides the currency they hunger for."

Dayena cleared her throat pointedly over party chat. *"If you two are finished with the social commentary, I count a total of eight Sect guards. Only six are combat Classes with the final two an Appraiser and an Actuary. That last pair and two of the other guards are standing beside the Dungeon portal now."*

I thought for a moment as I looked over the armored gate and the watchtower. *"Mark a spot where Lyrra and I can sneak over the wall. We'll hit the group at the Dungeon, put them down while they're split off on their own. Then we'll deal with the rest of the guards as they respond."*

A waypoint appeared on my minimap as Dayena highlighted one of the turrets halfway around the side of the compound. *"Cross at that turret. I have disrupted it and you will be out of the firing arc of the guns on either side."*

"On our way," I replied, creeping through the trees of the park beyond the line of sight from the defenses on top of the wall.

Lyrra followed in my wake until we reached a position in the treeline opposite the designated turret. I darted out over the open ground surrounding the Sect base and covered the killing field in less than a dozen strides. Planting my back against the smooth face of the concrete-like wall, I crouched with my hands cupped at waist level in front of me.

My Movana companion was only a pace behind me by the time I was in position, and she hopped lightly onto the offered foothold with no hesitation. I threw the elf toward the top of the twelve-foot barricade as she pushed off my hands like a springboard. The nimble elf landed atop the wall, deftly avoiding the razor wire strands that angled to the interior.

I backed away from the wall, giving myself a single stride to build momentum before leaping. Lyrra grabbed my wrist as my other hand landed on top of the wall. With the Movana's aid, I scrambled the rest of the way up and the two of us hurdled the razor wire to jump into the compound.

Good thing they were so focused on the inside; they didn't even spend a little extra to point the razor wire outside too, or else our entry would have been a touch more painful.

Rolling as I hit the ground, I popped back upright with both pistols drawn but I needn't have bothered. There were no signs that our arrival had been observed. Unsurprisingly, Dayena had picked an excellent spot for us to cross the wall as the ramshackle bunkhouse blocked sight of our position from both the tower at the main gate and the rest of the compound.

We crept along the rear of the building, and I noticed there were finger-sized gaps in the thin metal of the structure's exterior, allowing the wind and snow to flow freely through the cracks. The only way a System building could be this poorly built was an intentionally faulty design.

Peeking through the slats revealed a dimly lit interior with metal frame bunks, threadbare blankets, and a space heater far too small to provide any meaningful warmth with the flimsy construction of the building. Anyone inside would find the structure barely provided any protection from the elements. While most people should have a decent enough Constitution after two years under the System, I suspected the Sect was likely restricting the advancement of anyone stuck here.

Once I reached the rear corner of the bunkhouse that was only a few feet from the edge of the reservoir, I carefully peered out.

The shimmering of the Dungeon portal sat less than a dozen yards away through the swirling snow. The quartet of Sect members stood in an arc facing it as if waiting for someone or something to emerge. The pair with non-combat Basic Classes were both human and armed, while the other two were extremely alien.

Crythis Hive Sentinel (Level 24) (A)
[Binary Eclipse Sect]
HP: 980/980
MP: 860/860
Status: Sluggish

The Crythis stood eight feet tall, a hard-shelled insectoid with four legs and four arms, bearing some vague resemblance in form to a praying mantis with a mottled blue and purple carapace. The insect wore gray armor plates that looked riveted or bolted to the major sections of its carapace. The way the creature hunched in on itself combined with the status to indicate that the cold was taking its toll on it, despite the glowing heat coils affixed to the armor plates on its shoulders and back.

The final Sect member waiting by the portal was a humanoid feline with the head and curved horns of a ram.

Satyr Blade Dancer (Level 16) (A)

[Binary Eclipse Sect]

HP: 840/840

MP: 740/740

Status: Inner Fire

Shit.

The Satyr wore a dark red bodysuit with thin, form-fitting armor plates of the same color overtop.

Beyond the guards stood another structure that appeared more solidly constructed than the longer hovel that I currently hid behind.

"Want to bet there's a group of their prisoners inside the Dungeon?" I asked as I pulled back so Lyrra could see the base layout for herself.

"No bet," Dayena replied without hesitation.

Lyrra took a quick look and then moved back. *"I'll pass."*

"Where are you?"

Dayena chuckled. *"On the other side of the compound. I just finished setting up a present for anyone coming out of the guard shack when we start the party."*

I appreciated her forethought. *"Three inside their quarters, one in the tower, and four in the open. The truck we followed is parked inside the gate, with none of the guards nearby. Am I missing anything?"*

"An accurate summary."

"Give me a boost," Lyrra said, tapping my arm and then pointing to the top of the ramshackle prisoner bunkhouse.

I helped the elf to the roof the same way we'd climbed the compound's exterior wall. Once she slipped out of sight overhead, I posted back up at the corner with a pistol in one hand and a plasma grenade in the other. *"If Dayena is ready, give us the go signal when you're in position, Lyrra."*

"Copy. It'll just take me a minute. I'm trying to keep the cheap metal from creaking loudly as I get to the peak." Frustration tinged the elf's tone.

"Don't take too long. I doubt these guys are the type to stand around in the cold without a good reason."

"I'm at the top of the roof. Dayena, you ready?"

"Affirmative. The Blade Dancer is mine to deal with," the Countess replied.

"Going hot in three. Two. One."

I tossed the grenade around the corner with an underhand throw, aiming just between the Crythis and one human Sect member, both with their backs facing me. The grenade detonated with a roar as the sharp crack of a rifle from the rooftop above me broke through the howling wind.

The blue-white flames of the explosion wrapped around the energy shields protecting the two Sect members, which flashed red for an instant before failing under the plasma's intense heat. The human also being shielded came as a surprise since the Sect seemingly cared less about their local recruits, though the defense hadn't held against the force of the blast anyway.

I joined Lyrra on the offensive, stepping fully around the building and opening fire on the Sentinel with Last Word as I pulled Ace from the holster on my right hip. My second handcannon barked as I fired at the human Actuary, who was still screaming and attempting to put out the plasma flames.

The Sentinel turned to face me, and a trio of rounded energy shields blossomed from three of the insectoid's arms. The fourth arm held a machine pistol with a lengthy magazine protruding from the grip. The alien wove the shields in front of itself, constantly rotating the shield taking damage after every couple hits so that my shots never managed to break through. The damaged shield was hidden behind two fresh force fields and regenerated by the time the insectoid brought it to the fore again.

From in between the complex weaving of the circular shields, the alien's machine pistol poked out just far enough to burp out a handful of shots before the shields covered the weapon again. The rounds thudded across the armor of my chest hard enough to bruise but a small enough caliber that they spalled off, leaving gouges and scrapes behind instead of punching through.

The damage to my health was minimal but the bigger problem was the way the alien kept changing out its shields. Expose was only effective when I could consistently attack the same shield or armor. Without consistent attacks on the same defensive barrier, my Class Skill's damage bonus reset each time.

Two more rounds from my right-hand pistol dropped the human and I sidestepped closer to the water's edge as I brought Ace to bear on the alien. The insectoid stalked forward and I shifted my aim, snapping shots around the shields that protected its body.

One projectile broke through the segmented chitin that covered the ankle joint above the alien's front foot, or whatever that was called on an insect. The alien's leg crumpled slightly, and it spread the shields to cover itself more thoroughly instead of just protecting its core.

For a moment, the alien's pattern faltered as it began limping and a gap between the shields exposed its gun hand. I drove my fire into the opening and orange ichor splashed as my rounds shredded the limb. The gun dropped as several finger-like appendages were severed, but the weapon continued belching fire from one jammed down on the trigger. Rounds sprayed from the out-of-control autopistol, raking the inside of the alien's shields before the weapon hit the ground.

The alien hopped and danced above the gun as it continued bucking with each round fired. The weapon spun in a circle, bouncing along the ground as the Crythis jumped backward to put its shields between itself and its lost firearm.

I couldn't imagine how poor the creature's Luck must be for this particular chain of events to occur, but I capitalized on the alien's distraction.

Picking my shots carefully, I drilled several rounds into exposed joints between carapace segments. More orange ichor splashed out until the gun fell silent.

Despite the damage I'd dished out, the insectoid was only down to about half health as it turned its attention back to me. It started for me again, moving slower now with a hitch in its steps from the injuries plaguing its front legs. I had no desire to let the multi-limbed alien close the distance, but I didn't have much room to fall back between the wall, the bunkhouse, and the water's edge.

Instead of retreating, I ran to my left, skirting along the front of the prisoner barracks and toward the front gate. It was a risk with the guard still in the watchtower there, but I couldn't get pinned into place with no room to maneuver. Despite my continued training with Dayena, my gunfu hadn't reached the tier where I was confident with solo confrontations at this level.

I continued firing at the Crythis as I went, my shots still splashing against its shields.

The Crythis limped along in my wake for several paces until it realized that it had little chance of catching up. The alien's hesitation offered me a moment to glimpse the wider skirmish and I took the break to reload the cylindrical magazines of both pistols.

The second human non-combat Classer was down and Dayena was trading blows with the Satyr. Streaks of blood covered the area around the pair and new splashes of crimson arced out as their blades flashed over one another, leaving behind ragged cuts and slashes through both combatant's light armor. The hot liquid flung free of the weapons to steam across the white ground, quickly disappearing as snow continued to fall.

The Crythis opted to engage the Countess alongside the Blade Dancer but kept two of its shields between us to intercept my attacks. The insectoid moved the third shield to its front, which left its back open for Lyrra, who had been biding her time atop the bunkhouse since her opening volley to avoid giving away her position.

The Movana's rifle barked out single shots so quickly the echoes overlapped in one long peel of thunder. The Crythis staggered under the barrage as the rounds tore into the back of its head. Its legs buckled and it dropped to the ground, fully exposed as its arms instinctively attempted to break its fall.

I reversed direction and charged toward the stricken alien with my reloaded guns blazing. To further slow the Crythis, I activated Hinder and added a casting of Frostbolt alongside the Skill usage.

The jagged shard of ice formed between my pistols and streaked across the short distance that separated me from the insectoid alien. The icy lance drilled into the Crythis between two of the armor plates that protected its side, cracking through the carapace as it dug deep. Rime spread around the wound as orange ichor streamed down the alien's side.

The combined weight of fire from Lyrra and me stripped away the last of the insectoid's health before I reached it. The Crythis collapsed and a flood of experience accompanied a notification that pinged for my attention at the corner of my vision.

I ignored the update and readied another use of Hinder for Dayena's foe, but the dark elf didn't need my help. The Satyr was on his knees with one of the Truinnar's blades shoved through his chest. Dayena planted a foot on the alien's chest and pulled her weapon free, leaving the alien to slump onto his back.

With no immediate threats in view, I automatically swapped magazines on my handcannons again. The final set of Sect members hadn't ventured out from the security of their barracks and with the combat over, only the wind blowing through the compound made any noise, whistling through the cracks of the rickety prisoner bunkhouse.

Chapter 11

A glance through the snowfall at the watchtower beside the front gate showed no sign of the sentry there. I reached out with Greater Observation. Even pushing on the Skill full force without my usual subtlety found nothing. Either the sentry had a high tier stealth Skill or had abandoned their post when things went poorly for the other Sect members.

The door to the guard's dorm behind Dayena opened and a human stepped out, a black-haired man with a curled handlebar mustache and a pointed goatee that practically screamed cartoon villain. He didn't even look up from fastening the straps of an armored chestplate. "Are any of the plebes still alive now that you've finished with the usual post-Dungeon beating?"

Angel Rivera (Flashing Fencer Level 6) (A)
[Binary Eclipse Sect]
HP: 860/860
MP: 600/600
Status: Fleet Feet

When no one answered, Angel paused in adjusting the strap under his arm and finally looked up. His jaw dropped and his face went pale as he took in the bodies lying around the Dungeon portal with the Countess and me standing over them.

I shot the man in the face while he stood stunned. The round sent him staggering back into the open doorway before he could draw the rapier on his hip.

A golden-furred alien of medium-height dashed out the door, wearing nothing much but holding up a thick rectangular shield of riveted metal to block my attacks. The werejackal took a single stride before falling over face first with a high-pitched scream as it encountered Dayena's little surprise.

The Truinnar's mono-molecular tripline strung across the walkway had severed one foot completely and left the other leg torn to the bone before the strand snapped. Despite the severity of the injuries and the purple blood spurting from the stump of its left leg, the alien rolled upright with a scream of pain and managed to get its shield back into position. With the rectangular base of the shield planted on the ground and a Skill kicking in, making it glow, the werejackal was covered once more. Though not before I managed to grab an Identify.

Jarack Shield-Bearer (Level 48) (B)
[Binary Eclipse Sect]
HP: 418/610
MP: 400/480
Status: Regeneration, Bleeding, Crippled

Behind the Jarack, the human rushed out of the guardhouse with his rapier in hand. The final Sect member, another human, posted up just inside as they used the doorway for partial cover with the barrel of a rifle extending out of the building.

Tiana DuBois (Huntress Level 44) (B)

[Binary Eclips Sect]

HP: 440/440

MP: 220/220

Status: Falcon's Grace, Steady Hand

The muzzle of the rifle belched fire over the edge of the shield of the injured werejackal and a round snapped past my ear with a high-pitched whine. I returned fire at the gunman, or gunwoman it turned out, and she shrieked when my rounds hit home.

Lyrra also opened fire and her first shot scraped the doorframe, spalling off to catch the gunner with the ricochet. Our combined attacks forced the woman to edge further into cover behind the doorway, but she kept firing despite her wounds.

I sidestepped rather than remain an unmoving target in the open. Even with my movement, several rounds hit and punched through my armor as we exchanged shots.

Since the arrival of the System, I'd been shot, burned, stabbed, bitten, shocked, and had limbs torn off. As the Jarack proved, one could push through the pain with sufficient Willpower. The System would heal most damage eventually if you survived whatever caused the injury.

Hell, for some Classes, Skills grew more powerful the more you were injured.

My health dipped but the bullets hadn't hit anything vital, so I kept throwing a stream of fire back at the shooter. I dropped an occasional shot at the Shield-Bearer to keep the alien huddled behind its hunk of metal. Of course, the way the shield kept glowing, I was anticipating more Skill surprise at some point.

The Fencer bolted out from behind the Jarack and rushed toward me, his feet moving so fast that their motion blurred. Dayena slipped between us and engaged the swordsman, while I continued moving farther left to angle around the werejackal's shield.

When I got a side view of the Jarack, I activated Rend to take further advantage of the alien's bleeding condition. My attacks pounded into its flank and more purple blood appeared to mat the werejackal's fur. The alien staggered to its feet using the shield as leverage and then turned to stumble straight for me with the bulwark now blocking my shots.

Though twenty feet separated us, the alien lunged forward and crossed the space in an eyeblink with the activation of a Skill. The shield knocked my pistols out to either side and slammed into my chest.

The impact sent me flying backward, rolling ass over teakettle for a dozen yards before I skidded to a stop against the inside of the compound's front gate. I pushed off the wall and stood as the Jarack hobbled after me, now with a falcata in one hand. The golden-silver metal of the forward-curved shortsword seemed to glisten with a flashing energy that flashed over the area as the light reflected from the snow-covered ground.

"A little help, Lyrra? The Jarack's back should be wide open."

The Movana grunted. *"Kinda busy keeping this sharpshooter pinned. I can give you a couple rounds."*

True to her word, the Jarack's advance toward me jerked to a halt as the elf lit up the alien's back. The alien pivoted to face Lyrra's position atop the bunkhouse.

With only a limited window of opportunity, I unloaded the full rotation of my most effective abilities. Frostbolt and Hinder joined the hailstorm of rounds from my handcannons as they hammered straight into the alien's exposed back. The attacks nearly knocked the Shield-Bearer over onto his face, but the alien miraculously remained on his feet–probably courtesy of some knockdown resisting Skill.

As the Jarack teetered and regained balance, I charged to close the distance. I didn't particularly want to get close to that nasty looking sword, but I couldn't give the alien the chance to use another shield bash or control the range with its defensive abilities. Distantly, the fight continued with Lyrra returning to her exchange of fire with the sniper inside the barracks.

I dismissed Ace into my Inventory rather than holster the weapon and grabbed hold of the alien's sword arm with my free hand. The Jarack struggled against my grip, unprepared for my Strength to rival it with my Class masked and Levels showing below its own. I pinned the blade across its chest and triggered shots into the alien's already bleeding side until I emptied the magazine of my other pistol.

The alien activated a Skill that shrouded its body in a translucent shield, just in time to block the final few rounds, but the ability failed to dislodge my grasp. Despite the hasty save and its earlier regeneration potion, the Jarack's health showed only a third remaining and the bar ticked downward as the bleed effect of Rend continued.

The Shield-Bearer twisted and interposed the edge of his still-glowing tower shield between us. A blast of energy erupted from the front face and launched me away. I spun in the air and landed on my feet, fortunate that I'd only caught the edge of the accumulated energy despite the damage that further lowered my health.

I charged back at the Shield-Bearer, noting that the shield no longer glowed and that the alien was struggling to raise his sword arm. Taking advantage of the momentary weakness, I feinted a straight-on charge, and the Jarack braced himself behind his shield.

I sidestepped just before I reached the alien, replacing the empty pistol in my hand with my combat knife and lunging around the planted tower shield to stab the energy shield protecting the alien's bleeding side. Expose stacked with each jab until the barrier failed and the blade plunged into the Jarack's torso.

The Jarack let out a noise somewhere between a moan and a sigh as purple blood poured out of the wound to coat my hand. I sawed the knife through the alien's flesh, and it scraped between the werejackal's ribs.

The werejackal's struggles weakened, and it lost the grip on the shield. The bulwark thudded heavily to the snowy ground as I worked the knife further into its chest. The alien's health zeroed out and it sagged against me.

I pushed the body away and it fell, the blade sliding out of the ragged wound I'd left in the alien's chest with a tearing squelch. I stood above the dead alien with purple blood dripping from my hand and knife as I confirmed the notification for its death.

Certain of my kill, I turned back to the rest of the fight. Unsurprisingly, the mustachioed fencer was down and Dayena stood with her hands on her hips as she faced down the open doorway into the guard barracks. "Throw out your weapon and emerge with your hands in the air."

The command in the Truinnar's voice brooked no argument, but for a moment nothing could be heard over the wind. Then a wet cough came from inside the doorway. "You'll just kill me anyways."

"If we are required to come in after you, then your death is assured."

A moment later, the rifle soared out of the open door and clattered across the ground. It left behind a furrow through the snow until it came to rest. The Countess glanced at me and then nodded toward the weapon, signaling that I should pick up the loot.

Before I headed to the rifle, I stripped the Jarack. Then I trudged over to the long gun and brushed off the snow as I examined it.

The rifle resembled the old standard issue M4 but bore the hallmarks of System enhancement, especially in the silvery runework that circled the muzzle of the barrel. I'd have to check whether it would be an upgrade to Lyrra's current weapon before I offloaded it at the Shop. With all my extra Inventory spaces, I was the designated pack mule for our party, so I stowed the rifle away before looting the Fencer's gear.

While I was still crouching in the snow after touching the dead man, storing away yet another corpse in Meat Locker, the rifle's owner finally emerged from the barracks with her hands raised. The dark-skinned woman with box braids glanced between Dayena and me before looking for her missing rifle on the ground. Tiana frowned but remained silent when she saw the empty depression in the snow where I'd picked up the weapon.

Dayena waited until Lyrra dropped down from the roof to join us, then gestured to the shimmering Dungeon entrance. "What is the purpose of this compound?"

The woman's face shifted uncomfortably, clearly hesitant to answer. Her eyes lingered on the Countess and locked in on the gleaming blade of a shortsword at the Truinnar's waist as the dark elf began to slowly inch the weapon from its sheath. "City Dungeon. Farming low-tier materials."

"With slave labor."

The woman flinched at my tone but didn't deny the assertion.

Normally, I didn't care much about what happened to people who managed to get themselves in trouble with signing a short-sighted contract of servitude or indenture. People who reneged on those agreements formed the bread-and-butter assignments for bounty hunters like myself under the System, and I'd brought in my share of warm bodies in exchange for tidy sums of Credits.

Still, those contracts had obligations on the other side too. Serfs and servants required food, housing, and usually involved working in the relative shelter of a Safe Zone.

Whatever bullshit was going on here was something else entirely. The state of the bunkhouse was one thing, but being forced to delve into a Dungeon as a non-combat Class was pure insanity without appropriate support from a proper party and advanced equipment. I doubted the Sect assisted their Dungeon farmers with anything remotely resembling appropriate support.

"What happens to the materials?"

In response to Dayena's question, the woman pointed one of her raised hands to indicate the lakeside corner of the guardhouse.

"Show us," Dayena commanded.

Tiana led us around the corner to where another building was set back against the wall. The solidly built structure resembled the guard barracks more than the drafty prisoner bunkhouse but completely lacked any windows. The vehicle we'd followed through the storm was backed up to a loading dock off to the left side of the building, opposite the waterfront. Besides that sealed entry, a single-entry personnel door directly in front of us was secured with a System-tech lockplate.

Tiana stopped just before the door. "I don't have access."

"Not a problem." Dayena grinned confidently as she strutted past the woman and leaned over the lockplate. Her fingers danced over the panel as she activated a Skill. For a moment, nothing happened and then the panel flashed green. The Truinnar stood with a smirk and gestured for the woman to open the door.

When Tiana hesitated before stepping up to the entry, I drew my pistols, remaining out of sight behind the Sect member. Whatever waited inside was either a threat to her or a threat to us.

The door slid open as the Huntress touched the deactivated lockplate, allowing dim, yellow-orange light to spill out of the opening and revealing a deceptively large interior. The System shenanigans that permitted "bigger on the inside" construction were in full effect here, as the rear of the warehouse faded into gloom beyond row after row of shelving units. Several waist-high tables stood in lines on either side of the entryway and a frail woman shot to her feet at the far end of the metallic workbenches.

Camila Hernandez (Housekeeper Level 23) (B)
HP: 230/230
MP: 280/280
Status: Shackled, Enslaved

Between the lack of a Sect association and the effects listed in her status, I dismissed the middle-aged Hispanic woman as any kind of a threat. Though I wasn't sure what role exactly she played here, the spotlessly clean tables and her Class hinted at a portion of her duties.

Camila appeared terrified when Tiana walked through the door and then froze in alarm when the rest of our group entered with weapons in hand. A black metal collar encircled the Hispanic woman's neck and glowed with ominous red lights which flashed intermittently. She also wore shackles around each wrist that connected with a thin chain, just long enough that she could pick up one of the uniformly sized crates that filled the racks populating the warehouse.

"Cover the Huntress, Lyrra. I'm going to see what's on the shelves," I informed the party.

The Housekeeper shrank back as I strode beyond the end of the tables and moved past her, but immediately froze and stared down at the floor when I glanced over. I kept a wary eye on her as I continued over to the nearest shelf and holstered Last Word before popping open the lid on one of the crates.

The box was filled with hunks of metallic ore, each a little larger than the size of my closed fist. Crystals glinted from within the unrefined chunks, and I fished one out, holding it up as I examined it with Greater Observation.

Chunk of Glacial Ore

Weight: 5.15 lbs

Glacial Ore is a raw material that can be refined into Glacial Iron and Glacial Steel. Particularly adept at accepting Frost, Ice, or Cold-based enchantments, Glacial metals are highly desired by Artisans wishing to advance their Skills in these domains.

Checking another crate beside the first, I discovered stacks of what appeared to be fish-scales larger than my thumb. I turned and looked between the Housekeeper and Huntress. "Crafting materials?"

Camila nodded enthusiastically. "Yes, sir. The Dungeon crew offloads their materials onto the tables, and I sort the loot into the appropriately labeled containers. Once everything is sorted, I clean the area until the next batch is brought in. Is everything to your satisfaction, sir?"

The explanation showed the reason for the Sect's use of humans with the Auditor and other similar Classes. They were the mechanism that prevented the prisoners from hiding anything in their Inventories and forced the turnover of the Dungeon loot. Though the biggest problem right now was that the poor woman thought I was just another Sect goon. "No, there's one thing bothering me. Dayena, get that thing off her."

"Wait, sir. What?"

The Countess walked up beside the Housekeeper. "This shall only take a moment."

The woman froze with a wide-eyed expression, breathing deeply as she attempted not to hyperventilate. She let out a squeak as Dayena placed her hands gently on the device around her neck. "Please don't make my head blow up."

"She'll take care of you, don't worry," I reassured the woman.

"Don't do it. The Sect won't take kindly to you releasing their property," Tiana warned.

Still holding the ore, I raised the pistol in my other hand to point at the Sect member. "When I want your opinion on anything, I'll ask for it."

She sneered. "You're a dead man walking."

I shook my head. "Better beings than you have tried."

That gave her pause. Before Tiana could respond further, the collar around the Housekeeper's neck clicked and popped open. Dayena eased it from around the woman's neck then the collar disappeared into her Inventory. "You are free."

Tears glistened in Camila's eyes as she rubbed her neck where the device had been, too overwhelmed to speak.

"We should check the Dungeon," Dayena sent over party chat, unheard by the Sect member or former slave.

"Yes, but I don't trust this Huntress not to cause problems if we have to haul her along," I responded.

"Then take out the trash."

She wasn't wrong. We couldn't just leave the woman to her own devices when she'd been trying to kill us not long ago. I replaced the ore in the crate and closed the container before I started back to where the others waited between the tables by the entrance.

Without warning, the Huntress bolted for the open door. Lyrra opened fire, her rifle thundering in the enclosed space of the warehouse. One round clipped the fleeing woman's hip and she bounced off the frame of the doorway before making it out the door.

I sprinted past Lyrra as the elf fired out the entry portal. Once out of the building, I found Tiana had a significant lead. I activated Hinder, feeling the ability somehow slide off, leaving her unaffected as I managed to snap off a shot that caught her in the side. The hit twisted the woman around and she fell, rolling across the ground directly in front of the Dungeon portal.

She scrambled up to her hands and knees as I continued shooting, hitting her twice more before she lunged through the shimmering portal and disappeared.

"She made it into the Dungeon."

"I'm sorry, she moved too fast for me to take down," Lyrra apologized as she came out of the warehouse.

I shook my head. *"Don't worry about it. We should have restrained her."*

"Either there are more Sect members escorting the prisoners or she plans to take whatever weapons they have to arm herself," Dayena interjected.

"Well, we planned to enter the Dungeon anyway. Tell the Housekeeper she's free to leave and we'll hit the Dungeon entrance once you're ready."

I reloaded my handcannon as Lyrra joined me and seated a fresh magazine into her rifle. Dayena joined us a minute later and nodded. Without another word, I stepped forward and led our trio into the Dungeon.

Chapter 12

Dungeon Located!

You have entered a Level 20+ Dungeon.

Warning! The current Dungeon has not been fully cleared. Successful completion of the Dungeon by a System-registered individual will generate increased rewards.

The first two notifications were about what I expected. The third message was surprising.

Why the hell wouldn't the Sect members take the extra experience and Credits for completing the Dungeon?

Leaving those bonuses on the table for their forced labor seemed like a poor way to keep their victims in check. Unless the Dungeon scaled radically, beyond the ability of even the mid-tier Advanced Class combatants that the Sect employed for the compound.

"Stay on your toes. Something seems off, if the Sect hasn't cleared their own private Dungeon," I warned my elven companions as I took in the space just inside the Dungeon entrance.

The waterfront of the reservoir appeared similar to the view from outside the Dungeon, except for a narrow arc in the frozen surface of the lake where the ice had been hacked open to reveal a patch of water. The bottom could be seen near the shore but dropped away into darkness as the depth increased further out.

Lyrra sighed as she stepped up beside me. "Looks like we're getting wet. And my rifle won't fire underwater."

"Nope. Got a backup?"

The blonde elf scoffed. "Of course. And I'll hit you both with a water-breathing spell before we go under."

She summoned several knives from her Inventory and strapped the sheathed blades to her forearms before adding a second set to each of her calves.

I glanced at Dayena, who gave me a thumbs up. The dark elf had already donned a helmet that completely encased her head and appeared confident in her ability to use her short swords underwater.

I followed suit, grimacing as I summoned a never-used helmet from my Inventory and seated it over my head. The water-breathing spell would be a good backup option, but I'd rather keep water out of my lungs in the first place.

While the pair of elves might feel comfortable getting up close to whatever nasties were in the water, I opted for something with a little extra range. From the veritable armory I kept stashed in my extra Inventory spaces provided by Right Tool for the Job, I summoned a short spear. A narrow, leaf-shaped blade stretched out eight inches atop a shaft four and a half feet long, with the entire weapon standing just a couple inches over five feet tall.

Before entering the reservoir, I stored all of my projectile pistols away in my System Inventory. No sense getting water in the barrels of the weapons. Though they'd probably be fine if I left them out, some old habits died hard. I also stowed my poncho. Loose fabric and water was another poor combination.

Preparations completed, I marched into the reservoir. Though my sealed suit kept the water out, a faint chill still seeped through the material as I plunged beneath the rippling surface. Under the water, I found that the ice on the surface that surrounded the narrow passage extended all the way to the bottom of the lake. The only path forward was into a narrow ice cavern that was lit with an ethereal blue glow that seemed at odds with how unnaturally dark the water had looked from above.

I swam into the passage with my spear at the ready. The channel was mostly circular and large enough that I could have walked through if standing on the bottom, but the walls weren't uniform. Bumps and ridges ran throughout the ice cavern without any kind of recognizable pattern and the flow of the water through the passage had worn all the edges smooth, leaving the white surface stuck like waves frozen in time.

The channel descended at an angle for maybe twenty feet before climbing back upward for about twice as far, then ending in a circular pool that rippled and glinted from a light source overhead.

I swam for the surface, building speed and kicking hard as I broke out of the water. My free hand caught the lip of ice and I propelled myself up onto the ledge with my spear readied for an attack.

Instead of finding myself on the surface of the reservoir, I was inside a giant ice cave with an arched ceiling five stories overhead. Judging from the arch of the ceiling, the space was at least the size of a football field, if not larger, and my current position was nowhere near the outer edge of the cavern.

More blue light glowed at random intervals from spots at the top of the vault. Icy walls and stalactites climbed from the uneven floor, blocking sightlines and preventing me from seeing the exact size of this chamber of the glacial cavern. The jagged embankments and broken columns cast long shadows in different directions, only adding to the chaotic atmosphere throughout the jumbled crystalline alleyways.

My minimap remained empty of immediate threats, though gray dots appeared at random intervals near the extreme edges of Greater Observation's range. The movements confirmed that monsters still lurked within the Dungeon and hadn't been cleared by the delving prisoners. I summoned a pistol, replacing the spear, as I examined the ground around the ledge while Dayena and Lyrra climbed up out of the pool to stand beside me.

A fluffy blanket of fresh snowfall covered the icy surface of the cavern floor, but the area lacked any tracks left behind by the fleeing Sect member. Snow flurries swirled inexplicably through the chamber, though there were no gaps in the glacial cavern's ceiling for the precipitation to actually fall through from the sky. Snow falling in an enclosed environment, more fun System bullshit at play.

"Which way?" Dayena asked as she pulled out a beam rifle. Lyrra kept her knives in place but summoned her own rifle from her Inventory.

I paused for a moment while I considered our options. I wasn't sure whether we'd encounter Dungeon monsters or hostile Sect members first, so I kept a beam pistol in my right hand and Last Word in my left.

On the other side of the pool behind us, another ice wall climbed up over twenty feet which left only a split passage ahead of us as the way forward. The left side of the Y-split led down a slightly wider path.

Without any visual clues left to follow, it was time to use another sense. Before I answered the Countess, I pulled off my helmet and stashed it away in Inventory. I was more than happy that this wasn't an underwater Dungeon. For one thing, I preferred the boost to my natural perception offered by Keen Senses, rather than inputs filtered through a helmet system.

Now free of the brain bucket, I closed my eyes and activated a Skill that I hadn't used in quite some time. Blood Scent, a purchased Skill from outside my Class, provided the ability for me to identify and track almost any living thing that left an aroma behind. The Mana cost of the ability had initially left me only able to use it in short bursts, but now my attributes were high enough that I could keep the Skill running nearly indefinitely if I wasn't using any other active abilities.

Inhaling deeply, I pulled the crisp, cool air into my lungs for any traces that didn't belong. First, I worked through the odors of myself and my party, both natural and those from our activities throughout the night.

Stale blood and ichor from the enemies we'd slain, sweat from our exertions, gunpowder from my pistols, the ozone from beam weaponry and burning plasma grenades were all cataloged and discarded. A heady batch of feminine pheromones from the elves on either side sent my heart pounding and provoked a reaction that I forced down before moving on.

Once I got my hormones under control, I ignored the tightness in my pants before finally locking onto the coppery tang of fresh blood in the air, an open wound still bleeding. I sniffed carefully and stepped forward, turning my head to either side as I tested the air down either passage. "Blood is lingering in the air this way. We go left."

The snow crunched beneath my boots as it compacted with each step. I stopped after a dozen paces and looked back at the pool we'd emerged from, only to find that our initial footsteps were fading in our wake.

The sight reminded me of the old shooting game I'd played in the VA clinic while recovering from my wounds. The game graphics could only make so many bullet holes when you fired at a wall and so they would disappear as you continued to shoot. A bit of nostalgia for a bitter time, but the System seemed to be doing the same thing now, as each new step caused the farthest remaining step to disappear into undisturbed snow.

The phenomenon explained why the wounded Sect Huntress hadn't left a trail of footprints and blood through the pristine white snow. Maybe because it was in the air and not on the ground, the Dungeon hadn't absorbed the injured woman's scent. I wasn't going to complain since it provided us with a trail to follow.

I took the lead with the elves hanging back far enough that we couldn't all be caught in a single attack. They spread wide so that their overlapping fields of fire could support me if the fecal matter hit the rotary impeller.

Despite our caution, the first several passages felt like a walk through a winter wonderland. Surreal and peaceful, the only noise our steps crunching on the fresh snowfall.

The juncture of the path split again and a flicker of movement down the left branch froze me in place. A silver-white eel floated several feet above the ground, its four-foot length sinuously waving side to side as it swam in a circle through the air.

Frost Zepheel (Level 25)
HP: 301/301
MP: 305/305

At twenty Levels below me, the monster showed up gray on my minimap in an indication that I'd fail to gain any significant XP whatsoever from slaying the beast. Neither of my companions would gain much from it either. I slipped by the left passage and sniffed as I continued on, confirming that I still followed the correct path in pursuit of the fleeing Sect member.

"Damn, it spotted me," Lyrra warned after I'd made it several paces down the other path.

I looked back just in time to see a swirling storm of finger-sized hail pieces streak across the passage. The elf dove out of the line of fire and the attacks followed in her wake.

A crimson ray of energy lanced out from Dayena's beam rifle, searing across the monster's flank. The single attack stripped almost half the creature's health in an instant. Two blasts from my energy pistol finished it off.

Lyrra stood and dusted away the powdery snow from her jumpsuit before slinging her rifle over one shoulder. Not finding any holes in the armor, she gave a thumbs up and I continued down the passage.

If we'd been here to clear the Dungeon, following the path where the monster had been would be the best option. Instead, the cleared path should have been the route we needed to follow to the Sect party.

We advanced through the labyrinthine glacial channels carved through the cavern, sometimes crawling over or under broken ice columns that lay angled across the path. More of the floating Zepheel popped out from random side passages occasionally and the monster's Levels increased as we worked our way deeper into the Dungeon.

As those Levels climbed into the mid and upper 30s, they even started offering experience to our group. Split three ways and over-Leveled as we were, the experience gain wasn't much, but it still counted.

A flash of lightning and a crack of thunder from not far ahead sent us scrambling for cover as we assessed whether the sounds were a precursor to an ambush. The whining energy beams, gunfire, and explosions that followed indicated that our search was nearly complete.

We'd caught up to the Sect group.

Chapter 13

Though the combat ahead provided covering noises, we slowed our progression to a crawl to sneak up on them as we readied our weapons. It wouldn't do ourselves or any Sect prisoners any favors if we just blundered into a fight unawares.

At the next turn, I peeked around the corner to find that the ten-foot-wide passage spilled out into an open area that looked about fifty feet wide and a hundred long. The floor of the chamber lay cracked open with multiple crevices and numerous smaller ice columns that offered ambush positions for the Zepheel that swarmed the room.

The Sect party had been forced away from the entryway by a horde of floating monsters. Two human bodies lay smoldering between the entry to the chamber and where a writhing curtain of the Zepheel circled the cornered group. Only three under-equipped human prisoners wearing little more than rags remained but the Huntress we'd been chasing stood behind them with two other Sect enforcers.

A Scrofalori with a bulging potbelly and orange-red hair used a pump shotgun to sweep swaths of Zepheel from the air, while an androgynous Movana flicked throwing knives out from a bandolier that skewered a monster with every snap of the wrist.

Krenegrat (Heavy Gunner Level 24) (A)

[Binary Eclipse Sect]

HP: 823/880

MP: 567/720

Status: Run and Gun, Hot Shot, Resist Cold

Ryr Brynna (Trickblade Level 21) (A)

[Binary Eclipse Sect]

HP: 571/620

MP: 511/600

Status: Hawkeye, Resist Cold

Between the two aliens, the Huntress, unsurprisingly, used another rifle as she fired above the arc of melee fighting humans who formed a shield between the monsters and the Sect members. The two non-combat Basic Classers were a Miner and a Grocer and used short spears to fend off a darting swarm of the Zepheel. In between the two spearmen, a frenzied Nurse rushed back and forth as she attempted to patch up the worst of their bloody wounds. The poor woman's efforts seemed futile, and the injuries kept accruing under the onslaught.

A barrage of pointed ice shards coated the Grocer's torso in a jagged white coating that seeped pink as blood leaked from the multiple punctures. The Nurse sobbed in desperate frustration, trying to heal the wounds that accumulated faster than her Skills could keep up with.

It stood out that the three humans lacking the Sect tags in their status fought with simple weapons while wearing little more than rags. In contrast, the much better armed and armored Sect trio fought casually, seemingly unworried by the tide of monsters that pelted their frantic meatshields.

While most of the attacking Zepheel were the same ice-based ones we'd encountered through the cave system so far, a trio of significantly bigger monsters floated throughout the open area. Electric current visibly jumped across the surface of their shimmering scales and the sparking was likely the source of the lightning we heard earlier.

Storm Zepheel (Level 39)
HP: 823/1113
MP: 943/1304

The new monster variant looked tougher than their smaller, more numerous counterparts and that was validated by their significantly larger health and Mana pools. They circled through their brethren, peeking from their midst to discharge a heavy lightning attack before retreating back into the cover of the other Zepheel. A moment of observation showed three distinct groupings of the monsters, each centered around one of the Storm variant elites.

"This could get tricky," I signaled over party chat before ducking back into cover to quickly fill Dayena and Lyrra in on what I'd seen. With the clock running out for the human prisoners under the monster onslaught, our plan was rushed. As usual, I'd play bait in the hopes of drawing the Sect goons away from their prisoners while Lyrra covered me and Dayena played sneak. Still, the chances for the under-Leveled and under equipped humans weren't great.

I checked my pistols were fully loaded before I slipped them back into my holsters. It was time to bring out the big guns.

Or, in this case, the System equivalent of a Javelin launcher. My Hastati-VI Launcher Control System appeared from my Inventory, and I called out a disposable firing tube. The red band around either end of the cylindrical launch tube indicated that the missile inside was of the anti-monster variety.

I snapped the tube onto the control module and set the weapon onto my shoulder before glancing at my companions. They both nodded, then

Lyrra pulled her rifle tight to her shoulder as Dayena nearly disappeared from view with the activation of a stealth Skill.

Though I lacked a similar Skill, I could still use cover and concealment to find a better position. Crouching low, I sprinted around the end of the passage and out into the open area at full speed.

With the number of moving Zepheel between my position and the Sect party, the chances of getting spotted immediately were low. Still, without knowing the Skills in effect, it was best not to remain in the open.

I dropped to one knee as I slid behind a jagged column of ice, placing myself out of sight from the Sect. Then I scanned the packs of monsters. My first target was the most injured of the three Storm Zepheel, huddling in the middle of the host of monsters.

After dropping the reticle from the launcher control module onto the floating creature, I squeezed the trigger when it blinked to confirm the target was locked. The missile popped free from the launch tube and whooshed upward as the rocket engine ignited. At the apex of the missile's arc, it flipped over and shot down at the monsters below.

A firestorm of plasma engulfed the swarm but I wasn't watching the show. Practiced movements, smoothed from numerous attribute increases, popped the spent tube and snapped the fresh reload from my Inventory into place as I kept an eye on my next target, the second Storm Zepheel.

The metronome precision of Lyrra's rifle fire cracked over the explosion of my missile as the Movana joined the fray. Her shots threaded through the maelstrom of monsters, flying ice shards and bolts of lightning to thin out the Zepheel threatening to overwhelm the human fighting line. While she covered the more exposed humans, the elf left alone the creatures circling around to hit the actual Sect members.

I fired again and the missile launched, but a metallic clang against the armored bicep of my vambrace tugged me partially out of cover. I ducked as a silver flash nearly missed splattering my skull, slamming into the column of ice. I glanced at the impact, and found a knife embedded in the pillar. The distant detonation of my missile was eclipsed by the more immediate threat.

I dismissed the launcher to my Inventory and dropped prone as another blade flashed by in front of my face. Tracing back the flight of the weapon, I spotted the Movana Trickblade leaping across the gaping ice flows and bounding onto the top of a broken column to get a better angle on my position.

Before the nimble Sect member could send another throw my way, a veritable swarm of a half dozen smaller Zepheel swirled toward the dancing elf's precarious perch, followed by the healthiest remaining Storm Zepheel. The monsters presented a more immediate threat for the Trickblade to deal with and their attacks against the elf kept more knives from flying my way.

The rest of the Sect party remained in cover, though my peek in their direction was rewarded by a spray of steam exploding from the ground in front of my face. The near miss from the energy ray showed that the Huntress and her beam rifle were also keeping an eye on my position.

I'd confirmed that none of the Zepheel were focused on me as I scrambled back into cover. Instead, the monsters injured from my rockets surged toward the Sect's defensive line in a furious throng. A new glowing effect surrounded the smaller Frost Zepheel with a reddish hue of sparking current, speeding their movements as they darted around the defensive perimeter and pelted the prisoners with a cloud of jagged hailstones.

Since we hadn't encountered the frenzy ability yet, that indicated a group buff provided by the Storm Zepheel–the Storm Zepheel that hadn't quite been finished off by my explosive attacks.

Oops.

One of the human prisoners was down and the Nurse crouched over him, holding the fallen Grocer's spear in one hand to ward off the monsters. Glowing energy drifted from the fingertips of her free hand, falling like sparkling snowflakes toward the injured man and bathing his torso in light around a bloody shard of ice lodged in his stomach. Only the Sect Heavy Gunner pushed back the horde of creatures with each blast of the thundering wide-bore shotgun.

Though I knew the attack would draw the monster's attention, I needed to do something about the elite monsters. Summoning out my hybrid rifle, I eased around the opposite side of the column and aimed at the Storm Zepheel with the lowest health.

The injured monster barely remained in the air, with the rear half dragging a furrow through the snow that covered the ground. The rifle whined as the Mana capacitors charged. Agonizing seconds passed and then it discharged with a snap. A coruscating lance of energy speared the monster with an exploding projectile that cut the wounded Zepheel in half, coating the area around it with a layer of sparking gore.

I'd seen a lot of strange sights in the two years since the apocalypse started, but monster blood that crackled with electric current was a first.

Shocking.

In the meantime, the group of Zepheel nearest my deceased target slowly lost the glowing indicator of a frenzy ability.

Of course, no good deed went unpunished.

The Huntress ignored the creatures surrounding her, choosing instead to continue sniping at me through the ranks of Zepheel. The floating monsters absorbed most of the shots headed my direction, but a few still got through. The rays streaked across my armor and burned through where they hit the exposed sections of my jumpsuit. I hissed as I shifted to aim at the second of the larger Storm Zepheel, ignoring the minor damage. Instead, I squeezed the trigger as I settled the sights of the rifle over the other injured elite.

The physical manifestation of the Banshee's scream tore through the monster, removing the creature's head—along with the frenzy buff from the second grouping of Zepheel. That left only the third cluster still empowered by their elite, but they were tying up the Trickblade, so I dismissed my concerns over that last group and focused on the major combatants of the Sect party.

Another energy beam from Tiana seared along the left side of my head. My outer ear disintegrated with a spike of agony and the scent of roast pork filled my nose. Eyes watering from the pain, I rolled back behind the ice column. The Huntress just moved herself to the top of my priority list.

Instead of moving to the other side of the column, I stood and leaned out from a higher perch. The rifle whined, Mana capacitors spooling as I snapped around the column and lined the weapon up with the Sect markswoman.

She'd aimed at the other side of the ice column, expecting me to reposition there, and jerked her weapon back toward me.

Too slow.

The Banshee finished its charge and I fired. The round from the hybrid rifle flashed between us on a swirling beam of energy, right into the middle of the woman's chest. The hit knocked her off her feet and stripped away half of her remaining health.

When Krenegrat saw his teammate tumble backward, the boar-like Heavy Gunner roared and charged toward me. Though the reduced Zepheel throng pelted him with attacks, the Scrofalori lowered his shoulder and batted several of the monsters aside on his way through them.

A shot from my hybrid rifle punched into the orange-red furred alien's chest but caused little more than a hitch in his step. With the Constitution of an Advanced Class, the Scrofalori shrugged off the worst effects of the hit and charged on despite the drop in his health. The monsters continued their attacks, pelting him with ice shards that shattered against his armor and created a cloud of mist which surrounded the alien.

I fired again before ducking behind the pillar as Krenegrat extended his shotgun toward me and a loud boom echoed through the glacial cavern. The side of the column erupted from the force of the weapon's attack and a hail of ice shards pelted my back and side. The damage shaved off a bit of my health, but I escaped the worst of the blast zone.

The minor injuries barely slowed me as I circled around the pillar.

With my minimap, I could see the hostile red dot still charging at my former position, so I continued the rest of the way to the other side of the icy column. Hip-firing the Banshee, my attack caught the rushing Scrofalori beneath the armpit unexpectedly. A whuff of air escaped from the boar-like alien's snout and he staggered sideways a single step.

Krenegrat's head snapped to the other side as a round from Lyrra hit just behind the stocky alien's ear. Two more projectiles hit in rapid succession and the Heavy Gunner stumbled, dropping his weapon but somehow staying on his feet to lean against the column I'd just circled.

Even Lyrra's triggered concussion Skill hadn't dropped the resilient alien.

Before I could finish off the injured Sect member, I was engulfed by attacks from the crowd of Zepheel which pursued the alien. The jagged hail tore at my exposed skin and a large shard glanced off my cheekbone, rocking my head back.

I shook off the blows despite the continued assault. Knowing I could no longer ignore the monsters in favor of attacking only the Sect, I dismissed the Banshee rifle back into my Inventory and drew two of my holstered pistols.

The beam pistol in my left hand flared with red light as it burned a stream of energy into the closest of the Zepheel. Ace thundered out from my right hand as I fired at Krenegrat. The Scrofalori grunted as the shots slammed into his back and should have knocked him against the column, but what could only be some kind of steady footing Skill aided his attempt to stand. It made sense that a Heavy Gunner would need a stable firing platform.

More of Lyrra's rifle fire cracked through the cavern but Krenegrat showed no reaction, nor did any of the nearby Zepheel, so the Movana was firing at another target. I'd find no help there, for now.

The hirsute alien pushed off the pillar and launched himself at me. I spun away from him and jumped across one of the broken ice flow crevasses that ran through the chamber. The Heavy Gunner pulled up short, barely avoiding plunging into the ten-foot-wide gap that dropped to a jagged bottom twenty feet below.

The Zepheel showed no similar restraint, flying easily above the fissure as they swirled around and indiscriminately attacked both Krenegrat and me. I alternated my fire between the circling monsters and the Scrofalori.

My beam pistol dropped the floating eels one after another while Ace sent a barrage of armor piercing rounds tearing into the Sect member.

He pulled another weapon from his Inventory, this one a long gun that looked more like a crew-served rotary cannon than anything that should be carried around by a single person. The unwieldy weapon featured a forward handle above the barrel and a rear grip with inset trigger mechanism that looked like something out of a sci-fi model kit that was trying too hard to be cool.

The multiple barrels spun for a moment and then roared out a tongue of flame as the Heavy Gunner fired the weapon. An unnaturally precise firestorm spoke to a Skill in use as it swept through the flocking Zepheels and knocked them from the air in a single pass. Then the weapon swung toward me.

Without time to swap out my own weapons, I fired both of my current pistols at Krenegrat. The initial ray from the beam pistol struck the alien's face and the Heavy Gunner's eye evaporated under the pulse of energy. At the same time, Ace pounded a line of rounds into the Sect member's torso as each shot climbed higher, tearing first into the alien's throat and then ripping into his protruding snout.

Krenegrat screamed in pain, and I dodged as the cannon swung in line with me, carrying the barrel beyond instead of steadying to point at me. A jackhammer pounded a diagonal line across my chest and my health dropped in chunks with each painful hit as the Heavy Gunner twisted off target.

I kept shooting as the blinded Sect member turned in a vain attempt at keeping my attacks from savaging the rest of his face. Just before Krenegrat's health bar bottomed out, a shield deployed around the grievously wounded alien. My shots glanced off the barrier and he sagged in relief.

I growled in annoyance. I hated to see these sort of Last Stand-type Skill activations when I was on the cusp of victory. Protected temporarily, the Heavy Gunner hit himself with a potion injector before raising his cannon to point at me once more.

Though the weapon was aimed directly at me, Krenegrat held his fire and I realized the barrier blocked him from shooting at me as much as it prevented me from shooting at him.

I grinned at the alien, trapped in the barrier and tossed a smoke grenade at the base of the spherical shield. I kept my smirk as the cloud surrounded the shield. Once hidden from the Heavy Gunner's view, I circled around the barrier, and I readied my master-crafted pistols for the final stage of the encounter.

An unaimed stream of projectile fire swept from the smoke and announced the end of the shield's duration. Locked onto Krenegrat's position with Greater Observation, I fired through the obscuring cloud from behind the alien.

By the time the Scrofalori stumbled out of the smoke, the damage from my pistols erased the gains from his potion and the alien collapsed just outside the cloud.

A new experience notification pinged in the corner of my vision, and I ignored it for the moment. I may have defeated one of the largest threats in the glacial cavern, but the fight was not yet over.

Chapter 14

With the Scrofalori dispatched, I swung Ace to point at the nearest Zepheel, but the pistol clicked on an empty chamber. I holstered the weapon, scowling in disgust with myself for losing track of the remaining ammo count, and pulled out a beam pistol. The death of the Sect member meant that I was the sole target for the remaining monsters nearby and I spent a frantic minute dancing around the edge of the crevasse as I shot down the rest of the creatures. When the final Zepheel of the cluster flopped to the ground, I hit myself with a healing potion as I scanned for the nearest threat.

The swarm of Zepheel near the Sect party's original location was almost completely gone and the Huntress was down, a combination of Lyrra's rifle fire and support from the Sect prisoners. Of the prisoners, only the Nurse remained on her feet as she skewered the last monster with a spear. The two other men were still alive. One lay on the ground with only a few points of health remaining and the other knelt, treating a variety of his own injuries. After the Nurse dropped the spear, she turned to provide assistance to the pair.

The only Sect member who still remained a threat was on the far side of the chamber, crouching atop the carcass of the final Storm Zepheel and glaring in my direction. The Trickblade looked charred and moved stiffly as they pulled bloody knives from where they were embedded across the body of the dead monster. Electric current arced between the carcass and the throwing knives as they were yanked free, but the effect didn't seem to bother the Movana. Not that it particularly mattered, but I still couldn't tell whether the elf was male or female, even with several sections of their armor burned away.

Nearly a hundred feet separated the two of us, but the Trickblade had already proven capable of launching precision attacks at that distance while on the move. I raised an eyebrow in return and calmly reloaded my handcannons before also replacing the spent beam pistols on my harness with fully charged spares.

The Movana stood with a throwing knife in each hand, and I waited with my hands resting on the grips of Ace and Last Word. The elf sneered, apparently still thinking they had a chance since we both had only about a third of our health remaining. The problem with that assumption was that I wasn't alone and the location of the dots on my minimap told me that this fight was almost over.

The Trickblade blurred into motion and then froze with one arm drawn back for a throw. Surprise widened their eyes as a pair of silvery blades emerged from their front through their kidneys from behind. The Countess materialized behind the elf as her camouflage ability faded away. She'd been there for some time, waiting for an opportune moment to strike.

Dayena withdrew her shortswords and stabbed the elf in the back again before the initial stun of the kidney-shot and Skill combination wore off. By the time the Trickblade managed a spin to swipe at her with one of the throwing knives, only a sliver of the Movana's health remained. The dark elf parried the wild strike and sank her sword into the Sect member's side, burying the blade almost to the hilt under the elf's armpit.

The Movana turned as if to flee, but Dayena wrenched her sword from the elf's side and swept her second blade across the Trickblade's hamstring. The attack ripped through armor and flesh, leaving a trail of blood behind as the Movana's lifeblood drained away from the gaping wounds. The Trickblade took two hobbling steps and then collapsed to the ground. After a single twitch, the body quit moving entirely.

Leaving the Countess to loot the Trickblade and marking the location of the Heavy Gunner for later, I headed toward the battered prisoners. The two conscious members of the trio looked up warily as I approached but neither of them made any hostile moves when I scanned the group with Greater Observation, first analyzing the most gravely wounded of the three.

Larry Muller (Grocer Level 21) (B)

HP: 11/250

MP: 82/310

Status: Unconscious, Frostbitten, Fatigued, Starved, Enthralled

A foot-long shard of bloody ice lay on the ground beside the prone Grocer. Without the steady rise and fall of his chest, the man could have passed for a corpse. He was a balding, gaunt skeleton of a man with the knicks and cuts across his scalp still trickling blood, since the wound in his stomach had been treated first.

Emi DeVile (Nurse Level 23) (B)

HP: 78/230

MP: 12/380

Status: Mana Depletion, Frostbitten, Fatigued, Starved, Enthralled

A short, curvy young woman whose blonde hair was matted with sweat and blood, the Nurse still maintained a spark of defiance in her eyes.

Stephen Orrsey (Miner Level 24) (B)

HP: 46/290

MP: 68/300

Status: Frostbitten, Fatigued, Starved, Enthralled

Down on one knee and leaning heavily on his spear, the black-haired Miner still breathed heavily from the exertion of combat and his body shook with the aftereffects of adrenaline leaving his system.

The combined status effects of the three humans told the story of their suffering under the Sect and accounted for their sorry state. The System would heal most of the negative effects with time or active healing, but the final affliction concerned me. While I could draw some implications from the situation, Enthralled wasn't an effect I'd encountered before.

A weak cough from beyond the prisoners pulled my attention away. The Sect Huntress lay against a ledge in the glacial ice with her head twisted at an odd angle. Blood seeped from numerous bullet wounds and the fist-sized hole in her chest left by the hybrid rifle. A crimson pool slowly spread out around her.

I walked over to the dying woman and pulled Ace from the holster as Tiana looked up at me with hate burning in her eyes. She glanced beyond me at the prisoners and her mouth worked as if trying to speak.

Blood trickled from her lips as she finally croaked out a few words. "Kill him."

Ace belched flame as the round from the weapon obliterated the last of the Sect enforcer's health pool and splattered her head across the ice ledge. But it was too late, the order had been given. An order to the prisoners, one they had to follow from whatever hold still gripped them in the Enthralled state.

I spun back to the prisoners just in time for the Miner's spear to rip through my armored jumpsuit and plunge into my side. The man's face was wide-eyed in terror but he still followed through with the order forced upon him by the dying Huntress.

The Nurse also charged toward me, carrying the spear she'd taken from the unconscious Grocer.

"I'm sorry, I'm sorry," Emi repeated over and over, the words running together as she lunged.

I growled in frustration. The easiest way to deal with the pair would be just to unload Ace into them a couple times, but neither deserved that fate after everything they'd suffered.

I dropped my pistol and batted aside the Nurse's awkward thrust. It was clear that she wasn't trained or skilled with the weapon, so I should probably have been grateful for that. I twisted free of the Miner's spear, tearing the tip from my side and dropping my health more with the action than the actual attack.

Raising my left arm to point at the stumbling Nurse, I activated the grapple system in the bracer of my vambrace. The coiling cable shot out and wrapped itself around the woman, briefly reminding me of the last time I'd pulled the trick, against an angry dark elf. The memory brought a smile to my face as the Nurse toppled over, out of the fight for now.

Blood poured from the aching wound in my side and I knew I needed to end this soon. Fortunately, the Miner was only minimally skilled with the spear, and I soon had the man disarmed. I held him pinned to the ground before shackling his wrists and ankles. The manacles clicked into place, and he finally quit struggling.

"What exactly is going on here?" Dayena asked before I could stand up from on top of the restrained man.

"Enthralled," I growled, standing and jerking my head at the slain Huntress. "The bitch ordered them to attack, and they had to follow the command."

Any sign of mirth left the Truinnar's face as disgust twisted her expression. "Repulsive."

I shrugged. "How do we break it besides killing them?"

"Eep! You don't want to do that," Emi chirped before Dayena could respond. "I'm being a good girl, right? I'm not trying to kill you anymore."

The Nurse grinned up at us and shifted her weight so that her bound legs skewed to the side. "You like me all tied up and at your mercy, don't you? I could stay this way, just for you…"

I blinked in surprise at the clear insinuation filling the woman's voice. I'd never had a target react in this way, but it made a sort of sense when considering trauma responses as a whole. Fight, flight, freeze, fawn, and the first two options were ruled out by the restraints. That left freezing, which had no active appeal when the threat had already been stated, and finally the attempted seduction.

For a moment, I almost wished it had been Dayena's cousin making the offer but I shook off the thought. Why the hell was I thinking about that elf now?

I looked over at Dayena, who considered me with a raised eyebrow. "I like this one, Hal. Can we keep her?"

Lyrra, who had arrived in time to overhear the Nurse's plea, just laughed while I shook my head and sighed. "She's not a pet."

"I'm already wearing a binding collar. I can be *your pet!*"

Her last two words dripped sultriness and nearly short-circuited my brain.

"The only words I want to hear out of you right now are either 'Yes, sir' or 'No, sir' until I tell you otherwise. Do you understand me?" I replied without looking at the Nurse.

There was a hiss of indrawn breath before the nurse chuckled. From the corner of my vision, she wiggled her shoulders back and forth within the bindings. "Yes, Sir…"

I rubbed a hand over my face as Lyrra and Dayena cackled in unrestrained laughter. That one was on me. I should have known better than to say something like that.

If this kept up, things would start turning out like one of those men's adventure novels that some of the guys in my unit had passed around on deployment. While I'd admit to having read them out of boredom, the one where the guy controlled dinosaurs was cool, as was the one featuring a seer with future-sight who used a naginata.

"Enthralled. How do we negate it?" I asked in an attempt to move to a more productive topic as my elven companions continued to snicker.

"There should be a control key or keys held by those issuing orders," Dayena finally replied, once she restrained her amusement.

I marched over to the slain Huntress and began searching the corpse for anything that could be the control. A necklace with a ruby gem inset seemed the likeliest prospect, though the chain was coated in gore after I pulled it from around the dead woman's splattered head. I also found a bracer, two rings, and an enchanted belly button piercing.

I held up the ruby necklace with one finger as blood dripped from the chain. "I'm guessing it's this."

Binary Eclipse Domination Pendant of Controlled Intent

Effect: The wearer of this necklace may give orders to any individual bound by a reciprocal "Binary Eclipse Choker of the Enthralled" – who must follow those instructions to the best of their ability. Commands from any Domination Pendant holder must be attempted by the wearers of the Chokers regardless of any detrimental effects that may occur in the course of following those instructions.

Note: The Binary Eclipse Choker of the Enthralled are enchanted to only be visible to those wearing either their own Choker or those wearing a Domination Pendant.

Part of me wanted to immediately fling the item away in disgust as I read the description but that wouldn't help the enthralled victims of the Sect.

Dayena confirmed with a nod as I shared the item's depiction over party chat. "That would appear correct."

I held the necklace out toward the dark elf. "Since only the wearer of this necklace can even see the bindings on the enthralled, would you want the honors?"

"Fine," she replied, but I could tell the Countess wasn't thrilled with the idea. Still, she was our best chance at removing any restraints from the Sect prisoners.

I tossed her the necklace and the dark elf shuddered when she caught it. Then she cast Cleanse to remove the blood before settling the silver chain over her head. She blinked a couple times and then looked around at the three prisoners. Seeing the Grocer still unconscious, the Truinnar headed for him first.

With a nod to Lyrra to keep an eye on the Countess, I returned across the cavern to where I'd slain the Heavy Gunner. Looting the alien took a bit of work, since the bulky alien hadn't grown any lighter in death. The smell wasn't great either.

The alien's gear included another Domination Pendant, and I stowed it in my Inventory with the rest of his equipment before moving on to looting the Zepheel that littered the ground. Unsurprisingly after the stockpile found in the Sect warehouse outside the Dungeon, the loot from the monsters included scales and eel meat. I also ended up with several stacks of other monster parts that included bones, eel eyes, and fangs.

By the time I returned to the group, Larry the Grocer had regained awareness and was sitting up as Lyrra worked her medic Skills over the badly injured man. The health of all three former prisoners ticked upward under the effect of various regeneration and healing spells. Though they still suffered from starvation and fatigue, frostbite no longer plagued them and Dayena had removed the Enthralled status.

The two other prisoners were no longer restrained and sat on a nearby ice floe that provided a convenient bench. The Nurse looked up as I returned and her pale cheeks flushed when she met my gaze. Even blushing, Emi still kept her blue eyes locked on mine as she slowly bit her lip.

Apparently, the earlier offer was still on her mind. I double-checked the woman's status to be sure, but there were no signs of any mental duress that my Skills could detect. Still, the middle of a Dungeon was not the time or the place to figure any of that out. I wasn't really sure I could trust the reaction either. Desperate people could do things they might regret later.

The Nurse wasn't the only one I counted as desperate.

After Adventuring with two extremely attractive elves for so long, my ability to think with the correct head was more than a little compromised.

Dayena stepped between us before things could grow any more awkward, holding the Domination Pendant in one hand and a trio of metal collars in the other. She thrust both hands toward me. Reluctantly, I accepted them and stored all but one of the collars away in my Inventory. That last one, I scanned instead.

Binary Eclipse Choker of the Enthralled

Effect: The wearer of this collar is compelled to follow the orders given from any individual wearing a reciprocal "Binary Eclipse Domination Pendant of Controlled Intent" to the best of their ability. Commands must be attempted regardless of the inherent danger or self-harm instigated by the direction. This collar is enchanted to remain invisible to anyone not wearing a Binary Eclipse Choker or Domination Pendant.

Note: This collar may only be applied to individuals with a Basic Class below Level 30.

I stowed the vile item and accepted a second Domination Pendant from Dayena as she pulled it from her Inventory.

"From the Trickblade," she explained at my questioning look.

Nodding, I dismissed the odious piece of gear away to my System storage and then turned to the former prisoners with a question that had bothered me since I entered the Dungeon. "Why has the Sect never finished the Dungeon for the completion bonus?"

"It scales too high in the final stretch for mid-tier Advanced Classes," Stephen, the Miner, replied.

Emi nodded. "This chamber is always where we ended our runs. Usually literally, for someone."

The Nurse pointed out into the middle of the glacial chamber to the two human bodies, prisoners that had fallen before any of my team had arrived.

"I'm sorry that we were too late for your friends," I said.

Larry shrugged. "We weren't really friends, but you get to know someone pretty well when you suffer beside them."

The Grocer's gravelly voice matched his gaunt appearance, but his words sounded hollow as if the suffering wasn't just what he'd experienced at the hands of the Sect. The same could be said of pretty much everyone in this post-System world.

Not everyone got cheat Classes or the Credits for overpowered weapons to help ensure their survival. I certainly wasn't sure what a Grocer would do with the System in place and all the technology that kept food preserved for transport. That forcefully leveling a Class like that in a Dungeon led to a certain number of deaths came as no surprise.

I looked at the three as they glanced between the multi-species members of my party with some apprehension. After the Sect, I couldn't blame them for being skeptical of a human in association with any Galactics involved.

"We can escort you out of the Dungeon, if that's what you want," I said.

The former prisoners glanced at each other, and Emi looked back at me.

"You make it sound like there's another option," the Nurse said.

I glanced at my companions. Both elves nodded, knowing where I was leading the conversation. "Finish the Dungeon. Take the completion bonus away from the Sect. If we leave now, there's no telling if there will be another chance but if we finish it then you'll be stronger, and we'll give you a full share of the rewards."

Stephen pinched the threadbare rags of his tunic and lifted it up. "I like the idea of taking all we can from those assholes, but we've got nothing besides a couple flimsy spears. You expect us to finish a Dungeon twice our Level, like this?"

"No, we've got spare gear plus loot taken from the Sect. We'll see what you can work with from that."

The Miner nodded and looked at the other two former prisoners. "That works for me. What about you guys?"

The pair glanced at each other before Larry spoke. "Payback sounds good."

"It sounds like a better way to make Credits and experience than putting on hotpants and working on Colfax," Emi agreed, nodding with enthusiasm.

The two men chuckled at Emi's exclamation, which I interpreted as an in-joke for the local Denverites. A little humor was good after everything they'd been through, so I let their amusement continue as I dug into my Inventory for spare equipment. With the extra storage space provided by my Right Tool for the Job Skill, I had plenty of extra kit stashed away. Once I laid everything out, it took several minutes for the former prisoners to look through the options and get themselves fitted up with their picks.

The burly Miner was too large for one of my jumpsuits, but he managed to fit into an older pair of my armored boots. Since the jumpsuits from the Shop were perfectly sized to their purchasers, second-hand use was rarely an option for the skin-tight armor. Stephen ended up mostly clad in the Scrofalori's armor and carrying the Jarrack's shield with both hands. He could barely lift the thing but felt more comfortable with it instead of a weapon.

Larry could fit into one of my suits but had to roll up the ends of the legs and arms in order to not have them dragging out beyond his hands and feet. The scrawny Grocer opted to wield the beam rifle used by the Huntress when she'd been slain.

Finally, the Nurse wore a spare set of Lyrra's armored coveralls, since her hips were too wide to fit into any of Dayena's spares. Emi also had to roll up the sleeves, since she was significantly shorter than the taller Movana, but proved too busty to fasten the suit entirely up the front. She reminded me of someone doing a cosplay of a B-grade sci-fi movie. In all the best ways. The Nurse chose the projectile rifle first used by the Huntress in the compound outside the Dungeon, probably preferring some distance from the monsters.

Couldn't blame her, though I made a note to spread them out and away from me just in case.

With the prisoners equipped the best we could manage with the limitations of our current Inventories, I led the way out of the large chamber deeper into the Dungeon.

Chapter 15

The next several passages proved more challenging than the beginning of our journey through the Dungeon. Since the Sect party was no longer clearing the way, the Zepheel populations remained in full force. On top of that, we took extra caution to ensure that the low-Leveled members of our party were in no greater danger than necessary.

While I remained out front with Dayena in support, Lyrra hung back in overwatch. Stephan followed behind the Movana, using his shield to cover Larry and Emi. The two used their rifles to potshot at the Dungeon monsters once they were firmly focused on either myself or the Countess. It was effective but not particularly fast and the strategy worked until we reached the room with the final boss.

The last chamber of the Dungeon was even larger than the one where we'd caught up to the Sect party and freed their prisoners. Four packs of the floating ray-finned monsters roamed the chamber, each with a Storm Zepheel in their midst, but the real creature that gave me pause was a giant pastel-pink tentacled mass that sat at the far end of the cavern.

Since the floating eel monsters were the Dungeon creature of choice so far, I'd expected the boss to just be another tier up from the Storm Zepheel elites. No such luck.

Actinia Glacialis (Boss Level 50)
HP: 2684/2684
MP: 3233/3233
Status: Extended Reach, Mutualism

A giant, glacier dwelling sea anemone was not on my bingo card of likely monster candidates for Dungeon bosses but that was just how things worked with the System. I also spotted a few more of the normal Zepheel floating amongst the pink creature's tentacles.

The core of the giant monster was a cylindrical trunk at least as big around as one of the old plastic-walled above-ground swimming pools common in backyards across the nation. Only this circular column stood nearly a story tall. On top of the trunk, a forest of intertwining tentacles waved as if they were floating in water instead of wafting through the air.

I reloaded my pistols and looked over my shoulder at the group. *"We'll clear one group at a time, if we can avoid pulling the others."*

Dayena stepped up beside me and nodded. *"Keep away from the boss until the rest are eliminated."*

I holstered my pistols and gestured to the former prisoners, who were also included in Dayena's Diplomatic Contact Skill for the remainder of the Dungeon run. *"You three hang back. Only engage with the normal Zepheel if the elite for that group is down and they're firmly focused on one of us."*

Emi saluted. *"Yes, sir."*

I didn't laugh. Everyone else did, except for Larry, who'd been unconscious when she used the phrase earlier. I just shook my head and turned back to observe the roving monsters with the hope of discerning some pattern that would allow us to pull a singular group away from the others. The movements seemed random though, which made sense, as the monsters were still living creatures.

A check of my minimap showed the rest of the party formed up and waiting for my move, so I drew my first pair of beam pistols and I stepped into the chamber.

Eight Frost Zepheel in the first pack turned into seven as I burned down one of the outermost members of the group. I stepped along the outer wall to clear the entry passage as the remaining monsters swam through the air toward me. Ice shards and hailstones swirled, pelting me with a furious storm of crystal that quickly grew so dense that my beam pistols stopped reaching through it.

Seeing that I was unable to damage the monsters with the ineffective energy weapons, I swapped the beam pistols in my hands for projectile pistols from my Inventory. As soon as I managed my first shots with the firearms, a lance of lightning tore through the icy deluge and raked across my side.

The Storm Zepheel's attack briefly cleared a line of sight through the incoming barrage of monster attacks, and I fired through the opening at the larger monster.

Storm Zepheel (Level 47)
HP: 1024/1337
MP: 1537/1617

As the window through the storm closed, Dayena appeared. The dark elf slid beneath the floating monster with her swords tearing into the creature's underside. Then my view of the elite monster faded within the swirling hail, and I shifted my aim back to picking off the smaller targets.

Two of the Zepheel attempted to flank me, which reduced their ability to hide within the turbulent hail. The stinging storm slowly sapped away my health, point after point, and I quickly dropped the exposed pair before my pool dropped below ninety percent.

I took out one more of the Frost Zepheel before I heard the sound of shots over the roar of the assailing storm. At least the rest of the party was making good use of my time as an icy pincushion. The lower-Leveled group joining in on the fight meant that Dayena had handled the elite.

The storm of hail surrounding me faded away, and the last couple Zepheel fell in rapid succession under the combined firepower of the entire party. I hit myself with a round of healing spells and a regeneration potion while the group reloaded and rearmed.

Once my health was topped off, we repeated the process for the second flock of Zepheel. Everything seemed to go smoothly as we worked through the third pack, only for everything to turn into a complete Charlie Foxtrot.

"Incoming!" Dayena screamed over party chat, cut off by a grunt of pain.

On the party overlay nested in the corner of my vision, the Truinnar's health bar dropped a chunk but her dot on my minimap kept moving.

Currently enveloped within the shroud of another monster-induced hailstorm, I could barely see the fourth pack of Zepheel streaking toward our party but the moving dots on my minimap told the story. The larger red dot of the boss that also drifted closer was concerning, but the faster Zepheel would reach us first.

"Lyrra, fighting withdrawal, back toward the entrance to the chamber," I ordered, moving to do the same.

Stretching out the time it would take for the boss to engage would let us deal with the smaller monster first. I threw mines out across the chamber to further slow the boss, annoyed at using actual munitions on monsters when beam weapons cost nothing.

I jogged backwards, firing shots from each pistol with every step. Once I cleared the worst of the hailstorm, I swapped the nearly empty weapons for the Hastati control module and attached a missile tube on the run. Mentally cringing at the Credits I was about to blow, I slowed but kept moving as I sighted in on the approaching pack of monsters and locked the targeting reticle onto the Storm Zepheel.

Halting only long enough to fire the weapon, I ran on as soon as the missile popped free of the launcher. By the time the warhead detonated amidst the oncoming monsters, expelling a rolling cloud of plasma and steam that sent blue light glinting across the icy surfaces of the cavern, I'd already discarded the spent launch tube and replaced it with a fresh one.

Intermittent shots continued to ring out as the rest of the party pulled back. Only Dayena remained behind, tangled up with the elite from the initial Zepheel pack. I planned to give her some covering fire as soon as I finished clearing the added spawns.

I retreated three more steps before the plasma storm subsided enough that I could sight back in on the seared Storm Zepheel. Around the elite, the smaller creatures writhed as the flames consumed them and they fluttered to the ground where they continued smoldering. Instead of burning up like the other monsters, the elite shook itself in the air and its scales sloughed off, carrying the burning plasma away as it shed its outer layer.

Before it could pick up speed again, I fired the next rocket. The missile whooshed upward to arch over near the cavern roof before streaking down and making contact, bathing the chamber in a second flash of bluish light.

"Feeling like a big spender today, Hal?" Lyrra asked.

"Beats letting you and your fire support get swarmed before we even damage the boss. The Sect didn't have any problem letting them take the hits."

Even though I was nearly five-figures in Credits poorer after firing the pair of missiles, my response quieted my critic in the peanut gallery.

By the time I swapped out the Hastati for the hybrid rifle and swung it over to cover Dayena, the dark elf was already mounted on top of the monster and repeatedly plunging her short swords down into its flanks. Arcs of electric current crawled over the Truinnar's legs as she clamped down like a rodeo bull rider, holding herself on the back of the writhing Zepheel.

The monster slowly floated closer to the ground, deflating like a punctured balloon as she tore away its health with every strike. Beyond the pair, the boss drifted closer with its trunk hovering a few inches above the snow-covered floor of the cavern. As I watched, the massive monster's tentacles started stretching out toward the dark elf.

"Watch out!" I warned the Countess over party chat.

One of the probing tentacles shot out at the Truinnar, but she was already in motion. The limb grazed the dark elf as she lunged out of the way and a flash of light snapped between them, picking the Truinnar up and tossing her a dozen feet away. The feeler seemed to ignore the elf as it speared into the carcass of the slain Storm Zepheel.

The boss reeled in the hooked eel and pulled it up where it disappeared out of sight over the top of the trunk, presumably where the monster's mouth was located. I had no desire to find out for myself.

Dayena popped up to her feet after skidding across the icy ground but her right arm twitched as it spasmed from the anemone's attack. Her right leg looked shaky too, as she staggered farther from the monster.

Another tentacle at least as large as my thigh unfurled toward the dark elf, and I fired the hybrid rifle at the threat. The round slammed into the base of the limb and tore away a huge chunk of pinkish flesh. The tendril drooped to hang limply from the top of the anemone's trunk, dragging across the ground as the body of the monster continued to float after Dayena.

One appendage down, only a hundred or so to go, and the boss' health seemed barely tickled. I took out another tentacle and then lobbed a plasma grenade up over the top of the creature. The blue flash from atop the monster announced the detonation, too high overhead for me to get any sense of the damage done, but the health bar dropped farther than it had from my hybrid rifle shots.

Seeing the effectiveness of my attacks, I reevaluated our chances against the creature. As much as I liked helping out the former prisoners, I still wanted to finish the Dungeon and claim the completion bonus myself. Instead of retreating back to the chamber entrance, I cut across the open space of the cavern. *"It'll be a grind, but we can take this thing."*

"What makes you so sure?" Dayena asked. The dark elf had sheathed her swords and fired a beam pistol over her shoulder at the boss as she moved farther away. Scattered shots from the former prisoners flew over her head, accompanied by more precise fire from Lyrra.

"It hasn't caught us yet."

The Countess hissed dismissively over party chat, but she broke off from her sprint toward the chamber exit and curved to run opposite me around the chamber.

"We're doing this, then?" Lyrra asked.

I fired the Banshee again and the rifle whined before taking out another tentacle. *"You want that Level 50, don't you?"*

The Movana growled back over party chat, and I grinned at her response as her rifle cracked out several times in rapid succession, providing a clear answer to the question.

With the combined firepower of our oversized squad, even though half of the team was under-Leveled, we chipped steadily away at the monster's health. Dayena and I kept the focus on ourselves, pushing our attacks at a pace just shy of complete recklessness in order to present threats the boss couldn't afford to ignore. The large size of the monster meant that its tentacle attacks were telegraphed, providing enough warning that the reflexes from our high Agility attributes allowed us to dodge the worst of the attacks.

After we trimmed off ten percent of its total health, like a volcano erupting, a storm of fog and icy hail billowed out, straight upward from the boss's unseen mouth before spreading out around the monster. The cloud descended around Dayena and I as we were both close enough to fall within the aura. Much like the attacks of the smaller Zepheel, the attack reduced visibility and limited the effectiveness of beam weaponry. It also stripped away health while pelting us with razor shards of ice, though more aggressively damaging than the ability used by the floating eels.

A curse slipped from the normally reserved Countess as the Truinnar was forced to swap her beam pistol for a projectile weapon and I chuckled. *"Not a fan of firearms? I didn't even know you had one."*

Dayena scoffed. *"Of course I have a projectile weapon. It would be foolish not to have at least the basics for adventuring on a Dungeon World."*

The crack of thunder which followed her response clearly illustrated that her idea of a projectile weapon resembled a cannon more than any simple rifle. *"Go big or go home, huh?"*

"I do not have the slightest intention to go home any time soon."

Sometimes expressions didn't smoothly cross the translation boundaries even with the System's help. Despite the sad state of the dark elf's family situation, I found her response far more amusing than it should have been and I snuffed out the laugh before it could slip out. I had no desire to explain my sense of humor in the middle of a Dungeon boss fight.

Lyrra broke in before I could respond to the Countess. *"We can't see the tentacles from back here with that icy haze around the boss. We're still doing about the same amount of damage but it's not as targeted."*

"We took out a bunch though!" Emi exclaimed.

A tentacle punched through the cloud around me and I barely dodged the spear-like tip. The attack still grazed my leg and the barbs along the appendage tore through the jumpsuit over my hip. An electric spasm caused my right thigh to clench as several status notifications appeared.

You are Poisoned!
-12 HP per second. Effect partially resisted.

You are Shocked!
-5% Agility. Effect partially resisted.

I pushed through the sensation of my leg falling asleep and skipped away from the recoiling tentacle, driving a shot back toward its base as another pink limb stabbed out through the icy cloud. I'd moved enough that the second attack missed, and I kept going, partially dragging my right leg, though it worked well enough to support my weight.

The poison concerned me. It felt like a fire burning through my veins, crawling up my side, closer and closer to my heart. My health was high enough that I could last for a bit, but my Constitution and resistances were working overtime to contain the spread.

I had no time to apply an antidote with an increasing number of the tentacles flashing out toward me through the fog. Within the aura, the appendages stretched farther and faster than they had before. Twisting and jumping across the icy ground, one misstep would send me sprawling and leave me an easy target for the monster that pursued.

At every opportunity, I fired back at the tentacles before they could retract out of sight or toward the body of the monster itself. Each disabled tendril was one less threat to worry about, but I remained so intently focused on avoiding the persistent attacks, I lost track of time. The only indicator I had was that I'd swapped out empty magazines on the Banshee at least twice.

"Half health," Lyrra called out.

Was that all? My prediction of this fight as a grind was proving far too prophetic. I kept the thought to myself as I finally found enough breathing room to hit myself with an antidote injector.

A white streak flashed through the hailstorm, gone before I could take a shot. I dropped the spent injector and gripped my rifle in both hands as a circle of red dots expanded out from the boss on my minimap.

"Zepheel coming out of the aura, the normal ones," Stephen warned over party chat.

The tentacles flew out through the cloud, and I was back to focusing on avoiding them once again. *"Kinda busy here. Prioritize any of them near you."*

I hoped they could handle the smaller monsters. I didn't want to drag the boss anywhere near the lower-Level members of the group. They lacked the Agility to dodge and the Constitution to live through the poison. Still, if they were close to getting overrun, I'd do what I could. *"Call for help if you need it."*

"We'll handle it. There are only a dozen or so and they're spread out pretty evenly around the boss for now," Lyrra said.

I had to trust the Movana's judgment. She, and the former prisoners, needed the strength and confidence to stand on their own.

The shock effect numbing my leg wore off and I let my reflexes take over as a tingling sensation announced the return of feelings in the limb. I flowed through the mist shrouded cavern in constant motion, dancing in a deadly ballad of fire and maneuver that would have looked insane to any pre-System observers of the battle if they could have seen through the cloudy aura of the boss.

Once I disabled a few more tentacles, the onslaught lashing out at me slowed slightly and I used the opportunity to launch several grenades onto the top of the boss. The faint blue flashes that flickered through the cloud of ice shards overhead confirmed my aim for the throws had been on target, so I threw a couple more for good measure.

Ryk was going to love handing me the bill the next time I hit the Shop to restock my spent munitions.

I kept up the harassing attacks, leading the boss around the chamber while making sure I left enough room for Dayena's dot on my minimap to also remain clear of the monster. The smaller dots of the Zepheel swarm slowly winked out, one by one, until only the boss remained.

With the added monsters eliminated, the boss's health pool dropped steadily. The monster repeated the attack patterns and spawning of new waves twice more, until it stopped floating around the chamber and sank to the ground. The hailstorm surrounding the monster faded as the creature sagged in on itself, like one of those children's bouncy castles deflating.

My suit was torn in multiple places and every bit of exposed skin smarted painfully with the deep red tenderness of a sunburn. Or iceburn, as the case may be. A few cuts still oozed blood but my regeneration would seal the wounds and see to the burn effect soon enough that I didn't bother to use a health potion.

Approaching the sagging mass of flesh in the middle of the chamber, I looted the boss and quickly stepped away from the smelly mess. The entire creature was way too big to store in my Meat Locker and I wasn't even sure there was anything valuable in it. Considering the other bodies I had in there, it made little sense to try.

Once away, I began reloading my various weapons as I headed back toward the entrance where the rest of the group slumped in exhaustion.

Dayena's jumpsuit was even more ragged than mine, since she lacked the hard armor of the vambraces that protected my arms and shoulders. The others seemed in fair condition, though I noticed a number of icy streaks on the heavy shield Stephen had planted into the snowy ground. The Miner sat with his back against the protective plate, his gaze distant with the common expression of a person reviewing their System messages. Similar looks crossed the faces of the Grocer and the Nurse as their eyes darted through notifications and Skill selections. They'd all gained at least a Level, while Larry had managed to gain two.

Lyrra stood protectively over the trio as she kept watch for any threats, but her foot tapped against the ground impatiently. It was easy to see that the elf couldn't wait to review the updates to her own status.

Dayena stopped beside me and grinned at the Movana's impatience. "The Dungeon is cleared, and my notifications are caught up. You two deal with your status."

Lyrra's eyes glazed over as she accessed her menus while making happy noises. I couldn't help but smile at the elf's infectious smile and brought up my own notifications.

After scrolling through the summations of all the slain monsters from throughout the Dungeon, along with additional experience for the deaths of the Sect enforcers, I finally reached the bottom of the window.

Congratulations! Dungeon Cleared!
+5,000 XP

First Clear Bonus

Having cleared the Dungeon for the first time, you have been awarded an additional +5,000 XP +1,000 Credits

Title Gained

For successfully guiding multiple individuals through the completion of a Dungeon beyond their Level range while keeping them alive, you have been awarded the title "Sherpa".

Effect: Party members within a Dungeon who are 10 or more Levels below your own will receive a 5% damage reduction from monsters and environmental effects while dealing an increased 1% damage.

Level Up!

You have reached Level 46 as a Relentless Huntsman. Stat Points automatically distributed. You have 2 Free Attributes and 11 Class Skill Points to distribute.

At last I'd hit the threshold for the last of my Class Skills and the reason I've been holding on to so many of my unspent Points. I immediately assigned a single point to each of the three Skills in order to unlock them but left the bulk of the points to figure out later.

"YES!"

Lyrra's joyful shout interrupted my perusal of the notifications, and I closed out of the blue boxes in time to find the Movana dancing excitedly. Dayena chuckled quietly as the others watched the cavorting elf.

A quick scan confirmed the reason for Lyrra's celebration.

Lyrra Valjyn (Combat Medicae Level 50) (B)
HP: 644/840
MP: 489/880
Status: Active Camouflage, Healing Aura

"Congratulations." I nodded to the Movana as she finally began winding down.

At my well wishes, Emi glanced from me to the elf. "Oh, she dinged! Congrats!"

The Nurse hopped to her feet and wrapped Lyrra into an enthusiastic hug, while the other former prisoners were slightly more reserved in their acclaim.

"Have you decided on your Advanced Class?" Dayena asked once she'd acknowledged the Movana's accomplishment.

Lyrra shook her head. "I'm debating between two options, and I want to consider my choices a bit more before locking in the selection. Whatever I choose will determine a significant portion of my future."

"I hope I have some better options when I hit Level 50," Larry said.

Stephen grunted. "I wouldn't mind seeing what the Advanced options are for mining. It's been my family profession for generations."

"I like being a Nurse, but I'd like some more utility in combat situations," Emi said.

"I can tell you about my Adventuring experiences and guide you to some Skills that might fit you from outside of your Class, if you're interested," Lyrra offered.

The Nurse eagerly agreed, but I cut them off before they got distracted by that conversation. "Let's get healed up and head out. We're still in a

Dungeon and we'll need to be alert for any Sect reinforcements until we're out of the compound."

That sobered the group up, which made me feel like a real buzzkill. Even if it was necessary.

Once focused on the task, our healers patched everyone up and we were on our way back out of the Dungeon within minutes.

Chapter 16

Frigid water lapped against my calves as I waited, standing in the gravelly shallows of the reservoir just inside the Dungeon entrance.

The trickiest part of getting out of the Dungeon proved to be the final stretch underwater. None of the former prisoners had helmets, so Lyrra used her waterbreath spell on the trio. Even then, the three struggled to swim with their hand-me-down equipment and looted gear with poor fits.

Before the swim, Emi explained that the underwater passage was another method the Sect had used to force them through the Dungeon, since the prisoners were dragged through it by the higher-Leveled Sect minders and the only way back out was with their help once the run was completed.

I held up at the edge of the lake until everyone had shaken off the effects of the swim.

"Weapons up and ready. There could be more Sect waiting outside," I said as I raised my pistols in both hands. A ray of moonlight shining through the clouds glinted off Last Word and Ace when I stepped out of the water.

Breaking into a run as I passed through the Dungeon entrance, I prepared to engage in a running firefight if anyone waited in ambush outside but slowed to a walk after several uninterrupted strides.

Despite a steady snowfall, a snowfall that hadn't affected the inside of the Dungeon, the compound stood as empty as it had been when we'd entered the Dungeon earlier. I found no sign of any Sect members as I reached out with Greater Observation. The only person I sensed through the entire compound was the Housekeeper who remained hiding inside the warehouse.

"Well, that was anticlimactic and I'm okay with that," Lyrra said, emerging from the Dungeon with the rest of the party.

"Same," Emi agreed. Larry and Stephen hurried to voice their agreement.

"Get the Housekeeper and then we can get out of here," Dayena said.

I started walking toward the warehouse and stopped when I saw the halftrack backed against the building's loading dock. I turned back to the group and grinned. "I have a better idea. I bet the gnomes will pay a decent sum of Credits for anything we haul out of here and hand over to their Artisans."

It didn't take all that long to fill the back of the vehicle with the crates from the warehouse, leaving only enough room that everyone could fit inside between the cab and the remaining space in the cargo bed.

Since Camila had been responsible for organizing the warehouse, her knowledge ensured that the most valuable crates were loaded first and that we didn't waste our time on the more common materials.

Once everything was loaded, Dayena opened the compound gate before scrambling up into the turret above the cab. The dark elf swung the cannon barrel left and right as she tested out the controls, then grinned down at us from within the gunner's compartment.

I grinned back. "Alright, I'll drive."

"I'll navigate then," Lyrra said.

Emi darted toward the cab before either of us could move. "I'm small, I can ride between you!"

I shrugged as I looked at the rest of the former prisoners.

Stephen sighed. "I guess we're in the back then. Let's just get the hell away from this place."

I helped them into the cargo bay before closing the rear door and climbing up behind the controls. The seats were a bench that ran the width of the cab and I only managed to get the door shut after I squeezed in next to Emi, who didn't seem to mind the close contact. At all.

Attempting to ignore the warmth of the woman beside me and the amusement of the Movana sitting beyond her, I looked over the driver's panel in front of me. Though there were manual controls, I connected my Neural Link to the console.

It was immediately apparent that the vehicle lacked all but the most rudimentary cyber defenses. Maybe if it had been a personal vehicle, it would have been better equipped, but it seemed the transport was intended to be used by whatever Sect member was seated in the driver's position and lacked any advanced security measures. It only took a moment for my wetware to convince the vehicle that I was the authorized driver, and the computer started the vehicle's motor.

The Mana engine purred as I throttled up and steered out of the compound, though I kept the speed down as I guided the vehicle along the access road that led to the highway. The windshield had enhancements in a center box that filtered out the swirling snow, so it seemed like nothing more than an early drive in the gray light of pre-dawn.

Once I turned onto the highway and headed north, I relaxed slightly. Our chances of encountering the Sect now that we'd escaped the compound without incident were significantly reduced. Only a purposeful intercept or roving patrol could catch us at this point, which seemed unlikely. The Sect had bigger problems than a lone vehicle.

"Lyrra, let Command know we're coming in a stolen vehicle."

The Movana blinked. "That would be good, so they don't blast us at the perimeter for driving a Sect vehicle."

"An armed Sect vehicle," I corrected.

"Yes, that." The elf tuned out from the conversation after that acknowledgement, subvocalizing into a communicator nodule pressed to her throat.

Emi chuckled. "I couldn't have imagined this morning that I'd be free from the Sect and driving away after committing grand theft auto."

"Hopefully, your shares from the sales from everything we've stolen will set the four of you up nicely."

The Nurse blinked and then turned to lean into me. "Really? You're just going to give us all an equal share. You and your party did all the work."

Only the fact that vambraces covered my arms made it possible to ignore what would have been the pleasantly soft sensation pressing on my upper arm. Her jumpsuit was still unfastened dangerously low and there wasn't any room to move over in the cramped confines of the cab. "Seems only fair that the Sect's ill-gotten gains benefit you after what they put you through. We've got plenty of Credits already."

Emi snorted in disbelief. "Plenty of Credits, sure. That's like saying you've got too many women or too much whiskey."

"No such thing as too much whiskey." I wasn't going to touch the first part of her statement.

"Nope! Have you tried getting drunk since the System took over? It's impossible."

I shook my head. "Not impossible. Just expensive."

I felt the Nurse's gaze as I kept my eyes on the road. Though we'd made it out of the compound, that didn't mean we were home free just yet. The Sect still owned the City Cores for this section of Denver. They might be pretty tied up with the Pharyleri on the offensive but there was always the possibility that we'd encounter a roving patrol or reinforcements headed somewhere else.

"How's our route looking, Lyrra?" I asked, derailing my conversation with the Nurse in favor of live intel on our return to Pharyleri territory.

"No reported enemies," she replied.

I held back a snort. Unreported enemies were the problem. That was the fog of war. Murphy's Law would screw anyone it could, so staying alert was the only way you had any chance. Over the last two years, I'd had more close calls than I could count, but I intended to put off that one-way trip to my Final Duty Station for a long while yet.

I kept my eyes moving from one side of the road to the other. "It's not whiskey, but Apocalypse Ale out of Duchess Kangana's territory in the Yukon is pretty good. The price keeps going up as demand increases out in Galactic territories though, so it's cheaper to drink the imported stuff most of the time."

"That makes sense. It's been a while since I was locked up, so I'm not really up on the local drink scene."

I glanced down at the blonde woman and met her blue eyes as she stared back up at me. It was an intense gaze, but it lacked the heat I expected after her antics in the Dungeon. Instead, it seemed like she was latching on to me as a human touchstone. A human connection, since it was me and two elves that rescued her, and a way to confirm that this was reality after so long under the Sect thumb.

It still made me a bit uncomfortable. Was this my Charisma at work? Were my attributes getting high enough that someone with lower resistances would be easily manipulated? I didn't have a problem if I could affect a target, but the idea of manipulating normal people felt off.

As conversational as Emi was, I got the feeling she'd brought the topic back to the subject of being locked up intentionally. If she wanted to unpack some of her experiences, I'd let her talk. "If you don't mind me asking, what happened for you to end up there?"

The Nurse went silent and, for a moment, I thought I'd misread her intentions. Then she let out a deep breath. "I used to work at a domestic abuse shelter and free clinic that was still kinda running after the System started. No real Safe Zones and monsters spawning all over. With everything going on, the clinic turned into something of a community hub for survivors.

"Everyone pooled Credits to buy the building from the Shop and we treated anyone as long as they were willing to help out. When the Sect first rolled in, things were still chaotic, but they tried to shut us down, just so they could tax and regulate everything. People formed a Resistance and fought back, but one of the first places the Sect hit was the clinic and I got nabbed pretty early on. If I'd been able to fight back more, I'd probably have higher Levels."

Lyrra leaned over and put her hand on the woman's arm. "No. If you'd fought back more, and been an actual threat, they'd have killed you. You did what you could. And you survived."

The elf spoke softly but there was the weight of truth behind her words. Her gesture conveyed comfort and the strength of someone who had survived their own trials.

Emi sniffed and then the tears flowed. I shifted my arm around to hold the sobbing woman as she buried her face into my side. Lyrra's hand slid from the Nurse's arm and rubbed her back to comfort her.

"Is everything alright down there?" Dayena asked on a private channel over party chat from the turret above, clearly able to hear the crying Nurse.

"Just processing trauma. And relief at finally being free, I think," I replied without anyone else overhearing.

I kept driving with one arm on the control yoke and the other around Emi's shoulders. As much as I'd have liked to offer more comfort, it wasn't a good time to split my attention. We were still well within Sect territory after all.

When Highway 83 merged into Highway 2, I continued north as I retraced the way back along our earlier route. Just before reaching City Park, I bypassed the broad highway of Colfax Avenue and turned west on East 17th instead, in the hopes of avoiding any fighting around the State Capitol when we approached downtown.

Emi sat up after we passed the park and rubbed away the last of her tears from puffy, red eyes. "I'm sorry. It all just hit me. Everyone that died there. Katie. Jason. Robert."

She hiccupped, caught up in the past once more. "I couldn't save them. Stuck in that place."

I shook my head and gave her shoulder a squeeze. "Don't apologize. None of that was on you. The Sect were responsible."

"I was just so helpless to stop any of it."

"You can't save everyone. You just do what you can," I shrugged. "And maybe make a few Credits along the way."

"You saved me," Lyrra interjected.

"It wasn't intentional." I grinned at the Movana's scowl, but a smile tugged at the corners of her mouth and Emi's laugh was worth the jab.

"Not intentional. Just soloing an Alpha. No big deal," Lyrra said with a dismissive wave. The sarcasm dripped from the elf's voice and the nurse continued chuckling at her antics.

"The Dungeon boss we just fought was worse."

"You also weren't solo."

"Point. I do have a somewhat decent team now. Ow—"

Dayena's foot had descended from the gunner's seat in the turret above the cab and lightly clipped the back of my head with the toe of her boot.

"Somewhat decent?" The Truinnar's voice was as frigid as the snow swirling outside the cab.

"Hey, I'm driving here."

"Your Neural Link can handle it."

I sniffed scornfully but didn't argue the dark elf's point. I still liked manual controls even when I could pilot a vehicle with my mind.

The moment passed and Emi looked between Lyrra and I before speaking again. "You have quite the team here. Why are you fighting the Sect?"

Thanks to the System's regeneration, any signs of her red and puffy eyes were gone. Now, they just gleamed brightly with curiosity.

"Guns for hire, for the most part. The Pharyleri pay well, and the Sect are targets none of us feel bad about taking out."

"But you're not from around here. And neither are the elves."

For the remainder of the drive, I told the abridged tale of working with the gnomes on the rail system that now stretched between Denver and Pittsburgh, including finding Lyrra and a brief summary of the multi-sided conflicts that occurred on the return journey.

The snow gradually eased, and the full light of morning reflected almost painfully bright from the shining fresh powder by the time we reached the Pharyleri headquarters compound at Union Station.

The Nurse looked at us like we were certifiably crazy. She gushed, "You are all nuts. Bad ass, but nuts. You should let me introduce you to some friends of mine."

I glanced at her with a raised eyebrow. "Friends?"

She bit her lip. "The Resistance, if they are still alive."

"I'm not going to make any promises. If your friends are fighting the Sect then maybe I can at least put them in touch with the gnomish command team. It might be a bit, though," I said as I stopped the vehicle and lowered the window.

Cold air poured into the cab and I leaned out to speak to the sentry on gate duty. It wasn't long before I closed up the window as the barricade retracted into the walls on either side of the gate. Driving through the wall, I followed the lane markings towards the central HQ building.

I parked the half-track in the open plaza that stretched out in front of the renovated train station. Though we'd been cleared to enter the base and passed through the gate, a squad of power-armored gnomish infantry still surrounded the vehicle with weapons raised. Their stone-faced squad leader gestured for us to exit the vehicle.

"Everybody out, but don't make any sudden moves. Looks like the troops are a bit trigger happy with everything going on," I signaled over party chat to the entire group, including the riders in the cargo compartment.

The cab door creaked open, and more snow swirled into the compartment. The burst of frigid air caused Emi to shiver as I pulled away from her and slipped out of the vehicle.

While another pair of armored gnomes remained on overwatch, two of the troops waved handheld scanners over me and then Emi. Lyrra and Dayena, as well as the remaining former prisoners, got the same treatment before they moved on to searching the vehicle. Though annoying, I was glad to see the Pharyleri stepping up their security processes.

Once the sergeant overseeing the squad seemed satisfied with their scans, a familiar quartermaster approached.

"Morning, Grylk."

The surly gnome grunted in response. "Command says you've got some pilfered materials from the Sect to sell off that might do us some good. Let's see what you've found, eh?"

The gnome gestured to the sergeant, who transmitted the squad's scan over to the quartermaster. The gnome stared off into the distance as he perused his invisible screen. "Hmm, Zepheel scales and Glacial ores, good for melting down into armor plating and conductive circuitry components. Enchanting materials. I'll give you sixty thousand Credits for the haul."

I folded my arms over my chest. "Eighty. And I'll throw in the transport for another twenty."

Grylk scowled. "Seventy and ten."

"Seventy-five and fifteen."

The gnome grunted and then gave a curt nod. A moment later the Credits were transferred over to me and I split the funds out to the party. Only Emi had known that everything would be shared out evenly, so the rest of the former prisoners went wide-eyed in surprise when the notifications hit them.

I chuckled at the shocked expressions. "I'm going to check in with Ismyna. Lyrra, see if you can get them food in the Great Hall. Maybe room assignments too, if the gnomes are interested in debriefing them for intel on the Sect in exchange. That'll give them a couple days to figure out what it looks like to get back on their feet."

"Careful bossman, someone might start thinking you actually care about something besides Credits if you keep this up."

I turned away. "I'm going to get some sleep if there are no emergencies."

It was a quick walk into the heart of Union Station and the heat inside brought immediate relief from the biting wind. The guards within the complex passed me through into the command center without any trouble.

The buzz of overlapping voices filled the chamber as recon drone operators relayed info from across the city to communications specialists and officers working with the troops in the field. Nesdyna stood on the raised platform that overlooked the holographic map table with Ismyna and several other Pharyleri commanders. On the image, several sections of the city flashed with red and orange lights in indication of the fighting taking place.

I went over and leaned against the outer railing that surrounded the command platform until Ismyna broke away from the group. She walked over to me, almost matching my height while standing on the platform above me. "Good work to your team on taking out the Sect forces at the armory. That mortar battery was just finding the range on our forces at Tech Center. It would have been real trouble if they'd kept up that fire much longer."

I accepted the Pharyleri's gratitude with a nod before replying. "I'm more concerned that they had a City Dungeon up and running. They had an entire warehouse full of the materials on site there. It's a guess, but it's likely they were shipping those goods to the manufactories at Tech Center."

"Our intel team is pulling data now. We'll also see what we can do for those folks you freed."

"I appreciate that."

Ismyna sighed. "We'll have to look into them, and they'll need to be watched. It wouldn't be the first time the Sect has tried inserting infiltrators."

I understood all too well, remembering the betrayal by a hired contractor and their halberd blade lodged in my chest. "Don't take any chances. I already suggested seeing if they'd trade a debriefing for a few days of food and lodging."

"Good idea! Now get some food yourself, and rest, if you can."

"My teammates should already have them headed for the cafeteria in the Great Hall."

Ismyna gestured to a lower-ranking Pharyleri, who hurried over. "I'll send an aide to escort them and get them settled."

I waited until Ismyna issued orders to the purple-haired gnome and then headed out, waving over my shoulder as I left.

I looked down at the aide beside me as we found our way to the Great Hall. "Ismyna gave you the job of being suspicious of the people we rescued from the Sect but try to be a little sympathetic."

The gnome looked at me wide-eyed and nodded enthusiastically. "Of course, Knight Errant Mason. I'll do my best!"

That blasted title. "Hal is fine."

The young gnome's expression turned to horror. "I would never dream of treating a storied Adventurer such as yourself with familiarity."

I sighed. If I ever saw Sheera again, I was going to kill that damned Demarcian. The Credits had been great, but the title was a massive pain in my ass. Always looking for a few Credits more, that's probably what they'd write on my tombstone, if burials were still a thing by the time something put me down.

After the owl incident, I knew I'd be far more likely to end up monster chow. But I still had a few tricks up my sleeve to keep that from happening, especially once I took the time to spend my stockpiled Skill

Points. I was burning to spend them when I unlocked the final tier of Class Skills.

My musings brought us back to the Great Hall, where I found the rest of my group. The former prisoners were seated at one of the long tables and enough empty plates already sat in front of them that their statuses no longer displaying the Starved trait. The System really obviated the need to ease starvation victims slowly back into eating regular solid foods.

Dayena and Lyrra had their own plates, but far fewer empties stacked. The elves both noticed my approach and looked quizzically at the purple-haired gnome beside me, until he bowed low before the table and introduced himself to the detainees.

"Good morning, human friends. I am Krimi Coilwizz. While you are guests with us, I will be your escort and guide around this institution."

Then the friendly expression on the gnome's face turned serious. "You are, of course, free to leave at any time, but you will need to be accompanied at all times while you remain here. I hope you will take advantage of our hospitality for a couple days while you recover from your ordeal."

While the gnome continued talking, I grabbed a couple breakfast burritos. The fact that I hadn't bothered taking a plate or tray earned me a dirty look from the kitchen staff. I had used tongs to pull the hot burritos from the platter on the counter—I wasn't a complete barbarian.

By the time I was back at the table the gnome was preparing to take Larry, Stephen, Camila, and Emi off for their debriefing. I shook hands with the two men while they thanked us profusely but Emi insisted on hugs for both elves. When she got to me, the short blonde wrapped her arms around me and squeezed my waist tight while resting her head on my chest.

Ignoring the looks I received from both Dayena and Lyrra, I returned the hug while still awkwardly holding onto the breakfast burritos with one hand. I wasn't going to reject Emi's apparent need for human contact, not after everything she and the rest of the freed prisoners went through. Whether or not she was sending some kind of signals with the prolonged physical contact, I wouldn't make any assumptions.

"If any of you need anything, leave a word with the front desk." I pointed over to the hotel clerks once the Nurse finally released me.

After another round of expressing their gratitude, the rescuees headed off with Krimi, and I was left standing beside the table as my partners went back to their own meals.

"I really am going to go get some sleep now."

As I walked off, I clearly heard Lyrra mumbling about a certain blonde wanting to get some sleep with me too, but I kept walking without dignifying her comment with a response. It only took a couple minutes to reach my room, where I peeled myself out of my armor and took advantage of the scalding hot water for a quick shower.

By the time I flopped onto the bed, I was feeling the exhaustion from the long night. Still, I'd waited long enough and I pushed sleep away to review the last of my notifications that I'd set aside in the Dungeon.

You have reached Level 46 as a Relentless Huntsman. Stat Points automatically distributed. You have 2 Free Attributes and 8 Class Skill Points to distribute.

I put the two attribute points into Strength and Willpower, shoring up my two lowest attributes, and getting them out of the way before I got into the good stuff—the final tier of Class Skills that had been grayed out in my Skill tree for the last two years. Before I made any further decisions, I brought up the new Skills acquired when I dropped a point into the three of them inside the Dungeon. The abilities appeared on the blue System screens floating in front of me.

Class Skill Acquired

More Where That Came From (Level 1)

The Relentless Huntsman is now more efficient with their use of weapons, ammunition, and supplies, drawing directly from their stockpiled equipment in the heat of battle.

Effect: When a Relentless Huntsman fires a charge-based or ammunition-based weapon, the weapon magazine will automatically replenish itself from Inventory storage so long as that type of reload is available. Single use items summoned from storage (such as grenades, mines, and rockets) will be 25% more effective in strength. Designated Personal Weapons double the effect of this Skill. Mana regeneration reduced by 5 Mana per minute permanently.

Another passive Skill hampering my Mana regeneration but the benefits couldn't be ignored. No longer worrying about the firing capacity of my ranged weaponry meant more damage faster. I wouldn't be worried about reloading my projectile pistols or swapping out my energy weapons ever again. As long as spare ammo remained in my Inventory, that is.

Fortunately for my Mana regeneration, the Skill atop the Pursuit tree was an active one and the description waited in the next blue box.

Class Skill Acquired

Apprehend (Level 1)

On rare occasions, the Relentless Huntsman is assigned to bring in their prey warm instead of cold. This Skill ensures the target remains alive until they are brought to face their fate.

Effect: Creates Mana shackles on a target within line of sight from the user. Shackles restrict the target's movement, spell, and Skill usage. The user must specify how the shackles take form to restrain the target as part of Skill activation. Strength and durability of Mana shackles increases for each negative status effect on target at the time of casting. If the target is incapacitated at the time of casting, the strength and durability of the bonds are doubled. Shackles last for 4 hours.
Cost: 100 Mana.

That Skill certainly would have proved useful on numerous occasions over the last year. At least now, I could restrict targets at range a little easier. I also wouldn't be completely reliant upon equipment to keep bounty targets compliant while bringing them in for the reward.

The final unlocked Skill came from the Combat tree, and it was the one I'd looked forward to the most, since I lacked much in the way of direct damage dealing abilities.

Class Skill Acquired

Kill Shot (Level 1)

Sometimes, bringing the target in cold is the only way.

Effect: The Relentless Huntsman's next attack hits the target for 200% damage. This damage is increased by 5% for each debilitating effect or negative status on the target when the attack lands. This damage increases an additional percent for each effect applied by the Relentless Huntsman. Cost: 100 stamina + 50 Mana.

Kill Shot complimented Apprehend, since both abilities became more effective if I'd properly stacked my other Skills like Hinder, Rend, and Expose on the target before going for the capture or the execution.

While I certainly felt thrilled about all three of my new Class Skills, I recognized Kill Shot filled the largest hole in my repertoire. Most of my skill set revolved around taking advantage of having the right equipment prepared ahead of any fight and applying abilities that drained my opponent slowly, without much for directly boosting my damage output. Kill Shot closed that gap by providing a single attack damage boost that built upon the way my other Skills negatively affected my opponents in combat. Instead of grinding my foes down slowly, now I had a knockout punch held in reserve to finish the fight in a burst.

You have eight unassigned Class Skill points. Would you like to assign them now? (Y/N)

I grinned, selecting "yes" and immediately dropping all eight available points into Kill Shot. The stamina and Mana cost for the ability more than doubled, in exchange for a scaled increase to both the base damage and an additional two percent for each negative status effect I applied personally.

Closing out the rest of the blue screens, I kept my finalized status screen up as I finally let myself succumb to slumber.

Status Screen			
Name:	Hal Mason*	Class:	Hunter*
Race:	Human (Male)	Level:	46
Titles			
Dungeon World Delver*, Galactic Bronze Bounty Hunter, Knight Errant of Demarcia, Sharp Eyed*, Sherpa, Slayer of Kobolds* (*Title hidden)			
Health:	1440	Stamina:	1440
Mana:	1030		
Status			
Normal*			
Attributes			
Strength	79	Agility	155
Constitution	144	Perception	93
Intelligence	103	Willpower	77
Charisma	102	Luck	24
Class Skills			
Apprehend	1	Efficient Trail	1
Expose	1	Greater Observation	3
Hinder	2	Implacable Endurance	1
Keen Senses	1	Kill Shot	9

Meat Locker	3	More Where That Came From	1
On the Hunt	5	Quality Over Quantity	2
Rend	1	Resilient Nature	2
Right Tool For the Job	2		
Non-Class Skills			
Blood Scent	1		
Perks			
Gut Instinct			
Combat Spells			
Earth Spike (II), Firespray (II), Frostbolt (VI), Frostnova (IV), Greater Healing (I), Greater Regeneration (I), Howling Blast (I), Ice Armor (I), Lesser Disguise (V), Minor Healing (IV), Minor Renew (II), Whiteout (I)			

Chapter 17

The pounding beat of a fist against the door of my hotel room jolted me awake only a couple hours later. Despite my grogginess, I remembered to throw on a fresh set of coveralls and slid my feet into my armored boots as I made my way to answer the incessant knocking.

I yanked the door open. "What?"

A young, pink-haired Pharyleri jumped away with a nervous squeak as I stuck my frowning face out of the doorway. "I-I'm sorry to disturb you, Knight Errant Mason! Your presence is requested in the command center."

She blinked innocently, but the way she extended her hands toward me as she held up a steaming cup of black coffee told me that she knew exactly how to bribe grumpy mercenaries who would rather be sleeping.

I acknowledged the offering with a grunt. "Fine, I'm coming."

Still scowling, I grabbed my vambraces from the room before giving myself a once-over to make sure I wasn't forgetting anything else. Then ensuring the door sealed behind me, I put on the armor as I followed the gnome down the hall. Only after I was fully armored did I finally accept the offered coffee with another grunt of thanks. With my attributes, the mundane drink was more habit than true addiction these days, but the placebo still worked.

The steaming cup was half emptied by the time we reached the command center. As soon as the door to the chamber opened, a clamor of panicked shouts emerged. I entered the room to find Pharyleri rushing between various consoles in a sharp contrast to the calm and controlled atmosphere from earlier this morning.

From the platform in the center of the room, Ismyna attempted to rein in the chaos, but her frustration at her lack of success showed from the clenching of her jaw. On the holographic map floating overhead, a cluster of red dots flashed. The pings demanded attention but there were no friendly forces anywhere near the new enemies, except for the small grouping that marked the defenders of the City Core at the Central Library. The threat popping up in the middle of the city, in what should have been friendly territory, was the likely cause for the furor.

A minute of searching located the rest of my team, standing with their backs against the wall to avoid the worst of the frenzy.

"What the hell is going on?" I asked over party chat as I joined the elves, not trusting my voice to carry over the noise that filled the room.

"The Pharyleri were not the only ones to hire mercenaries. The Sect have apparently been infiltrating a force into a safehouse and are now making their own play to take a City Core while the Pharyleri are otherwise engaged." An air of disappointment filled Dayena's voice at the way the command center had devolved into disarray. I couldn't help feeling the same. I'd thought the gnome's better prepared than this.

"Enough!"

The harsh command cut through the din and silenced the uproar as the hustling Pharyleri froze in place. The sudden hush was so quiet that it was possible to hear the hiss of the command center door closing behind Nesdyna as the scowling clan elder entered the chamber.

I thought I'd been cranky when I woke up. I had nothing on the glare that the old Pharyleri leveled on the room as she hopped onto the center platform. "This is not the way to victory. War is chaos. Things will not always go to plan and the enemy will do the unexpected. The Binary Eclipse Sect is well armed and trained, with Levels earned in combat Classes. But that experience has been gained as thugs and they are not prepared for a well-equipped and organized force to stand up to their predations. I have faith in our strength of arms and in the preparations we have made for this day. Stick to the plans that have been provided to your teams and follow the procedures of your assignments. We will prevail!"

A few cheers grew into a thunderous roar that filled the command center, until Nesdyna gestured sharply and the clamor died out. "Now get back to work!"

The clan elder's gaze scanned the room as the techs and specialists buried themselves in getting operations running smoothly once more. Her eyes landed on me, and she beckoned for my squad to join her at the center platform.

Nesdyna pointed to the red dots in the map floating overhead as we reached her. The gnome lowered her voice, barely audible above the more normal buzz of conversation that filled the chamber. "I need you to buy time for a response. I'll pay a twenty-five thousand Credit bounty for each one of those dots you take off the board."

It took everything I had to keep my face blank in the face of that offer.

"Try for thirty," Dayena encouraged silently over party chat.

"Thirty. And fifty for any Advanced Classes we take out," I counter-offered the Pharyleri.

Nesdyna's eyes twinkled and I knew instantly that she'd led off low with the expectation of my response. "Deal."

A notification appeared in my vision.

New Reserved Bounty offered to Hal Mason!

Bring Them in Cold: Eliminate Binary Eclipse Sect members participating in the assault on the Denver Central Library City Core.

Reward: 30,000 Credits per Basic Class target slain. 50,000 Credits per Advanced Class target slain.

Reserved bounties were bounties offered to specific members of the Galactic Bounty Hunter Guild and could only be completed by the individual to which the bounty was offered. It meant nobody else could get paid for the same targets, even if some other registered hunter took them out first—which could happen with bounties classified as Public.

Dayena smacked the back of my shoulder, also clearly seeing the elder's amusement, but I just grinned savagely as I confirmed the bounty notification that Nesdyna sent my way. I stared up at the map floating overhead, memorizing the streets and plotting out the routes the red dots would take to hit the Core. "Time to hunt. Send us updates if those forces move off the direct route to the Central Library."

I spun in a crisp about-face that would have made any Paris Island DI proud and bolted for the door with my teammates on my heels. Startled headquarters staff frantically scrambled out of our path as we raced out of the building. Jumping onto our summoned vehicles, our biggest impediment came as we tried to exit the compound. It took a long minute for the gates to retract out of the way, so we shot through as soon as the gap opened wide enough for our bikes to fit.

We flew down 17th, skimming along in anti-grav mode just above the level of the defunct stoplights that still graced the intersections. We angled onto Broadway, heading south after making the turn a block west of the towering Wells Fargo Center. The third tallest building in Denver was better known as the Cash Register Building for the way its curved upper floors resembled an antique sales register.

From Broadway, it was a straight, four-block run to the Central Library. Ahead of us, energy beams flashed back and forth between the Pharyleri defenders and the Sect forces working to encircle the building. I pushed out my map as we grew closer, getting a feel for the urban terrain and the angles the oncoming enemies were using to besiege the City Core.

"Dayena, swing east and pick off targets of opportunity in their rear line. I want them looking over their shoulders. Lyrra, hop off along the way and find an overwatch position in the courthouse across from the library."

The elves acknowledged my plan and split off as we drove through the parks that strung out for several blocks from the old State Capitol building. I swung off the street and into the treeline rather than charge straight into the firefight ahead.

Bypassing the Greek amphitheater in the heart of the park, I caught sight of an armed squad working their way around the Art Museum to the west of the library and approaching along 14th Street. The alien in the lead of the half dozen Galactics pointed a cone-shaped device toward the library that held a rippling curtain of distorted light between the squad and the structure. Some kind of stealth field generator to cloak their approach?

I could see at least two Pharyleri lookouts keeping watch from the front entrance to the library but neither appeared to see the Sect fighters working their way toward the building.

Not wanting to alert the squad, I used a quick scan of their leader to assess the alien's Binary Eclipse affiliation and moderate health pool before I pulled out my Hastati launcher from Inventory. Just in case the stealth field projector could mess with the weapon's targeting lock, I focused on the second member of the squad, a green-scaled humanoid with a protruding snout and four arms.

The firefight on the far side of the building covered the noise of the launcher and the Sect squad had no warning of their impending doom before they were engulfed in a maelstrom of fire as the rocket detonated in their midst.

One of the gnome lookouts spotted me as I left cover and rushed toward the inferno. I waved to the sentry before swapping the launcher on my shoulder out for Ace and Last Word. It was time to see how well my new Skill worked at replenishing spent ammo directly from my Inventory.

The firestorm subsided, revealing all six members of the Sect squad still on their feet. My raised handcannons roared out a storm of projectiles as I swept my weapons over the singed and smoldering aliens.

One after another they dropped, though two managed to return fire ineffectively. The beams and bullets all missed by a significant margin as my movements turned me into a difficult target. The final Galactic turned to flee before I walked my fire over it, but I continued to fire into the center of its back until the corpse tumbled to the ground with its health depleted.

I frowned as that last alien fell. Something about the charred profile left me unsettled and I kept running forward until I reached the body. The shredded rear torso confirmed it was certainly very dead, but I hooked the toe of my boot under one shoulder and flipped it over.

For a long moment, I stared down at the corpse as weapon fire echoed over the city, both near and far. I ignored the sounds; my gut had been right to feel unease over the alien and it was not a reassuring sensation.

Sightless yellow eyes stared up at me from a blistered face of brownish-purple flesh and small horns protruded from both the forehead and on either side of the chin. For a moment, I flashed back to the first time I'd seen one of their kind, lying amongst a pile of executed human prisoners outside the rubble of a destroyed school building.

My old foes, the Krym'parke, were in Denver and they were working alongside the Sect.

Chapter 18

It couldn't be a coincidence, not after they'd worked with Dayena's cousins in an effort to return the wayward dark elf to face an arranged marriage.

"Dayena, watch your ass. The Sect are working with the Krym'parke."

For a moment, a chill ran along my spine as only silence met my warning over party chat.

"Are you sure?"

I breathed a sigh of relief at the Truinnar's question. *"I'm standing over one's corpse in the middle of a Sect squad. What do you suppose are the chances they're still working for your cousin's family?"*

The Countess paused again before replying. *"Creynora never left Earth to return home, so it might be possible."*

I shook my head and began looting the dead of any gear that survived my rocket attack against the squad. By the time I finished, both Pharyleri sentries inside the library had rifles pointed my way. They weren't firing though.

"Be careful. I'm going to talk down some anxious gnomes and then get back on the hunt."

The dark elf acknowledged my cautionary words and then the party chat fell quiet once more.

Holstering my pistols, I was pleased to note that the readouts on both weapons showed as fully loaded thanks to More Where That Came From. Pointedly ignoring the threat of the Pharyleri guns pointed my way, I knelt beside the body of the Krym'parke and looted it before working my way through the rest of the squad. A particularly long-barreled rifle was the only functioning weapon that, along with multiple pieces of enchanted jewelry, a variety of intact armor plates, and any equipped gear, disappeared into one Inventory space, while the stripped bodies disappeared into Meat Locker.

Only once the sidewalk was clear did I stand and start walking toward the library, keeping my hands well clear of my holstered pistols.

"Halt right there!"

The command came from a gnome who popped up from behind one of the cement barricades set outside the library entrance. He wore a set of black plates strapped over the olive Pistongrinder uniform and a black helmet with an opaque visor that amplified his voice.

Stopping in place, I held out my open palms, though that gesture really didn't count for much when weapons could be summoned from Inventory in an instant. "Easy, I'm not trying to come any closer. I'm a Bronze-ranked Bounty Hunter with a bounty to collect for every Binary Eclipse punk that I put down, so I just wanted to make sure that you all didn't start shooting me in the back as I moved on."

The guard conferred with his partner, and I kept motionless after I noticed that the two sentries outside were backed up by a crew-served turret hidden behind the glass of the library entrance. The glare of light on the windows hid the weapon from a distance, but I was close enough now to see through the windows and glimpse the additional defenders within.

"Alright, Knight Errant Mason. Command has verified the bounty. You're clear to continue."

Sketching a casual salute to the sentries, I jogged off along West 14th Avenue. The street curved around the park to the north, and I followed it to backtrack the path of the Binary Eclipse squad.

Working my way around the Denver Art Museum, I found a stone border around an elevated and overgrown yard on the corner of Bannock Street and West 13th Avenue. A layer of frost coated the thick overgrowth surrounding the two-story brick Victorian house, which a sign on the wrought-iron gate identified as the Center for Colorado Women's History.

Weapons fire in the distance continued, and I felt the need to get off the street. Getting spotted in the open was a death sentence. Despite the way sounds echoed off the buildings, some of that gunfire was close. Too close.

A quick leap from the stone border into the midst of the yard helped me avoid leaving an obvious path through the frozen foliage. I carefully forced my way through the tall grass and shrubs to the outer wall of the house before edging along to the other side of the building. When I reached a brick path that ran along the rear of the house and out to 13th Avenue, I peered out from my frozen concealment to find a cluster of Binary Eclipse forces setting up an entrenched position on the opposite side of the street.

The location the Sect had picked was out of sight from the library, hidden up against the angled building that had an oddly geometric protrusion sticking out over the street. The geometric building also connected back across the road to the art museum by a skybridge on the second story.

A steady stream of energy fire rained down towards the library beyond the weird geometric building from a Sect position on the skybridge. The side of the library facing this direction had been reinforced with solid stone for the entire first story, but it looked like the Sect were trying to drill through with their energy beams.

Ignoring the attackers in their overhead emplacement on the skybridge, I focused on the activities of the group across the street. A Scrofalori grunt hurried about, scattering several directional energy shields around the location in a rough arc that ended on either side against the walls of the building. Blue forcefields standing about eight feet high popped up from the mobile emitters to surround a heavily armored vehicle, but the haphazard spacing left several gaps in the defensive perimeter.

Harmecrat (Escort Driver Level 2) (A)

[Binary Eclipse Sect]
HP: 840/840
MP: 1020/1020
Status: Reflex Booster

The six-wheeled conveyance looked a bit like an off-road buggy crossed with one of those "van life" campers and the forest of antennas clustered on the roof spelled "mobile command center" to me. The vehicle itself resisted my scanning attempts, shielding the occupants from Greater Observation. At least, until the sides of the van folded down and exposed the interior.

The banks of monitors mounted within confirmed my command center guess, as did the flashy golden armor worn by one of the three passengers. Taking no chances and ready to withdraw at the first sign of alarm, I eased my awareness forward to encompass the trio of Galactics.

The first pair were a Tactical Technician and a Comm Specialist. Like the Scrofalori driver, both were barely into their first handful of Levels of the Advanced Class tier. The golden-armored third alien was more interesting.

Welven Yimishi, Favored Son (Sect Sub-captain Level 37) (A)

[Binary Eclipse Sect]
HP: 1840/1840
MP: 1890/2110

Status: Father's Favor, Armor of Nepotism

A decorative series of spikes ran in a line over each of the pauldrons of the gold plate armor, though I could hardly tell whether they were placed to protect the neck or just for the sake of appearances. With the spikes jutting out an impractical eight inches, it was almost amusing to watch the two others flinching and dodging away from them as the Sub-captain climbed out of the vehicle.

The Sect officer pulled off the armored helmet to reveal the brilliant golden hair of a Movana and a twisted sneer directed at the Scrofalori driver. "You incompetent hairball. Do you even know how to draw a straight line? What are all these gaps doing in the perimeter shields? Utterly useless."

Though I recognized the Sect officer's surname, the Movana's condescending voice was not the one I'd overheard in conversation before I completed the Pharyleri bounty on the Sect assistant manager. Still, the other elements of the status pretty clearly outlined a familial relation.

The hirsute driver hustled to adjust the spacing of the shield generators under the scowling gaze of the Sub-captain. It seemed beyond idiotic to me that the commander prioritized belittling and micromanaging his subordinate in the midst of an ongoing battle, but I wasn't going to point out the enemy's mistakes to them.

By the time the shields were moved to the satisfaction of the Sub-captain, the Comm Specialist had also climbed out of the vehicle and stood behind the officer while shifting nervously from one foot to another.

"What are you waiting on? Report already." Sect Sub-captain Yimishi snarled after turning to see the aide standing outside the vehicle.

"Yes, Sect Sub-captain. We've lost contact with the advance squad on the west flank. The east flank approach has stalled between a sniper pinning down a squad and an assassin-type stalking them whenever they try to circle around away from the sharpshooter."

Yimishi's jaw dropped and he gaped wordlessly for a moment. "Must I think of everything? Send another squad to the west to find out what happened to those slackers who are out of communication and get a sniper of our own. Deal with it."

The Comm Specialist exchanged a glance with the Tactical Technician, who remained safely inside the command van, before turning back to their commander. "Sect Sub-captain, all squads are already deployed. And the sniper allocated to the mission is no longer responding."

That explained the long rifle I'd looted from the dead Sect members. It was reassuring that the Sect's resources dedicated to this surprise attack were already spent and that there wouldn't be more turning up. Though that limited my potential payday from the Pharyleri. Good thing I still had a few more opportunities to collect.

With the Sect command group distracted as the Sub-captain fell into a bickering meltdown after the Comm Specialist's report, I eased clear of the overgrown bushes and hopped over the back fence that separated the Victorian house from the Art Museum. The noise of the battle covered my landing on top of a conveniently placed dumpster, then I leapt across the open stretch to the top of a loading dock where the roof jutted out beside the skybridge. Another quick jump and I'd passed out of sight from the command post below but found myself positioned less than a dozen yards from the Sect gunners operating the crew-served cannon that fired toward the library.

A human served as an assistant gunner for the tripod mounted cannon, feeding Mana batteries into a hopper on the side of the weapon, while a Truinnar operated the gun from behind by holding twin grips that reminded me of an M2 machine gun. The cannon spat out a stream of coherent light that tore into the wall of the Pharyleri-held City Center, where the library stood a block down the street.

Two more Sect members stood beyond the cannon, another boar-like Scrofalori and a Ceratophimi humanoid-rhinoceros. Clad in sleeveless armored vests, the pair laughed as they each shoulder-fired the energy beam equivalent of a light machine gun. If the heavy beam cannon was the equivalent of an M2, these were more like the M249 SAW.

Shards of glass from the long-broken windowpanes that ran along both sides of the elevated walkway mingled with frost underfoot, crunching beneath each step as I moved across the interior of the skybridge. I felt more than heard the noise, with the vibrations of the ongoing attacks by the gunners who still hadn't noticed my presence.

Sloppy.

A pair of my plasma grenades detonated in the midst of the Sect position, cutting off the streams of outgoing fire and engulfing the gunners in swirling plasma. The force of the explosion threw the burning human out of the broken window and knocked the remaining trio off their feet. The tripod of the heavy cannon collapsed, and the pair of light machine guns tumbled away from their operators.

My pistols barked as I closed the distance, firing projectiles into the unarmored limbs of the three Galactics in an attempt to keep them on the ground. My shots smashed into wrist and elbow joints, sending the Scrofalori and Ceratophimi sprawling. Though several of my attacks hit the Truinnar, he leapt back up and landed on his feet almost instantly. The dark elf launched himself toward me, a serrated machete appearing in one hand and a circular energy shield the size of a dinner plate snapping into existence on the other.

Shots from both weapons glanced off the translucent buckler, so I lowered my aim. Activating Hinder on the Truinnar and leaping away from the slashing blade, I drilled several shots into the lightly armored shins and ankles of the advancing Sect member. A cast of Frostbolt skewered the dark elf's thigh and further slowed his approach to a limp.

Normally, I'd have needed to reload about now, but both Last Word and Ace still registered as fully loaded thanks to More Where That Came From. I was really beginning to love this Skill. The handcannons continued to roar with every squeeze of their triggers, never slowing my assault.

When the Truinnar desperately tried to block my attacks against his legs by lowering his shield, I raised one weapon to blast away at his exposed face. The dark elf stumbled and used the forward momentum to fling the shield as an activated Skill. I twisted, but the glowing disc of energy curved with me and caught me in the stomach. The strike doubled me over and I retched as my stomach clenched. Bent over, I managed another flurry of rounds that finally dropped the dark elf.

One of the two hulks had climbed to their feet, and I shifted my fire to blast the remaining pair of Binary Eclipse goons. The second brute rose on one knee and scooped up a fallen light machine gun. The rising beam weapon leveled off to point my way and I barely managed to brace myself before the energy beams swept over me.

The rays traced over my thigh, and I felt the heat through my armor as the firestorm climbed over my waist and drilled into the center of my chest. Returning fire, I lunged to the side to dodge away from the attack, but the energy beam continued digging through my armor, hitting the same spot over and over as if locked onto a target. As much as I loved my own Skills, being on the receiving end was never as fun.

Beyond the alien hosing me down with rays of energy, the wounded Scrofalori scurried down the skybridge toward the other dropped light machine gun.

The rhino-like alien roared in triumph as my jumpsuit gave out and the beams seared into my flesh. I gritted my teeth against the pain and noted the way the closer Galactic flinched from my shots, even while keeping the energy gun focused on me. My rounds were chewing him up too and it was a race to see whose health pool would empty out first.

The Ceratophimi's expression turned to horror as the alien's health plummeted and I remained on my feet despite the punishing barrage. I bared my teeth in a predatory grin as the battered alien finally keeled over. On the far side of the new corpse, the Scrofalori finally picked up the other energy gun and I targeted the back of the boar-like alien's knee. Before it could turn, my rounds tore through the joint and the brown-haired alien toppled over. The energy gun skidded out of the Scrofalori's grasp, tumbling even farther down the skybridge when the alien slammed into the ground hard enough to shake the structure.

The alien managed to roll and pulled out an energy pistol to return fire while lying on its back. Compared to the damage I'd already weathered, the attacks felt little more damaging than hot water from a squirt gun left in the sun too long. My shots ripped through the last of the fallen Sect member's health and the arrival of another experience notification heralded the Scrofalori's demise.

Pulling a health potion from Inventory, I hit myself with the injector before scooping up the easiest bits of Sect gear lying about. Both light machinegun analogs and their big brother disappeared into my Inventory.

Then I peeked over the edge of the skybridge at the command center below, feeling a little surprised that none of the Binary Eclipse staff had shown up during the fight.

The spot where the command van had parked was empty. Only ruts remained in the frozen turf, where the all-terrain tires had dug through the frost to tear into the ground beneath. The energy shield generators still sat out, though the ones in front of where the vehicle had parked were knocked over by the apparent hasty departure.

The human blasted out of the skybridge lay in the street, directly in line with the tire marks. The hapless assistant gunner had been flattened by the fleeing command squad.

I shook my head and glanced around the area, pushing on my awareness and searching for anything that stood out in the sphere covered by Greater Observation.

Nothing stood out nearby.

Had the egocentric Sect Sub-captain panicked and fled at the first sign of a threat? That was a strong possibility.

Damn it.

That was fifty thousand Credits that scurried away.

Whatever the case, the Advanced Class command squad had left the field. Which meant I was free to quickly loot the rest of the Sect equipment from the firing position. It only took a couple minutes to strip any valuables from the corpses on the skybridge before I slipped back down to ground level, ready to continue the hunt.

There were Pharyleri bounty Credits still on the table, after all.

Chapter 19

Death stalked the Binary Eclipse forces besieging the City Core as Dayena and I circled the library from opposite sides.

Even with our link through party chat, the dark elf's position only appeared on my minimap intermittently. The short swords that the Countess wielded removed her foes far more subtly than the booming thunder of my pistols. She vanished from my awareness in between each of her kills, only to pop back up as another Sect member fell beneath her blades.

Mine was a more straightforward approach, taking advantage of the fact that the Sect combatants felt confident in the cover their emplacements provided against the defenders within the City Center. Those positions often left their flanks exposed and I exploited that using the doctrine of fire and maneuver still drilled into my bones from my time spent in the Marine Corps.

When the Sect vanguard set up emplacements firing from the upper stories of the civic center complex, I hit them from behind and took them out one by one. Another squad tried setting up inside the glass-paneled high-rise across the street and I grappled my way to the roof before sweeping through the building from above.

With the Sect command element absent after fleeing from the field, the lack of communication between the enemy forces meant that none of the groups warned their compatriots before being silenced.

I struggled with one group that included an armored healer and defender, paired in matching heavy armor. The healer repaired any health damage I dealt to other members of the party, while the defender always managed to get between my shots and the healer whenever I focused on the medic. That squad cohesion fell apart once I waded into the group.

Loaded up on my own healing spells and an expensive regen potion, I engaged at point-blank range. The defender couldn't match my speed up close, and I finally dropped the healer after bypassing the squad. The rest of the five-member party tore me up good in the process, but I was still standing when the last of them fell in a running firefight that traveled the better part of three blocks down Broadway.

After I finished looting the dead, weapons fire and spell explosions continued in the distance, but the sounds echoed off the buildings all around and made it almost impossible to tell where they were coming from—even with my enhanced senses. Rather than blunder into another firefight in progress, I hunkered down in a walled-off parking lot between two abandoned Mexican restaurants to let my depleted Mana and health pools refill and get a better sense of the battle as my minimap updated.

Before my pools filled back up completely, Dayena's status flashed as her position pinged for attention in the corner of my vision and the Truinnar's stressed voice sounded over party chat. *"You were right, Hal. There were more Krym'parke."*

The dot representing the Countess showed her near the intersection of East 13th Avenue and Lincoln Street, one block east and three blocks north.

"How bad is it?" I asked. Though my health pool was only half regenerated, the tightly held panic in Dayena's voice had me springing back onto my feet and I bolted out of the parking lot.

"Bad. My cousin is also here."

I ran north up Broadway at speed that would have any Olympic runner in the dust, only slowing as I cut across East 11th Avenue to take a straight shot up Lincoln. *"I thought she might be nearby if the Krym'parke were around."*

The dark elf paused and her voice dropped, so quiet it was almost inaudible over party chat. *"No, Hal. Creynora is not here. Rhegnah is."*

Rushing across East 12th in a flat-out sprint, my steps faltered. *"What?"*

Regaining my momentum, I passed half of another block in a dozen strides before I processed exactly what the Countess had said.

I'd blown up that Truinnar asshole.

The dark elf's armor had been evaporated by an anti-vehicle energy cannon and I'd fired a missile straight into his chest from the roof of a moving train. A missile which exploded with enough damage to bring down the Krym'parke vessel that Rhegnah had been riding. The train had plowed through the pillar of smoke from the wreck after the ship had crashed alongside the tracks.

"They have me. Get clear, Hal."

In that moment, Dayena's words distracted me as I was already preoccupied with figuring out how the Truinnar had survived when I'd earned experience for his death, and I missed the series of nearly invisible disks strewn across the sidewalk.

My foot landed on an unseen mine and the detonation catapulted me almost a dozen feet into the air. An instant of burning agony from my leg morphed into a sudden numbness as I crashed to the ground. I recognized the sudden lack of sensation from my lower leg. It meant I'd be regenerating a missing limb.

Again.

A quick glance down at my left leg confirmed the feeling as I rolled to a stop in the entry to a narrow parking lot between two larger buildings, less than a block from Dayena's position on my minimap. My foot was completely gone, and blood streamed out from the ragged flesh that remained of my calf muscle. Two jagged shards of bone jutted out from just above my ankle, but my foot was missing entirely.

I mumbled through a quick healing spell to stop the bleeding and summoned a health potion from my Inventory.

An armored boot appeared from out of nowhere and stomped down on my hand, snapping at least one of my fingers and shattering the potion injector before I could use it.

"Mines are not so pleasant when you are on the receiving end, are they?"

I looked up at the smiling Truinnar standing over me, her silver hair cut short in a wavy bob. She'd worn her hair much longer the last time we fought, on the roof of the gnome's train, but the new style still sparked recognition.

The black-suited dark elf wore the same haircut I'd seen disappearing from the bar in the Pharyleri section of the city.

I'd missed my chance to scan her with Greater Observation then, so I didn't hesitate to pull her information now. The Truinnar had climbed her way up to an Advanced Class since I'd kicked her off the moving train where we'd last fought.

Creynora Baluisa (Darkheart Guardian Level 3) (A)
HP: 1080/1080
MP: 1120/1120

"How long have you been waiting to say that?" I growled.

"Since you left me lying naked on the street in that dinky town."

I shrugged one shoulder, slowly grinning at the dark elf. Then I winked. "What can I say, you've got a cute ass."

Creynora's eyes grew wide, and her face flushed. I'd expected anger but flustered worked just as well. Either way, the comment still served as a moment of distraction, and I drew Last Word from its holster on my left hip unnoticed.

Firing almost as soon as I cleared the holster, my shots rocked the Truinnar and she stumbled, freeing the hand she'd been grinding into the sidewalk while we talked. I pushed up to my knees and pulled out Ace with my broken hand, ignoring the pain shooting through my fingers as I used my middle finger to trigger it.

"No, do not fire. His death is mine," Creynora shouted over her shoulder, despite the barrage I'd unleashed on her, and I realized there were two Krym'parke behind her with rifles at their shoulders.

A silver metallic shield unfolded from a bracer on the Truinnar's left arm, expanding out into a flat-topped barrier that curved down on either side to a point at the bottom. My rounds glanced off the heater shield and a saber appeared in the dark elf's free hand as she steadily advanced toward me. From her posture and the deliberate pacing of each step, I could see the way her muscles braced as Creynora waited for me to pull out the spell I'd used to knock her backward in our last encounter.

Missing a foot restricted my mobility to almost nothing and my stomach turned at the precariousness of my position, still suffering from the unhealed damage from my last fight. In my other fights against the skilled Truinnar, my higher attributes balanced out against the experience of her fighting techniques. Now though, my high Agility meant little, and the dark elf held all the cards.

I'd just have to play the hand I was dealt.

I skipped shots off the sidewalk to ricochet beneath the dark elf's shield, slowing her approach slightly. Creynora lowered the bottom tip of the shield, nearly scraping the sidewalk and limiting my ability to slide my rounds under it.

The lowered shield exposed the Truinnar's shoulders, and I unleashed a Frostbolt. The jagged shard of ice punched into her bicep and a sheen of rime crawled up her shoulder.

Then the dark elf was in range and her saber slashed toward me. Pushing off with my good leg, I threw myself to the side and rolled into the parking lot away from the street. I came up firing but left a trail of blood from my stump, despite my regeneration.

With Creynora expecting my use of Howling Blast as a knock-back, I cast Whiteout instead. The sudden blizzard engulfed the area, dropping the visibility to nothing in the mouth of the parking lot and concealing me from the stalking elf. I snapped off two more quick shots, then rolled to the side in an effort to throw off my opponent from my exact location within the swirling squall of snow and ice.

Before I could move further, Creynora appeared in front of me. She charged through the storm as if she knew exactly where I'd be, and her shield bashed into me. The impact of the rushing Darkheart Guardian hit my face and chest almost equally, picking me up and sending me flying through the air.

I hit the building at the end of the narrow parking lot, my head smashing into the cement block wall hard enough that it broke through the outer layer of the blocks, cratering the surface and sending shards of concrete flying out.

For an instant, I hung in place, stuck in the wall like a coyote on a Saturday-morning cartoon, before gravity reasserted itself and I toppled to the asphalt below.

The back of my skull cracked from the pounding, and sharp pain stabbed into my brain. The landing left me stunned and I blinked away stars. Concussion, if not outright brain damage, a strangely analytical part of my mind observed. My swimming vision made it hard to focus.

My health was nearly empty after the ambush and the beating that followed, but I had no intention of lying here and waiting to die.

Blood poured from my nose and a cut on my forehead filled my left eye with liquid. Barely able to see, I pushed myself up as the broken bones in my right hand protested. I struggled through the pain; it gave me something to focus on. If I didn't get up, I was a dead man.

A blow to my chest slammed me back against the wall once more. My head swam from the sudden movement and my stomach heaved as I flopped to the ground face first. The toe of a boot flipped me over as I hit the ground. I froze in place as the tip of a blade dug through the protection of my jumpsuit to scrape painfully against the bones of my ribs.

Blinking through the blood matting my eyes, my vision cleared enough for me to find Creynora standing over me. The curvaceous dark elf's saber lanced into the flesh of my torso, pinning me in place as she glared down at me.

A moment later, Creynora looked back over her shoulder to the mouth of the parking lot. I followed her gaze and watched as my spell-induced Whiteout faded, revealing a war party of several Krym'parke surrounding two more Truinnar.

Rhegnah held Dayena by one arm as the Countess fumed and struggled against his grip, but a Krym'parke pulled out manacles and began trying to force them onto her wrists.

My employer looked over at me with an imploring expression on her face, only to find me pinned down and skewered by her cousin's blade.

Dayena's gaze traveled up to the elf standing above me and some wordless communication seemed to pass between them in an instant.

Rhegnah was watching me with a maniacal grin on his face as his cohort prepared to shackle the Countess. It was as if the dark elf wanted me to witness this moment of his victory.

"Hal, I think Creynora is up to something. Play along—"

The party chat cut out as the manacles were clamped onto Dayena's wrists, one after the other. She looked wide-eyed and lost as access to her Skills were locked away.

"I will take care of this one," Creynora called over her shoulder before looking down at me again. "It will not take much to finish him off."

Then the dark elf winked, just before twisting the blade in her hand and driving it down into my chest.

Only that twist had set the cross section of the sword perpendicular to my ribs, so it painfully scraped off along the curve of my ribcage and plunged down along my side—instead of into my heart. It hurt like hell and my chest jerked as I flinched without thinking, which was almost exactly the same movement I would have made if the saber had slid between my ribs.

It hit me then. Creynora was faking my death.

Dayena screamed as I exhaled and then held my breath, locking my body absolutely still. Ignoring my employer's cries, I frantically activated On the Hunt. I tore my status apart to zero out my visible health and Mana pools while hiding all effects. As I stared up at Creynora unblinking, my status would appear the same as any other dead sentient scanned with the System.

An explosion rocked the buildings on either side of the alley and sounds of combat erupted nearby. The fight for the nearby City Core was expanding as the battle raged on. Pharyleri reinforcements appeared on the edges of my minimap, beyond a wall of red dots that indicated the Sect forces that we'd been trying to ambush—only to have ourselves ambushed in turn.

"Creynora, he's dead. Finish up so we can depart. We must clear out before the fighting reaches us, otherwise our allies will notice our misdirection and ask questions about why we insisted on this operation," Rhegnah ordered, apparently fooled by my disguised status. The Truinnar was already turning, dragging Dayena away with his hand wrapped around her bicep.

The deception only worked because Creynora had been the only one to deal me direct damage in our fighting. She'd planned this from the onset of the ambush, which is why she'd gone after me so hard to isolate us from the rest of her allies. Neither Rhegnah, nor any of the Krym'parke, would expect to receive experience from my slaying.

The dark elf with her blade in my side grumbled. "Not like we can just leave after contracting to fight alongside the Sect mercenary forces for the next two months. Just to get access to the city."

The elf pulled her blade from my side and flicked it clear of my blood before sheathing the weapon. Then she turned and strode over to the group, leaving the sightline of my unblinking eyes. "It's done. Let's go."

One of the Krym'parke spoke up. "Don't you want to loot him?"

Another explosion rattled the buildings around us and glass cascaded from broken windows nearby.

"Not worth it. We're in a hurry, as my brother already said." Annoyance crept into the Truinnar's voice as she finished speaking and the tone hurried the aliens along. Footsteps crunched through the debris of the alleyway, fading as the group marched off.

Leaving me lying in a pool of my own blood with my employer and friend captured and myself with more questions than answers.

Chapter 20

The dots on my minimap showed the Krym'parke and Truinnar moving away from the battle that continued a block in the other direction. The markers soon disappeared after they reached the limits of my Skill. I wasn't going to push Greater Observation right now. I was still playing dead, after all.

I wasn't going to repay Creynora's ambitious play by making a move too soon. She'd bought me the opportunity to stay alive with her foresight. Her ability to kick my ass had just literally saved my life, if the deception worked out. I'd already respected the dark elf for her drive and combat ability. Now I found that admiration growing into something else.

It didn't hurt that she was damned hot.

Shit.

Playing dead was probably not the best time for figuring out my emotional state. Potential romantic intentions aside, I had bigger problems right now.

Bile climbed in my throat at how spectacularly I'd just failed. I forced down the sensation, pushing away the doubt and dread of my defeat. I needed to regroup and then track down Rhegnah and the Kyrm'parke. I was sure that the mumbled griping from Creynora had been intentional, giving me the timeline I had to rescue my employer from Rhegnah and the Krym'parke before they'd be hauling Dayena back to her family.

I could already feel the strain of the contract that bound me to the Countess, pulling me to act. The sensation wasn't overwhelming, for now, but I suspected that the drive would increase the longer the elf remained imprisoned.

It didn't help that I'd found no clues to indicate where the Krym'parke were operating in the city. Though, it was clear from Rhegnah's words that they were working with the blessing of the Sect. I should be able to pry some intel from the Pharyleri, and perhaps even more if I could make a case for how taking out the Krym'parke would aid their efforts against the Binary Eclipse Sect.

Worst case, I'd see about buying the information from the System. Problem was, all Galactics knew of that loophole which meant they took precautions against such an easy out. And the cost of such a transaction might beggar me if I could even afford it.

I waited several more minutes as the fighting continued at the library less than two blocks away. The throbbing in my skull pounded away with each explosive spell effect. The noise mingled with the deep boom of artillery and the whine of beam weaponry, punctuated by the staccato tapping of standard gunfire. Nothing indicated which side might be winning.

When I judged enough time had passed for Rhegnah and the others to get well out of range, I finally blinked and then squeezed my dried-out eyes shut. Crusted blood on my eyelids resisted my efforts at first and I gently wiped away the residue. When I opened them again, they felt better thanks to the System's regeneration. Carefully sitting up, I gingerly explored the back of my head where my skull had slammed into the concrete wall. Again, my healing abilities were at work, so only the blood matting my hair and a few shards of bone that had been pushed out of my skin were left as the evidence of my cracked cranium and the lacerations from the shattered concrete.

I blew a disgusting mass of blood and tissue out of my broken nose, then leaned against the cracked concrete blocks of the wall behind me. Though the stump of my left leg had finally stopped bleeding everywhere, my foot was still gone, leaving just the shards of my tibia and fibia behind, ragged and growing out. That would be a problem until the missing appendage regenerated. That healing would take time; hours that I didn't have to sit around in a warzone.

I couldn't help the Countess if I ended up dead in the middle of the ongoing firefight between the Sect and Pharyleri.

Pulling a spare boot from my Inventory, I jammed my stump into the opening and fastened it as tightly around my calf as possible. When I put weight on the leg, I nearly passed out from the pain. I would have if the System-backed resistance to pain and Willpower wasn't propping me up.

I bit down on my lip, almost biting through completely as I stood and dusted myself off. I leaned hard to the left, since I was missing a good inch or so from the bottom of my leg, even with the boot strapped in place.

Hobbling around the area, it took a few minutes to locate the weapons lost when I'd slammed into the wall at the end of the parking lot. I found Ace underneath a dumpster next to where I'd smashed into the wall. Of course, Last Word had somehow fallen inside the open lid of the reeking container.

Garbage collection wasn't really a thing post-System, at least not for uninhabited businesses and parking lots. The foul odors rising from the rotting mess floating in the soup of rainwater inside the dumpster set my stomach roiling even with my advanced Constitution.

Jumping up so that I balanced with my stomach on the rim of the dumpster, I reached into the soggy mass and pulled the weapon out using just my index finger and thumb. The slimy mix dripped from the pistol's barrel and I gave it a shake to get the worst of it off before I heaved myself out of the putrid cloud that filled the bin's interior.

Fortunately, once I'd recovered the wayward weapon a cast of Cleanse removed whatever the goop was that had coated it. Despite the effectiveness and the visible removal of the slime, the stench lingered, and I was pretty sure I could still smell something foul even after casting the spell a second time.

I paused, then, noting the silence in my mind.

For over a year, I'd had access to party chat through Dayena's Diplomatic Contact Class Skill. Now that the ability had been forcibly shut down by the Skill-blocking manacles that imprisoned my employer, I no longer had access to the telepathic communication channel. No more could I banter or provide tactical updates with the effort of a thought. Nor could I easily coordinate with Lyrra—though I remembered that we both had Pharyleri communicators.

I summoned the device from Inventory and slipped it into my ear. It only took a moment to connect with Lyrra.

"Hal, party chat is gone. What is going on?"

I breathed a sigh of relief when I heard the Movana's voice. "Ambush. Dayena's cousins caught up with us and they took her."

"Cousins? I thought you'd killed one."

"I thought so too. I was wrong."

It didn't take long to fill in Lyrra on how Dayena had been led off after I'd been caught off guard and left for dead, though I couldn't offer any reasoning for why Creynora left me alive. When I finished, the elf was quiet for a moment.

"Dayena told me some stories from her childhood. They were close once when they were younger. Maybe she's had a change of heart on Dayena standing up to her family's wishes," Lyrra explained.

"Whatever the reasoning, we've got two months to track Dayena down and cut her loose. Or she'll be dragged home."

"That doesn't make sense to me. They got Dayena, why wouldn't they leave immediately?" Lyrra asked.

"Creynora grumbled something about a contract with the Sect, but beyond that, I'd be guessing."

"What do we do now?"

I grinned, though the elf couldn't see it. "The same thing we've been doing. Kill Sect members and earn Credits. Then we find out where they've got Dayena locked up."

"Alright. I'll go back to playing overwatch on the library and sniping at Sect members, but there's a new wave of forces coming up from the south."

"I'll see what I can do. I'll meet you back there when things die down."

"Be safe out there, Hal."

I glanced down at my empty left boot. "A little late for that, but I'll try."

With Last Word in hand, I limped out of the parking lot. A spike of pain from my severed foot jolted up through my leg with every step. Rounding the corner onto East 13th Avenue, I headed toward the library and the sound of combat. Keeping to the south side of the street, I approached carefully, wary of friendly fire from the Pharyleri defenders who might mistake me for a Sect member in the heat of battle.

At least no one opened fire on me as I crossed the block, but streams of fire flashed in both directions ahead of me. Though I'd cleared it once, more Sect now reoccupied the civic center to the south of the library housing the City Core.

That was fine with me as the pain in my leg brought me focus. I'd have to play this smart, something I had spectacularly failed at today. Deep down, I knew I'd be better off withdrawing from the field until I healed up, but I felt the need to kill something after my last disastrous encounter. I needed to get stronger if I wanted to have any chance of rescuing Dayena, though I couldn't see any way to reach Master Class in the span of two short months. Especially not when I also had to first hunt down the location of my foes and that was sure to be a time-consuming process.

Throwing myself just into killing monsters on the regular would have been so much simpler.

For now, the Sect offensive against the City Core continued and I still had a chance to rake in a few more Credits from the active Pharyleri bounty. I pushed thoughts of my Truinnar companion out of my mind and focused on the fight ahead of me.

I ducked through the broken lobby doors of the mirrored-glass tower and twisted through several hallways until I reached a side entrance alongside a loading dock, which faced out toward Broadway. The Sect firing positions in the civic center, which would have easily spotted me if I'd stayed on the street, were almost out of view from here.

Before any of the Binary Eclipse reinforcements noticed me peeking from the door, I slipped outside and left the shelter of the building, hopping a dozen yards down the sidewalk so that the corner of the civic center blocked the view from across the street. Only once the gunners were out of sight did I hobble over the four lanes of Broadway, still favoring my bad leg and doing everything I could to keep my weight almost entirely off that limb.

The jokes about a one-legged man in an ass-kicking contest flashed into mind, but they were far less humorous when I was the subject of the gag.

Though I'd crossed the street, I still needed to get inside the building. My first yank on a service door at the side of the civic center tore the handle free, leaving me with a useless piece of metal in hand. With a grunt of annoyance, I tossed away the scrap.

Two shots into the deadbolt solved that little problem. I wasn't too worried about anyone overhearing, not with the sounds from the ongoing battle out front to mask the noise. The overlapping bullet holes served as finger holds to tear the door open and I was off the street.

It took a bit of working my way through the service area on the ground floor to work my way up to the second floor and the semi-familiar territory where I'd already taken out several emplacements on my last trek through the building. Fortunately, my habit of looting everything not nailed down left little evidence behind, and I found the Sect members unknowingly reusing the same positions.

My condition forced me to take extra care with each encounter. Instead of rushing through, like my first time in the civic center, I scouted each position carefully. I picked off a lone Movana sniper first, attacking from the flank as I came out of the stairwell. At the opposite end of the hall, a human mage paired with a Ceratophimi with an autocannon were my next targets. The mage lacked the Constitution to withstand my barrage and fell to a concentrated burst.

The rhino alien noticed their human partner drop but failed to realize where the attack had come from and reacted too slowly to my presence. They managed to only get a couple shots off before they dropped too, though one cannon round did hit and dealt a decent chunk of damage when I was unable to dodge.

After I had taken out the two emplacements, the next position was up a flight of stairs. The third floor was held by a squad with four members, all close enough to cover each other and supported by a healer. An Alchemist sat back from the outer wall where the other three launched attacks toward the library. I might have been able to take out the Alchemist first, but the Grenadier, Ice Mage, and Sniper would make me pay for it.

Rather than engage, I eased back into the stairwell and moved up to the fourth floor instead. I'd only made it through taking out a squad with a healer earlier due to my ability to maneuver around the squad's defenders to target the healer and I no longer felt confident I could pull that off with my limited mobility.

On the fourth floor, I found two more solo Binary Eclipse members and eliminated them before the intensity of the combat below ramped up. Two groupings of friendly dots appeared on my minimap and began closing in on the front of the civic center, exchanging weapon and spell fire with the Sect squad on the level beneath me.

As I locked onto the Binary Eclipse squad, I felt them start to withdraw. Hurrying my limping self down the hallway, I beat them to the stairwell and slid down a flight of stairs to where I had a line of sight on the door to the third floor. Summoning several mines from my Inventory, I tossed them onto the stairs below the door before easing out of sight on the landing halfway to the fourth floor.

The door below slammed open. Footsteps pounded on the third-floor landing and then the stairs. I swung around and dropped my sights onto the Alchemist. I opened fire in the same instant that the lead member of the squad tripped the first of my mines.

A blinding flash of plasma fire flared in the stairwell, followed almost instantly by a second flash as the Grenadier's momentum carried her onto a second mine. An inferno swept over the entire flight of stairs and back into the third floor, through the door held open by the Sniper at the rear of the squad. The Grenadier and Ice Mage screamed as they burned within the plasma, but I ignored them to focus on my primary target.

My shots drilled into the surprised Alchemist, tearing through the man's health even as his boosted regeneration attempted to push it back upwards.

212

Between the raging plasma fire and the damage from my pistols, it was a futile battle and the healer collapsed. A health potion the man had pulled from a bandolier across his chest fell from his limp hand before he'd managed to take it, rolling away across the landing as I shifted my aim to the Sniper in the doorway.

Only singed from the plasma that burned in the stairwell, the Movana unlimbered a ridiculously big rifle from her back and pointed it my way. I lunged out of sight as the weapon thundered in the confines of the stairwell.

The round blasted through the steps and grazed my hip as I rolled, spinning me around and bouncing me off the wall. I staggered back as a second round exploded through where I'd been an instant earlier and punched through the exterior wall of the building.

The power of the Sniper's attacks clearly illustrated the difference between cover and concealment. The elf was tracking me despite not having a visual and I didn't have the mobility to get out of her range.

That left one option. I kicked off the wall before launching myself off the stairs as a third shot blasted through the floor—taking off the empty boot from my missing foot. Airborne over the three-story drop at the center of the stairwell, I stashed my pistols away in my Inventory before I hooked the railing with one hand at the last moment and swung back toward the sniper below.

The Movana's eyes flared in shock as I crashed into her foot first. Her rifle went clattering off as we tumbled into the third-floor hall. I twisted around and grabbed the elf's harness with one hand to keep her from slipping away. With the Sniper pinned beneath me, I summoned my soulbound knife into my free hand before stabbing away.

The blade scraped across the bones of her ribs as I plunged the knife into her side repeatedly. Hot blood splattered onto my hand with each blow against the shredded flesh of the elf's torso. The Sniper's struggles grew weaker as her life drained away and I slashed my blade across her throat to finish her off.

That was half the Sect squad down, now I needed to finish off the final pair before they recovered from the mines. I pushed myself up and stood with one hand against the wall. Since the Sniper had shot off the boot from my missing leg, I couldn't even hobble along.

The door to the stairs had shut after I knocked the Sniper down, so I pulled it open as I drew Ace back out from my Inventory. Heat poured into the opening from the plasma flames that still burned in the stairwell, but I stepped onto the landing.

At the bottom of the flight, the Ice Mage writhed with their robes engulfed in flames. Next to the screaming mage, the Grenadier scooped up a launcher with a drum magazine that reminded me of the old M32 MGL.

He climbed back to his feet, and I opened fire before he oriented on me. Leaning against the wall to support myself, I pulled out Last Word and hammered my target with both of my master-crafted handcannons.

The rounds drilled into the already injured Grenadier and drove him backward until he hit the wall. The structure gave him something to brace against and the launcher swung in my direction. With one last burst of strength as my attacks tore him apart, the Grenadier fired.

Limited by my injuries, there was no chance of dodging the projectile. The grenade smacked into my chest and detonated. Intense flames wrapped around me, burning into my nose and throat, blinding my eyes, and slamming me backward until I was the one hitting the wall from the force of the attack.

Coughing through my seared throat, I fought to stay upright and return fire. Only the awareness of my opponents through Greater Observation kept me on target and I triggered Kill Shot with my next round. The massive burst of damage finished off the Grenadier.

Barely able to breathe and gasping for air, I dropped to my knees and crawled to the edge of the landing. Though I couldn't see, the Ice Mage was still losing health, but slower than they had been, and I needed to end this before it turned into any more of a fight.

A half dozen shots and it was over, the health of the last Binary Eclipse member zeroed out. I dropped both pistols back into their holsters and hit myself with another health potion before gently probing my face with my hands. My eyes were still there, so the System's innate regeneration combined with Resilient Nature should have fixed them up shortly and my eyesight would return, provided I didn't get myself into any more trouble.

The scent of smoke returned as my nose healed, reminding me that the stairwell was still burning from the combined explosions of mines and grenades. I crawled over to the door and reached up to open it, but pounding footsteps echoed up the stairwell. The dots on my minimap showed the approach of the Pharyleri sweeping out from the library as they shifted from defense into a counterattack.

"Friendly," I croaked, feeling like someone had just stabbed my vocal cords, with my throat still seared from the point-blank grenade explosion.

A grunt from below acknowledged the call, but the team still charged up the stairs with weapons trained on my position. I kept my hands clear of my holsters just the same. I was ready to be done getting shot for the day.

A gnome paused next to me and grabbed my shoulder with surprising strength, easing me down to sit against the back wall of the stairs. "Well,

Knight Errant Mason, I take it we have you to thank for the reduction of the Sect forces hereabouts?"

Lieutenant Lenyka Stormfluke (Drop Commando Level 44) (A)
[Industrial Alliance]
HP: 1480/1480
MP: 1393/1520
Status: Storm Surge, Shared Suffering, Mantle of Leadership

I tried to speak and gave up after another jab of pain. My voice was still too rough for speech, so I just nodded.

The Pharyleri officer tsked at me. "Ease up lad, we've got it from here."

I wasn't sure I felt much like a lad, but when Lenyka called up a medic to address my wounds, I wasn't going to complain either. The burns soothed at the medic's touch and my eyes watered as I blinked to clear my blurry sight. The sensation of a belt sander tearing through the inside of my throat eased and I found I could speak again.

"Thanks for patching me up," I said, nodding in gratitude to the Pharyleri wearing a ubiquitous red cross on a band around her arm.

"No problem, big guy. Can't do much about your foot though, I'm afraid."

I shook my head. "All good. It'll be fine in a few hours."

The medic exchanged a glance with the officer standing over me. "Regen Skill?"

I nodded without speaking and the medic patted my knee, just above the missing section. "Those are pretty rare. Usually takes a Shop visit to fix those problems. Anyways, this should help you out until you're back on your feet."

The medic pulled a crutch out of her Inventory and leaned it against the wall beside me before the pair helped me up. I thanked them for the healing before seating the crutch under my left armpit.

Lenyka scoffed. "Don't thank me yet. These were your kills, so we'll leave you to clean up the bodies. We've got to continue our sweep and make sure we've routed the Binary Eclipse completely."

"I can handle that. How's the rest of the battle going?"

"We took the easternmost core with little trouble, but the Sect are holding onto their battlelines around Tech Center and the old University campus."

Binary Eclipse still held three City Cores and maintained control over half of the city. That meant my search area to locate wherever Rhegnah had taken the Countess would be significant.

I nodded to the gnomes. "I'll clean up my mess here and head to the library."

"You did good work here, Knight Errant Mason. Take care of yourself," Lenyka said, before the two gnomes followed on after the rest of their squad.

Even with the crutch, it still took me a couple minutes to hobble around and loot the dead Sect squad. I started with the Alchemist and Sniper, since they were still on the third floor, and then hopped down the stairs to the landing for the Grenadier and Ice Mage.

The bodies disappeared into Meat Locker with a touch, and I chuckled at the gnome's presumption that I would have any problem dealing with them. The damage to the stairwell remained, but that fix needed the attention of an Architect or some other construction-focused Class. Or the new owner could pay for a self-repair function, if and when anyone purchased the building from the Shop. Either way, not a problem I could address, so I left the civic center and started for the library.

Sounds of combat echoed in the distance to the south, signs of the Pharyleri counterattack continuing to push the Sect back. Plenty of gnomes were visible around the library now, looting fallen attackers and performing repairs to the defenses within a perimeter of bronze-armored Steamspanner defenders.

The closest pair of the heavy infantry turned to face me when I stepped out of the building. One pointed an arm-mounted cannon and lightning sparked between the hands of the second. The spell flickered out as the caster identified me as an allied combatant, but the gunner kept their weapon pointed in my direction.

The cannoneer kept me covered while the mage shifted from their position to intercept my path as I limped toward the library. The bronze-plated power armor covered the mage entirely, hiding any visual details not revealed by Greater Observation. She checked on me, verifying that I was actually Hal Mason, and then directed me towards an aid station set up inside the library for those crippled during the battle.

I gave up arguing that I'd be fine and just followed her instructions. Inside the library, there were only a few of the most severely wounded survivors. With the System's resistances and regenerative abilities, anytime a fight was intense enough to cripple, there was every chance that the enemy would just finish off their opponent.

In larger scale battles with Skills and spells flashing about, a target might only be caught at the edges of the effects or allied forces could come to their comrades' aid before it was too late. I'd also noticed a lack of Sect melee fighters in this engagement, so the battle had mostly taken place at range instead of up close. It was certainly much harder to finish someone off from a distance if they fell behind cover, out of sight.

When I limped into the triage station, a red-haired medic rushed over to me from a group of three healers in the middle of treating an unconscious gnome who was missing both legs and a section of torso where their shoulder and arm had been blown off. Blood stained the cot beneath the injured Pharyleri and discarded pieces of bronze power armor lay scattered on the floor where the trauma team had stripped the mangled plates away to get to the injuries.

I held up a hand and waved back at the grievously wounded patient. "I'll be fine, focus on someone who needs the help."

The medic narrowed his eyes at me but turned and hurried back to assist the surgeon and trauma specialist working on the triple-amputee. Two other cots held other injured gnomes, one missing a leg and the other an arm, but both were bandaged up with fluid-filled capsules over the remaining portions of the partial limbs.

Limping away from the doorway, I eased myself down onto a bench and leaned back. For the first time since leaving the headquarters earlier in the day, I forced myself to relax. The tension eased as I sagged against the wall behind me. I closed my eyes and kept my thoughts from turning to the Countess. There was nothing I could do for the moment besides let myself heal, and dwelling on my failure wouldn't help anyone.

Fatigue weighed on me and threatened to pull me into slumber, despite the fact that it was only late afternoon. The hours of sleep I'd managed to get this morning had carried me so far, but my numerous injuries demanded rest.

To stay conscious, I pulled up my notifications. Most involved the usual experience gains from my rampage through the Sect forces. Toward the bottom of the list, things got interesting.

Diplomatic Contact access to party chat inhibited.

That lined up with the ambush and when Rhegnah and his Krym'parke minions had manacled the Countess.

Contract Quest initiated–Rescue the Countess.

Your contracted employer has been detained against her will and is due to be shipped off Earth in two months, when the Deputy Adjudicator Rhegnah Baluisa ends his term of service with the Binary Eclipse Sect. The Countess must be freed before that term expires.
Duration: 1 month, 27 days, 16 hours, 21 minutes, 17 seconds.
Rewards: Variable XP and Credits.
Penalty: Permanent 20% reduction in attributes.

Damn. That contract had teeth and those fangs were sharp. That penalty for failure would strip away a significant portion of the attributes that allowed me to thrive in this System-changed world. I'd already planned to do everything within my power to rescue my companion and employer. It was more than that now.

Now my future was on the line.

Chapter 21

A tap on the shoulder roused me from sleep and I cracked open my eyes. Lyrra stood over me and held a finger to her lips in the universal gesture to remain quiet.

Beyond the elf, the three injured gnomes lay in their cots as they slept peacefully under the watchful gaze of the same medic I'd turned away earlier. The white sheets on the cots were clean now and showed no signs of the blood spatter from when I'd first entered the trauma center.

The windows to the outside were dark, showing that I'd slept for several hours, and a tingling numbness from my left foot pulled my attention downward to find that I'd dozed long enough for my foot to regenerate. Mostly, at least. My calf muscle and foot appeared emaciated, little more than flesh over the bones, but it was far better than a stump. Presumably, the regrowth of the limb was why the trauma staff had just left me asleep rather than treated me with one of the capsules that stuck out from beneath the sheets covering the Pharyleri patients.

Summoning another spare boot from my Inventory, I slipped my bare foot into it and stood while ignoring Lyrra's smirk at the replacement not matching the rest of my current armor. I'd worry about coordinating later. For now, I was just happy walking normally again.

"How'd you find me?" I asked as we left the library.

"Not many humans around hopping about on one leg."

I grunted in response. She had a point.

"What are we going to do now?" Lyrra asked.

I sighed and brought up the information on my latest quest, flicking the blue box toward the Movana to share the screen with her. She read quietly for a few moments before a sharp breath indicated she'd found the penalty clause. When she looked over at me from the window floating in front of her, I dismissed the blue box and kept walking. "I'm going to find her."

"She's my friend too. I won't let you do this alone, not after what you've already endured today. Also, why are we still walking right now? You have a bike," Lyrra complained as she hurried after me.

I chuckled. "Walking is nice when you haven't been able to for a bit, but you're right, my leg is still recovering and I shouldn't push it too hard just yet."

I summoned Outrider from the dedicated storage space in my Inventory. When I climbed onto the sturdy bike, Lyrra clambered on behind me.

"You really need to invest in a transport of your own." I waited until the elf was securely seated and holding onto my waist before I throttled up.

She sighed sadly from just behind my ear. "I know. I just liked riding with her."

"We'll get her back."

The conversation died off after that and I hoped my confidence wasn't misplaced. I had a couple ideas floating around in my head, but I wanted to see if I could pry any information from the Pharyleri intel teams before making any moves.

Distant thunder rippled through the air at irregular intervals, but the frenetic combat from earlier in the day had given way to what sounded more like cautious probing as the night wore on. Our route back to the headquarters kept us well away from those clashes.

A few civilians hurried furtively along the streets on whatever errands required them to be out, but they were the exceptions. Most people stayed hidden away in their homes, secured behind System-registered structures that would resist most collateral damage. Direct attacks would still get through, but the Sect wasn't targeting the civilian population.

Not yet, anyways.

I'd heard plenty of rumors about other countries, and even some cities within the US, that made it clear not all Galactics believed in the System equivalent of the Geneva Conventions. From what I've seen of the Binary Eclipse Sect, it wasn't any moral code that kept them from going after non-combatants. It was far more likely that they just wanted to make sure a healthy population of workers remained after they took control of the city.

The gate guards at the Union Station compound triple-checked our identities before allowing us entry, though that was something I expected. After the surprise force of Sect and mercenaries turned up to hit the library, the Pharyleri troops were on alert, and I was glad to see they were taking the potential threat of infiltrators seriously.

Since part of my plans for Dayena's rescue so far hinged on doing exactly that to the Sect, I hoped the guards on the other side were less diligent.

After I stored my bike, Lyrra stayed on my heels as I navigated through the headquarters to the command center. The guard outside the room wouldn't allow us access at first and only relented after Lyrra contacted Ismyna to relay our presence. A call to the guard post from inside the command center had the guard sweating and hurrying to usher us in.

Ismyna looked over at Lyrra and me when we approached the center command platform. "Where is your third?"

I stepped forward to lean on the railing around the platform as Lyrra gestured for me to take the lead. It took several minutes for the story of the afternoon to unfold, and it left Ismyna scowling by the time I finished. In the midst of my tale, Nesdyna stepped over from where she'd been conferring with some of the other Pharyleri command staff. The clan elder didn't say anything and just listened quietly while standing behind her daughter.

"So you're telling me that most of the force hitting the library were mercenaries, influenced by your Truinnar's cousins, in an effort to ambush your party, and that they captured her with the intent to take her back to her homeworld."

The green-haired gnome rubbed her temples with both hands as if trying to massage out a headache.

I moved over to the holographic map and pointed out where I'd flanked the first Sect squad and then traced my path around the block to where I'd found the command post. "It was a combined force. Most of the fighters I took out were actual Binary Eclipse members. There was a Sect Sub-captain with the same family name as the Regional Manager, but he fled while I engaged a nearby firing position."

"It's too bad you didn't take out the officer," Ismyna said with a frown.

I shrugged. "I didn't want a heavy weapon hitting me in the back while I was trying to deal with the Sub-captain and his command staff. By the time I'd taken out that squad, the command vehicle had high-tailed it out of there."

Nesdyna moved to stand beside her daughter and looked at me with a piercing expression. "You have a plan for recovering your comrade?"

I glanced between the pair of gnomes and nodded, though my thoughts were more along the lines of a rough idea than any fully realized plan.

The elder smiled. "Then I'll pay out for the bounties you've completed so far and I'll keep the posting active. The extra Credits should motivate you to cause additional chaos for our enemies, since it seems like this conflict isn't going to be over quickly."

Nesdyna waved her hand toward me and a status notification pinged for my attention.

Bring them in Cold—Reserved Bounty Updated!
Your party has successfully slain a total of 48 Basic Class and 2 Advanced Class members of the Binary Eclipse Sect.
1,540,000 Credits Awarded
Reserved Bounty remains active!

The sheer sum of Credits left me momentarily stunned. It was the largest single payout I'd ever received, and the most Credits I'd ever held at one time.

I'd only taken out about thirty of the Sect's Basic Class fighters, so the remaining kills were the contributions of Lyrra and the Countess. With my tendency to charge into combat contrasting Dayena's stealthy approach to picking off targets one at a time, the numbers looked about right to me. Even if our party was currently missing one member, it had been a team effort to make the kills and I still intended to split the proceeds three ways. I'd just have to hold onto Dayena's until the dark elf was free.

It took little more than a thought to split out a third of the Credits and transfer 513k over to Lyrra. The Movana frowned at the notification, and I grinned as her face morphed into shock.

She looked over at me, still wide-eyed. "No. What? Why?"

"Even split, three ways."

Lyrra shook her head in disbelief, but I ignored the elf's continued reaction and turned back to the Pharyleri. "I'll put those Credits to good use, so make sure you're ready to pay out for the next round."

Nesdyna nodded solemnly before walking away and returning to the group of gnomish officers she'd been huddled with earlier. Ismyna watched her mother for a moment and then faced me. "As much as I'd like to know what you'll do next, I know better than to ask."

I chuckled. "You probably won't see much of me for a bit. Since Rhegnah thinks I'm dead, I'll have to lay low and keep things quiet. I would appreciate if you'd pass on any intel you get, if you hear about Truinnar and Krym'parke operating with the Sect."

"I'll stay in touch with Lyrra and look forward to your return."

Her words were a dismissal, so I departed from the command center. I had to tug Lyrra along after me, since the elf was still stuck staring at the notification with her new Credit balance.

"Come on. It's just Credits."

My words finally pulled the Movana from her daze as we left the secured area. "Just Credits?!"

The sharp tone of Lyrra's question drew the attention of several onlookers in the hallway and I hushed the elf before she said too much out loud. I missed Dayena's party chat ability, though it had allowed us to ingrain some bad habits that we needed to stamp out immediately with the loss of the Truinnar's Class Skill.

Advertising sudden wealth wasn't any more beneficial to one's long-term health than it had been before the System's arrival on Earth. Though, I had to admit that there was a certain amount of irony in the fact that I was the one downplaying our new fortune when I was the one who tended to push too far in the acquisition of more Credits.

My scowling expression cut off whatever Lyrra had been about to say and she remained quiet until we reached the hotel section, where I led her back to my room. I locked the door behind me and gestured for Lyrra to take a seat on the couch before flopping in the desk chair.

I raised an eyebrow at the elf and she finally exploded.

"You just handed me half a million Credits and expected me to play it cool after everything that happened today!"

"Yes."

"Argh," Lyrra growled in frustration and bounced up from the couch. The Movana paced back and forth across the room, though there was only enough space for her to take a few strides. I leaned back in the comfortable chair and let the elf get it out of her system, until she stopped pacing and sank back onto the couch. Lyrra folded her arms and stared at me. "What's the play, Hal?"

"Rhegnah believes Hal Mason is dead, so step one is to not be Hal Mason anymore."

Activating On the Hunt, I reached into my status and tugged on the fields that listed my name. The adjustment to my first name was easy, but I felt the System push back ever so slightly when I altered my last name. Only the added ranks I'd purchased to the Class Skill let me get away with the modification.

"Clint Westgrove?" Lyrra asked and I chuckled at the elf's reaction to my changed status, since it was clear the inspiration for the nom de guerre went over her head. I expected most Galactics to miss it, unless they had spent a fair amount of time over the last two years catching up on pre-System cinema and Spaghetti Westerns.

"Like I said, step one. Step two will require a visit to the Shop."

The Movana raised an eyebrow. "And step three?"

"Pound the pavement. Talk to people and put the puzzle pieces together. Figure out where Rhegnah and the Krym'parke are hiding out, and then hit them when they won't see it coming."

Lyrra nodded slowly, while I toggled my status back to normal. I intended to hold off on keeping the change until I left the Pharyleri headquarters. Getting myself shot as an infiltrator by the gnomes at this point would just be embarrassing and more than a little ironic.

I kicked off my boots and stretched out my legs, wiggling my toes as I compared my regenerated leg against my uninjured foot. The new one still looked a bit on the skeletal side, so my body probably needed more fuel to continue the process. As if on cue, my stomach grumbled, and I summoned a ration from the supplies stashed in my Inventory before tearing into the calorie dense bar.

"How do you eat those things?" Lyrra asked with a shudder.

"I'm laying low as much as possible, so hitting the mess hall isn't an option."

The elf rolled her eyes. "Well, I'm not playing dead, so I'm going to get dinner. You have my comm channel, let me know if anything comes up."

"I'm going to sleep a little more and then hit the Shop. I might be out of contact for a while after that, but I'll call you when I find something."

I walked the elf out and locked the door behind her before I finished off the ration bar. I really didn't get what the Movana had against the rations, there were plenty of flavor options for those who were picky and this one tasted like chocolate peanut butter.

I stripped out of my armor and took a shower, then shut off all the lights and crawled into bed. After the long day, I was out for the night as soon as my head hit the pillow.

Chapter 22

"Knight Errant Mason, welcome back! It has been far too long since your last visit."

The shopkeeper's warm words greeted me as I materialized in my instance of the Shop. It really had been a bit since my last appearance, and I spotted a couple new additions to the displays that lined the large hall. Exhibits of weapons and armor from cultures beyond counting were mounted on the walls behind the display counters that stretched out of sight in the distance.

Between the fact that I could offload monster parts locally for about what the Shop paid and the Pharyleri crafters producing ammunition for my common projectile pistols on the cheap, I had only been hitting the Shop for armor upgrades and advanced reloads, like the Hastati missiles.

"It's good to see you too, Ryk. How's the life of the merchant treating you?" I replied, matching the shopkeeper's warmth. It was always wise to stay on the good side of the people selling you things that went boom.

The ram-horned quadruped shrugged. "Business is booming, for the most part. Exports from your Dungeon World are really picking up as more settlements are upgrading their facilities. Though there are still territories changing hands with some frequency."

"That's got to make some opportunities for you."

Ryk smiled. "Perceptive as always, Knight Errant Mason."

I sighed and rolled my eyes as the shopkeeper chuckled. After the Credits I'd spent here on upgrading On the Hunt, Ryk was well aware of my feelings about that title.

"Well, what can I do for you today? Your usual restocking?"

"Yes, but I'd also like to discuss how to make some adjustments to my physical appearance."

"Ah, physical modifications. Are you looking for permanent adjustments or more temporary options? You are no doubt aware, as I'm sure that you have done your research, the expense of those will scale depending on just how drastically the alterations modify your nature. For example, turning someone as lean and nimble as yourself into a muscle-bound hulk would be quite pricey."

I shook my head. "Nothing quite so significant. I just need the ability to alter my appearance enough that I'm not recognizable as Hal Mason. For a while, at least. But I'd like the option to return to normal afterwards."

"In some trouble, are you?" Ryk's eyes narrowed as the shopkeeper peered at me intently.

"Well, I'm supposed to be dead, and I'd like for certain people to continue operating under that presumption."

"I see, I see. A disguise, then. One that won't require ongoing Mana for upkeep."

The shopkeeper rubbed his chin with one hand as I nodded in agreement. Ryk remained silent for over a minute as he considered me while deep in thought. Then he held up a finger. "I think I have something that fits."

The shopkeeper gestured to one of the displays on the counter as a Class Skill description scrolled over the screen.

Silver Fox Mimesis (Level 1)

Named for the pinnacle deity of the Ruidian kitsune pantheon, this Class Skill allows the user to alter their appearance nearly at will. While the outward characteristics of the user are mutable under the effect of this Skill, Attributes remain unchanged. At higher Levels, this Skill may even allow the user to mimic an entirely different species.

Effect: User may alter their physical form to change their outward appearance. This includes height, weight, bone structure, and muscle mass within 10% of their base form.

Cost: 100 Mana + Variable rate dependent on changes made.

An image on the screen below the text showed a red-furred female humanoid with fox ears and tail, clad only in simple clothing that resembled athletic shorts and a sports bra. After a moment, the alien began shifting to appear more human as the fur, ears, and tail seemed to withdraw under the kitsune's skin, leaving behind smooth, pale skin. The tail had disappeared and her head sported normal human ears that the kitsune wiggled with a smile.

Then the facial features of the kitsune started to change. The pert nose went from rounded to flat, the nostrils widened, and the bridge grew higher. The mane of fiery red hair shifted to midnight black and the brilliant green eyes dulled to brown.

The new appearance remained in place for several moments before the changes reversed themselves and the red-furred kitsune was centered on the screen once more.

Just as the vision began fading from the view, the kitsune winked suggestively as she leered out from the display before disappearing entirely, fast enough that I questioned whether I'd even seen that last flickering expression.

I looked up at Ryk, who grinned as if knowing what I was about to say.

"I think that Skill is exactly what I need. How much will it set me back?"

"Seventy thousand."

I winced but paid the cost regardless. Advanced Skills from other Classes weren't cheap. At least this was an active Skill that wouldn't be burning out more of my passive Mana regeneration.

Once the new Skill appeared on my Status at Level 1, Ryk nodded and snapped his fingers. "Come with me, before you activate that."

He turned away, leading me deeper into the museum-like hall until we reached a room with a chair in the center. The padded chair's rubberized surface reminded me of the patient chair in a dentist's office, complete with a headrest. It was the sort of chair that could be easily hosed down to clean. I raised an eyebrow at Ryk after looking around the large space and glancing pointedly at the chair.

"Changing one's physical form can be... disorienting. It's best to not be standing the first time." The shopkeeper's attempted reassurance wasn't exactly comforting, but I took a seat.

As soon as I triggered the new Skill, a visualization of my body appeared in my mind. Floating against a black background, the image of myself slowly rotated with my arms spread and my feet shoulder width apart, like some kind of personalized Vitruvian Man. Oh, and the vision was completely naked.

A panel of options and sliders appeared, off to the side of the slowly spinning vision of my physical body. Bumping the first few sliders up and down started distorting the body. Taller and shorter. Fat and skinny. Bulky and lean muscles. Skin tone.

At the top of the options menu, a counter tallied up the modifications and the Mana cost climbed up with each change before zeroing out as I reset the slider bar after each experiment. Eventually, I found that I could focus the visualization on different sections of the body and make more minute adjustments.

Yes, there was a slider for *that*. Yes, I experimented with it. No, I didn't keep the changes.

Most of my adjustments I made when zoomed in on my face. My cheekbones became a little sharper and my chin a little wider. I modified the angle of my jawline by adding a little extra width. My nose also widened, and I enlarged the nostrils before flattening and tilting up the tip of the nose just a hair.

Speaking of hair, I grew out a medium length shag that was about as far from a regulation high-and-tight as I could comfortably conceive. Then I lightened the color from my average brown to a dirty blond.

Right now, the updated appearance of the visualization looked like a surfer ready to catch a wave. For a moment, I considered using Swayze instead of Westgrove as my disguised name, but I moved on to facial hair instead. Since I was trying to change the overall appearance of my face, I extended the growth of my usual three-day-stubble into a full beard.

The menu for facial hair popped out from there and gave a number of pre-configured options that were already named. Van Dyke. Short Boxed. Anchor. Balbo. Klingon. Gunslinger.

I stopped on the last one. The sideburns extended along the jawline into a horseshoe-shaped beard that left the chin bare in a unique look that was a far cry from my usual appearance, so I kept it.

From the beard, I moved to my mouth. I widened the edges and slimmed the lips. Eyes came next. I certainly wasn't going to go blue after changing my hair to blond, so I went with a deep emerald green instead. I adjusted the width so they were slightly wider and shifted the angle a degree or so, then set them a little deeper.

The face staring back at me within my mind's eye was no longer my own and I felt confident that part of the disguise would hold up.

Pulling back out from the face, the rest of my body still looked the same. I shifted the height slider and scaled my body so that I dropped four inches of height. Then I added some bulk to the muscles to make myself a slight bit thicker all over. My once lean and wiry frame now morphed into the figure of a gymnast with the changes. The final touch of adding a bit of extra thickness to my neck really pushed my body's appearance beyond recognition.

The Mana count at the top of the menus wasn't exorbitant, but then, I really hadn't made any serious changes to my physique. The most significant expense was reducing my height, as that had the greatest impact. Still, it was only a few hundred Mana and a more efficient disguise than using a spell because it was a one-time activation each time the Skill was used. And making the changes physically meant I could still cast spells over top, in order to layer my deceptions, if needed.

I confirmed the adjustments and the menu bars shifted to gray before slowly fading out of the visualization. A moment later, I opened my eyes and found myself seated in the padded chair.

"Ah good, you're awake. Don't try to stand up just yet. You'll need to let your body adjust to its new configuration, though I don't see any changes that are too drastic."

Ryk's voice came from behind me, back by the entrance to the large room, and I shook my head as I slowly pushed myself up using the arms of the chair. A handrail rose from the ground, and I used it to pull myself to my feet, despite the shopkeeper's warning.

My movements felt just a little bit off, which made sense when considering the changes I'd forced on my body. Ryk moved over and I realized that I was now significantly shorter than the ram-like centauroid.

Dropping from a couple inches over six-feet tall to a couple inches below was certainly a shift in perspective.

The shopkeeper watched me with concern as I stepped away from the chair, still holding onto the railing for support. I now understood the room's size.

"The room's big enough to move around and get comfortable with the physical changes." I nodded to the longer end of the room as I spoke, still looking at Ryk.

The shopkeeper nodded. "Yes. You'll want to walk, jump, and run."

"I don't suppose fighting and shooting are options?"

"No, you'll have to figure that out on your own." Ryk chuckled.

"I'll manage."

I took a couple steps along the handrail and then let go, walking forward for several halting paces and gradually picking up speed. With each stride, I settled into my new physique until my gait smoothed out as I reached the wall at the back of the room.

I spun and dropped prone, then rolled twice before leaping back to my feet. I pushed off, jumping as high as I could. For the next several minutes, I ran and jumped, sometimes literally bouncing off the walls as I got comfortable with the changes to my body. Without the System – and the resulting high attributes – I knew I would have had a lot more trouble getting settled. With it, it was a matter of minutes not years.

Finally, I settled down. Returning to where Ryk stood beside the chair, I gave the shopkeeper a nod.

"Your appearance modifications aren't like the Genome Treatments that scrubbed and optimized your DNA. These are true cosmetic changes, and they can be reverted or modified further as you develop your use of the Skill.

"Are you ready to go now?" Ryk asked, after the brief explanation.

"I'm satisfied with the changes for now, but I need to offload a collection of corpses, restock my special munitions, and upgrade a few things."

The shopkeeper smiled warmly at the prospect of additional Credits heading his way. "Of course, Knight Errant Mason."

"That's first on the list. It does me no good to change my face and body if that damned Title is still proclaiming itself to the world."

Ryk rubbed his chin in thought as we left the room and returned to the main hall of the Shop. "I know you've already tried upgrading your Class Skill with purchased Skill Points and that hasn't helped."

I glared at Ryk, grumbling at the reminder of the hundred and fifty thousand Credits spent in vain on the effort of upgrading On the Hunt. Though, I really couldn't be upset with him. Ryk made clear beforehand that he had no way of knowing whether the increase to the Class Skill would work or not.

The shopkeeper chuckled. "Well, I'm certain we can find other options."

I sighed, knowing that anything I could say would just give the jovial merchant another bit of leverage when it came time to haggle for whatever pricey item he came up with. And pricey it would be since I'd already looked into the ineffective cheap options.

We reached the shopkeeper's main workstation near the entrance to the museum-like hall and Ryk started flicking through screens on a display console.

"I think this is your best bet. I can look for other options if this is beyond your budget range."

An image of a chain necklace floated in the center of the viewscreen. Zooming in on the surprisingly simple piece of jewelry, I could make out stylized and unintelligible glyphs decorating the inside of each link. At a touch, the Shop provided the System display for the item.

Brumwell Necklace of Anonymity

While the Brumwell Necklace of Shadow Intent is the hallmark item of the Brumwell Clan, this lesser trinket is still the work of a high-tier Journeyman. Constructed as part of the Journeyman transition to a Master Crafter, the Clan's signature enchantments work to layer the wearer with a shroud of anonymity. This shroud prevents any Titles or Class Features from being identifiable on casual examination. Often used by nobles out for a night on the town, this trinket is perfect for illicit affairs and back-alley dealing.

Effect: Persistent effect of Anonymity (Level 3) results in the shrouding of any titles displayed by the wearer, but also disables any status effects provided by shrouded titles. Effect is persistent in hiding all titles while necklace is worn.

I frowned after reading the text. "The description mentions a Brumwell Necklace of Shadow Intent. Would that be better?"

Ryk chuckled again and toggled the display to the referenced item. "It doesn't have the same effect, so it's not what you need. And it's way out of your price range."

No kidding. I blanched as I read the eight-figure price tag on the simple chain that looked nearly identical to the first item I'd examined.

"Insane."

Ryk smiled. "Not when you own multiple settlements that have been upgraded to City-classification. They're rare, but not out of reach for the connected."

"What are we talking about for the Necklace of Anonymity?"

"Two hundred thousand Credits."

"Oh, is that all?" I sighed. The more Levels I earned, the more my equipment costs increased. It shouldn't have come as any surprise. I'd been pouring Credits into armor and weapons since Day One of the System's arrival on Earth. "I'll take it."

"Anything else today?"

"Besides the special ammo I already mentioned, I'll need the next two spell ranks of Lesser Disguise, the initial spell rank for Greater Disguise, and the remaining pieces of the armor set that match my vambraces."

The shopkeeper raised an eyebrow. "I'm sensing a theme with most of your purchases today."

"Don't think about it too much. And don't mention it to anyone."

Ryk nodded solemnly. "Everything you say here is as confidential as it can be within the System. To purchase the words spoken within a Shop would easily fund one of those necklaces beyond your reach. Nothing is impossible, but there are far easier and cheaper ways to obtain the information."

"Thanks, I think."

Ryk bleated with laughter and clapped me on the shoulder. "I'll prepare your order. It will only take a couple minutes to get everything together for you."

The quadrupedal shopkeeper's hooves clattered across the floor as he strode off out of sight. While he was gone, I perused through some of the displays and scanned through other spell options available for purchase. Some were tempting, but I wanted to keep my repertoire limited. In the heat of battle, it was already too easy to forget some of the newer Skills and spells I'd obtained.

Though I knew better, I still asked the Shop for information on Dayena. It was no surprise when the terminal responded with a sum beyond my reach. No matter how I rephrased my inquiry—searches on her, Creynora, Rhegnah, and Krym'parke—the staggering total for locations and movements remained excessive, despite my recent influx of Credits. It had to be that the Truinnar were covering themselves with multiple Skills, Shop purchases, and stealth equipment.

I took a deep breath and accepted that I would have to search the hard way. Investigating, info gathering, tracking allies and supplies. A test that would push my abilities and intuition. Deep down, I knew I would succeed. I'd come too far, sacrificed too much, to fail under the System now.

Ryk returned shortly with everything I'd requested. Before I completed the purchases, we spent several minutes unloading Meat Locker of all the Sect bodies I'd been collecting. I got more in exchange for the weapons and the selection of armor than I received for the bodies, but there were always necromancers and scientists looking for corpses in various conditions, so it was a steady bit of extra income.

I started a second pile with a couple sets of the Sect armors that I'd stolen from the Armory, along with a few pieces of loot that survived in good condition and a handful of weapons that were different from my usual armaments. I hoped to use them as props to assist my disguises as I worked behind the Binary Eclipse lines to discover where Rhegnah and the Krym'parke were hiding.

I pointed to the secondary stack. "I'd like those scanned for any trackers or tracing mechanism that would report the gear as stolen or looted."

"I can take care of that for you. I assume that you want the wearer to appear as a genuine member of a certain organization?" Ryk asked with a raised brow.

"You assume correctly."

The shopkeeper hummed for a minute and the pile glowed faintly. "I'll add the service fee to your account for repairs, along with the tab for affixing the appropriate badges and slicing the identity databanks."

I shook my head. I was spending Credits like water, but I didn't have much choice with the quest weighing on me. Instead of worrying, I continued picking out a few attachments to complement the new armor pieces Ryk had selected. When the trades were finalized, I ended up paying out over two-thirds from my portion of the Credits received from the Pharyleri bounties.

Easy come, easy go. That outlook beat the old adage about a fool and his money.

Brushing off the thoughts of the sum of Credits I'd just spent, I took out the Brumwell Necklace of Anonymity and draped it around my neck before tucking the silver links out of sight beneath my jumpsuit. I'd never been much of a necklace guy, but the chain reminded me of the ID tags worn beneath my digicam uniform during my service.

I shook off the memories of my former life and stowed the harness securing my holsters away in my Inventory. Then I started pulling out my new armor suit, putting the rest of the pieces on over my usual jumpsuit. Each section of the dark smoke-colored armor locked into place by securing itself to the next piece. Now that I was equipping more than just the vambraces that covered me from shoulder to wrist, I brought up the full description for the suit, noting that the System already showed the battlesuit integrating with my current equipment.

Tyrfing Semi-Powered Assault Armor

Designed for surviving the rigors of a Dungeon World by a team of human game-designers-turned-engineers and crafted by a Gimsar Master Armorsmith of the Ares Corporation, this exoskeleton is the perfect fit for human combatants seeking to increase durability without sacrificing mobility. The suit is specially augmented to take advantage of the high Mana density on Earth, allowing the Core to combine ambient Mana collection with the movements of the wearer to power the battlesuit's motion and provide limited shield regeneration. When used in conjunction with most standard adventurer coveralls, the battlesuit is able to seal for use in toxic environments or extra-vehicular activity in a vacuum.

Core: Class III Blam Physics Mana Engine

CPU: Class D Roland Core CPU

Armor Rating: Tier III

Hard Points: 6 (5 Used - ProTek Grappler G4, Promethium II Wrist Flame-Projector, Modified Elysian Drop Harness, CMN, Ares Type IV Shield Generator)

Soft Points: 3 (1 Used - Neural Link)

Battery Capacity: 180/180

The suit included greaves that served as boots and armored all the way up my shins. Knee guards connected the greaves to the thigh plates, which in turn hooked to the groin armor. A segmented section of thin, overlapping scales protected my waist and stomach while preserving my ability to twist and turn. A slightly thicker plate covered my upper chest and back, buckling over the collarbone to the vambraces that already protected my arms.

With the armor covering my body, I pulled out the customized drop and fastened it in place. Since the harness was already designed with military application in mind, the adjustments to get my holsters into the proper positions went smoothly.

The final piece was a helmet with a black-tinted visor that completely hid the face of the wearer. One of the attachments I'd added was already affixed to the side of the helmet. The Command Network Module copied the comm channels saved in my neural link and upgraded the range of the standard Pharyleri communicator that I'd been using. With Dayena's party chat currently unavailable, the CMN would help me stay in touch with Lyrra when I used the helmet in combat.

For now, I stuffed the helmet back into Inventory. I much preferred using my natural senses instead of data transmitted to my neural link from the suit's sensors. If I didn't need to use it, I probably wouldn't, but it was better to have the option if necessary.

Done with the armoring, I bounced on my toes and shifted my balance from one leg to the other before moving through a range of stretches. From there, I bounced into a couple small skips and then larger jumps. The suit moved seamlessly along with me, and each motion remained perfectly silent thanks to minor enhancements in the greaves that deadened the sound of each footfall.

Ryk watched my movements from behind his main Shop kiosk with arms folded across his chest. He nodded in approval when he saw my glance in his direction. "Looks good on you, Adventurer Mason."

I grinned at the shopkeeper, who had finally stopped using my ridiculous Title now that it was obscured by my new necklace. Ryk gestured to a full-length mirror that stood off to one side of the Shop and I moved over to it. Without really recognizing my changed face in the mirror, the vision of myself fully armored in the dark gray battlesuit looked like some kind of futuristic supersoldier badass from a sci-fi movie or video game. The new suit was awesome and worth every Credit that I'd spent on it.

"Thanks, Ryk. I love it."

The shopkeeper beamed at my satisfaction. "Perfect. I'm sure you'll be back for your next round of upgrades in the future."

"You know it." I sighed. There would always be more upgrades to my equipment, spells, and Skills.

"Then I will see you soon. Please don't go so long between visits."

The hopeful tone in Ryk's voice caused my eyebrow to arch as I considered the shopkeeper. "Maybe if I wasn't spending all my funds every time I came in here, I'd be inclined to stop by more frequently."

"This Shop has wares, if you have the Credits."

I rolled my eyes and prepared for my exit, only to pull up short. I wouldn't want to go back to the Pharyleri headquarters while wearing my disguise. That would just cause confusion and draw attention that I didn't need. I stowed the complete armor set, along with my original vambraces, into Inventory. The drop harness securing my holsters tightened down over my standard jumpsuit automatically, which was a nice touch.

Activating Silver Fox Mimesis, I found the menu somewhat easier to navigate this time. It took a couple tries, but I located several slots to save preselected appearances—one of which was already occupied by my natural appearance. I saved my current appearance under a new slot and labeled it "Clint Westgrove" before selecting the option to return to my default normal appearance. Since my Mana pool had refilled while I'd done the rest of the shopping, there was no issue with the cost to revert my changes.

A wave of vertigo swept over me as I opened my eyes and the room seemed to spin around me for a moment while I adjusted to suddenly being four inches taller. I kept my balance, probably due to my high Agility and Perception attributes. Fortunately, the armor shifted with reversion to my normal appearance, seeming to stretch ever so slightly across the whole suit to accommodate the change in my build and height.

My swaying caused Ryk to chuckle. "You'll get used to changing with practice, but until you do, you might want to be sure you're out of sight from observers when you do that."

"Good call. I didn't think the change would hit me that hard. I didn't notice anything the first time, probably because I was lying down." I shook off the last of the dizziness and with a farewell wave, I disappeared from the Shop and returned to Earth at the node in Union Station.

I slipped out of the headquarters building without notice and the guards at the gate barely batted an eye as I departed the compound on foot. The lack of Titles in my Status and On the Hunt's innate reduction in my System presence rendered my passage as innocuous as possible—even with the compound's wardens on high alert. They all gave me nods before I left, but no one seemed perturbed.

Leaving Union station behind, I walked a half dozen blocks southeast at a leisurely pace before slipping into an alley with my Mana pool topped off.

Once out of sight, I used On the Hunt in conjunction with my new Silver Fox Mimesis to transform myself into my Clint Westgrove persona. The vertigo that accompanied the shift still felt pretty significant, but less debilitating than the last metamorphosis—if only because I'd expected it this time.

Four inches shorter and wearing a new face, I summoned my bike from Inventory and cruised out from the alley. Drifting low enough to the road that the hovering bike could have been in ground mode, I rode casually through the streets. It was a risk using my bike, but the model was in common enough use that it shouldn't draw any extra scrutiny.

Despite the sporadic echoes of weapons and spell explosions from the distance, a fair number of Denverites were braving the town. While they hurried about their business purposefully, the locals weren't marked by the same nervousness and uncertainty displayed by the civilians I'd witnessed on the streets of Pittsburgh two years ago.

Everyone had been running scared and jumping at shadows back on that first day of the System's introduction. Now though, the human survivors, and a fair number of Galactics, carried on with the knowledge that unless the warring factions targeted them specifically, then there was little chance of permanent harm.

That might not be true everywhere, but, at least here, one side wanted to profit from the locals while the other wanted to exploit them. Not a particularly benevolent outcome in either case, though it beat wholesale slaughter and forced relocation.

The population grew sparse as I reached Colfax and headed straight east, intending to swing wide of the city and return to the Sect-held districts from the south. With the Pharyleri pushing out their territory to encompass Aurora, the perimeter around the new city limits was still in flux with sparse checkpoints.

I paused to briefly scale a building that overlooked one of the checkpoints guarding the highway that was my target.

It was little more than an armored box that couldn't fit more than a handful of defenders, a squat, pre-constructed building alongside the road. Greater Observation only picked up a pair of occupants inside, through the heavy shields that defended it. The shields around the armored bunker wouldn't hold against a concerted assault, but it might keep the pair of occupants safe from a harassing sniper.

With most of the gnome's forces engaged in offensive and defensive actions, the skeleton crews managing those few checkpoints were more canaries than true defenders at this point.

I shook my head as I slipped out of range of the closest guard station. I didn't envy those gnomes in the slightest. I'd rather stay mobile and take my chances fighting out in the urban jungle–though that hadn't worked out so well for me yesterday.

Then again, I'd failed to stay mobile, so that was on me. My hands clenched down on the handlebars of the bike as I recalled the feeling of firing up at Creynora from my knees. I'd come a long way since the System's takeover, but I needed to get stronger still.

Leaving behind the outskirts of Aurora, I pushed the bike a little higher to fly about twenty feet in the air. The elevation offered by the anti-grav allowed me to cut the corner of the interchange between I-70 and skim onto E-470, the toll road that circled the eastern perimeter of the metro area.

Several monsters pressed their luck and found themselves added to the morbid collection in my Inventory, but none were as challenging as a pair of mutated sawtooth robins. A mutated kangaroo rat, a bobcat, and a swarm of green insectoid worm creatures with praying mantis claws that Greater Observation labeled M'rimul Worms, all fell before the steady fire of my beam pistols. The fights barely offered much in the way of experience but the growing stockpile of carcasses, but they provided a plausible method of infiltrating the Sect territory once I finished circling the city.

Every Dungeon World settlement thrived on the processing of monsters and loot brought in by Adventurers. The Sect holdings in Denver were no different. Sure, I'd probably get forced into paying fees or giving a cut to their enforcers, but, if I played the part well, I'd have an established reason for leaving and entering the city. That should get me into the Sect-controlled territory, at least. After that, the real work started.

I took a deep breath and smiled, the wind rushing through my longer hair as I rode further south on my bike. It felt like a good plan, playing to my strengths and not relying on stealth. I'd be just another Dungeon World drifter, a simple man looking to make his way in the universe.

Chapter 23

"Name. Class. Purpose of visit."

Boredom infused the voice of the Ceratophimi bruiser half sitting on the waist-high Jersey barrier wearing heavy plate armor that left only the pebbled gray skin of his face and the rhinoceros horn on his snout exposed. Raised panels above the open face looked like they could close on command, leaving only the tip of the horn protruding. A ridiculously sized tower shield, four-foot wide by six-foot tall, leaned against the end of the cement barrier and a mace hung from a loop on the alien's belt.

__Ko'shal'sar, Stone Bulwark (Heavy Myrmidon Level 44) (A)__
HP: 1210/1210
MP: 810/810
Status: Strength of Stone, Squad Link, Shared Pain

The power-armored alien out front demanded attention and drew the eyes of everyone in the short line outside the western entrance to the Sect-held Lakewood district, but I felt confident that was the point. While the travelers focused on the hulking alien, less attention was directed to the supporting members of the squad manning the checkpoint.

Behind the approach through the offset barriers, a three-story tower looked down over what had been the intersection between Highways 8 and 391. Stretching off to the right and left from the checkpoint, the northbound lanes of 391 were now just a fifteen-foot wall with the southbound lanes a path for Sect patrols.

The rest of the Sect fireteam waited near the gate at the base of the tower, and I took a subtle sweep over them as I eased my bike to a halt at a gesture from the Myrmidon. Three of the four were the expected mix of standard Classes–mage, ranged attacker and support–but the fourth gave me pause.

Difelin Varmink (Field Auditor Level 33) (A)

[Binary Eclipse Sect]

HP: 730/730

MP: 823/990

Status: Baggage Scanner, Inventory Filter, Comm Link-up

When I swept Greater Observation over the Field Auditor, the wide, pointed ears of the gaunt, slender alien twitched. I quickly cut off the Skill as the motion of its ears displayed the webbed flesh that connected the upper and lower tips to the side of the alien's head. While I managed to discover the species could commonly be called a Siren, I hadn't picked up the official classification for the type of aliens.

The humanoid figure with ghostly pale, almost translucent white skin and wide eyes blinked before looking around warily. I made sure I appeared like the rest of those waiting in line when the Siren glanced over.

I was one of only two humans in the line and the rest were a wide mix of Galactic species. Most notably, while I wasn't the only individual lacking a Binary Eclipse tag in my Status, those tags were in the clear majority. The fact that not everyone was affiliated was the only reason I'd decided to chance the line to enter the city.

Since the presence of the Field Auditor implied the ability to scan into my Inventory, I was relieved that I'd buried most of my notable combat gear in a hidden cache back in Bear Creek Lake Park before approaching the checkpoint. As with most bits of System storage tech, the Cicada Gear Locker was bigger on the inside and fit the munitions with ease. After the locker buried itself, a couple of alternating casts of Howling Blast and Whiteout smoothed the snow cover over.

Without the multiple sets of armor, master-crafted handcannons, Hastati missile launcher, and Banshee rifle to give me away as a combat-focused individual, I hoped to appear exactly as simple a Hunter as my masquerading status presented me to be. I'd also left behind all of my gnomish communications gear in the stash, so I'd be out of contact with Lyrra and the Pharyleri commanders for a bit.

"Clint Westgrove, Hunter. I'm looking to sell off some monster carcasses, resupply, and uh, get some repairs." At the last part, I ran a hand over the slashed section of my jumpsuit's chest, wiggling the flap of armored fabric that hung from the tear. I hoped that appearing a little worse for wear would lend a bit of authenticity to my narrative as a Basic Class struggling to survive in the wilds.

The Ceratophimi only grunted in acknowledgement, looking me up and down. The move had a bit more scrutiny than shown to the last few travelers, but I wasn't quite ready to start worrying.

"Difelin. Got anything on a Clint Westgrove?" the heavy called out over his shoulder while keeping his eyes fixed on me.

I looked over at the pale alien, noticing now that I was closer that the Field Auditor was just as heavily armored as the Ceratophimi. Difelin's armor was far more subtle, which made sense if they were attempting to protect a fragile asset. At least, as much sense as it made for having a non-combat Classer exposed outside the walls.

That could very well be the point though: the Field Auditor was the obvious weak link. Almost too obvious. Anyone targeting him first would be exposed to the rest of the squad and any support hidden inside the tower overlooking the gate.

"Westgrove. Clint. No record found," said the Field Auditor in a high-pitched, staccato speech pattern.

The report only elicited another grunt from the Heavy Myrmidon, who then remained silent for several seconds before speaking again. "No record, huh? Ever been to Denver before?"

I shook my head. "Before the System, I flew through the airport but nothing since."

Another grunt from the Stone Bulwark. "Check him."

A sensation like ants crawling under my skin swept over me as the Field Auditor approached from the gate. The pale alien was escorted by the security team's mage, a very busty female Movana in silver armor with a runed headband holding back her long golden hair. "Multiple Inventory storages located. Sweeping."

Difelin stopped just behind Ko'shal'sar and the crawling sensation intensified, lasting for several long seconds. "Many monster carcasses. Excessive amounts of projectile ammunition. Excessive amounts of charged Mana capacitors for beam weaponry. Excessive numbers of weapons, projectile and beam weapons ranked Tier II to Tier IV. No contraband pharmaceuticals. No prohibited items. Scan completed."

The uncomfortable sensation finally ceased, and I choked back an involuntary sigh of relief that nearly slipped from my lips, causing the Heavy Myrmidon to chuckle in amusement. "What are you doing with so much weapons and ammo?"

I raised an eyebrow. "It's a Dungeon World. Gotta kill monsters somehow if I want to make a living, and I'd prefer to do that from as far away as possible."

He chuckled again. "If you want to keep those weapons, you'll have to pay for the license to stay armed in town."

"How much is that going to cost me?" The shakedown didn't surprise me. The Sect would want to keep tabs on anyone who could represent a threat.

"One thousand Credits."

I sighed and forked over the Credits, hoping that the Field Auditor hadn't scanned my total balance along with my Inventory.

The Ceratophimi stretched out a hand, summoning a gray badge from his Inventory. "This is a temporary visa that marks you as a visitor. Wear this at all times in the settlement. It will last for a week and then turn red. You'll need to visit a Binary Eclipse Sect admin office or another checkpoint to renew it, if you stay in the city or return after it expires."

I took the badge, which was the twin sun insignia of the Sect, and pressed it to the shoulder of my jumpsuit. It adhered in place and the alien nodded in approval.

The badge wasn't much of a surprise after Ryk's comments in the Shop. The Sect was putting some effort into tracking both civilians and their own forces in their territory. Whether that was due to the war with the Pharyleri or just their usual mode of operation was still up for debate.

The question was, how sophisticated the trackers were.

"Binary Eclipse is always looking for capable recruits. You can clearly survive in the wilds, but if you're looking to enjoy more of the comforts of civilization, our admin office's also houses our recruiters."

I nodded. "Send me the office waypoints and I'll think about seeing what the benefits are. Comforts are nice, but the people part of civilization isn't always great."

The Heavy Myrmidon chuckled again, and a notification pinged as he sent me the map update. I'd take the free intel and maybe visiting the Sect admin offices would provide some leads on where I could find Rhegnah and the Krym'parke.

I goosed the throttle on my bike, easing forward and passing by the rest of the squad guarding the entrance without them paying me any extra attention. Behind me, I heard the alien summoning the next individual in line.

"Name. Class. Purpose of visit."

I was in. Now the real job began.

Chapter 24

Coasting my bike forward, I rolled through the open gate and found myself fully inside Sect territory for the first time since the raid-turned-rescue from the Cherry Creek Reservoir City Dungeon. I kept my speed down as I continued, and traffic picked up the further I got from the walls. Pedestrians kept to the sides of the road while the few vehicles commandeered the roadway, especially after I turned north on Highway 121.

Occasionally, Binary Eclipse vehicles, half-tracks similar to the one we'd stolen from the Dungeon compound, patrolled along the roadways. Instead of a closed rear compartment, these vehicles were open-sided, allowing the combat squad stationed in the back to continuously scan for individuals without the proper badge authorizations. I also spotted occasional foot patrol units, who walked the sidewalks in pairs or alone.

Everyone, human and alien alike, wore one of the ubiquitous Sect badges on their chest or shoulder. All species gave the Sect patrols a wide berth, unwilling to do anything that might draw attention or single them out. Only those with the Binary Eclipse affiliation in their status moved around with any confidence, though I noticed the humans who sported the tags tended to eye their surroundings with accusing glares that almost dared their fellow homosapiens to call them out for joining up with the Sect.

The furtive glances and hurried movements of the unaffiliated reminded me once again of the early days after the System arrived on Earth. Or a warzone, though this far to the southwest there were no immediate signs of the ongoing conflict with the Pharyleri on the northern side of the Sect territory.

Thanks to the helpful Heavy Myrmidon, who I felt certain got a bonus for referring any recruits, my map showed several of the administrative centers for Binary Eclipse operations in the settlement. Though I doubted those locations were all of the Sect positions, they would give me a few places to expand my search if I failed to uncover any other leads.

I also needed to keep my cover identity intact alongside the search, which meant following through with everything I said I would do at the gate. There was little doubt that the Sect would check up on my activities in the settlement, so my information gathering had to occur alongside finding a place to sell off monster carcasses, buying basic ammunition, and finding a crafter able to repair my armored jumpsuit.

For a while, I followed the flow of traffic, quietly scoping out the frequency of patrols as I took in the area and noted other Sect activity. Despite their focus on ruthless control of the city and restricting the Pharyleri trade, significant efforts appeared underway to facilitate local economic growth.

The largest of those signs was an open-air farmers market in the parking lot of a former strip mall, set up beneath a series of popup canopies. Despite the cold wind and scattered snowflakes, a mixed-species crowd paid little mind to the weather thanks to resistances and passive regeneration rates, filling the plaza and flowing between rows of tables filled with produce. A plume of smoke drifted up through the flurries from a large cylindrical smoker, roasting some kind of meat that smelled amazing and caused my stomach to growl.

Two of the Sect half-tracks sat backed together in an L-shape on the far side of the lot, while the infantry manning the vehicles lounged casually in and around them. There seemed to be little caution as they only half paid attention to the crowd, who ignored their presence in return.

I pulled over and stored the bike away in Inventory before drifting into the edges of the crowd. Most people wore regular clothing, covered in thick coats, hats, and gloves to ward against the chill in the air, but there were enough System-tech wearers, especially among the Galactic species in the crowd, that my jumpsuit wouldn't stand out by itself. The slash torn across my chest drew some glances though, as most people's gear was in better condition than mine.

Walking through the aisle beneath the canopy, I got a better look at the goods on display. While I recognized some fruits and vegetables, others were completely alien in color and form. Less unusual were the number of tables offering a wide variety of baked goods that ranged from cookies, cakes, and pies to loaves of bread and bags of dinner rolls.

One thing that stood out was the sheer number of babies. I didn't see any toddlers capable of walking on their own, but well over half of the human couples carried an infant bundled up against the cold. Even a fair few of the women who weren't holding a baby showed signs of swollen belly. With the System having pretty much taken care of the obesity epidemic, large stomachs in women generally meant they were carrying—especially since pregnancy rates seemed to have drastically increased since the System's arrival.

Listening to the conversations around me, I soon got the sense that life was continuing more or less normally for most people. At least, as normal as things got after the System's arrival and aliens showed up from all over the Galaxy.

When I worked my way through the crowd and over to the smoker with the mouthwatering aroma, I discovered a family operation selling burgers and sausages on homemade buns. While a trio of smaller grills cooked the meats with Mana-imbued flames for use in the smaller sandwiches, the larger smoker contained slabs of monster meat that were visible through a window in the side of the cylindrical cooker.

I stood in line for a couple minutes and watched while the human family served up a brisk business, almost giving the enterprise the air of a barbeque at a family reunion. The father, a bearded man in his forties wearing an apron, wielded a flashing set of tongs and a spatula to flip the burger patties and rotate the sausages on the hot surfaces of the grills. The three children, two girls and a boy no older than 12, served the food to the customers after paying the mother, who took care of the financial transactions.

"Monster brisket'll be a couple hours yet, but we've got burgers and home recipe sausages. What'll it be?" asked the woman when I reached the front of the line.

"Two of each," I replied.

She raised an eyebrow. "You're a hungry one then. That'll be twenty Credits, or an equal value in trade if you don't have the funds."

I nodded. At five Credits a sandwich, that wasn't a terrible price. "I've got Credits for the meal, but I'd be interested in selling off monster carcasses for butchering too."

"Talk to Uncle Carl when you return your plate. He'll set you up." She made a gimme gesture and then smiled when I sent over the Credits.

One of the girls had been listening when I gave my order. She already had a plate filled with two burgers on round sandwich buns and two sausages on longer sub buns. "Here you go, mister! Condiments are at the end of the table and please bring your plate back to the bin when you're finished eating."

"Thank you," I replied, smiling at her enthusiasm as I accepted the fully laden plate and then moved over to the condiments.

The options appeared to be a large red bottle of ketchup, a yellow bottle of mustard, and a smaller red bottle of hot sauce. I applied the three in varying amounts to my burgers, put hot sauce on one sausage, and left the other sausage plain as a control variable. Then I stepped clear of the line to allow the next patron to reach the condiments.

After I took the first bite of the plain sausage, it was so delicious that the next couple minutes disappeared in a food-induced fugue state, but I apparently inhaled everything. I only realized the plate was empty when I licked a last bit of hot sauce from my thumb.

A woman with a burger of her own had paused mid-bite, blinking with eyes wide in either shock or horror. I looked at my plate mournfully, regretting the lack of additional food before shrugging at the astonished woman, "Sorry, I was hungrier than I thought."

She shuddered and looked away, finally chewing her own meal.

I followed the instructions of a sign at the end of the stand, directing dirty dishes to a spot beyond the end of the smoker. A trailer hitch at the far end of the cylinder was rigged up to support a wash basin by the enterprising family.

A bald man, up to his elbows in the soapy water, glanced over when I rounded the smoker before continuing to wash plates in the bin. "Just put your plate in the bin with the other dirty ones."

I complied with his instruction. "Are you Uncle Carl? The lady out front said I could speak to you about selling some monster carcasses for butchering."

The man looked over at me again, more intently this time. "That'd be me alright. Whatcha got?"

"A couple sawtooth robins, a giant kangaroo rat, a bobcat, and a whole swarm of M'rimul Worms."

Carl seemed impressed, pulling his arms free from the soapy water and wiping them with a towel. "M'rimul Worms, huh? Those are some nasty bugs. Not too many dare take them on, but they make great steaks. I'll take everything you've got, even the robins."

We haggled over the Credits for a bit and settled on a compromise, though the bulk of the exchange went towards the M'rimuls. The rest of the monsters would actually be used toward a community food bank and given out to those in need, instead of going into the luxury category like the burgers and sausages sold from the stand at the other end of the smoker.

The overall amount was nothing like the bounties collected from the Pharyleri, but it was a reasonable income for the trivial amount of time spent on it. If I were just the Basic Class that I pretended to be, it would be possible to scrape by just bringing in food supplies for the community. Fortunately for the locals, the contacts were worth more to me than whatever I could get for the carcasses themselves.

Carl stepped out from behind the table with the bin of dirty dishes and we shook hands on the agreement. Then he called out to the front of the stand. "Hey sis, I'm going to take our new friend over to the shop to offload his catch. Send Junior over here to keep up with the dishes."

The woman running the booth responded with a thumbs up and a gentle push on her young son's shoulder to send him our way, never breaking off her chatter with the customer currently at the front of the line. The boy hurried over and stripped off his winter jacket before plunging his arms into the steaming wash basin. It was impressive that the kid pitched in without complaint, but it said just as much about the way the System had forced children into maturity.

I shook my head and followed after Carl as he walked away from the stand. The bald man led the way over to a refurbished pickup parked nearby and paused by the driver's side of the extended cab. "Hop in, it's a quick drive. I'll give you a ride back after, if you need it."

I circled around the vehicle, noting the US Army decal on the cab's rear window and the expired veteran plate on the rear bumper, before hopping up into the passenger seat.

"You served?" I asked as Carl started the Mana engine and pulled out of the lot.

The truck eased onto the main street and Carl grunted. "82nd Airborne. Iraq."

He glanced over at me and raised an eyebrow in a wordless question.

"3rd Battalion, 5th Marines. Afghanistan," I responded.

The man nodded and continued to drive, turning off the main street after only a couple blocks and pulling into a residential neighborhood. We pulled over next to a recently installed sign constructed of different colors of stone that read "Butcher and Smokehouse."

Carl got out of the truck and beckoned me to follow up to the two-story garage, where he pulled up the sectional door that rose on roller tracks to either side. The coppery aroma of blood and slaughter rolled out as the door opened, mostly originating from a half-butchered, oversized monster hanging from the rafters. A man and a woman in blood-spattered aprons were carving away at the unidentifiable carcass but they paused their gory work when the door rolled up.

"Becky and Todd, got some M'rimul Worms for you to work on next, along with a few other things," Carl called out to the pair.

The woman looked from Carl to me, then raised an eyebrow. "M'rimuls?"

Carl nodded and transferred over the Credits we'd agreed on earlier, then pointed to the other half of the garage where the door remained closed. The open floor space within had several evenly spaced chain hoists hung over drains in the cement floor. "M'rimuls first and then we'll figure out where to put the rest of it."

I followed the instructions and laid out the ten green insectoid mantis-worm-hybrids in a line across the garage bay. The other carcasses followed until almost every available space of the garage floor lay covered by dead monsters.

Todd whistled. "Damn, that's a haul. It'll help the community to look forward to something besides Sect ration blocks."

"For a day," snorted Becky.

The man opened his mouth like he was about to say something in response, then cut himself off with a glance at me. I ignored the interaction, though I sensed that it related to the Sect control over the area.

'If you're interested in more meat, I can probably stop by after my next round of hunting. I do need to run a few errands before I head back out, like finding a local repair service," I said, holding the slashed section of my suit.

Carl rubbed his chin in thought. "It'll take a day or so to move this much meat, so I'd probably only be able to make you an offer in two days. For the repairs, try Valkyrie Leatherwork first. Val might have the Skills and equipment to help you out. She's where we sell all our hides after skinning and she's been ranking up her armoring. I don't think she could make a full Adventurer's suit of that quality, but she should be able to at least stitch it up. Or she'll know who might do better."

Noting the crafter's shop on my map, I thanked Carl before walking down the driveway to the street. The shadows were growing longer as the sun dropped toward the mountains to the west.

The bald man followed me partway. "You need a ride back?"

"I'm good." I shook my head and summoned my bike from storage.

"Damn. Slick ride, Marine. I miss taking out my Harley."

"Get a mechanic to stick a Mana engine on it. Shouldn't be too expensive," I said, throwing a leg over the bike and settling into the seat.

Carl snorted. "The wife would kill me."

I shook my head and engaged the throttle. "Take care of yourself, Army."

"You too, jarhead."

I smiled as I cruised away. For a moment there, things had almost seemed normal. Even the System couldn't diminish inter-service rivalry.

It only took a couple minutes to follow the directions Carl provided, and I soon found myself outside another home-turned-workshop. In this case, the "sign" was a 10-foot mannequin clad from head to toe in armor sourced from a variety of monstrous sources.

Chitin plates in shades of brown and dark blue covered the torso and shoulders in a manner similar to a suit of medieval plate. The surface textures of the different colored sections suggested they originated from different insectoid species but had been smoothly blended together at the seams by the armor's crafter.

A thick leather gorget protected the figure's neck and appeared to match the material as the basis for a brigandine skirt that reached down to the knees. The playing-card-sized plates of the brigandine were more chitin held in place by bone rivets, though I couldn't tell if the black panels were the same material used in the torso plates.

Rounded monster skulls protected the knees atop greaves of studded leather. I recognized the boot construction as bison leather, though I suspected that the source of those goods were more of the mutated variety I'd fought through on my first visit to Denver.

Despite the variety of armor types and the solid craftsmanship displayed by the full set of gear, the most impressive and eye-catching part of the exhibit was the pair of wings spreading out to either side of the mannequin from an attachment point on the back. The layers of feathers sewn into the fully extended wings started with shorter dark brown, growing both lighter and longer as they moved away from the leading edge.

A part of me wondered if the wings were decorative or if they were actually functional. Though it lacked the wingspan of the owl that had almost killed me, or even the robins I'd slain earlier, they looked structurally sound enough to at least allow a wearer to glide. Not that I needed something that flashy when my drop harness performed the same duty with significantly less bulk.

The wings certainly looked cool, but I left the display behind and pulled open the door to the house-turned-shop, ringing a bell attached to the top of the door. I stepped into the front room of the shop and heard the voice of a distant woman calling out over the thump of a mallet pounding on something that dampened the sound. "Be right there."

While waiting for the proprietor as the pounding continued, I scanned the wares on display. A glass counter took up the rear of the room, with a narrow gap between it and the wall. Smaller armor pieces filled the case, mostly matching sets of bracers and gloves that appeared already equipped with weapon attachments.

A couple normal human-sized mannequins were placed in opposite corners of the room. One wore a full suit of chitin armor that showed subtle bits of System-tech added between the black plates. A jumpsuit covered the other, though it looked a bit more primitive than the one I currently sported.

Arrayed on open shelves along the wall, individual pieces of varying materials and types showcased the progress of the crafter's talent and Skills. A few cruder pieces of rough leather, bone, and sinew marked the armorer's earliest works, while the latest included more advanced metals and integrated tech.

The pounding from deeper in the home, which had carried through an open doorway behind the main counter, cut off and footsteps followed. My reflexive scan of the brown-haired woman who emerged provided a few details about the shop's owner.

Valerie Smith (Organic Armorsmith Level 13) (A)

HP: 690/690

MP: 433/870

Status: Mana Drip, Focus Time

That Valerie had reached the Advanced tier with an Artisan profession said the woman was pushing her craft.

"Sorry to keep you waiting. Welcome to Valkyrie Leatherwork and Armor, I'm Val!" the woman exclaimed as she emerged from behind the counter and extended a hand.

"Clint." I shook the offered hand with a firm grip.

The brunette's eyes narrowed slightly when she scanned my status, but she let the moment pass and focused on the gaping slash torn in the chest of my jumpsuit. "Need a bit of repair then, do you?"

I nodded. "Carl, from the butcher shop a few blocks down the road, thought you could do the job. Is this something you can fix?"

Val stepped closer and peered at the tear as she pinched the torn edge of the material between her thumb and index finger. She hummed and then used both hands to pull one end of the ripped section, pressing her palms firmly against my chest as she pinched the edges of the tear together.

A gentle green glow radiated from between her hands and her Mana pool began dropping. A sensation of heat ran along the rip as the material flowed together like ice melting into a slow-flowing stream. The Armorsmith slowly inched her hands across my chest and the muted glow traveled with her movements, sealing the slash.

Val pulled her hands away after a moment and then leaned in to eyeball her work from only an inch away from my chest. After a few seconds she stood and held out a hand with the palm facing up. "That'll be fifty-seven Credits."

I ran a finger over the repaired section of the suit and, while I could visually see the slight change in the material, I couldn't feel any imperfection. I nodded in approval and transferred the odd number of requested Credits over to the woman.

"Sorry that the fused section is visible—I still need a Skill for truly seamless work with advanced synthetic materials. I'm much better with natural stock, like leathers, furs, and carapaces."

I waved away the apology. "For less than sixty Credits, it's good enough, so thanks. At least my chest isn't hanging out in this cold anymore."

Val raised an eyebrow with a wry expression. "Carl sent you, so you must have unloaded some pretty decent chunks of meat from outside the walls. Anyone running around out there on their own isn't going to be bothered by a little cold."

"There's a vast gulf between being bothered and actually liking it."

The Armorsmith laughed. "Is there anything else that you need? More repairs or new gear, perhaps?"

"Thank you, but that was it. Unless you know anyone selling Galactic standard projectile rounds?"

I summoned one of the common rounds used with my backup pistols and held the bullet up between two fingers.

Val shook her head, but she refused to meet my eyes and I caught a glimpse of her uncomfortable expression in the moment before she answered. "I'm on the protective side of crafting things and I mostly work with natural sources, so I don't work with the weaponsmiths or have much overlap with their material suppliers."

I slipped the projectile back into my Inventory, even though my gut said she was lying. Since I was an outsider in the community, it wasn't surprising that they'd be wary of an unknown like me. It wouldn't do me any good to confront her. "Understood. I'll shop around and see what I find."

I thanked Val again for her repair work and let her know I'd be back if I needed further fixes to my armor before leaving the shop.

Only dark orange and bits of purple light remained on the horizon with the sun already behind the mountains. With night closing in and the hour growing late, I doubted that I'd find many opportunities for the last remaining cover task of restocking ammo.

If I put that errand off until the morning, then tonight could be used for a little information gathering disguised as a night on the town. I'd just need to find an appropriate watering hole, preferably one frequented by a majority of Sect patrons.

It was time to find myself a drink.

Chapter 25

Night fell, enveloping Denver in darkness as I found myself back on my bike and riding deeper into the settlement. Cruising as casually and aimlessly as possible to avoid drawing any undue attention from the patrols, I kept my heading toward the lake at the heart of the district which held the primary Sect base and the City Core.

A silver tower, brightly lit with white lights reflected from the uniform material of the glossy metallic surface, climbed skyward from the center of Kountze Lake. Protrusions of decks and weapons platforms sprouted from all sides of the fifteen-story building at irregular intervals. As I got closer to the structure and approached the grounds of the former park, I could see that the foundation of the building eclipsed the tiny island and had artificially expanded the surrounding lake into a moat.

With the lake frozen over in a solid layer of ice, its effectiveness as a defensive measure was questionable. At least the Sect had taken the effort to clear the grounds of the park, turning the area around their headquarters into an open killing field.

I skirted the edges of the park and turned north on 121. The wide thoroughfare that ran north and south through the heart of the settlement was lined with numerous shops and businesses. Though most were shuttered and dark with the lateness of the evening, they appeared lived in enough that they were clearly well populated during the daylight hours.

Music rang out from a bar on the corner of one block. The establishment still sported a circular yellow sign with a winged buffalo, though the sign lacked the name of the popular pre-System restaurant chain.

A fair number of Sect transports hogged the parking spaces closest to the bar, though plenty of trucks, bikes, and personal walkers filled the rest of the lot. The Binary Eclipse half-tracks were in the best condition, while the remaining vehicles ranged from well maintained and freshly washed to battered and dented beaters.

Stowing away my bike, I headed inside. The heavy synth beat of some Galactic pop tune grew to nearly deafening levels when I opened the door, and I knew that if it weren't for the System's resistances I'd have earned a pounding headache in short order. The noise told me right away that I'd be unlikely to overhear anything useful, but it was somewhere to start.

A smoky haze filled the interior of the dimly lit establishment. Strobe lights flashed over a dance floor in the front corner opposite the entrance, populated with a small throng of gyrating figures. A mix of high-top tables without seating surrounded the dance floor and a bar counter ran from the edge of the dance area to the back wall. Booths lined the remaining walls, while the rest of the floor space was occupied by more normal seating arrangements.

The gloomy atmosphere made visually identifying any of the individuals within the bar nearly impossible, but Greater Observation pierced the murk and allowed me to obtain a better picture of the patrons. Binary Eclipse members occupied most of the booths around the perimeter of the bar and several of those tables were built with oversized furniture to offer comfort for the larger species like Ceratophimi and Scrofalori. My Skill even tagged a couple of Yerrick, though I wasn't thrilled to see the minotaurs after my last encounter with one of their species.

Nobody paid me any attention as I took in the room from just inside the doorway and I was fine with that. My gray jumpsuit blended in with the equipment worn by the rest of the crowd. If anything, my armor felt bland by comparison to some of the gear sported by a few of the Binary Eclipse elites.

One suit stood out in particular, my eye drawn by golden plates and ridiculous shoulder spikes. Even clouds of smoke and the bar's dim lighting couldn't hide the distinctive armor of the Movana Sect commander who fled the raid on the Pharyler-held City Core. Welven Yimishi, the son of the Binary Eclipse administrator who managed Sect affairs for the settlement.

The coward. He could be a source of information or exploitation.

A subtle glance around showed that no one was paying any attention to me, so I started working my way over to the bar. Once I reached the counter and climbed onto an open stool, it took a couple minutes to get the bartender's attention. The backlit sign above the bar made ordering easy despite the intensity of the music and I exchanged a handful of Credits for the cheapest whiskey on the display.

When I took my first sip of the watered-down whiskey, it took all of my self-control to keep the grimace from my face. The drink was terrible, so bad that I had no idea how the distiller could have possibly messed up the spirit.

I sighed and kept drinking. Hal might prefer the good stuff, but I was Clint right now. Clint couldn't afford top shelf booze on the paltry income of a lone Hunter.

Though I never looked in his direction after I'd spotted him initially, part of my attention remained on the Sect Sub-captain as I pretended to enjoy the music and continued cautiously scoping out the rest of the bar.

The music suddenly dropped to muted background noise and several holographic displays on the walls lit up, much like the widescreen TVs prevalent in sports bars before the System. A cheer roared from the alien patrons as a running line of script in Galactic scrolled along the bottom of the display announcing the preliminary rounds of gladiatorial matches for the Irvina Open. Apparently, a one-on-one fighting tournament was about to begin.

My attention wandered from the display as the man on the next barstool turned to me and blinked at me with bloodshot eyes. He took a deep breath and the exhale utterly reeked of booze. "Hey man, you got anythin' ta brin ma goarin va."

I blinked as he looked at me expectantly and I just sat there, trying to process the utterly slurred gibberish that poured out of his mouth. After a moment of being unable to make any sense of whatever he'd asked, I just shook my head. "Sorry, no."

"Aww, thas okay." His head drooped and then he belched loudly before continuing his drunken mumbling.

After about fifteen minutes and moving on to a second drink as a variety of aliens duked it out in magical combat on the displays, I managed to keep up the pretenses of a conversation with the drunk by using a half dozen rotations through the classic combination of "dang," "yup," and "man, that's crazy." Unfortunately, no one else in the bar registered as high ranking beyond the Movana. Certainly no one else was wearing ostentatious golden armor.

I noticed the Sect Sub-captain moving across the bar floor toward the rear of the building and I slipped from the stool before cutting through the crowd. I'd started off closer to the hallway leading to the bathrooms and it was simple to time our paths to intercept.

Stumbling a bit like a drunk, I bumped into Welven as we squeezed into the hall and I clutched at his shoulder to steady myself.

"Get off me!" Welven snarled at the jostling before shoving me into the corridor wall.

I bounced off the wall and then leaned back against it, holding up my hands defensively as I slurred out an apology. "Sorry, man. Jus' tryin' to take a leak."

The Sect officer only sniffed dismissively and didn't respond before stalking off toward the bathroom. I affected being shaken by the experience and eased back from the hallway, waiting around the corner for several minutes before the Sect Sub-captain returned. Only then did I follow through with using the bathroom myself, just in case anyone observed the interaction.

So far, it seemed I had gotten away with planting the nearly invisible tracker on the underside of the spike pauldron when the two of us bumped together.

If anyone in the Sect knew where Rhegnah was hiding, either Welven Yimishi would or he would know someone who did. I just had to track him long enough. Without getting caught.

When I returned to the bar, the drunk had his head down on the counter and was passed out. I had no idea how the man had managed to get that intoxicated after how watered down I'd found my own drink. Two Scrofalori bouncers arrived as I climbed back onto my stool. The pair of hairy aliens grabbed the man and hauled him over to the door where I lost sight of them.

On the wall-mounted holographic displays, a four-armed alien was dueling against a serpent-tailed mage. Shimmering clouds swirled defensively around the snake-alien as the bipedal opponent circled, barraging the spell shields with a hail of fire from a brace of pistols in its upper limbs. The lower pair of arms held a sword and shield combo that alternated to block and slice through attack spells from the serpent mage.

The gunslinging swordsman won after battering through the mage's shields faster than he could recover enough Mana to recast them. As commentators began a post-fight analysis, I ordered a dozen hot wings from the bartender and idly wondered how I would have fought against each of the two aliens.

After only a few minutes, a human server dropped off my order of wings and I tipped her a few Credits as I settled in to watch the next bout. The variety of combatants and their utterly alien abilities gave me plenty to think about by the time a half dozen matches were finished.

My biggest takeaway was my lack of a true combat movement Skill. Efficient Trail was great for covering the distance out in the wilds, but the Skill only offered minor application in combat. It took plenty of setup—or luck—to earn an advantage there. Against a foe who could step through shadows, ride along on a bolt of lightning, or explode themself through the air, that wouldn't take me very far.

On the other hand, watching all the different tools that were being used, I also started considering how I could potentially handle movement Skills now without one of my own.

As I edged closer to the Master Class tier, I hoped that my upgraded Class held something to meet that need. My gut told me it would, but I still felt nervous about all the unknowns that lay ahead of me. For now, I could only focus on my current quest and on not turning into a crippled contract-breaker if I failed. I could not and I would not fail, so I pushed those doubts away. Instead, I let my focus drift over to where Welven Yimishi sat with a table of his cronies. Now that the lights weren't so dim, I could tell that none of his companions were the team I'd spotted him with during the library assault.

One by one, I scanned their statuses as subtly and carefully as I could to ensure my presence wasn't noticed. It turned out that my effort was wasted, except for the value of the practice in itself, since not a single one was anywhere near the Level of the Sect Sub-captain. Lower-ranked toadies, brown-nosing for social status with the boss's kid and supplying him with drinks.

By the time most of the crowd started filtering out of the bar, I'd gotten a recommendation from the bartender on a place to stay for the night, and Welven was absolutely shitfaced drunk. I managed to pay my tab and exit the bar before the staggering group of intoxicated Galactics made it to the door themselves.

In the rear corner of the parking lot, I summoned my bike and took my time checking over my ride while I waited for the stumbling crew to reach their own vehicles. It would seem that the Sect patrols weren't enforcing DUIs, at least against their own members. Hopefully, that meant the inebriated aliens wouldn't worry about anyone following them either.

The vehicle that Yimishi and his cronies piled into looked more like a limousine than the command transport that he'd used before on the battlefield. The limo swerved wildly as it swung right onto the street and headed south. I waited a few moments for the vehicle to get about a block away before I pulled out after them.

Hardly any traffic flowed through the streets at this late hour, and I kept the lights of my bike turned off to reduce the chance of being noticed.

I thought they were heading to the Sect headquarters building, but that was proved wrong when the limo turned east opposite the fortified structure. After a couple short blocks on a road that curved past several apartment buildings, the vehicle paused while an automated gate into a fenced lot opened up, then they pulled into the compound.

Only the lower half of the wall was solid, with cement rising up about six feet beneath another four feet of what appeared like wrought-iron bars with pointed tips. The gate closed back up before I reached it and I continued on the street while keeping track of the limo's shining lights through the fence.

The parking area separated the street from a series of brightly lit apartment buildings which overlooked a small lake that lay beyond. The walled compound curved to circle the lake and I pulled over as soon as the gate was out of sight, hopping onto the sidewalk and peering through the bars. I quickly took note of where the limo pulled to a stop and the drunks were piling out.

As the distinctive golden armor of the Sect Sub-captain led the group into the building, the limo turned to leave the lot. I'd seen everything I needed to for now, so I climbed back onto my bike and retraced my way back to the highway. From there, it only took a few minutes to find the hotel recommended by the bartender.

The front desk attendant in the lobby leaned on the counter, half asleep until he noticed me and bolted upright.

"Can I get a room for the night?" I asked, ignoring the man's struggle to wake up.

"We've got suites available for five hundred Credits," he replied.

I shook my head at the attempt to upsell me; Clint didn't have the funds to get fancy. "Just a standard room."

"Oh, that will be one hundred Credits then."

I nodded and in exchange for the Credits received a room key that appeared no different than the card keys used before the System's arrival.

"You're in room 127, just down the hall there." The man pointed in the indicated direction.

274

"Thanks."

I found the room and swiped the card to enter. Inside, I found a standard hotel room with a bed and a cramped bathroom that included a shower.

I stripped down and showered quickly, then put my armor back on before lying on top of the bed. This wasn't a Pharyleri stronghold where I could afford to relax. I was in the heart of enemy territory, and I had a job to do.

But my luck had held out so far and I had at least one lead to follow.

For now, I could get a few hours of sleep before continuing my undercover investigation.

Chapter 26

It took a week of daily hunting with nothing remarkable in my Inventory besides monster carcasses before the gate guards stopped auditing every one of my reentries to the settlement.

After the routine relaxed, I started smuggling the pieces of stolen Sect armor into the city. Even though I got scanned on the second day of bringing in the armor, only having pauldrons and boots buried in with the rest of my usual gear drew no additional scrutiny from the auditor. Ryk's treatment to anonymize the gear had done the job, but I still took a few days to slowly assemble the full set.

While waiting, I kept a low profile. I acted like an average solitary Hunter whenever I remained inside the settlement. I visited shops, ate at decent restaurants within my budget, and only made minimal effort to interact with the local population.

Once I had a full armor set within the city, I started taking risks. I needed information and the clock was ticking.

That night at the hotel, I took off the jumpsuit with the Sect badge and slipped into a fresh one. Then I pulled out the smuggled armor that I'd taken off one of the humans assaulting the City Core. Thanks to Ryk's repairs, the light infantry armor showed no sign of the damage dealt when the previous owner was slain.

The plates of the suit were a lightweight material that provided protection from beam weaponry and shrapnel but proved little defense against projectile weapons. The hideous shade of ochre also detracted from the suit's appeal. Thankfully, I had no more intention of getting into a fight while wearing the disguise than of relying on the armor to pick up ladies.

With Mimesis still in place, I cast Lesser Disguise to look like my normal alter-ego before I headed out into the night. Once I was several blocks away, and out of sight from any observers, I let the spell fade. I replaced it with Greater Disguise to morph my facial features into a generic human template with black hair and green eyes.

For the next several hours, I mimicked the actions of the lone Binary Eclipse members I'd seen on patrol over the previous week. I walked confidently through the streets, nodding in acknowledgment as I passed the vehicle patrols that were out late.

A gentle snowfall picked up as the night wore on with flurries slowly drifting down from the clouds overhead. For once, there wasn't much wind, so the tiny flakes fluttered almost peacefully as they fell.

In contrast to the relaxing snowfall, flashes in the night sky and distant explosions to the east and north marked the violent continuation of the conflict between the Pharyleri and the Sect. Though it hadn't been my original plan for the night, I drifted in that direction in the hope of catching sight of the Krym'parke on the battlefield.

Both sides employed airborne flares that floated in the night sky overhead and illuminated the no-man's-land between the battle lines in an effort to expose infiltrators. Several blocks of rubble stretched out on either side of the cratered sections of the city, so damaged by the constant use of Skills, spells, and explosives that even the System's regenerative properties for purchased buildings proved unable to cope with the destruction.

I kept a block or two back from the rear of the Sect battle lines, not wanting to get dragged into the fight. I caught sight of several troop formations hurrying between positions, but they were the more common forces, like those I'd fought at the armory, units sporting the usual mix of human cannon fodder with Scrofalori and Ceratophimi elites in their midst.

After watching two such units, I realized that unless I got lucky, my chances of finding the Krym'parke or signs of Rhegnah were slim. I pulled away from the front line and returned to the Sect stronghold in the Lakewood district with only a couple hours left until dawn.

I snuck back to the hotel, once again using the disguise spell to look normal–if a bit drunk, to explain my night out–as I returned to my room. Hidden in the safety of my room, I stripped off the stolen armor and undersuit before storing them in Inventory and taking a shower. Then I put on the suit left behind on the bed before collapsing on top of the covers to catch an hour of shut eye.

The blaring alarm on the bedside table dragged me to blurry wakefulness as the gray light of dawn peeked into the hotel room windows. I hauled myself out of bed and gave the room a quick once-over before hurrying to check out at the front desk. Out in front of the hotel, I summoned my bike and raced through the light early morning traffic to the settlement gate.

I managed to join the trailing end of the hunters and gatherers departing the Safe Zone, pulling into line behind a tow-truck with the tow rig replaced by a drilling mechanism and a crew of rough looking miners in tan coveralls.

The overnight guards watching the gate, and closing in on the end of their shift, looked at all the traffic flowing out into the unclaimed territory surrounding the city with apathetic expressions. The lack of concern shown toward the outflow contrasted sharply with the precautions taken for those entering the settlement, especially newcomers.

Well worth noting, and I kept tabs on each guard surreptitiously as I worked on an exit plan. After all, we would need to get out after I found the Countess. Sneaking out with the normal flow of traffic was definitely my preferred exit strategy right now.

The other option was trying to run through the front lines, hoping not to get shot by either side.

Outside the city walls, the wind picked up sharply and the biting cold slashed through the crowded streets. Those with low Constitution attributes and lacking in elemental resistances hunkered down in open-top vehicles. Insulated headgear appeared on many as the wind whipped through the line and I followed suit, summoning an encased helmet that offered an environmental seal.

Most of the traffic broke apart and spread out without ranging too far from the protection of the Safe Zone. While the Sect kept an eye on the area immediately surrounding the settlement, the monster density was manageable for most Basic and low-level Advanced Class tiers.

I left most of the groups behind and continued west beyond the signs that advertised Red Rocks Park and Amphitheatre. The snow-covered slopes that lined the sides of CO-74 offered a scenic ride as I cruised along the winding highway. Several rockslides blocked the road, and I converted the Outrider to hover mode to traverse the route as the elevation continued to climb, slowly but steadily, along the way.

Just beyond a small green sign welcoming me to the abandoned ruins of Kittredge, a sudden avalanche of rock and snow swept down toward me from the slope on my right. The wave of destruction hit the side of the road and sent a spray of ice and gravel into the air as I reacted by pushing my bike's anti-grav to the max. The Outrider whined, lifting straight upward as the avalanche passed underneath.

As the rocks and snow settled across the road below me, a small pack of goblinoid monsters rushed out from several nearby building ruins just beyond the edges of the slowing tide of earth. The gray-skinned creatures, clad in ragged furs and primitive leather armor, were even uglier than the Gribbari from Pittsburgh.

The monster's dismayed cries revealed the avalanche as an attempted ambush when they saw me floating in the air above the rockslide. That disappointment turned to anger and pain as I began picking them off with a beam rifle.

If I'd been injured by the rockslide or stuck on the ground, it might have turned out very differently, but most of the creatures were only armed with primitive clubs and spears. They proved little threat to me in the air, though a few attempted attacks with bows and arrows. Fortunately, my basic jumpsuit was enough to repel the flint-tipped weapons.

A pair of goblin shaman showed up after I had slaughtered a good chunk of the monster population. Their lightning and fire spells forced me into evasive maneuvers, but I took them both out and went back to killing the rest of the monster colony from the air.

The beam rifle's barrel steamed red-hot by the time I finished, and I left the weapon sitting out on the back of my bike to cool down while I landed to loot the slain monsters. Other than the two shaman, I didn't bother storing any of the scrawny little creatures in Meat Locker. As frail as the creatures were individually, I doubted there was much value in the carcasses, and I hoped to find better on today's hunt.

I spent the rest of the day roaming the slopes of Bear Mountain, bagging a giant elk and a handful of mutated rattlesnakes that seemed to thrive in the cold. It was a reasonable haul, so I headed back to town by late in the afternoon.

The usual gate guards waved me into the city without a word, though the Field Auditor stopped a silver-haired Movana ranger behind me for a more thorough search. The elf's complaining followed me through the gate and I cruised on without concern.

I followed my routine of offloading my catch at the butcher shop and getting a room for the night, then went out for drinks at one of the several popular bars in the area. I avoided the wing place I'd visited the first night, since the Sect Sub-captain's preferred that bar as his prime choice of evening hangouts and I didn't want to chance another direct encounter.

Not yet anyways.

If I failed to find more actionable intelligence on Rhegnah and the Krym'parke, my current backup plan involved a very direct conversation with the Sect officer.

For tonight, I cased out a different bar, only a block away from the wing joint. Quiet music greeted me as I entered the dive, and I found the place sporting a relaxed atmosphere with soft mood lighting.

The bartender, an older man with graying hair and a full mustache, greeted me as I took a seat at the end of the bar. I placed my order for a neat whiskey and asked for a menu when the man nodded in approval.

While waiting for my drink, I scanned the mostly full interior of the bar. As close as we were to the Sect tower in the heart of the settlement, the number of Binary Eclipse members was no surprise. However, among the patrons were an equal number of civilians, crafters, unaligned hunters, and hired mercenaries. I even spotted a couple of the miners I'd seen leaving the gates earlier this morning, their tan coveralls now streaked with grime as their table conversed over a round of pint glasses filled with an amber lager.

The bartender returned with an old-fashioned cocktail glass filled with a standard pour of whiskey and sat it down on a napkin before sliding a laminated menu across the bar. I thanked him before my growling stomach focused my attention on my options for dinner.

I ordered a barbecue bison burger, done medium rare, and steak fries, casually listening in on the conversations around the establishment while I waited for the food to arrive. Topics ranged from complaints about the weather, "always winter and never Christmas," to available mercenary contracts and gram-per-ton mineral densities for newly discovered System metals in nearby ore deposits. While everything besides the complaints was interesting and offered more detail about local conditions, none of the conversations offered any new information that led me closer to my goals.

When my burger and fries came out, the mouthwatering smell of the homemade barbeque sauce sent my hunger into overdrive, and I dove into the meal with gusto. I still listened with half an ear to the talk around the bar, but my focus stayed locked onto the food until I'd mopped up the last of the savory sauce with the fries. I let the flavor linger for a moment before I washed down the meal with the last of the whiskey.

I signaled the bartender for a refill and leaned back in satisfaction as I let the food settle. I took my time with the second whiskey, listening in to more conversations around the bar while slowly sipping the drink. Nothing else caught my attention over the next hour and I paid my tab before heading back to the hotel.

The next day, I repeated the routine, though I stopped at my buried equipment cache for another set of Sect armor and used the communicator to check in with Lyrra.

"Hal, it's great to hear from you. How deep are you in over your head?"

"Hilarious. I've managed to get into the Lakewood district with my cover intact, but the intel gathering has been slow. I've only managed one night of scouting out the Sect side of the front lines. Do the Pharyleri have any reports of Truinnar or Krym'parke fighting with the Binary Eclipse forces?"

Lyrra hummed as she checked her notes. "The only mentions of Krym'parke are when the Sect deploys their mercenary units. Those forces have been much more cautious than the conscript units that they've been sending into the meat grinder at the front lines."

I frowned. "They're recruiting hard down here and I stopped at one of their depots to check out what they're offering. The pay is pretty tempting for anyone with a Combat Class, but there's a non-payout clause hidden in the contract amendments."

"Looking to sign your life away a second time, Hal?"

I scoffed. "I was never going to accept their offer, but I needed to look like I was considering it to keep my cover going down here. Seriously though, no updates on Rhegnah?"

"Sorry, nothing from my end. Intel doesn't have enough sightings to put together any patterns and Shop costs for all information related to the Sect took another jump."

Pulling up my quest log, I saw the timer had continued to count down and now showed eight fewer days than when it started. I sighed. "I'll keep searching down here. I've got one lead I can force if I run out of other options, but I don't want to play that card unless everything else comes up dry."

"I'll talk to Ismyna and see if she'll put an analyst on it. Things are pretty tense with the gnomes in the command center right now, with the stalemate bogging down their forces."

Part of me wished I could do more for my Pharyleri friends, but I was stuck looking out for myself until I resolved my current quest. "I'll see if I can find any opportunities to disrupt the Sect if it won't blow my cover.

No promises though. Until we can get Dayena back, she has to be my priority."

"I get it, Hal. I miss her too, even if I know you won't say it like that."

A grunt was my only response and Lyrra chuckled. "Yeah, I figured. You stay safe out there."

I bid her the same and signed off from the call before burying the communicator with my stashed equipment once again. A few casts of Howling Blast smoothed out the area and spread enough snow over the ground to disguise the cache hidden below the surface.

The rest of the day was spent hunting, and I returned to the settlement just before dusk. Another pack of M'rimul Worms filled Meat Locker, but I ran away from the Alpha instead of killing it–hoping that this group would repopulate in a few days and I could farm them for a premium.

At the family shop, Carl and his meat market crew were thrilled with my haul, though the butcher's raised eyebrow expressed his wordless skepticism that I'd managed to slay the pack of a dozen monsters solo. To return the favor, I pointedly avoided observing the decidedly lethal weaponry hidden amongst the tool racks. Even with monster meat often coming in larger forms than the pre-System pigs or cows, the butchers had some decidedly extra-curricular tools like claymores and katanas mixed into the collection of bonesaws and boning knives.

After exchanging the monster carcasses for Credits, I asked the Army veteran to suggest a few restaurants for dinner. With a week of bar hopping only landing the single lead with the Sect Sub-captain and no clues for the Kyrm'parke, my hope was that a change of tactics and venues might turn up something new.

Though a Thai place a couple blocks north of the Sect HQ turned out worthy of the endorsement in food quality, I came up empty on useful intel once again. Returning to the hotel for a couple hours of sleep, I snuck out to recon the front lines once more.

After another night of cataloging patrols and fruitless searching for Krym'parke, and two particular Truinnar, amongst the Binary Eclipse units, I returned to the hotel exhausted.

The days blurred together as I repeated the cycle of hunting monsters, selling off goods, repairing my equipment, and then spending the nights mapping out patrol routes as I sought Rhegnah's hired help.

The settlement guards only scanned me every few days and even backed off further to only once a week, but I remained cautious about the contents of my Inventory nonetheless. I caught sleep in stretches of no more than an hour or two, checking in every few days with Lyrra to see if the Pharyleri turned up anything useful.

For four more weeks, I hunted in vain. For four weeks, I bided my time and watched the countdown on my Contract Quest tick lower.

With less than two weeks left on the clock, I decided that I could no longer wait. I had one lead, and I could only hope that a risk with it would pay off.

Chapter 27

"It's getting late for you. Another successful hunt?"

"My armor is in one piece and I've got a load of monsters to sell, so I'll call it a win." I half-shrugged with my response to the Stone Bulwark's question as I rolled to a stop and did my best to hide my exhaustion.

Five weeks after my first use of this gate, I'd fallen into a regular routine and the Sect squad on duty had grown used to my evening arrivals, but I'd sacrificed sleep to stick to that routine and my body was paying the price. This evening was later than most and the guards were already relaxing as they prepared for the end of their shift.

"Have you given any more thought to joining up?"

I bit my lip and shook my head. "It'd probably be a bit more enticing if you lot and the gnomes weren't tearing up the city. I'm not keen on jumping into the middle of a war."

Ko'shal'sar rumbled in laughter. "The monsters you hunt every day are just as dangerous."

"And I'm good enough that I see them coming. I don't have to worry about artillery rounds dropping on my head in the middle of a fight or stealth drones laying mines on my patrol routes. Or worse, more System shenanigans that I can't even imagine."

The rhino-like alien scoffed. "The shorties aren't that much of a threat."

"Then you'll have the fighting wrapped up soon?"

A snort was the only response as the alien waved me on through the gate. I coasted forward and gave a friendly wave to the rest of the squad as I passed. Then I was through, and I held back from showing the relief I'd felt at the Field Auditor's lack of attention.

I hadn't been subjected to a search for over a week and a half now, but if there was a time that I didn't want my Inventory checked, it was today.

Most of my Inventory would now be considered prohibited combat weaponry after retrieving the entirety of my stash from the park outside the city.

With the gate checkpoint behind me, I followed my usual routine and headed for Carl's butcher shop to unload. It was a familiar route after weeks of hunting trips outside the walls. The only difference was that this time I carried a veritable armory in my Inventory that would definitely draw the attention of any patrol that could scan my storage.

But the chances of that were slim, since the Auditors and Analysts with those Skills were mostly stationed at the gates and major trade hubs. A backyard barbeque joint shouldn't rate high on the list of priority targets.

I reached the suburban butcher shop without encountering any patrols and pulled into the driveway. After returning my bike to Inventory, as was my habit in Sect territory, I knocked on the front of the garage and waited for one of the staff to raise the door.

I frowned when I heard no response from within. Usually, someone was in the garage-turned-butchering station and I knocked again, just in case no one had heard my first attempt. After waiting for another minute and still hearing nothing, I walked over and rang the bell at the front door of the attached house. The doorbell rang audibly inside the house, but still no one came to the door.

Part of me worried that something had happened to the family, but a glance at the setting sun allayed those fears. I was far later than usual due to my maneuvering with the gate guards, so it was just as likely that they'd made other plans for the evening and closed up shop early.

The local community probably needed the extra food more than I needed the Credits, but if no one was around then there wasn't much I could do for now. I couldn't afford to wait around though; there were other things that I had planned for the night now that I was fully armed once again.

Back on my bike, I left the quiet neighborhood behind and took a slightly longer route to the center of the district. The indirect course avoided the most common routes for the Sect patrols that I'd mapped out during the previous weeks, without looking too much like I was actively avoiding those same patrols.

I skipped the bar and went straight to my room at the hotel. Instead of stripping down for my usual hot shower routine, the only thing I removed was the Sect patch that I'd worn for most of my time inside the city walls.

It hadn't been hard to confirm the little emblem also served as a tracking device, allowing the Sect to keep tabs on the civilian populace. The encounters I'd observed after covertly following Sect patrols revealed that they were rarely used as active trackers. Instead, the patrol's sensor operator would bring up a display that showed patch users traveling through an area during a selected timespan or they would enter the patch of a detained subject into the console to reveal the target's movement history.

There were only a few places within the settlement where sensors would trigger alarms if they detected a Sect patch. The blindspot within the Binary Eclipse defensive strategy was believing that the fear of being caught without a patch would keep the locals scared enough to wear them.

I tossed the removed patch onto the bed so that if anyone checked on the location, it would appear that I'd slept the night away. A muttered incantation let me cast Disguise on myself to show an illusionary Sect patch in the same location on my jumpsuit where I'd removed the real one. It wouldn't stand up to any scrutiny, but it would suffice for any visual checks from a distance.

Then I used Greater Disguise to alter my appearance to closely resemble another man that I'd seen in the hotel lobby early this morning. It didn't really matter if that person was still staying here, just that it wasn't my face that walked out of the building when I was supposedly asleep in my room.

No one took any notice when I walked straight out the front door of the hotel and into a snow squall. The wind whipped around, swirling the white crystalline flakes around me, and I couldn't help but smile at the sight. The weather would help cover the actions I planned for tonight.

I continued down the street for over a block before bringing out my bike. Without any concern of being tracked, I used side streets and back alleys to fully avoid the nighttime patrol routes through the city. It took about twice as long for me to reach my destination, but with the deadly arsenal in my Inventory I felt more comfortable in the shadows away from the main streets.

When I reached the rear of the Sect Sub-captain's apartment complex, I stored the bike and walked casually along the curving fence. There were a couple people walking the opposite direction on the far side of the street, and I kept a sharp lookout for anyone else as I waited for them to get out of sight.

As soon as the coast was clear, I took off in a running start. At full speed, I reached up with both hands to grab the top bar of the decorative fence. Throwing myself up and over, I vaulted the spiked tips at the top and dropped down on the inside of the fenced area.

A quick glance showed no one outside who might have noticed my jump. I straightened up and walked through the property, doing my best to look like a building resident out for a bit of fresh evening air. Since the buildings were reserved for the middle- and low-ranking Binary Eclipse functionaries, humans were uncommon but not enough that I would stand out.

Moving between two of the apartment towers, I headed toward the building where the Sect Sub-captain lived and circled around the edges of the frozen lake that sat in the middle of the ring of apartment buildings. The ice sported a rectangular section scraped cleared of snow and smoothed out into a skating rink, though the wireframe and net goal cages at either end suggested that hockey was the sport of choice for the skaters. The rink would soon disappear under a blanket of white if the snow continued falling at its current pace.

Reaching my target building, I didn't bother checking the rear patio door. The security lock that flashed on the latch served as a warning, even if I had intended to risk encountering any residents inside.

I had another route in mind.

Retrieving my vambraces from Inventory, I slid my arms into the gauntlets one at a time. I missed wearing the entire suit, now that I'd made that investment, but military-grade armor would definitely stand out when I was trying to keep a low profile.

Once I secured the armor in place, I pointed my left arm toward the roof and picked a spot with no windows in line with the ground below. The wrist-mounted launcher fired with a hiss and the monofilament cable unspooled before the grapple latched on to the wall just below the crest. The line snapped taut and began reeling in at a steady pace, allowing me to walk up the wall as the cable pulled me upward.

I might have hummed a certain 1960s TV show song under my breath.

Reaching the spot where the grapple attached to the top of the wall, I pulled myself over the crown with my free hand and released the hook as I rolled onto the angled roof. A couple inches of snow covered the surface and I carefully steadied myself before reeling in the rest of the cable. Then I cautiously crawled over to the southwest corner of the building, directly above the penthouse suite belonging to Welven Yimishi, Sect Sub-captain.

From there, it was an easy crawl to the corner balcony under the cover of the nighttime darkness and falling snow. Though the tinted surface of the door blocked my vision, my other senses and Skills detected no one in the apartment beyond. I summoned my Pharyleri lockcracker from Inventory and placed it on the balcony door. Lights on the device blinked green a moment later, and I stowed it away before sliding the door open just enough to slip inside.

I was momentarily blinded by the inside illumination, and a burst of wind and snow accompanied me through the opening until I slid the door shut. Heart pounding at the brief blindness, I blinked my vision clear and relaxed as Greater Observation found nothing in the apartment with me. A quick casting of Cleanse removed all the ice and snow stuck to my armor after my trek through the city. A second casting of the spell cleared the mess melting inside the doorway.

No longer concerned with leaving a dripping trail through the suite and with my vision adjusted to the bright lights, I stepped deeper into the apartment. A cautionary sniff revealed a faint lingering smoky scent, something between vanilla and black licorice.

The balcony was just off a sitting area with two couches, with a dining table on the opposite side of the space next to a galley-style kitchen. An opening on the wall to my right led to a hallway, and I knew from the floorplan that the suite's two bedrooms lay down that passage, along with the bathrooms.

A conspicuously placed armor stand stood empty in one corner, while tasteful artwork decorated the walls. The two couches were handcrafted with leather upholstery, showing the Sect Sub-captain had spent a fair sum of Credits on the decoration of his living space.

The idea of spending Credits on furnishing and art felt horribly foreign. For the last two-plus years, every Credit I owned went into investing in Skills and better gear to ensure my survival. The height of luxury was a higher-tier gun or stronger armor.

Maybe I indulged occasionally with an intoxicating beverage or two, but my drinking habits had decreased, slightly. At least, they'd improved from the borderline alcoholic tendencies I'd fallen into while drifting around the western reaches of Pennsylvania doing odd bounty hunting jobs. Dayena's surprising arrival changed the course of my life when we met in that seedy rural bar.

I might never tell her, but her enforced Contract had been for the best. Probably.

Thoughts of my Truinnar employer brought me back to the task at hand. I had a job to do if I wanted to rescue the Countess from her overbearing family. Still, I noted the well-stocked liquor cabinet and smiled at the thought of liberating it once I obtained the information I needed.

After sticking a covert transmitter underneath one of the kitchen cabinets with a line of sight on the apartment's entry hall, I headed into the master bedroom. There was plenty of open space in the lavishly decorated chamber for me to summon the remaining pieces of my semi-powered armor and slip into it.

Once I settled the helmet over my head, I ducked inside the walk-in closet that connected to the master bathroom and moved behind several of the one-piece adventuring suits suspended on hangers. Before I shut off the closet light, I noted that the suits were higher quality than mine and mentally added them to the growing list of things to loot from this place, if I didn't have to leave in a hurry.

I connected my helmet's display to the transmitter planted in the kitchen and leaned against the wall in the darkness of the closet to wait for my prey.

Chapter 28

It was well after midnight before Welven showed up. I straightened up from a crouch after stretching my legs as his golden-armored figure walked through my transmitter's field of view. I readied myself to act, but hesitated when I saw that two additional toadies followed the Movana into the apartment.

Of course, he wasn't alone.

Watching a human woman and a female Movana traipse into the kitchen, all I could think was that at least it wasn't the six-person entourage that usually trailed the Sect Sub-captain. With the transmitter's limited field of view, I couldn't see where the trio went, but the audio pickup transmitted giggling and the clinking of glassware. It sounded like they were continuing to hit the booze.

"You ladies take a seat. I need to take off my armor, I could not abide damaging the Ingolian hide leather on the couches. I hunted those beasts and harvested their skins myself, you know."

The women fawned over the boasting and then made appreciative noises as the elf apparently stripped down right there in the room with them. I rolled my eyes at his antics.

While I might have been able to handle Yimishi and one of his partners, a total of three targets was too risky for what I had planned. If any one of them got away, that would cut my undercover work short and ruin my chances of finding where Dayena was imprisoned. I sighed and resigned myself to hiding for a while longer, doing my best to tune out the tonsil-hockey being played in the sitting room.

One of the floozies finally said something that grabbed my attention. "You're so strong, you're clearly one of the best commanders we have. Why hasn't your father given you another chance at the Pharyleri?"

"That incompetent Truinnar and his pet mercenaries blamed me and my forces for not taking the City Core at the Central Library."

"The dark elf? He's like something out of a fantasy movie!" The human woman was floozy number two and not the sharpest tool in the shed.

Welven's subsequent intoxicated recounting of the attack on the Pharyleri-held Central Library bore little resemblance to the reality of the battle. His rendition left out a few details, like the fact that he'd fled without firing a shot, so I could see why his father might have taken Rhegnah's side if there'd been an argument in the battle's aftermath.

The yarn ended with more face-sucking noises that led to other sounds that I did my best to ignore. Thankfully, Welven was only up for a short performance and passed out drunk not long afterward, leaving the two ladies more than a little disappointed as they left the apartment on their own.

The door clicked shut behind the pair and I closed the feed from the transmitter as I hurried to take advantage of the new opportunity. Slipping out of the closet and the master bedroom, I cast Ice Armor on myself and quietly approached the front door, where I both activated the electronic locking mechanism and flipped the deadbolt to ensure no one else could enter the apartment.

I crouched low before sneaking into the kitchen, where I activated the Pharyleri anti-teleportation device. Along with that, I added a one-use communicator disruptor that worked on Skills too. It was incredibly expensive since it didn't just stop transmission but also ensured that, to cursory observation, Skills like Party Chat or Diplomatic Communique or the like appeared to be working. I'll admit, I winced while making use of it, but needs must.

I placed the items on the counter and crept the rest of the way to the sitting room.

The place showed the signs of a party. A trio of wine glasses sat partially filled next to several shot glasses and a couple half empty bottles of booze. The golden armor that the Sect Sub-captain usually sported sat on the display stand in the corner of the room, while the owner of the armor sprawled shirtless on one of the fancy leather couches with his lounge pants around his ankles. Not a pleasant sight, but one that would make what came next significantly easier for me.

Pulling a silenced projectile pistol from Inventory, I activated my attack Skills to trigger both Rend and Hinder. Then I flipped the insensate Movana over and pressed his face into the couch's decorative throw pillow as I placed the weapon over his kidney and opened fire.

The projectile from my first shot punched into Welven's torso accompanied by the gasses from the firing weapon. The gas pressure damage at least equaled the damage of the projectile and the explosive forces tore through the Movana. Internal hemorrhaging and gas expansion with nowhere to go inside the body forced a bloody mist back out the entrance wound to splash over my armor.

Contact firing a pistol before the System was a dicey proposition with certain models of semi-automatic firearms. If too much pressure was applied to the end of the barrel, the slide could be forced out of battery and either fail to fire or fail to cycle after a single shot. With System technology and the prevalence of melee combat, it was a guarantee that a projectile weapon would be fired in contact with the target at some point, so those weapons were designed to avoid such drawbacks.

Welven screamed and thrashed under me, but my knee in his back kept him pinned in place. Obviously, someone hadn't put as many points into

Strength as he did Charisma. I continued to fire, and the elf's health plummeted from the repeated shots.

Welven began sobbing into the pillow as his life pool dropped below half. More than once, I sensed the flicker of Mana as he activated his Skills, but none of them did more than rock me around. I assume most had to do with his position, which meant tactical overview, some personal defense, a retreat skill, and maybe a communication skill.

None of which worked.

Sensing I had him where I wanted him, I activated Apprehend and flipped the fully restrained Movana onto his back.

"What do you want? I'll give you anything. Credits. Gear. Contracts. Just don't kill me."

"Rhegnah Baluisa."

The Movana blinked in confusion at my words. I pressed the scorching hot muzzle of my pistol against his junk and he screamed. "What? What do you want with the Truinnar?"

I shifted the pistol to the meat of the elf's thigh and pulled the trigger, then waited until the screaming quieted once again. "I'm asking the questions. Tell me where he's hiding. Tell me where I can find him and his force of Krym'parke."

Welven panted in pain. "They're downtown. He's got a Pharyleri commander in his pocket. One that he's paid off for a safehouse, along with passage in and out of their side of the settlement as long as he's not directly fighting in that area."

Well, that certainly explained my inability to find any sign of Rhegnah and the Krym'parke in the Sect settlement over the last five weeks. I'd been looking in the wrong place entirely. "Which commander?"

"I don't know. Can you stop hurting me?" Welven whimpered.

I ignored the plea. "Tell me more about the safehouse."

"It's just off Broadway, a few blocks north of the old State Capitol building. Some historic hotel-turned-museum."

"And the address of this hotel-turned-museum?"

"I don't know," he whined, and his eyes went wide as I lifted my silenced weapon to point at his forehead.

"Wait–" The pistol coughed twice more, splashing brain matter and shards of bone over the fancy leather couch. The corpse of Welven Yimishi slid to the floor and I dismissed my pistol into Inventory.

I stared down at the dead elf, the body's releases at death already stinking. While I wanted to strip the place bare, I couldn't afford to leave signs of pilfering behind without giving away that Welven no longer lived. Despite the fact that the younger Yimishi had demonstrated he lacked the confidence of his father and most of the Sect forces after the failed Central Library attack, any commander suddenly disappearing in the middle of a warzone could impact morale. Hopefully, in a negative way, if it looked like the commander had fled.

The corpse disappeared into Meat Locker and my eyebrows shot up at the sum of Credits looted. If Welven hadn't been skimming off the Sect operations, then his father was giving him quite the allowance.

It took several castings of Cleanse to remove the bodily fluids from the couch and rug, along with the blood spatter from the furniture and the wall behind it. With no sign of the slaying left behind in the sitting area, I returned to the kitchen to collect the pair of devices set up there and swiped two bottles of expensive bourbon from the liquor cabinet on the way. A little nudging of the remaining collection disguised the empty spots on the shelf.

After I removed the transmitter and the dimensional jammer, I pilfered two of the adventuring suits from the closet. They wouldn't fit me, but I could sell them for their material value the next time I hit a Shop. I removed the pair of empty hangers and spaced out the other suits evenly, so that the ones I took wouldn't leave an open spot in the closet.

I took another pass through the empty apartment, confirming that no signs of my presence remained. Back in the sitting room once more, I paused in front of the armor stand that held the Sect Sub-captain's suit of golden plate. I was certain that Welven never went anywhere without that status symbol and leaving it behind would be a red flag that something was amiss to anyone who came here looking for him. Piece by piece, I sent the armor into Inventory and left the armor stand as bare as it had been when I arrived.

A glance through the balcony doors showed that the night's snowstorm had died out at some point while I was waiting, leaving a fresh blanket of snow on the dark platform outside. The fresh snow had erased my earlier tracks, but now I had to get out of the apartment without creating new ones.

I slid the door open and then turned around, holding onto the side of the door frame as I leaned backward and fired my grapple up to the roof. I reeled in the cable enough to lift myself off the ground and gently swung out onto the balcony. Bracing myself on the wall, I slid the door shut and used my lockcracker to secure it behind me. I dismissed the device back into Inventory before reeling in the line a little further to raise my height enough that I could clear the balcony rail.

I walked a couple steps along the wall to clear the balcony and then I reversed the reel to rappel down the side of the building. Another command to the grapple when I reached the ground released the tether's hold on the top of the structure. The reel mechanism whined as it retracted the cable into the housing on my wrist.

As soon as it finished, I headed for the wall of the dark apartment complex and vaulted the fence. It was still a couple hours before dawn, so I couldn't leave the settlement directly just yet. I also needed to retrieve my badge, so I retraced my route back to the hotel. The lobby attendant, asleep at the front desk, never noticed me passing through and I went straight to my room.

I dispelled the disguise spells, then replaced the real badge on my jumpsuit before taking a hot shower and collapsing on the bed. Tight muscles I hadn't even realized were clenched loosened up as I sprawled. Finally learning useful information and possessing a new lead relaxed me for the first time in weeks. My exhausted head hit the pillow and I fell into a solid sleep.

Chapter 29

The first rays of daybreak glinted off the white-covered Rocky Mountains to the west and the city itself remained shrouded in predawn gloom as I departed the settlement gate amidst the steady stream of other hunters and prospectors who braved the wilds daily.

The gate guards watched aloofly as the fortune-seekers rode out in a variety of transports. My bike crawled behind a refurbished pickup with double rear wheels with a harpoon mechanism mounted in the bed. I idly wondered what the dually's occupants were hunting with that kind of setup, but I wasn't curious enough to follow when our paths diverged outside the walls.

A quick stop at the park allowed me to retrieve my cached Pharyleri communicator, the only thing remaining in the hidden stash, then I followed Highway 8 west until I hit 470 and turned north at the edges of Sect-patrolled territory. After about fifteen minutes of cruising on the old highway, I felt safe enough breaking my cover to pull out the comm and signaled Lyrra.

"I haven't heard from you in over a week, Hal. You better have news." Annoyance filled the words, but I felt her concern beneath them.

"Don't complain, I kept you updated on my lack of progress," I replied. I grinned at her tone even though she couldn't see it.

The Movana scoffed. "If you're just comming to tell me that you still don't have anything, I will kill the transmission right now."

"I've got news."

A sharp hiss of indrawn breath was the only indication that Lyrra had heard me, so I waited for her to respond. "Tell me."

"I don't have an exact location, but the reason I couldn't find any sign of Dayena in Sect territory was because she was never there."

I continued until the elf was filled in on the rest of the details I'd learned.

"So, with Pharyleri command compromised, we can't go to Ismyna for help on this. We need a local who might know about an old hotel-turned-museum." Lyrra commented after I finished with my update.

"What happened with that crew of civilians we pulled out of the Sect Dungeon?"

Lyrra hummed. "That might be a good place to start. The Alliance intel group cleared them and they were released a few weeks ago. I know where the Nurse has been working, since she left the contact details for her clinic with me—just to give to you…"

I rolled my eyes, but otherwise ignored the insinuation that trailed off from the Movana's last words. I still wasn't comfortable with that whole situation. "Great, send me the location. I'll meet you there."

The coordinates popped up on my neural link as the elf killed the comm. Of course, the clinic was on the complete opposite side of the city—with a warzone separating me from it. No shortcuts, I'd have to circle around and enter the Pharyleri territory from the north to avoid the battle line.

Leaning low over the Outrider's handlebars, I pushed the throttle and streaked north along the highway. It took over an hour to circle around the outskirts of the city and the sun had climbed well above the horizon by the time I reached the abandoned construction of the Pharyleri starport.

Despite the snow cover, the frozen ruins glinted as I streaked between buildings entirely encased in ice. The late morning sunlight lanced down to glare from the crystalline white carpet of ice and snow that lingered on the ground. Even if the city should have been due a spring thaw, the dragon-disrupted weather patterns from the nearby Rocky Mountains kept a chill in the air and the cold was even more noticeable over these cursed grounds.

Leaving behind the graveyard of silent icy towers and entombed starships, it wasn't long before I reached the perimeter for the Pharyleri portion of Denver. An expanded settlement shield covered the area and it had been reinforced in the weeks since I'd left the territory. A ten-foot wall now ran along the cleared stretch that had once been Interstate 70 and I continued until I reached a gate, one no less guarded than the Sect side of the city.

Rather than risk the Pharyleri tripping up on my false identity, I pulled over and hopped off my bike long enough to shift both my physical form and status back to Hal for passage through the checkpoint. Since I was going back to my normal self, I equipped my semi-powered armor set, minus the helmet, and my good weapons. It felt good to have Last Word and Ace holstered on my hips once again.

Once I'd cleared the entry scans, which were far more thorough than the Sect's, despite my identity appearing in the Alliance databank, I resumed my journey toward the coordinates sent by Lyrra.

The waypoints led me to the campus of the former University of Colorado Hospital. With the System naturally regenerating most injuries and ailments within minutes, healthcare institutions were pretty much out of business. The large structures now frequently served as mental health clinics, community centers, or dormitories for individuals unable to afford their own housing from the System.

In this instance, the campus and the neighboring children's hospital now housed many of the refugees from the destruction caused by the ongoing conflict between the Pharyleri Alliance and the Binary Eclipse Sect. With a line of wreckage and rubble that stretched for miles through the middle of the city, hundreds of homes had been demolished as collateral damage.

I found my elven friend with her arms folded over her chest and leaning against the wall outside the entrance to the former emergency room, where the posted signs showed that it now primarily served as a limb replacement clinic.

Lyrra Valjyn (Combat Chirurgeon Level 2) (A)
_HP: 940/940_
_MP: 1020/1020_
Status: Active Camouflage, Death from Above, Steady Hands

I stored my bike and nodded to the elf as she pushed off the wall. "I see that you finally picked your Advanced Class."

"A keen eye and precision movements are just as important for servicing targets as they are for stitching up wounds in combat," Lyrra replied.

I grinned. "As a regular victim of your stitching, I'm in favor of any and all improvements in that field."

The elf glared at me in annoyance, smacking the side of my arm. My smile remained despite the abuse, since it was so good to see my friend again after so long alone in Sect territory. Another friend still needed our help though.

I jerked my head toward the hospital doors. "The Nurse we rescued is working here?"

Mention of the Nurse erased the elf's scowl and she smiled, suddenly cheerful. "Emi's putting her healing talents to work in the recovery ward for patients who opt for cybernetic limb replacements and upgrades."

The abrupt shift in Lyrra's mood alerted my suspicions. She was up to something. I wasn't sure exactly what, but we needed help if we wanted to rescue Dayena. "We'll see if she can give us anything on what I learned."

The two of us headed into the building and crossed through a waiting area filled with humans across a wide age range to approach the front desk. The woman working behind the counter glanced up and saw us approaching. She immediately looked away nervously, her wide-eyed reaction seeming a bit out of place. While we were over-armed for a hospital waiting room, it wasn't like either Lyrra or I were wearing a mech suit or brandishing our weapons. Staying armed was just a fact of life, especially in a warzone.

I reached the counter and placed both hands on it as I leaned forward. "We're looking for Emi DeVile. She's a friend who asked us to find her here."

The clerk stammered for a moment. "There's no one by that name here."

"She told me I could come find her at the clinic, since we were the ones who freed her from Sect captivity. Just let her know that Hal is here," Lyrra said with a smirk, stepping up beside me and smacking a hand down onto the counter.

The woman jumped at the sharp sound and pursed her lips as she recovered, then picked up the handset for the phone on the desk. "I'll call the back and ask. I don't know everyone who works here."

I rolled my eyes as she swiveled her chair to turn her back to us and began talking to someone at the other end of the line. She was actually telling them that we were here, which gave lie to her earlier words, but I didn't call her out since we were getting what we asked for.

While waiting, I looked around the lobby and noticed that several of the occupants scattered throughout the room were observing Lyrra and me closely. A half dozen men stood out, despite their appearance of casually browsing books or magazines, from the way they each kept one hand free of their reading material. Either hidden out of sight down at their sides or under a coat draped across their lap; I suspected that they were all holding onto a weapon aimed in my direction.

Keeping my face blank, my mind raced as I tried to figure out why there would be armed guards hanging out undercover in the clinic waiting room. The nervous glance from the clerk on our arrival had clearly been to ensure that at least one of those guards was keeping an eye on us, but the reason for her concern still eluded me.

And why would Emi work in such a place?

After I asked myself that question, the answer came to me immediately. With the Nurse's heavy involvement with the local human resistance prior to her capture by the Sect, it seemed more than likely that she'd gone right back to working with them after regaining her freedom. In that case, the sudden appearance of Lyrra and I as heavily armed mercenaries would understandably invoke a response from an underground cell of the resistance.

The receptionist behind the counter ended her phone call and I tagged the guards with Greater Observation to keep tabs on them. The men were all decently high-Level Basic Classes, but none stood out as a threat. I turned back to the desk and the woman fidgeted for a moment when I fixed my gaze on her. She finally spoke up after I raised an eyebrow in a wordless question.

"The back-office staff is looking for your friend, if she's here. Please have a seat over there." The clerk gestured to a spot off to the side of the main lobby where a few hard plastic seats sat isolated from the rest of the waiting room. I couldn't help but notice that the spot would be under clear lines of fire from the hidden guards without any cover whatsoever if a fight broke out.

"I'll stand right here, thanks," I responded, giving the woman a stern look that had her blinking wide in fear. I mentally winced at the unintended effect. My high Charisma was a little too good for intimidation against those without mental resistances. Lyrra gave a curious look, not having picked up on the undercover guards or the potential killbox.

"I'm sorry, sir, but I still need to be able to assist our other patients." The clerk recovered enough to respond, and I stepped away from the counter, moving a couple paces off to the side and folding my arms over my chest.

Lyrra followed but gave me a questioning look. I shook my head, shaking off her question. Not for the first time, I lamented the loss of the party chat offered by Dayena's Diplomatic Contacts Skill.

After we'd waited for a couple minutes, a scrub-wearing nurse came out and called a name. A guy in the waiting area, not one of those I'd marked as a guard, stood up and followed her out of sight down a hall that led deeper into the facility. The process was repeated a few more times over the next half hour as occasional patients returned to the waiting area. The returnees checked out at the desk before departing the facility.

My patience was starting to grow thin as the wait dragged on. I fixed the clerk with a scowl and the woman pretended to ignore me. Unfortunately for her, the sweat that appeared on her brow belied her act.

"How long are we going to wait?" Lyrra asked quietly, stepping in front of me and keeping her back to the waiting area so her voice wouldn't travel.

"Not much longer."

I growled and then raised my voice loud enough that the clerk could hear from a few steps away. "I'm almost ready to go look for Emi myself."

If this was a resistance base, they definitely wouldn't want Lyrra and I roaming around the back halls. Their choice would be to offer up what we wanted or potentially let things get heated.

The woman at the desk swallowed nervously after hearing my declaration and hurried to grab the phone again. Lyrra turned to face the desk at my louder tone and then smirked as she saw the clerk's panic. Keen Senses ensured that I overheard enough of the ensuing conversation to confirm they really were looking for Emi this time.

One of the guards I'd tagged started moving across the waiting room and I dropped a hand onto the grip of Last Word as I glanced his way. The man was doing his best to be subtle, but the way his jacket hung over his left arm clearly hid a weapon.

When a second one of the guards also started moving, I sighed. "Seems they didn't like my idea."

Lyrra followed my glance and frowned at the poorly disguised weapons before stepping back to clear enough space to deploy her rifle.

"Hal!"

The excited cry from the hall beyond the reception desk preceded a blond-haired streak that sprinted across the room with arms spread wide. My higher attributes kept me steady as the woman slammed into my midsection and wrapped her arms around my waist. I jerked my left arm away to keep it free from the hug and dropped my hand back onto the grip of my pistol. My glare kept the pair of guards from acting, though they seemed confused by the possessive actions of the new arrival.

I gently pried Emi away, greeting her while keeping one hand on Last Word and an eye on the uncertain guards. "We could use your help, Emi. We have some information that requires local knowledge."

The Nurse nodded in excitement as she moved over to Lyrra and gave the elf a hug, then she saw the undercover guards in position to confront us. She waved the men back to their posts and looked around the crowded lobby. "My local knowledge is quite high, but let's go somewhere less public for this chat."

The Nurse guided us out of the waiting room and down the hall, passing several nurses and doctors along the way. When we reached a nearby conference room, Emi led us inside and closed the door. Sealed off from the noise from the hall, it was surprisingly quiet as the woman rounded the rectangular table and slipped into a seat across from where Lyrra and I stood. She looked pointedly at the comfortable leather executive chairs, and I took a seat, despite having my back to the door.

Emi steepled her fingers under her chin as she considered the pair of us. "Why are you here, why now, and where is your third?"

Lyrra glanced at me, and I took the lead on filling the Nurse in on the highlights of the last few weeks, namely Dayena's capture by her cousins and my infiltration behind Sect lines in an effort to learn where she was being held. I finished off with the information I had gotten from the Sect Sub-captain, though I left off exactly how I'd obtained that information and about the Movana's demise. I also kept quiet on the fact that someone within the gnome command structure was covering for the property we were seeking.

The Nurse thought in silence for a minute when I finished before looking over at me. "There's really only one place that stands out for its savory backstory, which could be the place you're looking for. The Navarre building. Originally built as a girl's school, it became a brothel after the school founder passed away. Then the building went through several iterations as a fine-dining establishment before it became a museum, but I don't know what became of it after the System arrived."

"It's at least a place to start. Can you give us the location?" I asked.

Emi smiled. "I'll do you one better, I'll guide you there."

I raised an eyebrow, measuring the woman's reaction. "If this is the place we're looking for and Dayena is there, things will get very heated, very fast."

"I survived the Sect. Besides, I'm just a simple passerby." The Nurse nodded with confidence before giving an expression of complete innocence. She added a few blinks to sell the look.

I rolled my eyes at her behavior but nodded anyway. With the clock ticking down on my quest to rescue the Countess, I would take any advantage I could get and every bit of assistance regardless of the risks. "I doubt the Krym'parke will care, but I'm not going to turn down the help."

The Nurse grinned at my acceptance and then had us wait while she bounced cheerily out of the room to arrange leaving for the rest of the day. It wasn't long before she returned and we left the hospital.

Lyrra summoned a bike of her own from her Inventory with a flourish to draw my attention. The road bike was armored with sleek, matte gray panels that seemed to absorb the afternoon sunlight to disguise the vehicle's outline from a distance. Though it was narrower and less bulky than my ride, I recognized the anti-grav nodules on the wheels that would allow the vehicle to shift from wheeled operation to hover mode.

"Personal Assault Vehicle?" I asked after I scanned the bike with Greater Observation.

Lyrra grinned, clearly proud of her new acquisition. "It can transform into a power-armored mecha. Since the System classifies it as armor, I can store it in Inventory."

"I'm just glad you finally got your own wheels."

The elf scoffed and swung her leg over the bike's seat. "My main ride got herself captured and my backup went harrowing off on his own for weeks on end. I needed a way to get around."

I retrieved my Outrider from Inventory and then paused, glancing at the others. "So, since we're going hunting for Krym'parke, I'm going to do a thing. Don't freak out."

I activated Silver Fox Mimesis and shifted to my alternate personae, shrinking down about four inches as my facial features shifted along with the disguised form. Lyrra and Emi gaped open-mouthed while I adjusted my Status. I grinned at the pair before climbing onto my waiting vehicle.

"So that's the trick that let you stay behind enemy lines for the last weeks?" Lyrra asked and I nodded.

With Lyrra and I both on bikes, Emi was left standing alone on the curb outside the hospital entrance.

"You don't have a ride?" I asked her, pulling the attention away from the Skill I'd just used.

A sad look crossed her face as the Nurse shook her head. It reminded me that the days of nearly every American owning a car had disappeared along with the System's arrival. Now, only those with Skills or the ability to purchase Mana-powered vehicles had their own transportation, with bikes, riding animals, and good old fashioned shoe leather being the more common modes of transport among the human survivors of the apocalypse.

Lyrra shrugged with a pointed look over her shoulder at her smaller bike. "I don't have room, but you can ride with Hal. That way you can give him directions too."

The Movana's tone was neutral, but her expression showed that she was quite pleased with herself, and I sighed, jerking a thumb to the back of my bike. "Hop on."

I ignored Lyrra's smirk as the Nurse bounced happily over and climbed on behind me. As the woman grabbed hold of the back of my weapon harness, I just knew the elf had been maneuvering to set me up with the Nurse since our arrival at the hospital.

I punched the throttle and Emi squeaked in surprise as I suddenly accelerated away from the entrance. My abrupt departure left Lyrra hurrying to catch up, and it was my turn to give the elf a smirk as we raced off into the city.

Chapter 30

"That's the Navarre?"

I sipped from a frothy ale, looking out through the tinted glass of the corner tavern's muntin bar windows that kept our observation hidden from the outside. The chilled brew in a frosted mug was a specialty of the corner tavern, though the beverage seemed less popular in recent history with the perpetual chill of the Rocky Mountain climate. I liked it though.

Across the street and nestled in the middle of the block between two modern structures that towered more than twenty stories above, the historic red brick of the four-story building in question seemed tiny by comparison with its neighbors.

A narrow half-flight of stairs led up to a shallow porch with four white-painted columns that supported the decorative balcony above it. An arched full-height window on either side of the main entrance looked out onto the porch. Two additional matching windows bracketed the porch itself and their positions were mirrored directly above on the second and third floors.

I reached out with Greater Observation, but pushing the Skill to probe at the building felt like slamming into a wall. Though the building was within range of my ability, all I sensed was a condensed blank space as if the structure was a solid block of metal. I'd never experienced anything quite like the feeling before. While things had avoided my detection with various combinations of camouflage, stealth, and cloaking technology, I'd never found myself completely shut out and unable to examine an entire area.

"That's it. At various times a girl's school, bordello, jazz club, and museum," Emi replied. The Nurse sat next to Lyrra, with the two of them across from me in the booth.

Lyrra peered out the window. "Now we just need to confirm whether certain individuals are present."

"I thought you were looking for Dayena?" Emi asked, glancing between us with a puzzled expression.

Lyrra kept her gaze locked on the building across the street as she answered. "If she could come and go as she pleased, then she'd have gotten in touch already."

"It's her captors you need to confirm, then."

I nodded. "That's the hope. Then even if she's not here, there's a strong chance she's held nearby. And that's the confirmation we were looking for."

As I'd been speaking, two figures walked out of the Navarre's main entrance and descended the steps to the sidewalk in front of the building. The purple-brown skin and distinctive horns that protruded from both brow and chin marked the recognizable Krym'parke. The pair of aliens moved down the street and I watched until they'd traveled out of sight around the corner of the next block.

It took a conscious thought to relax my left hand from the grip of Last Word, holstered out of sight beneath the table.

"Now what do we do?" Lyrra asked.

"We need a floorplan, so we're not going in blind. We should be able to get an older one from the Shop, at least. That'll also let us know about any other ways in. It would also help to get an idea of how many Krym'parke are on site, along with whether Dayena's cousins are here too."

Emi fidgeted in her seat, like she had something to add, and I looked over at her with a raised eyebrow. The Nurse thought for a moment before speaking with some hesitation. "I can get you the floorplan. At least, from the pre-System blueprints."

It could only be a resistance thing, but that prompted more questions. "Why share it with us?"

"You two and Dayena got me out of that Sect prison, so I owe you. All three of you. You have to promise that you'll keep this between us."

I looked at Lyrra and the elf nodded back at me. "Alright. We'll keep your secrets."

The Nurse pulled a touchscreen tablet out from her Inventory and activated a privacy screen across the front of the booth. She swiped through several menus before placing the tablet in the middle of the table. A wireframe hologram projected up from the surface of the device, displaying the floorplan of the Navarre. From the screen of the tablet itself, I could see the Denver Community Planning and Development office watermark on the blueprints.

"Historic landmarks were all registered before the System, when the Navarre housed a billionaire's private art collection. Without a Shop purchase, there's no way of knowing the inside layout, but this is the data we've compiled for our use," Emi explained, glossing over exactly who was compiling that information.

We spent several minutes looking over the wireframe of the building, separating out each level to review each floorplan individually before Emi sent the files to our neural links. Unfortunately, the blueprints were more than two years old and wouldn't account for any System upgrades to the structure. Unless we were willing to fork over an insane amount of Credits, the cost to purchase any info from the Shop would be astronomical with whatever was in place that blocked my use of Greater Observation.

I pointed to where we had the wireframe of the ground and second floors floating side by side. "There are two doors on the front of the building, the main entrance up from the street on the porch and this gated entry that's a few steps down from street level."

"I don't think we want to use the front door, Hal," Lyrra said. A frown crossed the Movana's face as she considered our options. Emi also appeared pensive, but she wasn't really looking at the holographic blueprint.

I shrugged. "My gut says that if they're holding Dayena here, she'll be on an upper floor and it's a straight shot up the stairs from the front door. If we go in through the basement entrances, that's another level to sneak or fight through."

We cleared away the holograms and lowered the privacy screen as a waiter delivered platters of food to the table and the conversation lapsed while we ate. I'd ordered a barbecue bacon bison burger, the house special prime rib, and a fry flight that included a selection of potatoes—tots, garlic fries, steak cut fries, and sweet potato. After living lean for the last five weeks, I may have splurged on my order.

Emi and Lyrra were more reserved with their dinner selections, but I still finished scarfing down my meal at the same time. As soon as the staff cleared the empty plates, I paid the tab before Lyrra and I went back to quietly discussing our options.

Motion from the corner of my eye caught my attention and pulled my gaze across the street, where Rhegnah, Creynora, and a quartet of Krym'parke filtered down the front stairs of the Navarre and gathered on the sidewalk in front of the building.

I whispered a curse which caused Lyrra and Emi to follow my line of sight. The three of us watched while the alien party departed, traveling down the street in the same direction as the two earlier Krym'parke.

Lyrra looked at me. "Now would be the perfect time to hit them."

"I can get us in," I said, referencing my Pharyleri lockcracking device.

"No, I'll get you in."

Lyrra and I both turned to Emi in surprise at her comment. The pensive look on her face was gone, replaced with determination.

"Come with me." She stood from the booth and beckoned for us to follow. I drained the last of my beer as Lyrra slid out after Emi, then I followed behind the pair.

The Nurse led us out of the tavern and turned away from the Navarre. After walking several blocks in the opposite direction, she paused outside a general goods store with faded paint and a weathered wooden sign.

Emi stopped in front of us and held up a hand, halting us with a stern expression. "The resistance has been doing everything they can to keep the existence of what I'm about to show you hidden from the invading Galactics, which means that I'm trusting you both not to inform the gnomes."

The Nurse looked pointedly at Lyrra, before staring at us both intently until I nodded in agreement.

"We already agreed to keep the secrets of your resistance band, but you have my word," Lyrra pointed out, folding her arms over her chest.

Emi glanced between us again, weighing the sincerity of our responses before nodding in acceptance.

A bell affixed to the inside of the door rang as we walked inside, alerting the two men behind the counter of our entrance. The balding Grocer working the register had filled out since our first encounter, no longer appearing quite so skeletal or as pale as he had when I'd rescued him along with Emi and the Miner from the Sect compound. Larry Muller looked surprised for a moment before smiling and waving to Lyrra and me.

The second man was clean-shaven and wore denim coveralls with a flannel shirt, which disguised the look of the armored skinsuit peeking out at the unbuttoned collar. One hand remained out of sight beneath the counter, and it wasn't a leap to assume the presence of a heavy weapon hidden just out of sight.

The man's Class of Veteran Infantryman wasn't the only clue that something was off with the shop, just the most immediate, though he relaxed after exchanging a look with Emi and taking in Larry's reaction.

The Nurse waited until the door closed behind me before leading us through the aisles toward the rear of the store. I took a moment to greet Larry, but the man's good cheer faded into a more serious expression when I hurried after Emi and Lyrra.

A shadowed alcove in the rear of the shop contained several shelving units, stocked with various dusty knick-knacks. After a nod from the shopkeeper, who kept watch on the front of the store, Emi reached up under one of the shelves on the back wall and I heard an audible click. The entire rear section of the shelf swung outward from the wall on silent hinges, revealing the dark outline of a secret doorway.

The Nurse ushered Lyrra and me into the hidden passage behind the shelves before pulling the unit shut behind us. At Emi's direction, I continued ahead down a narrow stairway. The corridor was so tight that my shoulders brushed along the walls on both sides as we descended the steps. A bolt latch secured the door at the bottom of the stairs, and I slid the catch back before opening the door.

I stepped through into a dark passage, wide enough that two people could walk side by side. Pulling out a handheld lantern from my Inventory, I clamped the device onto the side of my bracer to keep my hands free as I looked around the underground space.

The tunnel extended to the left and right, fading out of sight in the darkness beyond the reach of my light. Old bricks lined the walls, crumbling with age, and the ceiling was only a few inches above my head. I was fine, especially in my shorter persona, but any of the larger Galactic species, like Hakarta, Ceratophimi, Scrofalori, or Yerrick, would find themselves restricted. Along the floor of the passageway, faint lines ran through the smooth surface of poured cement.

"This will get us to the Navarre?" I asked.

Emi nodded, lighting a flashlight of her own and pointing it down the passageway. "These tunnels run all throughout downtown. In the early days, they were used to move all the coal around to heat buildings during the winter. Of course, they got quite a bit of use for more nefarious activities too. Relevant to our current situation, the Navarre became a brothel in the late 1880s. Since patrons didn't want to be seen coming and going, the tunnel system allowed access from the Brown Palace Hotel across the street. The tunnel network expanded over the years and was used extensively during the Prohibition era."

With the tunnel's origin in mind, the impressions within the floor must have been the remains of the old coal car tracks beneath the surface.

She turned and led us onward through the tunnel. Doors of widely varying construction lined the sides of the passage at irregular intervals.

From the street addresses written on the doors in white paint, each presumably led to another building on the surface. Offshoot passages branched off at right angles to other parts of the tunnel system, the black maws opening to stretch out into darkness beyond the range of our lights.

We walked through the passageway without encountering anyone else. Without Greater Observation and my minimap, I would soon have been completely lost as the Nurse led us through the labyrinthine underground network. But I kept track of our route and felt confident I could retrace our steps back to where we'd entered the tunnel system, if necessary.

Keen Senses helped, picking up the faint sounds of activity from beyond some of the doors, but nothing especially near to the hidden entrances that would indicate active use. It seemed like most people weren't aware of the secret entrances or were content to leave them well enough alone.

Interestingly, the tunnels showed multiple signs of restoration. Places where the color of the walls shifted slightly, sections of the floor that weren't quite even, and areas that seemed suspiciously clean given the dusty signs of age that permeated most of the tunnel network. The details all added up throughout our underground journey, and it seemed clear that the resistance was renovating the tunnels for clandestine access across the city.

I was more than happy to benefit from their efforts. If this was the favor I got in return for rescuing Emi and the others from the Sect, it was well worth it to get a shot at rescuing Dayena from Rhegnah and the remaining Krym'parke.

The Nurse slowed and stepped up beside a labeled door that appeared no different than the many others we'd passed. She tapped a finger on the white painted street address and met my gaze confidently. "The Navarre."

I compared our underground location with the scouting I'd done on the surface and nodded when I saw the map centered in the middle of the block between Broadway and 17th Street. The mysterious blank spot to Greater Observation confirmed it. "This is it."

As I still couldn't get the Skill to provide a read on any of the building's occupants, I could only hope the layout hadn't changed significantly from the pre-System blueprints that Emi had provided.

I drew a pair of silenced pistols from Inventory, the same weapons I'd used to complete the assassination bounty on the Sect administrator upon my return to Denver. Lyrra readied a new weapon of her own. As much as I loved the firepower the Movana brought to the table as a sniper, I was glad to see something a little more practical for the situation. A matte black submachine gun filled her hands, a futuristic MP5 variant with a drum magazine and a large cylinder at the end of the barrel.

I raised an eyebrow at the elf. "Silenced?"

"Of course," she scoffed.

"Good. We'll need to take out any guards as fast and quietly as possible. The more we put down, the better our chances."

Emi worked the latch mechanism and then paused, bracing the now unlocked door closed before looking back at us. "Once this is open, you'll want to stay quiet since you'll be inside the walls and there's no telling how the sound will travel. Are you ready?"

I took a deep breath and hoped that whatever we found in the building over our heads wouldn't be anything like the last Krym'parke hideout I'd raided. Buried memories bubbled to the surface of my mind. Children. Locked up within jail cells. Awaiting their fate as meals.

I'd slain their captors and led them free, but while I figured Lyrra could handle that ugliness, I didn't want that experience for Emi. The Nurse was too kind-hearted for her own good. Between that and the danger of the higher-Leveled aliens against her lack of dedicated combat Skills, the Nurse had to stay behind.

I looked at Emi and shook my head. "Stay hidden and close up the passage behind us once we're through. We'll be going out through the front door and causing as much destruction as possible. That should keep the route secret."

"I can help!" Emi protested.

I gestured to the tunnel around us. "Are you willing to risk the resistance's trump card?"

"No, but I still want to do something." The Nurse sighed.

"You have done something. You got us this far. Now let us handle it from here."

"Fine."

Once the Nurse agreed, I looked at Lyrra. The elf nodded and I brought my pistols around, pointing them just over Emi's head. "Go."

The Nurse swung the door open to reveal a narrow stairway like the one we'd used to access the tunnels. I stepped lightly, silent as I climbed the steps.

The stairs ended at a small, square landing, barely large enough for me to stand and face the interior wall. If this access point was anything like the hidden shelves where we'd entered, then there should be a mechanism keeping the door hidden. I dismissed one pistol and gently felt for the latch.

The lever was right where I expected it. I slipped the catch with a slight click and eased the door open, swinging it away from me. Releasing my free hand from the door and summoning the pistol back into it, I stepped through with my weapons raised to find an empty room.

The elegantly furnished room looked more like a museum showroom than I'd expected despite Emi's description earlier. Framed artwork decorated the walls while display stands supported various sculpted works, though the platforms were all pushed back against the walls.

By the time Lyrra stepped out from the hidden passage, I'd finished sweeping through the building with Greater Observation. The Skill revealed a handful of red dots scattered throughout the four-story structure and a single green dot blazed on the top floor. Even though we had climbed stairs to reach the building from the tunnel, the basement level of the structure was only half above ground and three more stories rose above it.

"She's three floors up. Moving to the stairs," I said, keeping my voice low without looking back at the Movana.

"Copy, covering." The elf followed behind as I advanced, her footsteps whispering even more quietly than my own.

I kept my pistols pulled in tight as I rounded the corner, sweeping the next room as I stepped into it. I was pretty sure Greater Observation had picked up all the occupants of the building, but ingrained habits from CQB training still governed my approach.

Lyrra watched my back and covered our rear until we reached the stairs. The door at the top of the flight was only partially closed and I eased it open. I heard voices from a room or two beyond, but I swung around to the next set of stairs after crossing a hallway that led to the front door.

The curving stairway from the ground level climbed quickly and I kept the weight of my steps close to the walls to avoid any creaking stairs. When I reached the second-floor landing, the flooring transitioned to traditional wooden floors. I kept my footsteps near the wall in an attempt to keep silent and avoid any old flooring. Before I could take more than a couple steps, I heard a pair of Krym'parke growling to each other through an open archway that we would have to pass to get to the next flight of stairs. There was no way that we could slip by the two aliens unseen.

I posted up beside the arch and gestured my intentions to my elven companion. She nodded in understanding, and I stepped back to point my weapons at the hostiles through the wall. I took a single step to clear the archway, firing my pistols as the silenced weapons cleared the obstructing wall.

Only one of the two Krym'parke faced the opening and its amber eyes grew wide in surprise an instant before the pistol rounds turned that alien's ugly face into an uglier ruin. The silent shots hammering into its mouth cut short the alien's snarl and prevented any warning it may have been about to give. Purple blood sprayed across the room and spattered the second Krym'parke, who was just starting to turn.

I'd kept moving, stepping out of the way for Lyrra to follow. The Movana stepped into position with the SMG pulled tight to her shoulder and she fired an automatic burst into the back of the second Krym'parke. The rounds tore into the alien's shoulder as it turned, tracing across the arm and punching the last several rounds into its torso.

Grunts of pain, the impact from the shots hitting the aliens, and the mechanical clicks of our guns' firing mechanisms were the only sounds until the spent brass from the cycling projectile weapons tinged off the wood floor. Just like an assassin gunfight in a Hollywood movie. The System bullshittery defied physics since the bullets should have snapped through the sound barrier.

The first alien staggered back several steps from my shots but stayed on its feet. I activated Hinder on both Krym'parke, further slowing their responses to our surprise attack. A rifle appeared in the hands of Lyrra's target, and I knew we had to prevent that weapon from firing if we wanted to remain undetected.

I darted forward and slid beneath the line of my companion's fire, kicking out the armed alien's leg. It fell and the rifle clattered across the floor. I winced at the noise as Lyrra shifted her aim to my initial target while I took on the now prone alien.

My new target attempted to push up to its feet, but a single shot to each elbow took out the joints. The Krym'parke dropped back to the floor with a yowl of pain that was quickly cut off when its face slammed to the ground. The now desperate alien reached out and snagged my foot with a hand that glowed with electric sparks. The stun Skill jolted me but fizzled against my Advanced Class resistances.

Lyrra's target activated a barrier Skill, but it failed in moments when she countered with an increased damage Skill of her own. The pair never recovered after that, and we continued firing until both Krym'parke finally collapsed with their health depleted.

When they stopped moving, I hurried to dump both corpses into Meat Locker while Lyrra reloaded her weapon with a fresh drum magazine. The fight hadn't been loud, but it hadn't been especially quiet either. Between a strangled shout and the sound of bodies hitting the floor, it was only a matter of time until someone checked out the noise. Still, the one-sided fight was an illustration of the gap separating Basic and Advanced Classes—even when there might only have been a handful of Levels' difference overall between Lyrra and the Krym'parke.

Moving to the next stairway, I aimed both of my weapons at the doorway leading out to the main hall of the uppermost floor. There was no door sealing it shut and my greatest fear at this point was a grenade tossed down from above while we ascended the stairs.

Only three dots glowed on the upper floor, two of which were red and neither approached the stairs as we reached the top. The hostiles remained at either end of the hallway but were stationed so that they would both see us the moment we stepped out from the stairs.

I dismissed one pistol long enough to signal their positions to Lyrra with a few quick hand motions. The elf nodded and I readied my weapons once again. She stacked up on the doorway and we launched ourselves out in unison, each facing one of the threats.

My pistols rattled in my hands as I opened fire at my target, despite noting that the armored, pale-skinned figure was definitely not a Krym'parke. The human woman's black hair whipped around in a ponytail that pulled it back from her sharp-featured face as she spun toward me. The move pulled her away from the door that contained the friendly dot of the Countess on my minimap.

The woman's dark eyes narrowed in confusion as her soulless gaze locked onto my face. I grinned in response as my shots slammed into her. She couldn't identify me, not with my disguised face and status, but I recognized her, and a jolt of adrenaline ran through me as I scanned her with Greater Observation.

Madison Hughes (Blood Warden Level 31) (A)
_HP: 748/860_
_MP: 890/920_
Status: Hunger for Flesh, Life Siphon

Taking the moral high ground, especially when Credits were on the line, wasn't usually my thing, but some people just needed killing. The Warden was one such person. Back at the System's initiation, she'd overseen the Pittsburgh jail-turned-Krym'parke larder and base. A base that held imprisoned children while hiding that horrible fact from the street-level cops, who were still trying their best to patrol a city overrun by spawning monsters.

She tried to move out of line of fire, struggling to pull a weapon but getting jerked around by my bullets was doing a number on her.

"It's been a bit, Warden," I greeted her without slowing my attacks in the slightest.

The casual response threw off the Warden's reactions to my assault. Her health plummeted by over a third before she successfully deployed an energy shield to block my attacks. I triggered Expose in response as the translucent crimson barrier popped out to cover the Blood Warden.

The oval-shaped barrier consisted of translucent crimson energy that curved slightly around the Warden at the sides and rippled as my shots pelted it continuously. The woman huddled behind the shield, turning herself sideways to keep her profile masked behind the barrier.

"Who are you?!" Shock and anger filled the woman's surprised response to my greeting.

Expose would drop that shield eventually, but I needed to end this quickly and prevent Hughes from taking advantage of her Krym'parke-inspired Class Skills. Activating Hinder on the Blood Warden, I charged down the hall in a sprint with my silenced pistols still blazing. Just before I reached the woman, I angled to the side and then launched myself into the air. I kicked off the wall before crashing into the top portion of the Warden's shield.

She hadn't been braced for the impact and the top of the barrier tipped back to smack her in the face. I hooked my left arm over the shield, firing down on her head. I wrapped my other arm around the side and shot into her side.

Sometimes, the easiest way through is around.

The Warden staggered under the onslaught, then I heard the crackling snap-hiss of a charged weapon deploying. Hughes swung out with her free arm in a wild overhand blow, an energy baton clenched in her fist. The head of the weapon writhed with sparking currents of electricity, the entire thing sheathed in additional blood-red energy. At a guess, a Class Skill was being used with the baton to increase its effectiveness.

She overextended with the attack, reaching for my head.

With my arm overtop the shield and inside the blow, I batted the haft of the weapon to the side. I was just grateful she didn't hit my arm instead, a simple maneuver she could have done if she wasn't panicking.

The head of the weapon scraped along my shoulder, and I felt a tingle through the protective layers of my armor as the shock baton discharged its current. The glancing hit wasn't enough to cause a muscle spasm or weaken the arm enough to drop my pistol, though I felt a little of my health and blood drain as she struck.

I continued firing.

"How do you have so much ammo?" Hughes screamed in frustration. She attempted to push me back with a shoulder-check against the shield, but I hooked my wrist around the solid barrier and used it as a fulcrum to spin around before slamming her into the wall.

Hughes glared at me, her eyes turning bloodshot before going solid red, as if filling with blood. More angry red lines spread from around her eyes, stretching across her face just beneath her skin. Her muscles swelled suddenly, and she roared as she surged away from the wall.

Now I was the one getting bashed against the wall. The repeated impacts threw off my aim as I was tossed around and few of my shots landed. My armor absorbed most of the damage, but the battering put me on the defensive.

As bad as I was getting it, the wall was taking it worse. If it wasn't System-reinforced, we'd have gone through it by now.

With another angry grunt, Hughes hefted me up before throwing both me and the shield down the corridor. I bounced on my back, skidding across the wooden flooring before kicking my legs up over my head and rolling back to my feet as I came to a stop.

"I'm going to devour your flesh," Hughes growled through teeth that had grown out into pointed fangs. Between the sharp fangs and crimson veins pulsing near the surface of her pale skin, Hughes looked like a vampire in a budget sci-fi movie.

I didn't bother to respond.

Instead, I raised my pistols and opened fire once more as the Blood Warden charged. There wasn't much maneuvering room in the narrow hallway, but I backed away as I attempted to get off as many rounds as possible.

Just before Hughes reached me, the automatic rattling of Lyrra's silenced submachine gun echoed over the Warden's pounding footsteps. The enraged woman staggered at the hits from behind, but she kept coming. Though my elven companion had finished off her opponent and added her firepower to mine, Hughes seemed determined to reach me at any cost.

With my back against the wall at the end of the corridor, I had no space left to retreat. Bracing my heel on the wall, I prepared to push off as I waited for the perfect moment.

Hughes still carried the shock baton, and she hauled back a step before she reached me, swinging the weapon at chest level. I shoved off from the wall, ducking beneath the blow and dropping my pistols as I rammed my shoulder into the Warden's midsection.

I caught sight of Lyrra running down the hall behind the Warden as the air rushed from Hughes' lungs with a whoosh and I wrapped my arms around the woman. With my foot braced against the wall for added leverage, I took the Blood Warden to the floor.

Boards cracked as the back of her skull hit the wooden boards. Then Lyrra stood over us, firing her SMG down into the Warden's face. I could feel the passage of bullets near my neck and body, so close that I swear she clipped me a few times as the body beneath me writhed and jerked. If not for the System, I don't think we would ever have dared this.

Eventually, Hughes went limp.

Lyrra emptied her weapon's magazine into the woman's head for good measure while I untangled myself from the corpse. I scooped up my dropped pistols before dismissing them back into Inventory. There was no way that the noise from that fight didn't alert the rest of the Krym'parke.

"Thanks for the assist, Lyrra. Keep an eye on the stairs while I get the door here open."

"On it, but you better make it fast. They'll be here soon."

I nodded and stood, pulling the Pharyleri lockcracker from my Inventory and turning to the door that Hughes had guarded.

The heavily reinforced door and the System-tech of the lock mechanism were just two of the signs that the building had been upgraded. It also illustrated that the room held something valuable. Or someone.

The device blinked through a range of colors as I held it to the lock. After several long heartbeats, the cascading lights just seemed to repeat the same patterns. I started growing impatient and tried to think of other options. I could blast the reinforced door from its hinges, but that would put Dayena in danger.

Just when I thought I'd have to explore the more explosive options, the lights on the lockcracker all blinked green. A faint click from the door followed, signaling it was now unlocked. Pulling the device from the lock, I hauled the door open and felt only a little anxious at what I might find inside.

Chapter 31

The door opened into a simple room utterly devoid of decoration. The walls lacked any windows and the only natural light descended from a bar-covered skylight in the ceiling. Bare walls and a bare floor, constructed of some dark gray System material both solid and smooth. Off to one side of the cell, an open doorway without any door led to a small bathroom which included a sink, toilet, and shower.

A Truinnar, the room's sole occupant, lay on a bed little larger than a cot, directly opposite the door. Instead of her usual adventurer's armored jumpsuit, the dark elf wore a matching beige set of loose tunic and trousers. Dayena rolled up onto one elbow and she somehow made the motion look easy despite the presence of the shackles still locked around both her wrists. Apparently, the reinforced nature of the room had blocked the sounds of combat in the hall.

The Truinnar cocked her head in confusion as she considered where I stood in the doorway and observed her in turn. "I have not laid eyes on a human since they locked me in here. Who are you?"

With the shackles locking away Dayena's abilities, she couldn't use any of her usual Class Skills to identify me. Not that they would have helped in this case since I was still wearing my disguised persona.

"So, what's a high-class dame like you doing in a dive like this?"

Dayena blinked in surprise and her brow wrinkled. "Hal?"

I grinned. At least she hadn't called me short for a stormtrooper. Triggering my shifting ability, I transformed back into my natural self over the course of a few seconds while also returning my real name to my status with On the Hunt.

By the time I finished, Dayena was standing. "That is some trick."

"It should be, after all the Credits I spent on it."

"You are here to break me out, right?"

I gestured for the dark elf to hold out her cuffs and placed the lockcracker on them when she raised her arms. The lights on the device cycled through a few patterns before flashing green. The shackles unlocked with a snap and I swiped them out of the air as they fell.

Dayena rubbed at her wrists, and if there were tears glistening in her eyes, I wisely refrained from commenting. Instead, I stowed the shackles and the cracking device in my Inventory. A notification for completing a quest pinged for my attention and I breathed a sigh of relief but ignored the update to my Status. This wasn't over yet.

The sudden echo of weapons fire rattled from down the hall and jolted us both into action. Since Lyrra's weapon was silenced, the gunshots could only be the remaining Krym'parke from throughout the building. Part of me was surprised things had stayed quiet as long as they had.

I summoned a bundle of spare gear from my Inventory and tossed it over to the dark elf. I hadn't known whether Dayena's captors would pilfer her Inventory, so I'd brought the basics along just in case–a black armored jumpsuit wrapped around a pair of combat boots and held together by the belt that went with a sheathed pair of short swords.

"You good?" I asked, already in motion toward the hall.

"Is Lyrra with you?" Dayena responded, and I noticed she hadn't answered my question. There would be time later to deal with the aftermath of her captivity, but for now we needed to move.

"Of course."

The Truinnar's Diplomatic Contacts ability touched my mind, and I grinned as I felt Lyrra join in a moment later, the Class Skill linking us together as a party once more.

"Lyrra, status report?" I asked as I drew Last Word in my left hand.

The Movana responded without missing a beat. *"Two Krym'parke below us, a Fleshtearer and a Red Knight."*

I reached around Lyrra and flicked a plasma grenade around the wall with my right hand, putting a spin on the deadly little sphere as I released it to fly down the stairway. The intentional bouncing off the wall prevented the aliens below from just catching the explosive and throwing it back up.

An alien roar of surprise echoed from the floor below before it was cut off with the grenade's detonation. The gunfire chewing up the wall around the doorway also ceased as a wash of heat reached us, crisping the small hairs of my face. Moments later, I caught the smell of burning wood and concrete.

I jerked my head back toward Dayena as I stepped around Lyrra. *"Let me take the lead. Get Dayena into the armor in case things get ugly."*

"On it," Lyrra replied, but I was already rounding the corner and rushing down the stairs.

The floor and walls at the bottom of the steps burned with blue plasma flames. I didn't see either of the Krym'parke that Lyrra warned me about, but the red dots on my minimap showed them split to either side.

Summoning my armor's matching helmet from Inventory as I descended into the burning portion of the passage, I jammed it over my head. A flicker of the fire's intense heat seared the exposed skin of my neck before the armor sealed in place.

I drew Ace with my right hand in the midst of the inferno, then spread my pistols to either side to point at where Greater Observation revealed my targets standing on the level below. My foot hit the landing at the base of the stairs and I opened fire, surrounded by the flames climbing the walls of the stairwell.

Return attacks tore through the swirling wisps of blue plasma and slammed into me from both sides as the Krym'parke caught me in a crossfire. The grenade's explosion had forced the two aliens back from the stairwell, but I caught sight of the pair as I emerged from the flames.

The Red Knight wore crimson plate armor and hip-fired a submachine gun at me, a weapon strikingly similar to the one Lyrra carried. The Fleshtearer fired a less traditional projectile weapon, one that fired fist-sized disks of serrated metal that looked like miniature saw blades. Their armor was only a little singed and they lacked any significant damage from the explosion.

The Knight took a ponderous step forward and I guessed that he was the heavier and slower of the two. Activating Hinder, I charged the slow Krym'parke. Though the alien wore a helmet that hid his ugly face, I still heard its snarl of frustration as I ducked beneath the muzzle of its submachine gun and pivoted around the alien's back.

From point-blank range, I fired in between the armor plates and into the softer materials of the joints. I shifted through firing up under the armpit, into the back of the knees, and on either side of the neck—all while keeping the bulk of the Krym'parke between myself and the second alien.

In response to my attacks, the Knight's armor glowed with crimson energy and the damage began to seal. The bullet holes shrank as lethargic sensation settled over me and drained my health. The longer this fight wore on, the stronger the alien would become as I weakened. It also increased the chances of Rhegnah and the remaining Krym'parke returning. I needed to end this and get Dayena out of here.

I holstered my pistols to free my hands and kicked the back of the Knight's knee, knocking the alien off balance. With both hands, I yanked down hard on the back of the torso plate as the alien's leg gave out. Before the alien hit the ground, I slipped an armed grenade underneath the falling Krym'parke and leapt clear.

Felling the Knight left me exposed to fire from the second Krym'parke. Whining ricochets and the scraping of metal on metal echoed sharply through the landing as the sawblades from the Fleshtearer's weapon hit my armor. Some shots deflected off while others carved ruts or dug in to embed themselves in the plates. Each of the attacks seemed to dig in further than they should, a light glow around the tearing blades speaking of a Class Skill in use. The attack that got through the armor — little that it was — didn't stop bleeding, even when my System healing should have taken care of it.

Bleed effect from a Class Skill, I'd bet.

I closed with the Krym'parke, weathering the storm of whirling blades. A loud whump from behind indicated my deposited grenade's explosion beneath the Knight and the red dot on my minimap winked out. The alien in front of me snarled at his companion's demise, dropping the wide-barreled projectile weapon and producing a melee weapon in its place.

At first glance, the outline of the weapon appeared something like a longer version of a cricket bat. Then reflected light from the plasma flames behind me glinted off rectangular metallic teeth set around the edges of the flat club.

While I was trying to remember the name of the ancient obsidian-toothed Aztec weapon that this sci-fi version resembled, the Krym'parke swung, and I dodged the attack that narrowly missed tearing through my stomach.

The alien held the blade upright as I recovered. He stabbed a clawed finger down on an activation switch on the hilt and the weapon roared as a motor engaged. The rectangular teeth disappeared in a blur as they rotated around the weapon.

The Krym'parke wielded a damned chainsaw sword, not a macuahuitl.

I took another step back to ensure I stood beyond the reach of the weapon and raised my right arm, triggering the flame projector. Fire sprayed out toward the Krym'parke and now the alien was dodging away from me.

More importantly, the flames blinded the alien momentarily and I used the cover to fire the grapple from my left vambrace. The line shot out and snagged the hilt of the chainsword trapping the Krym'parke's hand in place as I yanked on the wire.

The alien stumbled, suddenly going from dodging backward to being pulled forward. I slipped to the side and whipped the slack in the grapple line around one leg as I stepped beside the Fleshtearer. With his hand bound to the weapon and the line now wrapped around his leg, the alien could no longer swing so freely.

Before he could use the whirring blades to slice the cable, I swung my arm over his head and wrapped the line taut around his neck. Then I rammed my shoulder into the alien's back before dropping low and using the line as leverage to hip-toss the alien.

The Fleshtearer cried out in pain and a shower of blood splashed out as I flipped the alien over my back before slamming him into the floor. The chainsaw weapon revved as it bounced on the floor before biting into the calf of the alien's remaining leg and eliciting another scream. The other leg had been sliced through just above the knee by the alien's own flailing weapon when I'd flung the Krym'parke through the air. The severed limb lay several feet away in a slowly expanding puddle of purple blood.

The wounded alien attempted to push himself upright and lunged off balance to swipe the whirring weapon at my ankles. I easily dodged the weak strike as the Krym'parke fell onto his back and then I darted forward, smashing my boot down onto the alien's hand. Bones crunched beneath my foot, but, more importantly, I'd pinned down the dangerous flailing chain weapon. The grapple's cabling was still wrapped around the hilt and bound the Fleshtearer's hand to the weapon, so I needed to do more than just break his bones.

Or I could just finish him.

I pulled out Ace and fired down into the Krym'parke's face until nothing but a gory mess of ragged flesh and shattered bones remained to leak purple blood across the floor around his body.

Rather than detach the line for my grapple, I pried the alien's lifeless fingers from the hilt of the chainsword and deactivated the motor. The teeth stopped their whirring, and I stowed the weapon in my Inventory before untangling the cable from the corpse. As I looted the aliens and tossed their corpses into Meat Locker, twin thuds sounded from the landing as Lyrra and Dayena jumped down the stairs through the flames of plasma fire.

I nodded to the elves and drew my pistols before leading the way to the next flight of stairs. Only two red dots remained inside the building, and both seemed intent on holding their position at the front door. That was fine with me since we'd be sure to deal with them on our way out.

I pointed my pistols down the stairway as we descended just in case my detection Skill missed out any stealthy Krym'parke who remained in the building and made the poor decision to face us head on. We encountered no one else and quickly reached the bottom of the steps.

Instead of turning down the hallway toward the front door, I flung myself straight across the hall and rolled into one of the well-decorated sitting rooms opposite the stairs. A storm of energy beams and a spelled bolt of lightning filled the hall. Only a fraction of the lighting jolted through me, catching my trailing leg before the remainder of the spell tore into the side of the doorway as I passed out of the caster's line of sight.

"A Flesheater Tactician and a Blazing Vanguard are at the front door and on their guard," I reported over party chat. Damn, I'd missed this ability, I thought while climbing back to my feet and preparing to return fire down the hall.

"I have them," Dayena responded, her voice cold. I almost winced at the promise of pain in her tone, but I figured the Krym'parke would be the most deserving targets the dark elf would find to vent the anger over her captivity.

A single note sounded through the building, the opening chord of a haunting melody that sent a chill down my spine. The Countess had managed to keep her relic instrument hidden from her captors this entire time. I shouldn't have been surprised with the luitsalin's ability to stay hidden and avoid anyone thinking about it. The semi-sentient relic was so subtle that I hadn't even noticed it when I'd broken Dayena out of her cell.

Across the hall, a shadow flickered from the stairwell, and I'd have missed it completely if I hadn't been watching. The screaming from the vicinity of the front door started a few moments later and signaled that the Krym'parke were more than a little distracted. I rushed out of the sitting room and charged down the hall with weapons ready as Lyrra bolted from the stairwell to join me.

It was abundantly clear by the time we reached the hallway that neither of us were necessary for dealing with the final pair of guards.

Flashes of light glinted off the lone short sword as Dayena danced in a graceful blur of motion around the only Krym'parke still standing. Purple alien blood sprayed from each delicate slice that cut into the joints between the Vanguard's ivory armor. His wrists, knees, and elbows leaked purple over the white plates and the alien's rifle lay discarded on the floor several feet away.

Meanwhile, the Flesheater Tactician slumped on his knees, weakly coughing up a fountain of purple blood that poured from his mouth. The hilt of Dayena's other short sword stuck up from the alien's collarbone, the blade jammed vertically down into his torso.

Jahgg'd Ot'lyke, the first Krym'parke that I'd met face to face when I'd infiltrated the Pittsburgh jail turned alien slaughterhouse. I raised my pistol to point at the Flesheater Tactician instinctively, but the blank look in the alien's eyes proved my caution unnecessary.

With an excessive pirouette, Dayena's blade flashed out and through the neck of the Vanguard. The severed head seemed to jump from the alien's shoulders. It arced through the air before splattering to the floor. The rest of his beheaded body collapsed as the Tactician toppled forward, also dead.

Lyrra shot me a glance as we both stood watching the finale of the macabre performance, but I just shrugged. Anything I could have said at that moment would just be trite or insensitive to Dayena's ordeal over the past weeks.

Instead, I stepped over to the fallen Tactician and pulled the sword free of the alien's torso with a squelch. A quick cast of Cleanse removed the gore from the weapon, then I grabbed hold of the hilt before flipping the weapon around and extending the grip to Dayena. The dark elf cleaned the blade still in her hand and sheathed it before forcing a thin smile and accepting the short sword from me.

I nodded back. "Now's not the time, but I'm here if you ever need to talk."

The dark elf's head jerked in acknowledgment before she started looting the dead. Then she looked pointedly at me, a clear signal to toss the corpses into Meat Locker. It seemed even her stint in captivity hadn't dulled her instinctive delegation, but I didn't mind my return to sherpa duty. Returning to the roles we'd held as a team would be good for Dayena.

Once the bodies were stashed away, I looked back at the Truinnar. *"Let's get you out of here."*

"I am more than ready to depart. The hospitality of this establishment is severely lacking."

Still smiling, I raised an eyebrow at the dark elf. The sarcasm was a positive sign: she felt able to let loose a little.

In preparation for leaving the building, Lyrra swapped out the silenced SMG for her sniper rifle. *"You're right, the service is terrible here. They didn't even offer us hot coffee or kipatchya."*

I snorted. Secret prisons and black sites weren't known for their amenities before the System. I doubted that Galactic powers left chocolates on the pillows for those "guests" deemed threatening enough to imprison.

"I'm just happy we're all walking away. Dayena, still have your bike in your Inventory?"

The Truinnar shook her head and pointed to an interior door off the foyer. *"Restricting my Skills and keeping me from accessing Inventory was not enough for them. They were confident that I could not escape the bindings on my own, but still took everything. Most of my equipment should be stored here though."*

Fortunately, most of her gear was collecting dust in the closet near the entrance, including her hovering bike that was folded into a space-reducing storage mode. The dark elf scooped the weapons and armor into her Inventory before giving her bike an affectionate pat.

I waited until the bike also disappeared into Dayena's storage. *"When we hit the street, you get on your bike. Lyrra, get the door and then mount up as soon as Dayena has the transport ready. I'll lead and cover you both."*

The elves nodded in agreement, and I posted up beside the door as they moved into position. The shielding that prevented Skills and technology from seeing into the building also prevented me from scanning the street outside with Greater Observation, so we couldn't know what we might be walking into.

While the entry door was reinforced by the System, it still used an old-school deadbolt and knob instead of a fancy biometric or magical lock. That made it trivial for us to leave.

Lyrra flipped the deadbolt and turned the knob, pulling the door open in a smooth motion that filled the foyer with a blast of cold Denver air.

Time to go.

Chapter 32

When I stepped outside, I discovered that Murphy always got his due.

A half dozen figures climbing the front steps looked up in surprise as I emerged unexpectedly from the door. A familiar suit of white power armor at the forefront of the group halted mid-stride, the onyx-skinned leader visible with the suit's helmet retracted. Rhegnah's eyes bulged in shock as I opened fire and launched myself off the porch.

I crashed into the dark elf feet first, delivering a drop kick that sent the Truinnar tumbling through the midst of the Krym'parke behind him. The party toppled like bowling pins with half the aliens falling over the railings to either side as he crashed down the stairs. The other two landed at the bottom of the steps in a tangled pile with Rhegnah and Creynora—she had been at the rear of the group. Despite the momentum of the dropkick, I still landed hard onto the stonework of the front porch before bounding back to my feet.

By the time I regained my feet, Dayena was already dropping onto one of the Krym'parke who had fallen into the narrow, fenced-in, flower beds beside the steps, and she plunged both short swords into the alien's chest. Lyrra stepped up to the side of the porch and fired her heavy rifle down at the Krym'parke in the other flower bed, activating multiple Skills to end that enemy before the alien could stand. Basic Classes, even high-Leveled ones, couldn't stand up to stacked abilities from an Advanced Class.

With my companions engaging the separated Krym'parke to either side, the task of keeping the remaining four enemies occupied fell to me. For the moment, they were reeling after having been caught by surprise and we had to capitalize on the advantage. If we couldn't even out the numbers fast enough, we'd have no chance against the group of Advanced Classers.

My handcannons thundered as I poured my attacks into the tangled pile of Galactics at the base of the steps. I activated Hinder on Rhegnah and started throwing indiscriminate Frostbolts into the mass. Every time any of them stuck out a hand or leg to climb free, I targeted the limb with a barrage of pistol fire. The targeted limb would rapidly jerk away from the shots, throwing the owner off balance and keeping the pile tied up.

The stacks of Expose and Rend on all four Galactics were ticking up, even if I wasn't inflicting significant damage to any single individual. My shots alone wouldn't keep the four pinned for long and I descended the stairs in preparation for the moment when things would inevitably turn for the worse.

The two red dots to either side of the stairs winked out on my minimap, and I felt a surge of optimism that my concerns weren't justified. Lyrra's dot moved laterally up the street, the sniper looking to open up the range to attack, while Dayena's faded as she prepared for a sneak attack.

The fight swung back the other way in an instant as the tangled pile of bodies erupted.

The pair of Krym'parke were flung violently through the air, arcing toward the sidewalk and away from the rising form of Rhegnah's armor. Bones cracked audibly and Creynora whined in pain from the bottom of the pile as the white suit pushed off her to leap upward. From the speed that the Truinnar steadied himself in the air, Rhegnah had activated a Skill that boosted strength and granted flight to his armor.

The Deputy Adjudicator hovered in the air for a moment before a massive two-handed mace appeared in his hands. The spiked cylindrical head of the weapon was larger than a propane tank used for backyard grilling and it started glowing. Then the dark elf swung it overhead, an instant before dropping straight for me.

I dove between the descending Truinnar's legs, snagging the prone form of Creynora and yanking her out of the blast zone as the mace slammed down before the Navarre's front steps. Shards of concrete and stone sprayed out like the detonation of a claymore mine and devastated the building's front porch.

Weathering the storm of debris, I released Creynora only a moment after pulling her clear and rolled into the middle of the street. I turned back toward Rhegnah and shuffled sideways, hoping it would appear that the blast itself had pushed her without any involvement from me. I wasn't sure where things stood between us, but she'd spared my life and Rhegnah wasn't concerned with hurting his own allies if they were in his way.

That was clearly evidenced by the six-foot section of the sidewalk that was just gone, obliterated along with the front stairs. One of the columns supporting the front porch crumbled and the awning sagged. The two Krym'parke had been caught up in the edges of the attack and lay just beyond the debris-filled crater of dirt, but I didn't have time to do more than a glance at them as Rhegnah spun. The mace whistled as it swiped through the air and I jumped backward, dodging farther out into the street for maneuvering room.

I kept up my handcannon fire on the heavily armored juggernaut and swept Greater Observation over the dark elf as he chased after me.

Rhegnah Baluisa, Fist of Judgement, Deputy Adjudicator (Dominator Level 38) (A)

HP: 1905/2100

MP: 1829/2310

Status: Accelerated Motivators, Armor Boost, Power Strike, Regenerative Injector

Most of the Truinnar's status enhancers and bonus attributes appeared linked to his fully powered armor. I'd have to render the suit inoperable in order to strip away those benefits.

Rhegnah swung the mace at chest level, and I hopped away, still firing a storm of projectiles from both pistols. The dark elf used the momentum from the missed strike to swing the weapon overhead before bringing it down toward me. The mace streaked by in a rush of wind as I stepped to the side. The impact blasted a hole in the street.

Any clean hit would likely end the fight on the spot, and I wanted to avoid that at all costs. Instead of lingering in range for risky shots, I took extra care to dodge further than normal, just in case Rhegnah still held any tricks up his power-armored sleeves.

His overhead strikes were the easiest to avoid since I just had to not be standing where the mace dropped. I danced away from the steadily raining attacks as those missed blows cratered the street, transforming the asphalt into more and more perilous terrain.

Horizontal sweeping strikes proved more challenging as they covered more range, but the dark elf still hadn't deployed his helmet and his snarls revealed the Truinnar's mounting frustration.

Expose climbed with every shot of mine that landed, but few hits managed to find the same spot twice in a row and it would take forever for me to punch through his armor at this rate. Rhegnah pursued doggedly on my heels, the menacing mace nearly catching me out multiple times, but I managed to avoid the sweeping blows.

Just when I started feeling optimistic about eventually wearing down the Deputy Adjudicator, the bulky protrusions on the shoulders of the dark elf's armor suddenly opened up. The newly revealed holes could only be for some kind of projectile weapon, which proved true when the holes belched smoke an instant after they opened and a swarm of jumbo crayon-sized micro-missiles fired out. The missiles spiraled as they homed in on me and I sprinted along the street in a vain effort to dodge the attacks.

The missiles slammed into me like a hailstorm, pelting into my armor and covering me in rippling explosions that sent me flying into an abandoned SUV alongside the street. The car crumpled around me as the last of the barrage drilled into my back. My armor deflected the worst of the damage, but my health dropped by a significant chunk.

The heads-up display in my helmet showed blinking red panels all across my backside. I pried myself free of the twisted wreckage, knowing I couldn't take another barrage like that to those sections again. Staggering away from the ruined car, I raised my pistols and fired at my foe through the surrounding cloud of smoke from the missile detonations.

A roar filled the street as Rhegnah ignited thrusters built into power armor and he flashed toward me in a sudden burst of explosive motion. My high Perception and Agility saved me, providing the coordination to avoid the incoming strike as I dropped onto my back. The mace passed less than an inch in front of my face and clipped my right hand as I failed to pull it completely out of the way fast enough.

Bones in my hand shattered with a crunch and Ace went flying into the distance, but the savage glee on the dark elf's face morphed into fury as he rocketed past me without landing a significant hit.

As Rhegnah slowed himself enough to turn into a three-point stance, skidding to a halt almost a dozen yards beyond, I jumped to my feet and opened fire once again, while casting a heal on my injured hand. Pure rage lit the dark elf's eyes when he turned around, gritting his teeth as he fixated on me.

A loud boom echoed through the street and the shot slammed into the missile launcher on his left shoulder. The weapon shattered into sparking wreckage that scattered across the street as Rhegnah staggered to one knee from the hit. His two-handed mace fumbled from his hands and clattered as it slid across the asphalt.

The supercharged rifle attack brought everything to a standstill, and I held my fire for a moment as the interruption broke the dark elf from his single-minded focus on me. In the pause, Rhegnah finally noticed that the rest of his allies were down. Of course, it had taken one of Lyrra's sniper rounds to wake him up to that fact.

The Movana knelt on top of an awning from the next building over with her rifle pointed at Rhegnah, while Dayena stood in the street behind me and pressed one of her blades against Creynora's throat. All of the Krym'parke who had arrived with the two Truinnar were already dead, finished off by my companions while I'd kept the Deputy Adjudicator occupied. The numbers now favored us, three to two—and one of the two was already down with grievous injuries caused by her sole remaining ally.

The mindless fury seemed to fade from Rhegnah's eyes as the Deputy Adjudicator evaluated the precariousness of his situation. His gaze flicked from me to Dayena before glancing up at Lyrra's elevated position. Then his eyes focused on Creynora, laying on her back at the mercy of her cousin, and his mouth twisted into a sneer.

That disgusted expression remained in place as the dark elf suddenly spun and took off in a sprint. I opened fire, but the sound of my handcannons was instantly drowned out by the roar of Lyrra's rifle. Her shot staggered the fleeing Truinnar, though it failed to drop him.

He recovered, and thrusters ignited from the rear of the torso and calf armor. Rhegnah jerked slightly as flames streamed from the jets. When he came down, the boots of his power armor seemed to float a couple inches above the ground as if skating on air. He hunched over and zigzagged from side to side. The evasive motions allowed Rhegnah to dodge Lyrra's next shot as he accelerated south.

I summoned my bike from Inventory. Mounting the vehicle, I focused on Rhegnah as the dark elf turned left onto 17th Street and headed toward Broadway. Greater Observation locked onto the Truinnar just before he disappeared around the corner. As long as I stayed close enough to keep him in range, I'd be able to follow.

Looking up at Lyrra, I pointed to Dayena. *"Get her out of here. I'm not letting him get away again."*

When I looked back at my dark elf companion, she locked eyes with me. For a moment, her expression appeared more haunted than it had when I'd rescued her initially. Then her face turned serious, and she nodded solemnly.

I knew then.

With the System logging every word spoken out loud, she couldn't say what she wanted. She couldn't even ask. It was something only I could do to give her a chance at freedom. I nodded back.

Squeezing the throttle and hunching forward over the handlebars, I shot off down the street. I couldn't remember the last time I'd ridden a bike while wearing a helmet, though it had to be back before my injuries. Injuries that the System had erased.

Now my helmet's heads-up display provided useful visual readouts of the bike's speed and direction. The Neural Link embedded in the back of my skull connected me with the armor and the bike, making both seem like extensions of my body rather than inanimate objects.

A gold circle surrounded Rhegnah's red dot on my minimap. The Truinnar was nearly a block ahead by the time I followed onto 17th. I cut the throttle and leaned to the inside of the turn as I took the corner, accelerating again when I emerged.

As much as I wanted to catch up and finish off Rhegnah, a part of me wondered where he intended to run with his hideout exposed. If all he intended was an escape to Sect territory, I had plenty of time to run him down.

The Truinnar armor in travel mode lacked the acceleration of a dedicated vehicle like my bike and I gradually gained on the fleeing elf. I eased off the throttle when I closed to half a block after Rhegnah turned south on Broadway.

We zipped across Colfax, and I saw an opportunity. I cut left, shooting diagonally across the park. Turning straight south onto Lincoln Street, I drew even with the elf, who remained a block to my west as we raced over East 14th. After another block south, I felt a chill as the dot on my minimap started turning toward me.

Maybe it was karma. Maybe it was fate. Whatever the case, we'd returned to almost exactly the spot where Rhegnah had ambushed and captured Dayena almost two months ago. Where I'd been left for dead.

I braked hard, suddenly stopping in the middle of the intersection of Lincoln and East 13th. There I swung around, my left hand resting on the grip of Last Word as I refreshed Ice Armor.

Though I missed Ace's presence on my right hip, it didn't deter me as I waited for my prey.

Chapter 33

Rhegnah rounded the corner and I smiled coldly at the way the dark elf's eyes grew wide when he saw me sitting casually on my bike, waiting for him in the middle of the street.

The Truinnar skidded to a halt as he disengaged his thrusters, his power armor worse for wear and health notably lower after our previous exchange of blows. For a lengthy moment, silence stretched out over the city block between us.

Then his amber eyes narrowed. "Will you give me the road? I have business elsewhere and I can pay you more Credits than your little mercenary mind can comprehend. Just step aside."

I chuckled darkly at the Truinnar's insinuation. He thought I was just another human mercenary. Sure, I could be bought. Every man has his price, but there weren't enough Credits in the Galactic Bank for this elven asshole to just buy me off after all the spilled blood that lay between us. "No."

"What are your intentions then?"

"I mean to kill you and leave your bloody corpse lying on this street."

The dark elf sneered. "I call that bold talk for a dead man. You are nothing but a Basic Class hired hack."

The spoiled Truinnar might have scraped his way to the upper range of Advanced Class Levels but, even after multiple combat encounters, he still hadn't figured out that I was punching well above the Basic weight class.

I grinned at the dark elf's overconfidence, but it was time to end our little conflict. "Fill your hands, you sonofabitch."

My words echoed through the street as I drew Last Word in my left hand and summoned my hybrid rifle into my right. Pushing the command through my Neural Link, I accelerated Outrider's throttle to the max while switching on all of my active Skills.

My pistol spat fire and rounds sparked off the armor plates protecting my foe. The smaller projectiles stacked instances of Expose on the Deputy Adjudicator's chestpiece. I held the Banshee on target as the weapon spooled up and the high-pitched whine of the rifle pierced through the staccato roaring of my pistol. The cacophony of attacks reverberated through the urban canyons of the war-torn city around us, shattering its rare moment of silence.

Rheghan snarled and the remaining micromissile launcher on the dark elf's shoulder belched smoke as it fired a volley. The rockets streaked upward and trailed fire across the sky before arching back down in a deadly hailstorm of explosives. A gatling cannon appeared in the elf's hands and the barrels spun up before spitting out a flurry of projectiles.

Amidst the storm of fire and titanium penetrators, I huddled low over the handlebars and my bike bore the brunt of the damage. The detonations rattled me enough that several of my pistol shots missed, but I kept my rifle on target and the cerulean energy lanced out, shooting an armor-piercing round at hypervelocity. The projectile hit the upper side of Rhegnah's torso and tore through the chestplate of the power armor, weakened after our last encounter. The elf's health dropped by a significant chunk, and he spun from the force of the shot.

The hit pushed the cannon out and rounds tore through the street before ripping into the side of a nearby building. With the heavy weapon no longer punishing my advance, my bike streaked across the distance between us before the Truinnar regained his footing.

Rhegnar recovered from the attack and turned back, looking up as I jumped clear of the bike. The shock and surprise on his face when the bike plowed into him at full speed would be a memory to be cherished.

In midair, I dismissed my rifle back into Inventory before I rolled to take the landing on my shoulder and skidded across the ground with my remaining pistol clutched to my chest. I'd have to track down Ace after the fighting ended, but I wasn't going to lose Last Word if I could help it. The broken and ravaged backplate of my armor provided little protection in the high-speed skid, the friction further shredding the back of my suit as I scraped across the asphalt. My health ticked down, but the road rash was a minor injury compared with the potential fusillade of attacks the Truinnar's power armor could pump out.

Sacrificing my bike was a big hit to my mobility, but looking at the smoldering wreckage in the middle of the street it seemed my reckless tactic had proved effective. The gatling cannon lay discarded at the initial collision point, and the momentum of impact had dragged the Truinnar over a hundred feet beyond.

I cast Ice Armor on myself again as I crawled to my feet and felt the soothing chill seal over the oozing warmth of the friction burn on my back. I staggered almost drunkenly for a few steps before speeding up. I raised the weapon and kept it focused on the wreckage as I approached.

The bike heaved upward just before I reached it, revealing that the front end of the Outrider had twisted almost ninety degrees from the collision and the forward anti-grav housing had entirely crumpled into ruin. Rhegnah's damaged elven power armor whined from the effort of lifting the bike off it. The suit gave a dangerous crack and the front panels of the armor popped open, ejecting the occupant before the armor collapsed again beneath the mangled frame of the bike.

Rhegnah's bloody and battered form tumbled across the ground, and I opened fire without giving him a chance to find his feet. I caught sight of the rose-and-fanged-skull emblem of the Baluisa House on the dark elf's shoulder as the shots tore into the pale gray undersuit with the yellow trim in the colors of his house. The elf had survived an anti-vehicle rocket to the chest, I wasn't going to allow him any opportunity to repeat that exploit.

My free hand flung a Frostbolt and I activated Hinder at the same time. The shard of ice caught the elf and speared through the meat of his thigh as he sprang to his feet in a smooth motion. Despite his injuries and the projectile rounds that continued tearing into Rhegnah's body, the elf only grunted as he managed to land upright with a natural grace that reminded me of his cousin.

The Deputy Adjudicator launched himself at me as another two-handed maul appeared. Air whooshed past as the elf's first swing missed caving in my chest by a hair's breadth. The weapon swung in a devastating circle, and I jumped away to get further out of reach as Rhegnah advanced.

In midair, there was nothing I could do when a wall of energy sprang up from glowing runes that appeared around me. My face and shoulder smacked into the barrier, and I toppled backward, throwing myself under another of Rhegnah's attacks.

With my head ringing from the impact, I flung another Frostbolt from my free hand into the whirling chest of the Truinnar before I summoned a spare projectile pistol. Trapped together inside an energy ring no more than five feet wide, I popped back to my feet and both my weapons belched fire at close range into the elf.

I recalled the first fight between the Deputy Adjudicator and my employer, so I was ready when the elf activated his Haste Skill in an attempt to catch me off guard. As the Truinnar blurred with increased speed, I cast Howling Blast directly into the elf's snarling face.

A cone of frozen wind blasted out in front of me and stopped the forward momentum of the charging elf, but it wasn't enough to stop the maul from lashing out. The weapon caught me solidly in the chest, crushing through my armor and driving the breath from my lungs as I was flung into the barrier. My ribs cracked at the impact, and I struggled to breathe, but I managed to land on my feet. Rhegnah managed to remain standing, his raw strength overcoming the worst of the spell's knockback effect as the rush of wind faded.

The dark elf grinned, his shining white teeth glimmering with menace from his onyx-skinned face. "Is that the best you can do?"

I smiled in response, coughing blood from the broken ribs that punctured my lungs. The spell had performed its purpose and bought me time. The barrier ring that trapped me faded away, its runes winking out, and I cast Whiteout without answering my opponent.

A chilled bank of fog enveloped us, dropping the visibility to nothing as the temperature within the frozen cloud plummeted. Shards of ice swirled through the mist chipping away slivers of Rhegnah's health. He let out a surprised breath and I quietly stepped away from where I'd cast the spell.

Though I no longer could see the Truinnar, Greater Observation still pinpointed Rhegnah's location.

"Coward. Fight me!"

I wasn't dumb enough to speak out loud before I triggered two shots into the elf's back. Instead, I continued circling and doubling back on myself as I fired at random intervals to throw off any predictions of where I hid within the fog.

As Rhegnah's massive health pool kept slipping lower from my unseen hit-and-run attacks, the elf's growling betrayed his growing frustration. Finally, he roared into the frigid mist. "Domain!"

I felt suddenly weighed down, as if wearing a full combat load with ankle weights while swimming underwater in a mud-filled pool. The shouted ability affected the area and even the spell-formed fog slowly dropped from the air as if too heavy to float.

Without the concealment of the fog hiding me, Rhegnah was on me in two strides. The hammer dropped onto my left shoulder and shattered the vambrace, along with my collarbone. My arm went numb and Last Word fumbled from nerveless fingers.

Rhegnah hauled back on the maul for another swing, and I launched myself forward. Slowed by the shout, I'd never dodge out of range in time, so the only option was to get in close. I flung my damaged arm out to wrap around the elf's waist and caught it with my good hand as I drove my body into the Truinnar.

The strength-based melee Classer might have had me beat in raw attribute points, but my lower center of gravity still allowed me to bring down the elf with a tackle that would have made my old high school football coach proud—though the knife I summoned into my hand would have sent Coach Morrison recoiling in horror.

The hilt of the blade hit the ground first and our combined mass drove the blade deep into Rhegnah's back. A gasp of air, little more than a faint whine, slipped out from the Truinnar's lips as my body slammed down on top of him. The hit sent a jolt of pain spiking through the numbness that filled my shoulder, and I winced as the grinding sensation of broken bone on bone as feeling began returning to the limb. I gritted my teeth against the pain radiating from my left shoulder, tugging my good arm free. I kept the knife firmly clutched in my hand as I pulled it out from the elf's back and I stabbed it immediately back into his side.

Blood poured out from the gaping wound, coating my hand. It was far from the elf's only injury and Rhegnah bled from multiple wounds. The afflictions from my Class Skills like Rend and Expose, along with the effects from spells like Frostbolt, were taking their toll on him.

Rhegnah bucked his hips and attempted to wrap his legs around my torso, but the Marines had drilled ground fighting techniques into me years ago and muscle memory enabled me to prevent him from assuming the guard position. It helped that his Haste had worn off while I'd bought time with Whiteout and he was slower now, though my injured arm was only about half functional.

Rhegnah took advantage of my weakness and punched upward. His first strike glanced off the side of my nose and bruised my cheek. The second hit full force, landing on the socket of my right eye. My head rocked back, exploding in pain, and my vision on that side went dark as blood flowed down over my eye from a cut on my brow.

In response, I clenched my tingling left hand into a fist and smashed it down into the dark elf's face. The crunch of his nose crumpling beneath my knuckles brought a satisfied smile to my face as I pummeled the Truinnar with fist and blade.

My ground-and-pound session ended as the lithe elf twisted beneath me and managed to plant a foot on my chest. He drove his boot upward and I nearly blacked out as the kick drove broken ribs deeper into my lungs. Fighting the pain, I could only let the motion push me back onto my feet. My moment of weakness afforded Rhegnah the opportunity to roll himself away before also standing.

Battered and bloody, the pair of us faced off in the center of the street. Both of our health pools showed barely a third remaining. We both breathed heavily from the exertion of our fight. Neither of us would back down at this point. Barring outside intervention, only one of us would walk away and we both knew it.

Another massive mace appeared in the dark elf's grasp. This one had a solid metal shaft about five feet long, with a head consisting of evenly spaced flanges that flared out wickedly around a cylindrical mass. I summoned two more projectile pistols from my Inventory.

Rhegnah lurched into motion, the head of his mace glowing with another Skill. The weapon shot forward, faster and farther than it physically should have been capable, and I twisted to avoid the attack. The mace caught the side of my hip and spun me around with a bruising impact. I managed to keep my footing as I darted away from the Truinnar with pistols raised and spitting fire.

I cast another Howling Blast and Rhegnah again resisted the knockback, but it bought me the space to maneuver away from the Skill-enabled mace. A Frostbolt joined the stream of projectiles pelting my foe and I kept the added effects of Rend and Expose activated despite their continued drain on my Mana. If I wanted to have enough Mana left for my big finishers, I'd have to cut them soon, but I needed to do a little more damage first.

The Truinnar chased after me as we danced up and down the empty street. He landed a couple glancing blows but my health only trickled lower while my relentless attacks reduced the dark elf to critical.

As I evaded another attack, I spotted Last Word laying on the edge of the street. My dropped pistol sat dangerously close to a storm drain built into the curbside. It took a frustrating minute of working around

Rhegnah's sweeping strikes to position myself with enough space where I could safely retrieve the fallen weapon.

I dismissed the projectile pistols I'd been using as I dove toward the curbside. Scooping Last Word up with both hands, I activated Apprehend on the pursuing Truinnar. The Mana shackles clamped into place around Rhegnah's torso, holding the dark elf in place and trapping the maul at waist height. With the dark elf's chest completely unobstructed, I engaged Kill Shot as I squeezed the trigger of Last Word.

Time seemed to slow as a gout of fire blossomed from the barrel of my weapon and a pitch-black round emerged in place of the standard projectile. The empowered round immediately absorbed the flames into itself and then time resumed as the shot streaked instantly across the space between the Truinnar and me with a peel of thunder that sounded like the firing of an artillery cannon.

The round punched through the upper right side of the dark elf's chest and a look of shock flashed onto Rhegnah's face. The dark elf's torso spasmed and then blood trickled out from his mouth as he coughed. The Truinnar sagged within the conjured shackles of Apprehend, and the maul fell from his limp hands.

A pounding headache bloomed inside my skull from Mana depletion, and I cut all my Skills as the pain threatened to drive me to my knees. With my active control of Apprehend released, the Deputy Adjudicator collapsed forward onto his face.

The hair-raising sensation of being watched crawled uncomfortably down my back, like cold fingers walking along my spine, as I staggered over to the fallen elf. Notifications clamored for my attention at the corner of my vision as I reached the corpse, but experience awards had appeared the last time I'd thought the dark elf dead too. This time, I was going to make sure of things myself.

An exit wound the size of a basketball showed where my Kill Shot had blown out the Truinnar's heart, most of his lungs, and his liver, or whatever the equivalent organs for a dark elf were called. Still, I knelt beside the body and summoned my knife into my hand.

With the sharp blade, I sliced through the tissues of flesh, muscle, ligaments, and tendons of the Truinnar's neck without issue. Reaching his spine, it took a bit of sawing to cut through the resilient discs between the vertebrae. All in all, the grisly work took a couple minutes before I hacked completely through the neck and stowed the dark elf's severed head in my Inventory. Then I looted the rest of the dead Truinnar's equipment and finally dumped the headless corpse into Meat Locker.

I had no idea if those measures would prevent whatever System effect kept Rhegnah alive the last time, but it was worth the attempt to ensure the asshole was dead for good now.

Standing up, I cast Cleanse to remove the gore that covered my hands, along with the blood, dirt, and gunpowder residue that coated my body in the wake of the fight. My regeneration was already healing the worst of my injuries, and the pounding ache of Mana depletion eased as my Mana pool refilled.

Only one last bit of post-battle cleanup remained.

The pile of wreckage that had been my Outrider lay intermingled with the ruined power armor of my slain enemy. A diagnostic query from my Neural Link reported that the bike was inoperable and required significant repairs to the anti-grav, propulsion drive, Mana storage, and steering systems. The nano-garage module still worked though, which allowed me to stash the wrecked vehicle in my Inventory. The ruined power armor joined it, though I'd probably be selling the broken equipment off to fund my other repairs or replacements for my gear.

It was time to look into stronger armor upgrades of my own. The semi-powered armor worked well enough, especially with the attachments like the grapple launcher, but a fully powered suit would provide better protection as my encounters with aliens and monsters seemed to be ramping up the closer I got to reaching the Master Class tier.

I looked over the street once again before turning away from the site of Rhegnah's final battle and heading north. I'd left the others outside the Navarre, and I wondered what Dayena had decided to do with her remaining cousin. I hoped that Creynora was still alive. She'd spared my life and that mercy had provided the opportunity to pull off this rescue.

It didn't hurt one bit that the dark elf was damned good looking. And more importantly, not my employer.

I broke into a jog as I reached the park. With every step, my boots plunged into the couple inches of snow and left behind a clear track through the white field. I already missed my bike, but going on foot was a small price to pay for finally ending the Truinnar's threat.

Chapter 34

After leaving the park behind, I was headed north on Broadway when Lyrra pinged me through party chat. I mentally cursed myself for forgetting about the ability. While it had once been second nature to use Dayena's Skill, I'd been without it so long that I'd have to get used to it again.

"I am. Rhegnah is no longer a problem. For anyone," I replied.

A sense of Dayena's relief flowed through the telepathic link. *"Thank you, Hal. You accomplished what I never could."*

"My brother will not be missed, at least by any here on Earth. Father's reaction back home shall be an entirely different tale."

Creynora's sultry mental voice over party chat was a surprise, but the Truinnar's communication addressed my earlier concern as it seemed that Dayena had added her to our group. Now that I remembered the ability was in place, I used my minimap to identify their location and quickly spotted the three clustered dots that still displayed near the Navarre.

"I'm headed your way, but it'll take me a bit to get there on foot."

"Do you need a ride, Hal?" Lyrra's smug tone carried clearly through the party chat. After giving the elf such a hard time about getting her own bike, I could practically feel her malicious glee that I might not have the use of mine.

"My bike may have been involved in a violent collision. With Rhegnah's face."

For a moment, silence reigned over party chat. Then a giggle from the Countess broke the spell and started the three elves howling in laughter.

I waited until their amusement faded before continuing. *"Is there a reason you're all still hanging out there at the Navarre?"*

Creynora answered first. *"With the slaying of the Krym'parke inside, none from this enclave remain."*

"Weren't there two entire ships full of them back when you assaulted the train?" I asked. My brow wrinkled along with the question, even though Creynora couldn't see it. I'd blown one ship out of the air with a missile after it had already been damaged by a mounted cannon and I'd wrecked the other when it landed to offload the alien troops, but if Rhegnah had survived then it seemed likely that others had as well.

The Truinnar grunted with a dark laugh. *"Ha! A large party stranded in the wilds? We were little more than a feeding frenzy for the countless monsters spawning from overflowing Dungeons. Of those who survived the train encounters, few walked all the way back to civilization. I will not miss those disgusting savages."*

The aliens that I'd fought in Pittsburgh and on the train had mostly been upper-Level Basics, so that explained Creynora's jump to Advanced Class and the preponderance of that tier amongst the Krym'parke we'd fought here in Denver.

If the Krym'parke were all gone and Rhegnah was dead, that left me with one question. *"What happens to the Navarre with Rhegnah dead?"*

"It was rented through a Truinnar merchant Guild transaction to disguise our presence and the payoff to the local Pharyleri settlement administrator. Since nothing tied the rental to Rhegnah directly, the building should remain available to use through the end of the term."

"I'm sure that the rental contract will be of great interest to our gnome friends in Alliance Command. I bet there'd be a nice reward for rooting out a traitor," Lyrra commented.

The talk of payment jogged my memory. *"Speaking of rewards. Dayena, I've got a few Credits with your name on them, after the bounty payout you earned right before you got nabbed by Rhegnah."*

"Keep the reward," Dayena commanded.

I frowned. *"We've always split bounties."*

"Consider it payment for your timely rescue, if you must. Rhegnah was counting the hours until his contract with the Binary Eclipse ended. He gloated about his great triumph at returning me to my parents for 'discipline.'"

"I did have a Contract Quest to break you free before he got you off planet, so I was invested," I responded. The unread notification still blinked at the corner of my vision, but it wasn't a secret since Lyrra already knew about it.

"You would have come regardless."

I wasn't convinced that I would have without the threat of the failed quest looming over me, but confidence filled the Truinnar's voice, and it was clear that her belief wouldn't be swayed by my denial.

"In fact…" Dayena's voice trailed off with a hint of amusement. A moment later, a new notification appeared and displayed itself across my vision automatically, bypassing my default status settings to suppress notifications.

Contract between Dayena Baluisa and Harold Mason has been terminated by the senior party.
All agreed-upon terms have been finalized and no penalty clauses for failure have been activated.

My feet halted in place as I read the glowing text. The message lingered in my vision before slowly fading away as I felt the inexplicable sensation of pressure being lifted from my shoulders, like the removal of a weight I hadn't even realized I carried. The feeling vanished and I breathed in deeply, unsure how to process what had just occurred.

I was free.

But that freedom only took me so far, I realized. Rhegnah was dead by my hand and even if I was no longer tied directly to Dayena, someone from that branch of her family tree would come looking for blood. If I didn't help the Countess resolve her situation, then I'd spend the rest of my life looking over my shoulder.

I growled to myself and started walking again for several paces before speeding back up to a run, still headed to the Navarre. Damned Truinnar, their labyrinthine politics, and their ridiculous Charisma. I was invested in seeing this through, and I'd probably never know whether or not my former employer had predicted my response when she dissolved the contract between us.

In her favor, the Countess had intentionally broken the contract from a distance. There were no external influences, like the dark elf's Charisma, to immediately sway my next decisions. There was nothing right now to stop me from heading out on my own if that's what I wanted. My Pharyleri starport connections could easily help find transport off Earth and offer the opportunity to explore the wider galaxy.

I wasn't strong enough to be running around out there on my own with no one to watch my back. Not yet, anyways. As much as Earth's violent introduction to the System fostered my growth over the past two years, we were only the 11th most deadly out of the thirteen Dungeon Worlds, and there were plenty of dangers in the galaxy at large. While a Master Class might open other options, I had a few Levels yet to go so I'd stick around Earth for a while longer.

I figured that Dayena had clued in the others to her actions, since party chat remained silent for the rest of my trek. Dusk fell over the city as I returned to the Navarre. By the time I reached the historic brick building, the sky overhead was painted in deep purple hues with only a sliver of orange-red light remaining above the mountains to the west.

The three elves waited outside the building, seated on the System-repaired stairway that led up to the porch. Though Rhegnah's attack had obliterated the steps, they had already rematerialized in the same gray and white painted woodwork, showing no sign of having been shattered into splinters and dust within the past couple hours.

The fact that the stairs were back in form but entire blocks of the city still lay in rubble between the Sect and Pharyleri territory illustrated the magnitude of difference between a small-scale skirmish and full-blow warfare between Galactic powers.

I stopped at the base of the stairs, glancing up and down the nearly empty street before locking eyes with the Countess. "Still hanging around outside?"

"I spent far too long stuck inside. I wanted to feel the fresh air on my skin," Dayena replied, closing her eyes and taking a deep breath.

I nodded in understanding. Her reluctance to return to the place of her captivity made sense, even with the temperature dropping as night rolled in. The dark elf opened her eyes and met my gaze again. This time, I could see the relief she attempted to hide behind her normally stoic expression.

Despite my cynical thoughts that the Truinnar's actions were a subtle manipulation, she really hadn't been sure that I'd return.

"Besides, you dropped something." Dayena raised her arm. She held Ace by the barrel, extending the pistol's grip toward me.

I accepted the weapon and grinned as I slid the handcannon home in the holster on my right hip. "Thanks."

"You two are adorable, staring at each other like that."

I raised an eyebrow at Creynora. A hint of jealousy in her tone implied that she thought there was something romantic between the Countess and me.

I looked back at Dayena with my brow still arched. "You didn't tell them?"

The Countess shook her head without answering.

"She terminated our contract," I explained, looking back at Creynora.

The dark elf glanced between the Countess and me. "So the two of you are not…?"

Dayena just smirked at her cousin's assumption.

I couldn't help but laugh out loud. "Together? No. Not like that."

"So what you're saying is that you are available?" Creynora bit her lip as her eyes swept over me.

The hungry look reminded me of the dark elf's expression on our first meeting on the opposite side of the country. Though Creynora and Rhegnah initially dismissed any thought of me as a threat, focused instead on preparing to ambush Dayena after a visit to the Shop in Hancock, they had come to regret that judgment after our fight in the small village in western Maryland.

"Get a room, you two," Lyrra interjected.

I glanced at the Movana and then up at the Navarre behind her before shaking my head. "I don't think I'd trust any of the rooms inside, knowing the Kyrm'parke."

The golden-haired elf winced, but looking at the building reminded me that I still didn't know who had rented the place out to Rhegnah and hidden their presence from the Pharyleri.

"Creynora, do you know who arranged the lease here?"

The short wavy locks of the Truinnar's silver hair reflected the exterior lights from the tavern across the street as she shook her head. "Rhegnah made the arrangements, and the payments went through one of the family corporate accounts to disguise the deal. I have no idea how he made contact with the property owner."

"Lyrra, can you use your comm gear to arrange a meeting with Ismyna in the morning? We'll want to keep it away from their HQ, so we can try to limit anyone overhearing anything. Then let Emi know we're still alive. We owe her that for her help."

"You should be the one calling Emi," Lyrra replied.

"You're the one with her comm details," I replied with a smirk. The elf glared at me but nodded before pulling a handheld receiver from her Inventory.

I zoned out for a moment, and I realized that my lack of sleep was catching up with me. Though my stamina, health, and Mana pools were full, just because the System restored the numbers on my status screen it didn't make up for the punishing schedule that I'd forced myself into while undercover. My body and brain only needed a few hours of sleep, but I'd pushed past that limit for too long.

I started up the steps and stopped halfway when a caressing hand pressed on my thigh.

"Where are you going?" Creynora asked, looking up at me from her seat on the steps.

I was flattered by the dark elf's attraction, and more than a little interested in return, but I was too tired to follow through on anything. For now.

"I'm running on an hour of sleep after an assassination, a rescue op, and killing a whole bunch of people. I'm going to get some shut eye."

"Want some company?"

I cursed mentally without letting any expression cross my face. If anything, my talk of assassination and killing only turned on the Truinnar even more. Which made sense, in hindsight. Dark elves.

Rather than answer directly, I winked at Creynora and continued up the stairs. I pushed open the unlocked door and walked into the museum. Inside, the gallery held several fancy couches and I stepped over to the nearest one, pausing only to cast Cleanse on it before sprawling across the plush upholstery.

While I wanted to sleep, the notification icon pulsing at the corner of my vision demanded my attention before I could nod off.

Rescue the Countess - Contract Quest Completed!
Your contracted employer has been freed from captivity and Deputy Adjudicator Rhegnah Baluisa has met his end, permanently. Congratulations, all failure conditions have been avoided!
100 Credits and 100 XP awarded.
-1000 Reputation with House Baluisa
-500 Reputation with Truinnar Noble Houses

Ouch. I recounted the zeros, but they didn't change with my second reading. The lack of Credits and experience hurt, especially when I'd spent more than five weeks on that damned quest, but successfully avoiding the penalty clauses offset the loss. At least I wouldn't be stripped of my abilities and attributes by the System-enforced contract.

Every time I'd brought in the bounty on a contract breaker, the target often seemed like a shadow of their former selves. Only the foolish and the desperate signed on to contracts with clauses that were detrimental buried in the amendments, but I knew from personal experience just how easily one could fall into that trap.

As good as it felt to no longer have the contract hanging over my head, the reputation penalty clearly demonstrated that there were still consequences for my actions and my interactions with Truinnar in the future would be affected by the blood on my hands.

I dismissed the notification and brushed off my morbid thoughts. Worrying about the future gained me nothing. All I could do now was continue to grow stronger. I planned to meet my fate as it came—with my weapons in hand.

Sprawled out on the fancy art gallery couch, I let my left palm rest on the grip of Last Word as I drifted off to sleep.

Chapter 35

Late in the night, my conscious mind registered the three elves slipping inside from the front porch, though I kept still as they passed through the foyer. A fourth figure joined them, and I recognized Emi's voice as the quartet whispered over the clinking glassware of the liquor stash in the back of the gallery. From the muttered conversation, Rhegnah had kept a well-stocked bar and the ladies deemed a celebration in order.

I snoozed through the festivities, only alert enough to keep watch for potential threats. They finally quieted several hours later and bedded down in one of the other galleries with camping gear from their Inventories.

The building remained quiet until the first light of dawn crept into the windows. Not quite yet fully awake, but still feeling significantly more rested than I had for the last several weeks, I pulled myself off the couch and moved to a clear spot in the middle of the floor.

Intending to get my blood flowing a little, I worked through several stretches and had dropped prone for a few pushups when motion caught the corner of my eye. Turning my head toward the movement, I found Creynora observing my workout and I held myself up with my chest only a couple inches above the carpeted gallery floor.

The Truinnar leaned against the wall, arms folded in front of her emphasizing her impressive bust, along with the cleavage revealed by the unfastened seam down the middle of her torso. The dark elf sported more curves than her more slender cousin. While the two shared similar facial features and narrow waists, Creynora's hips flared out into a more defined hourglass figure than Dayena's lithe build.

"Please, continue. Do not stop on my account," Creynora purred.

I slowly pushed up until my arms were fully extended before lowering myself smoothly back down to hold just above the floor. "What's your game here?"

"It is no game that I would play with you." The dark elf's pink tongue flicked out across her upper lip, leaving behind a glistening trail of moisture.

I pushed up into a front-leaning rest and considered the Truinnar staring at me with undisguised hunger. I couldn't tell if her blatant flirting was a trick or if she really was that interested in me. She hadn't hid it from Dayena last night, so my former employer was aware of whatever this was.

Hopping up to my feet, I looked the dark elf in the eyes as Creynora took a step back from my sudden motions and dropped her arms into a defensive posture.

"I killed your brother after you left me alive in that ambush weeks ago, but that doesn't seem to bother you. Why are you defying your family's wishes and why are you picking Dayena's side now?"

Creynora's eyebrows shot up. My direct approach clearly surprised her. Then the dark elf sighed and forced the tension from her posture. She stepped forward and it was my turn to tense, until the elf walked around me and took a seat on the couch behind me. The same couch I'd slept on overnight. I turned to face the Truinnar and folded my arms across my chest while staring down at her.

"When the arrangement was announced, I envied Dayena. Marrying a Duke? That was more power than I ever dreamed of having as a daughter in the cadet branch of the family. Only after Dayena fled was I able to see just how little regard her parents had for her as a person. My brother was just as bad, if not worse. His obsession with our cousin was always more than a little odd, but it grew to a disturbing level when she ran away and we were sent in pursuit."

The dark elf stared down at the floor, lost in the memories. I kept my mouth shut and let her continue.

"Once we reached Earth, I began to understand the value of freedom and I resented that Dayena had found it—while I was stuck with my brother chasing after you two for most of the last year. As long as Rhegnah lived, I was bound to follow his lead. When my brother learned Dayena would be coming back to Denver and began working with the Sect, I knew that his obsession with our cousin would make him overlook the threat you represented."

Creynora looked up. "With Dayena under his thumb, Rhegnah would focus on getting back home and become sloppy. That is why I faked your death. I trusted that you would come after her."

"That's a lot of trust to have in a guy who tried to kill you."

The dark elf shrugged and wiggled her eyebrows suggestively. "If you wanted to kill me, I would be dead. I think you like my ass."

I snorted in amusement. She wasn't wrong and I admitted as much.

Creynora smiled, her brilliant white teeth shining.

"If Dayena trusts you, there's not much I'm going to say to convince her otherwise. Welcome to the team."

The dark elf's smile grew even brighter as she bounced to her feet and threw her arms around my waist. The motion emphasized both her strength and bountiful chest as she pressed against me and pulled me into a hug. My arms wrapped around Creynora instinctively in response. Apparently, I was hungrier for physical contact than I'd realized.

The sound of a throat clearing from behind interrupted us before anything further could happen. Creynora flinched and we stepped apart as

I turned to face the sound, where I found Lyrra rubbing her throat as if massaging away a cough in an exaggerated manner.

"Something you want to say?" I asked.

The Movana just shook her head. "We've got a meet with Ismyna in two hours. Before that, Dayena and I promised Emi that we'd escort her back to the clinic first thing."

"She doesn't have wheels and neither do I, anymore." I thought for a moment and turned to Creynora. "Did the Krym'parke have any vehicles?"

"Out back, in the alley," she replied.

"I'll go see what we're working with then."

I ignored the whispering behind my back as I went deeper into the building and down the stairs to the basement. Now that the building's shielding effect no longer blocked Greater Observation, I had no issue finding my way to the door that led out to the back street. The narrow alley ran from 17th Street to 18th Street and divided the block, giving rear access to the buildings that faced out onto Tremont Place to the southeast and Glenarm Place to the northwest.

A blast of cold air smacked into me as I stepped out from the Navarre's back door and directly onto the alleyway, but the rear end of an SUV stuck out from beyond the wall to my left and led me to the small parking area that ran alongside the building. Besides the SUV, two old cars with broken windows were parked in a tiny lot marked with faded orange lines for ten available spots. Two non-Earth vehicles, both double-parked across multiple spaces, were the obvious Krym'parke transports.

The first was a three-wheeled, two-seater with an enclosed canopy that resembled the cockpit of the old Marine Corps' AH-1 Cobra attack helicopters, but the similarities ended at that point. The rear of the trike had a small, open truck bed that was only about four feet long. Since the bed was completely exposed and the tandem seating up front could only fit two people, I ruled it out as an option and turned to the second vehicle.

The four-wheeled transport sported off-road tires and a heavy-duty push bar, which wrapped around the front of the vehicle to protect the forward bumper and lights. The hood and windshield sloped at a matching angle, though it appeared heavily armored panels could drop down to reinforce any of the tinted windows around the transport. The vehicle lacked any external weapon mounts on first inspection, but the only thing I could think of to describe it was 'combat minivan.'

Unfortunately, the armor of the combat minivan was painted a burnt umber. Other than that, it was exactly the sort of vehicle that I'd hoped to hijack.

With a sigh, I tried the vehicle's doors and found them unsurprisingly locked. I pulled out the Pharyleri lockcracker and let it work its magic on the driver's door. The device flashed green lights after a few moments and the door clicked as it unlocked.

I pulled the door open and poked my head inside. Nothing seemed threatening, so I unlocked the remaining doors manually. The vehicle controls resisted connecting to my Neural Link, so I stuck the lockcracker on the center console and put it to work once more. This time, the device took longer to finish the cycle and I frowned as it flashed both green and orange lights to signal completion.

I read the update provided through my Neural Link. The hack had been successful, but the lockcracker would have to remain in place as long as I wanted to use the vehicle. Since the device wasn't really designed with its own security in mind, pretty much anyone who wanted to use the vehicle would be able to if I left it in place.

Still, it beat walking. Annoying, but I'd have to take the device with me whenever I left the vehicle and hack the combat minivan again the next time I wanted to drive anywhere.

The rest of the group made their way out of the building a minute later and I found their reactions to the vehicle amusing. Dayena's lip curled in disgust and Lyrra raised an eyebrow, while Creynora just nodded as if she'd expected which vehicle I would select.

"Shotgun!" Emi yelled, bolting around the front of the transport for the passenger door as the elves looked around in confusion. The Nurse grinned as she hopped into the open front seat beside me and began adjusting the navigator station.

The elves looked hesitant, so I jerked my thumb towards the back seats. "Climb in, unless you're using your own ride."

The three exchanged glances and Dayena shook her head with a shiver. Clearly preferring the enclosed vehicle to a bike ride on the chilly morning, the elves jumped into the back compartment of the transport. They all fit on the cushioned bench in the middle row, directly behind the driver and navigator stations.

Once everyone was inside, I sealed the hatches and put the vehicle into reverse to back out of the lot. The transport maneuvered smoothly, and it only took a few minutes to drive from the back alley to the clinic on the mostly empty roads.

Pulling up at the old hospital emergency entrance, the same spot where Emi had joined Lyrra and I, I marveled that it had been less than twenty-four hours since we'd launched the operation to rescue Dayena.

Emi climbed out and paused before closing the door. "I want you to come in. There's someone I think it would be good for you to meet."

I thought about it for a second. The help that Emi provided us in rescuing Dayena was more than worth doing a favor in return.

"How much time before our meeting?" I asked, looking over my shoulder into the rear compartment.

"We've got plenty of time," Lyrra replied.

"Let's go inside," I said and waited until the elves had opened the back door before removing the lockcracker from the console. The doors didn't lock behind us automatically, but no one would be driving the combat minivan anywhere without their own hacking ability.

The four of us followed Emi into the lobby and I faked a smile toward the receptionist when the woman behind the desk, who had been such a pain on our last visit, looked up. The woman paled at my expression and her eyes frantically scanned over the elves. Glancing around the waiting area, I saw none of the hidden security previously present and the room was almost completely empty. None of the previous horde of patients waiting to be seen were around, possibly due to the early hour.

"Emi, what are you doing?" the receptionist hissed as the Nurse walked across the lobby.

"I've got some friends to introduce to the boss," Emi replied.

The woman shook her head. "Now is not a good time."

"It'll be fine." Emi waved away the receptionist, who looked more concerned than she had when I'd threatened her on our last visit.

"Something is up. The undercover guards that were here the last time aren't around," I cautioned the group over party chat.

The elves acknowledged the warning but kept any alarm from showing on their faces to hide the outward appearance of increased alertness. Our formation shifted as we followed Emi into the hall beyond the lobby.

Creynora dropped back to cover our rear, while Lyrra and Dayena walked side-by-side to watch our flanks at any crossing hallways.

Emi led us past the conference room we used before and into an executive office suite, where I saw two of the lobby guards waiting outside a closed door. Emi waved them down with a casual movement, and before they could object, we stepped right in.

Far more alert than the hospital guards, a six-man squad that I instantly recognized as Special Forces operators stood around the executive suite. The soldiers all looked up as I entered, and started reaching for weapons the moment that Lyrra and Dayena followed me into the room.

Weapons appeared from Inventory and our party responded in turn. Emi halted in shock just a few paces in front of me as a blur of motion from the corner of my eye warned of another threat. My pistols flashed into my hands as I spun to aim at the oncoming warrior.

"Stand down!" a voice roared.

Mental Influence Resisted

The room froze at the shout, and I paused with my fingers on the triggers of Last Word and Ace. Somehow, my target had managed to smack aside Ace as she moved, bringing the blade of her naginata to rest against my neck. Despite the gun barrel pointed straight at her chest, the diminutive Asian woman seemed unperturbed by the obvious threat. The black-haired warrior wore no helmet, but spectral Samurai armor protected the rest of her body.

The intensity of her glare paled next to the killing intent emanating from the blade of the naginata that gently scraped on the ridge of armor that protected my neck. Without my gorget, I felt confident that the hungry blade would already have tasted my flesh.

"I said, 'stand down!'" The growl of annoyance that filled the words was the clear tone of a man used to having his orders followed. Combined with the presence of the spec ops troops, he was probably an Army officer.

The naginata lifted an inch from my neck and I eased my pistols away from the woman, then we both took a step away from each other. I took the moment to scan her with Greater Observation.

Mikito Sato, Blood Warden (Middle Samurai Level 17) (A)
HP: 1160/1160
MP: 750/750
Status: Ghost Armor, Haste, Honor, Sharpness

After stepping back, the Blood Warden bowed her head respectfully without taking her eyes off me and the naginata disappeared into her Inventory. I returned the nod, dropping my pistols back into their holsters and finally looking for the source of the shout.

Unlike the soldiers kitted up in System equipment over their Army Combat Uniforms, the officer standing in the now open doorway wore only camouflage fatigues. The subdued insignia of an eagle holding arrows and an olive branch on his collar marked the man's rank.

My eyes flicked from the officer to the other soldiers as I contemplated the Army colonel's presence. While the Sect had done their best to keep it quiet two weeks ago, the news had still leaked out amongst the human population that an allied human-Galactic force had freed Salt Lake City. I'd ignored it at the time, focused on the pressing nature of my own quest, but when combined with Emi's earlier comment about seeing "the boss," then the likely explanation was that the city's human resistance was involved in a meeting with the remnants of the American military.

Beyond the colonel stood several civilians, but a quick scan dismissed them as any threat and confirmed my suspicions. I stopped checking after finding a Mayor, a Strategist, and several aides, turning my attention back to the colonel as the uniformed man stepped out of the back office. The Aura of Command that I'd resisted meant that he was the key figure here.

The colonel focused on Emi and me at the front of our group, folding his hands behind his back. "Explain yourselves."

The Nurse appeared petrified by the threats surrounding her, so I stepped forward and nodded in her direction. "Our friend here was looking to introduce us to a connection, but I think that you're the one we should meet."

The officer arched a skeptical eyebrow as he looked me over with a critical eye. Despite the several paces between us and all the defenses hiding my status, like On the Hunt and the Brumwell necklace, it still felt like I was a fresh recruit back on Parris Island under inspection by a DI.

I returned the blatant probe by unleashing Greater Observation.

Octavian Wier, The Man in the Arena (Officer Level 9) (A)
HP: 620/620
MP: 940/940
Status: Aura of Command

"Colonel Wier, I presume? Allow me to introduce Countess Dayena Baluisa." My voice dripped with false politeness as I motioned to my former employer. The dark elf skipped up beside me with a warm expression, though she shot a glare my way as I forced her into playing the negotiator.

The two exchanged pleasantries and I stepped back, shifting my focus to the soldiers around the room as they conversed. Though the weapons remained on display, none were pointed directly at us anymore. I took my time scanning them a little more subtly, now that Dayena's interactions with Wier held the majority of their attention, only to find that one of them was actively using a Skill that blocked my probe of the troops.

The squad leader kept his focus on me and nodded my way with a hint of humor in his eyes when I failed to scan him with Greater Observation. The nametape on the front of his combat rig read "Johnson" and he wore the three chevrons and rocker of a Staff Sergeant. Since the Skill protected the squad and not the officer, there were some apparent limits to how the ability applied.

Though I couldn't get a read on the strength of the soldiers, the way they covered for each other and their earlier sharp reactions showed them as experienced troops. I had no doubt they'd seen a fair amount of action on the West Coast and wouldn't have been surprised to learn they were one of the Army's kill teams meant for Master Classes.

That did make me wonder who the hell the Japanese women was. Everything about her screamed civilian, from the hairstyle to the non-traditional weapon.

Only after Wier invited Dayena into the back room to join the discussion with the other bigshots did things seem to relax. The soldiers returned their weapons to their holsters, sheathes, and Inventories as the tension left the room.

I glanced over at the Samurai and found her watching me with a patient expression that warned she was just waiting for me to make a wrong move.

I knew that her deadly naginata hungered for my blood, even if it remained out of sight, for now. A chill ran down my spine. Her eyes held the look of a killer, the same eyes I saw whenever I looked in a mirror.

Though the Army soldiers might have the strength of a squad, I couldn't shake the feeling that the Blood Warden would give Dayena a run for her money as the deadliest female in the room.

Chapter 36

"You sure this is a good idea?" I finished parking the combat minivan at the designated location for our off-grid meeting with Ismyna and glanced at the rear-view display, frowning as I watched the Humvee pull up through a haze of windblown snow. I was sure that the multi-barreled weapon mounted atop the Army vehicle happened to stay pointed at us for the duration of the drive would just get dismissed as coincidence, if I bothered to confront Staff Sergeant Johnson.

The barrel projecting from the armored turret certainly wasn't the M2 machine gun that would have been standard before the System. Like the gear of the soldiers, the military mixed old and new as they adapted to the changing times.

"This should get the human military and the Pharyleri talking, at least," Dayena replied.

Keeping the display in view, I arched an eyebrow at the dark elf in the passenger seat. "And what do we get out of it?"

Dayena smiled at my cynical response. "You are learning."

Unseen from the rear seats, the Truinnar's eyes flicked meaningfully toward our passengers in the back. Emi now sat between Lyrra and Creynora, after Dayena successfully called shotgun when we walked out of the clinic.

"Hunters thrive with the cover of chaos. You know this, having used it to your own advantage," Creynora added over party chat.

Dayena nodded and looked out the forward windscreen. *"The Pharyleri tracked every individual that passed through their starport back in Pittsburgh. The troublemakers were monitored there, but things have been too unstable here with the ongoing conflict. If the gnomes can make peace with the humans, then both will be more productive and problematic elements like the Krym'parke will no longer have the cover of an ongoing war."*

"Sounds nice, in theory. But are we getting paid?" I popped open the door and climbed out of the combat minivan without waiting for an answer.

The cold waited for me outside the vehicle. The chill flowed around the plates of my semi-powered armor and sank through the undersuit beneath. It seemed worse here, amidst the abandoned and icy tombs of the failed Pharyleri starport on the north side of Denver. As much as everyone avoided this place, it served as a perfect spot for a covert meeting.

Walking out into the open between the unfinished terminal building and the snapped-off control tower, I folded my arms over my chest and waited for Ismyna's arrival.

It wasn't a long wait. A short figure, bundled in thick padded gear to ward off the cold, stomped out from the other side of the open space. The green strands of hair sticking out from the hood of the cold-weather gear would have identified Ismyna, if I hadn't already confirmed it with Greater Observation.

The Pharyleri didn't stop when she reached me, instead marching right up in front of me and growling as she delivered a sharp kick to my left shin. Her boot clanged as it bounced off the plate greave just above my ankle, but the gnome lacked the strength to knock me off balance.

"Was that supposed to hurt?" I asked.

"Yes!" Ismyna snapped, kicking me ineffectually once more. The blow barely shook my semi-powered armor and I let her work out whatever frustration she had built up.

"You disappeared for five weeks. Five weeks. I'm glad you managed to free your Truinnar friend, but I had to find that out from your aide, when she called to meet me in the middle of this graveyard instead of you bothering to get in touch directly."

I almost laughed when Ismyna labeled Lyrra as my aide. Not wishing to further antagonize the gnome, I kept my amusement hidden and my tone level. "Trust me, there are two reasons we needed to meet."

The Pharyleri clenched her gloved fists. "Tell me."

"The first is why we're meeting out here. You've got a rat in Alliance command."

Ismyna pulled down the scarf covering her face, revealing an expression of confusion. "A what?"

"A traitor. Someone on the take from the Sect."

The gnome's confusion turned to anger. "You better have evidence to make a claim like that."

I filled her in on the Navarre and Rhegnah's payoff to his unknown contact amongst the Pharyleri. The gnome rubbed a hand over her face when I finished catching her up. Her hand dropped away and Ismyna glared at me. Then she sighed. "This is a huge problem, but thanks for getting this info."

I dipped my head in acknowledgement as the gnome fell quiet and she stared off into the distance. She blinked several moments and looked back up at me. "You said there were two things."

"I did. There's someone else here you need to meet."

I waved toward the vehicles that were almost hidden by the icy haze that filled the derelict starport, also using party chat to signal my companions to send out the colonel. The Officer's outline was soon visible, trudging through the drifting snow that already filled my earlier footprints.

Weir's face showed no sign that the cold environment bothered him as he approached. Ismyna glanced at me questioningly, but I waited until the colonel reached us to introduce the pair.

"Colonel Octavian Wier, I'd like you to meet Commander Ismyna Pistongrinder. Commander Pistongrinder serves on the high command staff of the Pharyleri forces holding most of Denver. Colonel Wier is part of the human military leadership of the forces that have fought, and removed, several Galactic groups from the western reaches of the former United States."

The gnome and the colonel sized each other up as I gave the introductions. I measured their stares, feeling pretty confident neither was going to try to kill the other.

Yet anyways.

"I'll leave you two to chat," I said, turning to head back to the vehicles.

As I started walking, something in the air felt off. Though the curtain of snow swirled around me uninterrupted, feeling like home to my Ice Affinity, a portion of the snowfall failed to register on my senses. My gut churned in warning and my hand lashed out, a palm-strike into the falsely empty air.

The base of my hand impacted something solid as a figure materialized with a feminine grunt, like a shadow suddenly illuminated by a piercing light. Knocked back by my sudden blow, the human woman left a pair of troughs through the snow as she struggled to stay upright. She skidded to a stop like an Olympic skier ending a downhill run, offering me an opportunity to examine the newcomer.

Her raven-haired tresses were too short and her skin too tan for her to match the Samurai from earlier, her appearance more Native than Asian. Still, the woman's unflinching thousand-yard stare as she faced me down spoke to her own deadly experience. I pushed out with Greater Observation only to feel the ability slide over her without grabbing hold.

Ingrid Starling (Shadow Assassin Level ??)

HP: ???/ ???

MP: ???/ ???

Status: ???, ???

"This a friend of yours, Wier?" I called over my shoulder without taking my eyes off the Assassin. Resting the palm of each hand on the grips of my pistols, I flashed a warning over party chat as I prepared to draw the weapons.

"I think we'll be fine here, Ingrid," Wier responded.

The Officer's calm voice as he addressed the Assassin without answering my question was an answer in itself, and using her name clearly linked the two together. The woman scowled at me and then promptly disappeared in a flash of shadow.

I drew my pistols at her abrupt departure and waited for several seconds to see if the shadow-girl would return on the offensive. After no attacks materialized, I slipped the weapons back into their holsters and started back toward the vehicles once again.

When I arrived, almost everyone from both vehicles had disembarked and were standing around their respective transports in distinctly separate groups. The Assassin sat on the front of the Humvee with one leg stretched across the hood, buffing her nails with a file and ignoring the critical stares from the pair of Truinnar who leaned against the back of my hijacked combat minivan. The Samurai stood next to the seated woman, holding a posture that spoke to her wariness while engaging in a quiet conversation that failed to carry in the wind.

Staff Sergeant Johnson and his soldiers huddled with hunched shoulders against the cold, but the Assassin and the Samurai seemed unaffected by either the chill or the blowing snow.

"Is she causing any problems?" I asked.

Though she didn't move, I got the sense of a mental head shake from Dayena over party chat. *"No. She teleported in behind the soldiers before walking around them and hopping onto the hood."*

"Any idea how long she's been tailing us?"

"No way to tell."

I grunted an acknowledgement and walked over to the two human women. The soldiers watched my approach with concern but did nothing to stop me.

"Neat trick, Ingrid," I said.

The Assassin ignored me up until I used her name. At which point, she looked up and gave me a once-over, before returning to her nail file and breaking her silence. "How'd you spot me? A Skill?"

I couldn't place her accented English, though I had no trouble understanding her. While she acted like she didn't care whether I answered, I briefly debated whether or not to reveal how I'd noticed her. We were trying to make allies against the Sect here. "Affinity. The snow around you felt off."

A grunt and a scowl were the only thanks I got from the Assassin. The corner of the Samurai's mouth twitched as if suppressing a grin, but an awkward silence descended over the group after that solitary reaction.

"You're not military. How'd you get stuck with these doggies?" I asked, looking between the two women as I jerked my thumb at the shivering soldiers. From the corner of my eye, I caught the motion of Johnson's head jerking around and the NCO glaring at me. I cracked a smile at the muttered epithet cursing "crayon-eaters" as the Staff Sergeant turned back to his squad.

"Doggies?" Ingrid looked up from her nails.

The way the Assassin perked up as she said the word told me she was looking for a pet, not an interservice rivalry. I sighed and spent the next couple minutes explaining the plethora of derogatory terms the American military branches reserved for showing our affection for each other.

Creynora and Deyena moved over, listening as a "helpful" Staff Sergeant Johnson interjected himself into the conversation to gleefully explain the Army phrases used for Marines.

"Look, it's fine to say Leatherneck, Jarhead, or Devil Dog. Just don't call a Marine a soldier. And the green crayons are the best." I glared at the Army NCO as I wrestled back control of the discussion.

"Explains why the guys from Camp Pendleton got prickly when we called them soldiers," Ingrid said.

The Assassin glanced at Mikito, who just shrugged.

"You're from California?" I asked the Assassin.

"Much further north," Johnson replied.

"Canada? That's a bit of a trek. You're a long way from home." There was a story there, I was sure, but that explained the accent.

The Assassin snarled, exploding to her feet from the hood of the Humvee. Mikito's hand snagged Ingrid's shoulder in caution, though the raven-haired woman stood without stepping any closer. My hands dropped to my pistols, relaxing a moment later when I noticed the Assassin hadn't pulled her knives. The angry woman glared at the Samurai and shook off the restraint, before growling at Dayena and Creynora. "Don't talk to me about home. Thanks to the System and your dark elf friends, I don't have one anymore."

The Assassin's empty hands balled into fists as she struggled to calm herself, but it felt like the raw emotion was a surprise even to her. The two Truinnar recoiled from the anger twisting through the woman's face, stepping toward the combat minivan and putting space between them. Even the soldiers appeared unsettled by the outburst from the killer traveling in their midst.

Footsteps crunching in the snow announced the return of Colonel Wier and the apparent end of his discussion with Ismyna. The Colonel took in the tension. "Is there a problem here?"

Ingrid shook her head before spinning on one heel and marching off, disappearing into the windblown snow that filled the abandoned starport. None of the group looked at all concerned about the Assassin wandering off into the cold, so I figured she'd be fine. At least, as long as she didn't stick one of her knives into someone.

Wier cleared his throat, pulling my attention from the Assassin's departure. "Your Pharyleri friend wanted to talk to you again before she left."

Thanking the Officer with a nod, I headed over to meet back up with Ismyna. The gnome waited in the same spot. "It's too damn cold and creepy to hang out here any longer than necessary, so let's make this quick."

I waved for her to continue.

"I'm going to propose to Alliance Command that we cede the City Cores to the human forces, if we can come to a mutually beneficial trade agreement and contingent on kicking the Sect the rest of the way out of town. If we're going to make that work, whatever leak we've got within HQ needs plugged. I need you to hunt down our traitor."

"I'll need information and access. I'm not going to make any friends on a witch hunt."

Ismyna nodded. "That's why I need an outsider. Like an audit, your team is perfectly positioned for this kind of task. We'll get you whatever you need."

"Do you want the bounty brought in warm or cold?"

The gnome's jaw clamped shut as she considered the question before waving a hand in my direction, prompting a notification to appear.

New Reserved Bounty offered to Hal Mason!
Eliminate the Traitor: Track down and remove the individual within Pharyleri Alliance Command guilty of making deals with hostile forces.
Reward: 200,000 Credits
Bonus Objective: Obtain record of any transactions opposed to Pharyleri interests to determine how much damage has occurred.
Bonus Reward: Variable.

"Allowing Sect-allied forces refuge within our territory, especially after attacking us, was a complete betrayal. Do what you must."

Nodding to the gnome, I accepted the bounty notification and my status log filled with the text. The new lines showed up just beneath Nesdyna's contract since the bounty for slaying Sect members remained active.

"If that's all, I'll round up my team and meet you back at headquarters."

Ismyna waved goodbye and pulled her hood tight, covering her face once more. The wind died off as the gnome walked away and the snow began settling back down.

As I returned to the parked vehicles, Wier intercepted me a short distance from the others. "Do you trust the Pharyleri?"

"I trust their Credits."

"That's not what I asked." Wier stared at me with intensity, taking both my measure and that of my words.

"The gnomes are Artisans at their core. They want stability to practice their trades and sell their goods. If you make a deal with them, they'll keep it. Just don't break your word or stab them in the back—that's how the war with the Binary Eclipse Sect started."

The Officer stared at me expressionless for several long seconds after that. Then he nodded and extended his hand. "Thank you for making this meeting happen. I have some calls to make."

I shook the offered hand and then returned to the rest of my group, who were waiting by the combat minivan. Everyone piled into the vehicle to get out of the cold, and I rolled my eyes at the scramble for shotgun. Lyrra ended up beside me as I explained the new bounty, lurching the ungainly transport into motion and heading for the Pharyleri headquarters.

Chapter 37

"This was not how I envisioned hunting for a traitor." Dayena looked away from the monitor, closing her eyes and rubbing them.

It was late on our second day spent crammed into the dimly lit room. Buried in the bowels of Union Station, the chamber housed a backup repository of the Pharyleri databanks. Our access to the backups, approved by Ismyna and Nesdyna, were an effort to avoid any precautions or alerts the traitor may have arranged with the primary data storage systems. Though the computers now ran on Mana instead of electricity, the power still generated waste heat from the advanced technology. Not even the System fixed overheating server rooms.

The military forces from the west coast had managed to sneak closer to Denver than anyone within either the Sect or Pharyleri realized and now the headquarters building surged with activity in preparation for a renewed offensive in coordination with the new allies. The human military offered a force multiplier and a morale boost for the combat-weary Pharyleri.

Meanwhile, we sorted through data files in search of the traitor within the ranks of Alliance Command. There was so much data, our search was like hunting for a needle in a warehouse filled with needle-stacks.

I grunted to acknowledge the dark elf while staying focused on my own terminal, scanning through line after line of Credit transactions. The gnomes tracked everything that flowed through their territory and kept records of it all—including purchases and sales that occurred in the System Shops. I hadn't even known that was possible, but it made sense when considering that the territory owners linking to the Shops almost always taxed those activities.

Searching for abnormalities in the flow of Credits coming in to Pharyleri command staff and their accounts was just one search route.

Lyrra hunted through the comm logs for unusual intercepts. So many things were tracked by the Pharyleri gear that much of the intel was ignored unless it could be traced to a Sect-controlled asset.

I'd stuck Creynora on tracking down her brother's accounts and tracing through the transactions from that end. Until her family got wind of how things were playing out here on Earth, the Truinnar still had access to her family connections. We all expected House Baluisa would cut off both dark elves from any use of their court influence once news of Rhegnah's death reached their homeworld, so we opted to take advantage of those resources while we still could.

Back when I was bringing in bail jumpers, many of those idiots couldn't resist posting all their activities on the internet for the public to see and it made tracking them down so much easier. I never thought I would someday end up missing social media, but here we were.

Somehow, the equivalent of Galactic social media had never caught on, at least for those in Dungeon Worlds and Adventurers. Not in the same way at least. Not to say there weren't publicity hounds, or Adventurers who made their living and Credits – or even their Classes – by sharing their exploits. But it wasn't a common thing, partly because at the highest Levels, supposedly, it was impossible to stream one's battles. Something to do with unaspected Mana saturation and Forbidden Zones.

All I knew was that my System Quest ticked up when I heard that the first time, and then I'd promptly ignored it. Not an issue for me.

The door to the basement server room cracked open and I dropped my left hand to grab the pistol grip of Last Word, only relaxing after Emi pushed through the door carrying a tray full of sandwiches and drinks.

"They were out of coffee and tea, so you'll have to settle for kipatchya," she announced, kicking the door closed with one foot before setting the tray down on a tiny table in the center of the small server room.

"As long as it's hot," Lyrra growled, standing up from the console where she worked and stretching out her arms before twisting her torso from side to side.

Creynora shook her head and wiped her brow with a hand towel pulled from her Inventory. "Is it not warm enough down here for you?"

The Truinnar unfastened her jumpsuit even more as I stood long enough to grab a sandwich and a drink from the tray in the middle of the room. Thanking Emi for the snacks and returning to my station, it took focused willpower to avoid the view offered by the dark elf. Her jumpsuit was now unfastened all the way to her navel and threatened to spill her assets completely into view.

As much as I appreciated the show, too much rode on us hunting down the mole within Alliance Command for any of us to get distracted now. I glanced over at the smirking Truinnar and winked as I consciously met her gaze instead of looking lower. Then I dove back into the balance sheets and account information that filled the display at my workstation.

For all the Auditors and Accountants that we'd fought as part of the Sect occupation, I couldn't help but wish we had one on our side now. Not that we could trust any of the Pharyleri in those Classes, not when they could be in on the scheme. All we could do was hope that an AI or program hadn't compromised the backup databanks in the way that the main storage systems likely were.

The conversation lapsed as we dug into the refreshments. The sounds of chewing sandwiches and sipping drinks filled the room, just audible over the low hum of the databank servers.

"Son of a bitch!"

Everyone jerked around at Creynora's sudden shout as the dark elf shot to her feet and continued her cursing in Truinnar. Her hands balled into fists as her initial human phrasing devolved into very colorful expletives that demeaned everything about Rhegnah that covered hygiene to a preference for sleeping with foul-tempered quadrupedal animals.

"That was quite the outburst," Dayena said after her cousin's tirade ran out of steam.

"My fretreshken brother, may he rot in the deepest of the seventeen hells, was siphoning from my accounts to fund everything for our excursion here. He had someone blocking my access so they would seem untouched, but my savings are stripped empty, all to pay for those savage Krym'parke mercenaries and that damned house museum."

Hurt and anger filled the dark elf's voice. Before I realized it, I'd crossed over to her and pulled her into a hug. The Truinnar melted against me, but there was nothing sexual about the contact between us.

There was something here that I wasn't seeing. "Why would he do that?"

"She was not meant to leave this planet alive," Dayena answered. Her quiet voice prompted a choked cry from Creynora as the dark elf shivered against me, but I could tell the news was no surprise. She'd known that truth the instant she'd found her accounts depleted.

"How do you know that?" Emi asked.

Dayena shrugged. "The tactic is not an uncommon one, since most Credits are lost when an individual is slain. If you have someone you will be eliminating and can exploit their trust along the way, why not take all that they possess along the way."

While I certainly hadn't felt bad about slaying Rhegnah before, now I felt glad for taking his head and I was determined to let it rot in my Inventory for a while. Not that anything in Inventory rotted, but it was the principle of the matter.

Emi shook her head in shock. "That's pretty cold, especially to a family member."

Lytra nodded in agreement, before returning to reading through the mountains of logs on the screen in front of her. Creynora gave an extra little squeeze before releasing me and Dayena moved over to give her cousin a hug as I stepped back.

Before returning to my terminal, I paused. "I hate to ask, but does that information get us anywhere on our Pharyleri traitor problem?"

"I think so. Now that I have the source accounts, I should be able to trace outgoing funds. If they were regular payments to the same destination, it should show up."

I nodded. "Good. If we can identify that destination, then we can search for a match from there to anything sent to someone here."

Everyone got back to their silent work of scrolling through endless amounts of text on the databank access consoles. I finished another sandwich and emptied my mug of kipatchya while working my way through more Shop transaction summaries.

Then Creynora cleared her throat, speaking up once more. "Got it. The rent payments for the Navarre went to Steamspindlebus Holdings Limited of Irvina."

Everyone exchanged glances at the ridiculous name of the front company.

"That's our target. A name like that should stand out in the logs, hopefully. Call out if you find it anywhere," I ordered, putting my own words into action as I dove back into the console.

It only took a few filtered searches through the Shop transactions to find a purchase for a custom-built PAV, on behalf of "Steamspindlebus Holdings Limited of Irvina" and delivered to the care of one "Olgec Crankblast" more than five weeks ago.

"I've got one," I announced, at the same time as Dayena called out a discovery of her own.

I gestured for the dark elf to go ahead.

"I have a record of a steady stream of Credit transfers from Steamspindlebus Holdings Limited of Irvina to an Olgec Crankblast. Varying amounts and frequencies, but they add up to very significant sums over time and there is nothing to denote what payments are for services rendered."

I nodded. "That's suspicious and I've got something else for the same individual. SHL, for short, purchased a PAV for Mr. Crankblast."

"Ordering a PAV sounds like someone planning to get in a fight," Dayena commented with a raised eyebrow.

"Seems likely. That timing is right when the fight with the Sect escalated."

Dayena's jaw clenched. "And when I was captured."

I nodded. "I think we have more than enough to confront Olgec Crankblast. We just need to track him down."

Lyrra looked up from the comm station. "I just found a set of encrypted messages exchanged between Olgec Crankblast and a source labeled as 'Deathwalker,' less than an hour old."

"I'm guessing there are no Alliance contacts with that label?" I asked.

Lyrra shook her head. "Nothing that I can find. It also looks like these messages were wiped from the main databanks, but copied into the hidden backups before the deletion algorithm scrubbed the message queue. Thanks to the clearances from Ismyna for top-level access, I'm using the Pharyleri intel equipment to decrypt the text, but I don't know how long it will take."

The console in front of the Movana beeped a few moments later and she frowned. "It hasn't unscrambled the whole message chain, but I've got a set of coordinates and a date-time string. A meeting time and place?"

"Throw it up on the map," I said, pointing to an unused wall display that was large enough for everyone in the room to view.

The monitor blinked on and displayed an aerial map of Denver that slowly zoomed down from a suborbital altitude. A depressing amount of the city lay in ruins, having never recovered from the System's arrival. Also visible from above was the clear line of destruction between the Pharyleri sectors and the remaining Sect territory.

"That's Cheesman Park," Emi said as a marker popped up on the display and the view flew lower, centered on an open area in the middle of the city. The rectangular area ran north-south between East 13th Avenue and East 8th Avenue and was smaller by half than the Denver City Park to the northeast, where we'd eliminated the Sect mortar battery and cleared the armory at the Denver Museum of Nature and Science.

"When is the meeting?" Dayena asked.

Lyrra glanced down at her console. "Less than twenty minutes from now."

Everyone paused, seeing the clock in their minds watching the seconds tick down as they weighed the possibilities and whether we could reach the park.

I stared at the map, judging the distances and mentally cursing myself for not taking the time to fix my bike. If the meeting was with a Sect contact, then we were in a race against time to catch our traitor in the act.

Transportation was the problem. Dayena had her bike and could ride doubled up, but Lyrra's PAV only seated one. That left the burnt orange combat minivan, but the potential payday on the other end of this opportunity called for us to do what we could to get there.

I jerked my head toward the door. "Let's go."

Chapter 38

The combat minivan skidded over the icy surface of the unmaintained road as I slid onto the access road at the edge of the Cheesman Park picnic area. The tires crunched through a layer of snow with every movement. The white blanket covered the tables and benches, while a row of trees screened our vehicle from the main expanse of the park beyond.

"And here I thought that the city's snow removal was terrible before the System," Emi muttered from the back.

Dayena turned in the passenger seat. "Snow on this planet used to be better before the System?"

"Not noticeably," Emi replied, still hanging on tightly to the Oh My God Bar affixed to the vehicle's ceiling. It was an interesting cultural note that the bar seemed just as standard on Galactic transports as it was on terrestrial cars.

The grumbling from the passengers as I braked to a halt reinforced just how much my companions failed to appreciate my driving. "Reckless," "dangerous," and "menacing" were all used, along with several Truinnar descriptors best not repeated amongst polite company.

They weren't wrong. The Pharyleri forces, starting their push to take the remaining City Cores, filled the streets and slowed our progress, so I drove aggressively to reach the park in time.

That I turned off the headlights a few turns before we reached the park had only heightened the unease from the backseat riders as we finished the drive in near-total darkness. Thanks to Keen Senses the moonlight offered plenty of light for me to navigate the road, but my party members were not thrilled at the adventure.

"Time until the meet?" I asked, ignoring the complaints in favor of scanning between the trees to look out over the open field of the park.

"Two minutes to spare," Lyrra answered.

I grinned without looking back at the Movana, certain that if I did, I would find the elf glaring at me. Instead, I continued a visual search of the wide moonlit expanse of Cheesman Park.

Across the field, a trio of frozen reflections pools were separated by pathways that led up to parallel flights of stone stairs. The steps climbed the slight rise at the center of the park, atop which sat a large neoclassical pavilion constructed of white stone.

The slight motions from a handful of shadows within the elevated structure proved that someone was lurking about the park at this late hour. I pointed out the movement to the others, shifting my companion's focus to the reason for our presence here.

"Dayena, we'll approach from here, out in the open. You circle around and cut off any retreat," I sent through party chat as I climbed out of the vehicle and quietly shut the driver's door.

"On it," she replied. The Countess slipped out of the vehicle, then silently stalked off toward the edge of the picnic area. The Truinnar triggered her suit's camouflage and promptly disappeared into the shadows of the night.

I glanced at Emi. The Nurse wore a combat jumpsuit with a personal shield generator on one hip and a medical response kit on the other. *"This might get ugly. It's not too late for you to sit this out."*

"If the Sect is involved, I'm not staying on the sideline. They deserve some payback for the hell they put me through." She pulled out a beam rifle, one of the spares we'd handed out when assisting the prisoners' escape from the Sect compound.

Sighing, I pulled two fist-sized orbs from my Inventory, pointing out the activation triggers before fastening them on her armor. *"Web grenades.*

Use them if you need to clear some space, but don't throw them too close or they'll tangle you too. Stick with Lyrra."

I glared at the Movana, conveying without words that she was to keep the Nurse out of harm's way. Lyrra nodded her understanding before preparing her own weapon. The elf then summoned her bike, and I watched as the PAV folded around her, transforming into a mecha.

Creynora signaled she was ready, though her deployable shield remained in its housing within the dark elf's bulky bracer. I cast Ice Armor on myself and drew my pair of master-crafted pistols before starting off toward the pavilion in the heart of the park.

Snow crunched beneath our armored boots as we crossed the open field, our formation opening up to put enough space between us that any area attack was unlikely to hit more than one member of our group.

Despite the noise of our footsteps, I heard another sound that echoed faintly all around us. I stopped and listened, cocking my head to the side as I attempted to locate and identify the source. The others paused and soon heard the noise as it grew louder.

"What is that?" Creynora asked aloud, unsettled enough by the strange grinding noise that she hadn't used party chat.

The eerie sound of scratching seemed to fill the field and I looked down. Something was digging through the frozen ground beneath our feet.

On the ground, several paces ahead of me, a small spot writhed and heaved upward. Dots of dark brown earth appeared through the white snow as an ivory, fleshless fist punched up and out though the mound of dirt. The skeletal hand unclenched and waved in the air for a moment before clawing around to widen the hole.

Spots of churned earth appeared around us, spreading across the expanse of the field while that first skeletal hand clawed to free the top of its ivory skull from the ground. Another pair of skeletal hands burst from one of the other spots writhing throughout the field. Then dozens—and the count continued to climb.

From behind me, Emi gasped with a horrific realization. "Necromancer! The park used to be a graveyard—a necromancer is raising the skeletons!"

"What idiots placed a park over the resting place of the dead?" Creynora growled.

Before our local history expert could respond, a cackling laugh echoed across the field and a blue light shone out from the pavilion at the heart of the park.

Holding high a staff with a glowing blue crystal, the laughing figure threw back the hood of their dark burgundy robes to reveal flowing golden hair. Along with the hair, the pale skin and pointed ears of a Movana, I recognized similar facial features to the corpse of the Sect Sub-captain still sitting in my Meat Locker storage. A quick scan with Greater Observation confirmed the familial resemblance as I probed the robed elf.

Sect Regional Manager Vynn Yimishi, Deathwalker, Soul's Blight (Mortus Dreadcaller Level 8) (M)
[Binary Eclipse Sect]
HP: 793/1280
MP: 435/1090
Status: Dread Mist Shroud, Shield of Midnight, Ritual of Doom, Army of the Dead

Glossy black armor covered the elf's torso and shoulders overtop the robes, the smooth plates glinting in the light from the magical stave.

"You're all too late! With the Pharyleri pushing out on the offensive, my army of servants here will swarm over your meager party and overwhelm anyone left at your headquarters." The twisted laughter from the Mortus Dreadcaller rang out through the park.

A rain of dirt poured off the first skeleton as the animated bones hauled its torso free of the ground, only a half dozen yards away from where we stood. An ethereal blue glow filled the eye sockets as the skull turned towards us.

The roar of Last Word cut through the Regional Manager's laughter and the round glanced off a shield that protected the distant Sect leader. Growling in frustration that I couldn't eliminate the problem from here, not that a single shot would have ended the fight, I shifted my aim and the head of that nearby skeleton exploded. The blue light winked out and the torso collapsed to the ground like a puppet with cut strings, the bones clattering as the skeleton came apart.

"Aim for the head," I commanded. Without waiting for a response from the rest of the party, I strode out onto the field with my pistols blazing. Each shot shattered a skull or sent a cranium flying after punching through the spine at the base of the neck.

A storm of energy fire washed over the animated dead as Emi opened fire with her rifle. The beams left blackened streaks on the bones but failed to drop even a single risen monster.

I paused my shots long enough to scan several nearby skeletons with Greater Observation.

Animated Adult Human Skeleton (Construct)

Durability: 137/140

Status: Dread Mist Shroud, Army of the Dead

Animated Juvenile Human Skeleton (Construct)

Durability: 93/100

Status: Dread Mist Shroud, Army of the Dead

With no Levels and a durability stat instead of HP, the constructs were a threat from sheer numbers. Thankfully, the status descriptions showed no trace of the individuals that the bodies had once been, but I had a jolt of disgust at the realization that the smaller skeleton was a child's and only one of many tiny figures throughout the shambling horde. It should have been no surprise that the Regional Manager would use the bodies of children as casually as he'd thrown away the lives of his troops throughout the battles for the city.

Pushing away my revulsion and letting the anger fade into a cold rage that simmered in the back of my mind, I focused on the status conditions of the skeletal figures. They were the same status conditions sported by the necromancer, which meant that Yimishi likely also shared the risen dead's defenses against beam weapons.

Fortunately, the rest of my party picked up on the fact that the initial barrage from the energy weapons barely shaved single digits from the mass of skeletal foes. The booming roar of Lyrra's rifle echoed over the field as her shot blasted a line through the horde. It signaled the firing line to swap out their weapons for more effective options.

Not everyone carried projectile weapons for their backup, evidenced by a clash of metal on bone and the snapping of multiple skeletal frames as Creynora bull-rushed into the fray. With her shield held out in front of her, the armored Truinnar sent several bony appendages flying while smashing through the horde.

"My skills are best used up close," Creynora said, once again using party chat. Confidence filled her words now that the eerie sounds from earlier proved to be something she could fight. The words may have fit her charge into the skeletal horde, but the suggestive wink from the dark elf's twinkling amethyst eyes—thrown over her shoulder, out of view from the party behind us—implied a far different meaning just for me.

A smirk tugged at the corner of my lip at her antics, but I continued my steady barrage at the surrounding monsters as I blazed a path through the undead. The deeper I pushed into the skeletal ranks, the more the horde closed around us, but I forged my way forward and moved ahead of the Truinnar once more.

I spared Creynora a glance as I took the lead. "Watch my back."

"A duty I shall enjoy whole-heartedly," the dark elf purred as she moved behind me.

I just shook my head and kept shooting. As much as I enjoyed the dark elf's clear intentions toward me, I wasn't going to waste time trading double entendres while a Master Class threat waited ahead of us.

Afterwards, well, that was another story.

But we needed to survive first.

Covering fire from Emi and Lyrra protected our flanks and Creynora kept the undead off my back as I advanced across the churned field. The holes in the earth, left behind by the risen dead, forced us to watch every step. Any misstep would throw off the careful weight of weapon fire that held back the angry tide of skeletons lurching around us.

Halfway across the field and with dozens of shattered skeletons in our wake, it became clear that the undead alone wouldn't stop our push.

An angry orange glow filled the field with light and I yelled out a warning over party chat. *"Scatter!"*

I launched myself sideways to the left and sprinted away from the straight-line path toward the pavilion. Creynora darted in the opposite direction as a growing sphere of flame arched out from the center of the park. The flare briefly illuminated the structure and revealed a couple of Sect bodyguards advancing from where the Regional Manager stood as they joined the fight.

The fireball splashed down where I'd been only moments before, and a wave of heat swept over me as flames licked at my heels. The attack hit a half dozen skeletons and blasted them apart, their bones flying out like shrapnel from the detonation. A hail of shards pelted my backside, but none managed to pierce the outer layer of my Ice Armor, though I'd probably have a few bits to wash out of my hair if I didn't cast Cleanse before my next shower.

None of the health bars on the party interface even flickered, since I'd been well out in front of the group and the sole focus of the attack. Still, the threat broke apart our formation and forced us away from each other, leaving Creynora and I separated—and exposed to the mass of skeletons that surrounded us.

I ducked beneath the swatting arm of a skeleton and obliterated its skull with a single shot without stopping. Twisting and spinning through the horde of undead, I hammered out shot after shot into the swarm.

Claw-like fingertips scraped over my upgraded armor, but failed to tear through the plates, though the softer joints of the semi-powered suit proved more vulnerable. I hissed in pain when something lanced into the back of my knee, and I almost fell.

Before my leg gave out, I dropped into a forward roll and kicked the injured leg upward behind me. A partially dismembered skeleton, missing everything below the ribcage, swung overhead before I slammed the monster through one of its fellow undead. The two monsters disintegrated under the impact, and I popped back to my feet on my good leg.

A green glow surrounded my wounded knee and the torn flesh knitted itself back together, proving the worth of Lyrra's ranged healing abilities from her Class advancement. From the rapid-fire pace of the single rifle shots echoing over the field, the elf hadn't even slowed her sniping while keeping tabs on my health.

I quickly acknowledged the medic's contribution as I dove back into the desperate dance through the seemingly unending mass of skeletons with my leg fully restored. The army of the dead provided the cover we needed to hide from the Sect Regional Manager's elite bodyguards, and they howled their frustration as more indiscriminate attacks rained down across the field.

Fireballs, shards of ice, spraying acid, and explosions tore through the skeletons and sent clumps of earth flying alongside the hailstorm of shattered bones. The devastation filled the air with clouds of smoke and steam, only serving to further obscure my advance through the swarm of monsters.

Greater Observation pierced the fog of war and my minimap displayed the rest of my group. Only one dot remained back on overwatch, and I knew without looking who had advanced into the horde, while the other stealthy figure now circled wide around the fray. If we kept the Sect commander focused on our frontal assault, Dayena would strike from behind when the opportunity arose.

Through the clouds of smoke rolling across the field, I caught a glimpse of Creynora hacking her saber to either side as the mass of skeletons clawed their way around the shield braced in front of her. The curved blade sliced through skeletal torsos and necks with little resistance. Emi stood behind the Truinnar warrior, sheltering the storm of combat under the protective cover of the Darkheart Guardian's shield, having ignored my instructions to stay back in support. The Nurse kept one glowing hand on the dark elf's back, soothing her wounds with healing energy while the faint shimmer of an energy barrier protected her against attacks from behind.

At the edge of the park, beyond the swarm of undead, Lyrra huddled under the protective dome of a mobile shield generator. The shield held off the ranged fire from Yimishi's guards as the Movana fired her rifle into the skeleton horde from a distance.

Greater Observations still held a lock on the Sect Regional Manager at the heart of the enemy formation, despite the quantity of enemies currently between us. The Mortus Dreadcaller's health ticked down slightly with each shot from my pistols before climbing back up again under boosted regeneration. The effect hinted that the necromancer was linked to his creations, his health pool somehow fueling their animation. Army of the Dead wasn't just a status condition, it was the lifeforce that bound them all together.

Breaking through the final ranks of the undead, I reached the terrace in front of the pavilion. Ice crunched beneath my boots when I hopped over the knee-high wall of stone that bordered the northernmost reflecting pool and I chuckled as the skeletons pursuing after me clattered against the lip of stone but lacked the coordination to climb over the obstacle.

Then I caught sight of a hulking, rhino-horned Ceratophimi standing guard at the base of the steps leading up to the pavilion and my mirth faded. The warrior lacked the typical jumpsuit worn by most fighters, instead sporting individual plates of armor strapped directly over the gray pebbled flesh of its torso, thighs, knees, and shins. Thick, studded gauntlets covered the Ceratophimi's fists so completely that it didn't even appear to have articulated fingers.

La'khar'tas, Bastion of Redoubt (Warshaper Level 44) (A)

[Binary Eclipse Sect]
HP: 1860/1860
MP: 793/880
Status: Steelskin, Warcry, Dread Mist Shroud

The commotion from the undead drew the brute's attention and I immediately opened fire with both pistols as the alien's horn dropped to point at my chest and the Warshaper charged. The massive alien's arms bulged with muscles that seemed to grow larger as it rapidly closed the distance between us.

A slight bounce allowed the Warshaper to easily hurdle the lip on the far side of the reflecting pool and an explosion of ice erupted from beneath the alien's first pounding step on the frozen surface. The fact that the next steps also cratered several inches into the ice seemed not to bother the alien in the slightest.

Instead, the creature roared and leapt skyward, arching almost twenty feet into the air before plummeting down with one fist drawn back in preparation for a massive strike. The jump was fast, too fast to be anything besides an active Skill, and I barely dodged out of the way.

The pressure wave as the alien's fist swept by inches from my head nearly knocked me off balance, but I slid beneath the blow while firing my pistols into the Warshaper's side. Another eruption of ice shards exploded beneath the alien's landing, but I shrugged off the trivial damage and focused on hurting my opponent.

A casting of Frostbolt sent an ice shard of my own lancing out to spear the alien's flank and I activated Hinder to further slow my opponent. Blood spattered from the wounds as I blasted out gobs of flesh with each shot into the gaps between the armor plates that covered the alien's body.

La'khar'tas roared in pain, spinning around and lashing out with those deadly studded gauntlets. Each solid fist easily outmassed my head and any successful hit would shatter my bones on impact.

Backpedaling away from the huge alien, I thought I'd moved out of range when one of the Warshaper's arms suddenly stretched, growing larger and longer. The blow clipped my left shoulder and only the protection of my armor plates kept me from losing the arm as the Ice Armor overtop shattered.

My arm went numb below the shoulder as my bones cracked from the force and Last Word flew from my nerveless hand. The pistol skittered across the ice until it hit the stone barrier that surrounded the frozen pool.

The alien's second arm enlarged to match the first and the Warshaper's movements accelerated. La'khar'tas lashed out again with arms churning like pistons, but I danced through the storm of blows without the brute landing another hit. For all the Ceratophimi's speed, the bulky alien lacked the dexterity to truly pin me in place and pound me into oblivion. All the sparring I'd done with Dayena ensured my survival as I led the alien on a merry chase around the frozen pond, all the while chipping away at the Warshaper's health pool.

Feeling returned to my left arm with a tingle and I clenched my fingers into a fist a few times. Once I felt confident that my hand worked properly again, I summoned a spare pistol into my grip and added its firepower to my attacks.

The Warshaper shifted through several more body morphs in attempts to catch me off guard. When its legs lengthened to enable longer strides and cut me off, I slid across the ice right between them, firing upward into the Warshaper's groin. The rhino-like alien shrieked in pain.

Some things still hurt, no matter how high one's Constitution attribute climbed.

The Warshaper spun and the shriek turned to a bellow of rage. I dodged a wild backhand as I popped back to my feet, but a wave of energy poured off the fist and sent me tumbling across the ice once more. It took a moment to shake off the bitch-slap Skill while the Warshaper was recovering too. I ripped off a barrage, stacking Rend and Hinder with each shot.

The alien dropped to the ice as I circled around behind it. I triggered both weapons into the back of the Ceratophimi's head. The back of its skull disintegrated, and its hulking body slumped forward before smacking horn-first into the ice.

A quick touch looted Credits and sent the corpse into Meat Locker, though I'd have to strip the equipped gear later. Once the body disappeared, I only paused long enough to scoop up Last Word before hurdling the stone lip of the wall surrounding the pool and dashing for the pavilion.

Chapter 39

I sprinted up the white stone stairs, leveling my master-crafted pistols at the final pair of Sect members. Yimishi and one last bodyguard waited beneath the white roof of the open-sided pavilion. Behind them, a wide-eyed gnome watched my approach with mounting terror.

Before I could open fire, my weapons hit an invisible barrier, and my arms crumpled before I plowed face first into the unseen wall. Like a dog hitting the clear glass of a sliding patio door, I bounced backward and almost toppled over as the necromancer and his remaining bodyguard howled in laughter. Stumbling down two steps with my broken nose pouring blood, I regained my balance and raised my weapons to point at the two Sect members.

"You won't get through that shield with those little pistols," cackled Yimishi. The necromancer flicked his crystal-topped staff toward me, and a bolt of ugly green energy snaked from the tip. The energy bolt hit my armor in the chest without any sensation of impact pushing me backward, but the green energy hissed and popped as it spread across the Ice Armor protecting my torso.

I ignored the damage crawling across my chest and opened fire at the invisible shield. My rounds hit the point where I'd face-planted the barrier before slowing to a stop. The projectiles seemed to float in the air with nothing holding them in place, but they weren't falling or ricocheting like they would have after hitting something solid.

A glance down at my chest confirmed the green energy fading away. The attack had eaten away a hole the size of a dinner plate through the icy shell that coated my armor. However, the spell didn't appear to have affected the chestplate of my Tyrfing armor underneath.

I recast the spell to reform the extra protection and scanned the humanoid figure who currently stood laughing alongside the Sect Regional Manager. It was a spellcaster as tall as the Mortus Dreadcaller, but I couldn't make out any sign of their species with the hood of their dark blue robes pulled low over their face.

Quilllid Marrska, The Resplendent Barrier (Force Mage Level 49) (A)

[Binary Eclipse Sect]

HP: 840/840

MP: 1431/1670

Status: Shield Boost, Amplified Force

Not getting anywhere with my pistols, I dropped them into their holsters and summoned my Banshee hybrid rifle from Inventory. Sometimes, I just needed a bigger gun, and the Right Tool for the Job offered the storage space to carry the heavier firepower. The weapon's magazine was already loaded with anti-magic rounds, and I squeezed the trigger, hip firing at the barrier from only a couple feet away.

The rifle projected a swirling beam of energy which lanced into the invisible shield, carrying the hybrid round beyond where my pistol's projectiles hung suspended in the air. Translucent waves rippled around the larger projectile as it bore through the shield in a way that reminded me of videos of bullets fired into ballistic gel. The round gradually slowed before halting more than two feet beyond the smaller pistol projectiles.

The Force Mage shouted in alarm as I fired again. The second round pushed even further beyond the first rifle's shot as the specialized hybrid projectiles continuously drained the energy from the spell.

The two Sect spellcasters hiding behind the barrier threw out a fireball and a stream of ice shards, but I dodged behind the nearest set of columns supporting the open-sided pavilion's roof. Flames from the fire spell wrapped around the pillars and enveloped me in heat as the flying shards of ice glanced off the white stones, both outgoing spells completely unaffected by the barrier halting my attacks.

The desperate reactions of the Sect members clued me in that I was close to breaching their barrier, so I braved the oncoming magic and stepped around the column to fire once more. This time, the fist-sized projectile pushed through the invisible shield and thunked onto the ground on the far side. The other suspended rounds also fell, dropping to the stone deck with a clatter.

Before the rounds finished their first bounce on the pavilion's floor, I'd pulled the rifle tight to my shoulder and sighted the targeting reticle on the shadowy figure of the Force Mage. Shot number four flashed across the pavilion and staggered my target, the round drilling into the center of their chest. The stumble threw off the spell forming in their hands and a black ball of acid splashed across the floor at the mage's feet.

The floor steamed and bubbled everywhere the black liquid touched. The Force Mage jumped away from the growing pool, clutching their wounded chest with a gloved hand as orange blood seeped out from between their fingers.

Another green bolt of necrotic energy from the necromancer smacked into my left shoulder, but I ignored the hissing and popping as my Ice Armor melted away to fire another shot into the Force Mage. The attack threw off my shot slightly, punching the Force Mage in the gut instead of a repeated hit to the upper chest.

I snarled at the off-target shot as glowing green eyes stared out at me in horror from beneath the hood of the Force Mage's robes. In my expression, the Sect member saw their death. The mage spun and bolted, holding up one hand behind them and keeping it pointed toward me as they sprinted away. Instead of hitting the fleeing mage in the back, my follow-up shot stuck in a narrow forcefield projecting from the upraised hand.

Then I noticed the runner was headed almost directly for Dayena's dot on my minimap and I coldly shifted my aim to the Sect Regional Manager. The Force Mage wouldn't be a problem for long.

"Coward! Get back here!" Yimishi shrieked in anger before turning back to face me with furious green energy writhing over both hands. The Mortus Dreadcaller threw twin necrotic bolts that streaked across the space between us and sizzled as they ate away at my Ice Armor.

I responded with repeated shots from the hybrid rifle as I crossed the pavilion, angling closer to the necromancer. The attacks seemed to inflict less damage than they had on the Force Mage. It was just a guess, but it was likely that Master Class damage resistances were in play.

Hinder still took hold when I activated the ability on my target and the physical component of the hybrid rifle's rounds allowed the bleed damage of Rend to affect Yimishi. I added a Frostbolt for good measure, but speed didn't seem to be an issue when the spells and Skills of the Mortus Dreadcaller always landed despite any evasive measures I took.

Attempting to stop my advance, Yimishi waved a hand and a row of bone spikes erupted from the floor of the pavilion. I launched myself into a forward dive over the growing wall, scraping between two of the barbed ivory tines. Twisting in the air, I landed on my shoulder and rolled back up to my feet as another pair of the necromancer's spell bolts smacked into me.

The necrotic energy from the angry green spells consumed the last layers of my Ice Armor and seeped around the plates of my assault armor, eating away at my jumpsuit and the flesh beneath. I couldn't see the damage, but I could feel the pain as the spells ravaged my skin and muscles.

We both raced to apply detrimental status afflictions as our health pools dripped away with each round of firing spells and weapons that crossed the space between us.

Only, the Mortus Dreadcaller's Status showed his health ticking upward slightly in time with the waves of pain sweeping over me from the necrotic afflictions.

Shit.

The drain of my own health fueled my opponent's recovery. The more afflictions the death mage piled on, the more his rate of regeneration increased. My damage wasn't ramping up as quickly, despite multiple stacks of Rend.

Normally, the ability of Implacable Endurance to reduce Stamina spent on actions provided me a significant advantage in any fight the longer it went on. Now it didn't matter how much more Stamina I had in a battle of attrition if my lifeforce fed my opponent directly.

I activated Expose, even though the Movana lacked any shielding tech or abilities. He relied solely on the ability to drain health from his foes, instead of blocking out the incoming damage, but I needed to increase the number of negative status conditions to boost my top tier Class Skills.

My health dropped below half, and I knew that I was running out of time. Activating Apprehend, I visualized the shackles forming around the

Mortus Dreadcaller's wrists. Then I envisioned those restraints attaching to a belly chain to restrict the spellcaster's hands at waist level.

The ability snapped into reality, silvery light pulling down Yimishi's hands. The bindings twisted around his wrists to bind them in place, knocking the staff against the side of the necromancer's head as the cuffs drew his hands to his waist.

The Sect Regional Manager snarled in anger and pain, straining against the Mana shackles, and I immediately felt the strain of holding the Skill. I'd used the ability on a Master Class target and the innate resistances of the higher tier weakened the restraints. Apprehend was supposed to last four hours according to the Skill description and I could already tell that they wouldn't last anywhere near that long. I'd be lucky for four minutes, if that.

The shackles flickered and I revised the estimate downward again. Forty seconds.

In a fight, forty seconds was an eternity.

I cycled the Banshee as fast as it would fire, and the weapon's piercing whine filled the pavilion. Each hybrid round that slammed into the Sect leader left afterimages superimposed on reality, like repeated strikes of lightning hitting the Movana over and over. With each shot, I stepped closer until the end of my weapon was just beyond arm's reach, if Yimishi could have raised his arms.

"You are about out of ammunition for that weapon. By the time you reload, I will tear you apart." Blood dripped from the lips of the grievously injured Sect Regional Manager and his health dropped below a quarter. Apprehend weakened and Yimishi slowly pulled his hands away from his waist, my desperate hold on the ability the only thing preventing him from activating his own slew of Skills.

I grinned and fired again without slowing the barrage. "I'm not even close to running dry."

Not that I needed anything more than a single shot, but that one shot had to count. Stacking more applications of Rend and Hinder, I kept one eye on my Mana pool. I needed just enough to trigger one final ability.

An instant before Apprehend failed and with 137 Mana left, I activated Kill Shot and squeezed the Banshee's trigger.

The attack tore through Yimishi's torso in a fleshy explosion. Blood, entrails, and bone shards sprayed out from the Sect Regional Manager to splash down on the pavilion floor behind him like a gore-filled shadow.

For an instant, as the beam of energy from the hybrid rifle faded away, I could see beyond the Movana's torso through a blood-drenched hole large enough that my entire arm could reach inside. Then the elf collapsed, spine severed by the attack that tore out the center of his chest.

Determined not to let the restorative abilities of the necromancer's attacks repair the damage before I finished him off, I fired another shot as Yimishi hit the ground. The round knocked the elf flat on his back and tore through his shoulder, nearly ripping off the arm. Only a few shreds of ragged flesh remained to prevent the limb from falling away.

The Sect Regional Manager clawed the ground with his uninjured arm, trying to pull himself away as I stood over him. The elf glanced at the ground beneath my feet, and I hopped forward, clearing the space as another wall of bone spikes erupted in a last-ditch offensive.

I landed with one foot on Yimishi's chest, and the elf stared up with hate filled eyes.

"You've... won... nothing," he managed to rasp out.

I stomped my other foot down on his throat. Cartilage and bone crunched beneath my heel as the elf gagged from the blow. Dropping the muzzle of the Banshee to point at the Movana's forehead, I fired one last time and the upper half of the necromancer's head disappeared. Nothing remained above eye level with a vaguely concave line carved throughout. A pool of blood seeped out from the severed head to cover the smear of brain matter and bone fragments spread across the floor.

Under my feet, his body went limp. I kept the rifle pointed at the base of Yimishi's jaw until I confirmed the appearance of the notification that granted experience for the kill. I dismissed the popup as the sounds of fighting out in front of the pavilion died away.

I knelt and looted the body of the slain Sect Regional Manager before dumping the corpse into Meat Locker. Summoning a health potion from my inventory, I slipped the vial into the injector port built into the side of the thigh plate on my armor. The potion emptied with a barely audible hiss and entered my bloodstream, boosting my recovering health pool. The empty ampule popped out of the port and clattered to the stone floor as I stood back up.

At the rear of the pavilion, the small figure of a gnome attempted to slink away unnoticed while I was occupied with looting. I pulled the Banshee to my shoulder and the rifle whined, snapping off a shot that caught the Pharyleri in the side. The round punched through an energy shield, spinning the gnome. His baggy clothing flared out around him before he bounced off one of the stone support columns. The gnome was clearly staggered, though I expected more damage from the attack.

Olgec Crankblast (Comptroller Level 43) (B)
HP: 164/370
MP: 473/550
Status: Dazed

The gnome pushed off the column and turned to run, but my next round hit just above the knee. Sparks flared from the spot as the attack tore away the leg of the Pharyleri's pants to reveal the PAV armor hidden beneath the baggy clothing. The force of the shot still knocked the leg out from under Olgec and crumpled the armor enough that he fell onto his back.

The PAV held up surprisingly well to the first couple shots, but rapidly began to fail, and the gnome screamed in pain as I continued to fire the hybrid rifle. Olgec's attempt to flee ruined any chance of mercy I might have considered so I ignored his cries, content to complete the bounty by bringing in a corpse.

A final round through the chest of the now-broken PAV silenced the gnome and initiated a new round of pending notifications. I left them unopened and dismissed the prompt, anxious to check on my companions. I dumped the dead gnome into Meat Locker, receiving another notification that the storage space was now full.

I added a Shop visit to my to-do list. I needed to clear out some space and restock. And fix my damn bike.

Twin walls of bone from the Dreadcaller's attacks still separated me from where I'd entered the pavilion, but each crumbled with a solid kick now that the summoner of those barriers no longer supplied them with Mana. When I reached the edge of the pavilion and looked out over the field, the only figures standing were the battered and bloody members of my party.

The army of undead lay strewn across the park in piles, like puppets with their strings cut. Once I had severed that connection feeding the animated skeletons, there was nothing keeping them moving.

Only one figure was still missing from the group, and I glanced back at where the fleeing Force Mage had disappeared, but I saw no sign of the robed figure through the trees beyond the edge of the pavilion. Dayena's marker on my minimap showed her just beyond the copse lining the walkway that led to the botanical gardens east of the park and there was no sign of any other nearby threats.

"You good, Dayena?" I asked over party chat. It still felt good to access the private communication ability after so long without Dayena's Skill.

"The Force Mage has been eliminated."

I acknowledged the Countess and started down the steps, knowing the Truinnar would catch up. I wasn't going to admit that I was paying extra attention to Dayena with Greater Observation. Though Rhegnah was dead, Creynora had joined up with us, and every Krym'parke that we could find was slain, I had no doubts that we had not seen the end of the family's attempts to return the Countess for her arranged marriage.

Even if I was no longer bound by a contract, I'd been burned once ranging too far away and I wasn't going to repeat that mistake if I could help it.

When I reached the group beyond the frozen reflecting pools, they were patching up the last of their wounds and fixing up any gear that would accept field repairs.

A clang of metal on stone rang out over the park as Creynora smacked her shield against the rim of the nearest pool. Several nicks and gouges around the side edges of the deployable shield prevented the device from folding in on itself and retracting into her bracer. She growled and abandoned the effort after several attempts, slipping off the bracer and stowing it away in her Inventory.

The dark elf sighed before stepping over and wrapping her arms around me. I slipped an arm around her waist, surprised at how comfortable the casual act of intimacy felt in the aftermath of the battle. There was too much to do to hold on for long, but I gave Creynora an extra squeeze before dropping my arms reluctantly.

When I stepped away from Creynora, Dayena had rejoined the group and I ignored the knowing smirk that the Countess directed toward us. I wasn't going to let her get under my skin or I'd never hear the end of it.

Still, it was good to see Dayena finding amusement in something. She'd surely been deeply impacted by her imprisonment in Rhegnah's safe house, even if she put on a brave front. Getting back into action with the hunt for the Pharyleri traitor and bloodying her blades seemed to be helping her recovery. Fortunately, there were still plenty of Sect forces left around the city, though our actions tonight had removed the primary leader just ahead of the joint human and gnome attacks on the last Sect-controlled Cores.

By the time everyone was ready to leave, the skeletons throughout the park were beginning to crumble to dust. Whatever necromancer Skill animated the centuries-old bones and provided the strength to fight left them weaker now that the ability had run its course.

"Well, at least we don't have to bury them," I said, watching the final skeletons decompose like a digital special effect in a pre-System movie.

Emi shook her head, kicking at a raised clump of dirt where one of the undead had dug free of a grave below. "There are still all the holes in the ground. Someone is going to turn their ankle or break a leg."

Somehow, I wasn't surprised the altruistic Nurse was thinking of others possibly getting hurt.

"A few earth-magic spells should easily fix that problem, but that is not something I can assist with," Creynora interjected.

Dayena waved her hand dismissively. "Any City Planner or Groundskeeper can perform the landscaping. Not something that should be a priority during a conflict."

"I'm sure Johnson or Wier will find someone, or whoever they put in charge. I'm ready for a hot shower and a drink," I said, shrugging before heading back across the field.

The others readily agreed and trudged after me, the conversation lapsing into silence as the post-combat adrenaline crash swept over us.

Chapter 40

We dropped Emi off at the resistance clinic after multiple detours around burning vehicles that blocked main roads. The combatants had moved on, but the evidence of fighting was fresh through the northern part of the city.

When Emi climbed out of the combat minivan, the Nurse refused the offer of Credits as thanks for all the aid she provided over the last few days. Waving goodbye, I headed back to the Pharyleri headquarters.

Now well after midnight, the streets were almost entirely empty. Lights flashed over the city and the rumble of thunder echoed. The sounds of combat, both distant and closer than I would like. It was a bit surreal, given our own recent fighting and the knowledge that elsewhere in the city others were caught up in the struggle of life and death.

We parked outside Union Station without further delays. Dayena stuck with me as I reported to the command center, while Lyrra and Creynora headed straight for the cafeteria. With a major operation underway, it took longer than usual for the guards to clear us.

When Dayena and I were finally allowed in, the room bustled with activity that belied the quiet streets around the headquarters. Colonel Wier and another Army officer stood with the Pharyleri commanders on the raised dais in the center of the room. A scan of the city map showed that one of the City Cores was already well into the capture process, but none of the officers looked happy with that fact.

"Order the scouts from the 63rd Division to push out wider. I know they're not contracted for direct combat, but I want eyes on our flanks," Wier commanded with a glance at the other officer as I reached the command dais. The major began muttering into a headset, his words muted by a sound dampening field that encompassed his head like a bubble.

Nesdyna hunched over the center map with a worried frown. "They've always reacted faster to our probes in the past. I don't know why we've pushed this far without seeing a more organized response. The Sect is taking heavy casualties and our losses are trivial in comparison."

I caught Ismyna's eye and waved her over to the side. Wier tracked the green-haired gnome as she walked over, but none of the other commanders seemed to notice her step away. The colonel's eyes narrowed when he saw me, and I nodded to the Officer.

"I hope this visit is less disruptive than our last conversation," Ismnya said, keeping her voice low to avoid drawing any extra attention.

I leaned in close so that the gnome standing on the raised platform blocked the view of the others around the map display. "Your traitor problem is dealt with, but he made contact before we got him. I don't know if his contact passed any more intel on to the Sect at large before we got him too."

I briefly filled Ismyna in on our investigation and the likelihood that Olgec had been trafficking information on the Pharyleri for quite some time. I detailed tracking down the gnome, skipping over most of the battle in Cheesman Park. She listened silently until I got to the end.

"I also have a pretty good idea why the Binary Eclipse forces aren't showing a coordinated response."

"Why is that?" Ismyna stared at me suspiciously.

"Olgec's contact was the Regional Manager."

The gnome blinked before sighing and smacking my shoulder in frustration. "You could have led with that."

"I know." I grinned, barely feeling the tap through my armor.

Ismyna rolled her eyes and stepped away from the edge of the dais. "Hang on, while I spread the good news."

She returned to the command group surrounding the map table. I could tell when she informed them of the Sect leader's death and the identity of the traitor, since every head snapped around to look at me. I waved at the assembly, ignoring the glares sent by a few who were likely closer to Olgec. They'd get over it when their initial feelings of betrayal resolved themselves. Professionals that they were, they returned to the business of managing the forces in action.

On the map, the countdown clock continued ticking down over the southwestern City Core as the human Army closed in on the Lakewood district. At least one element had punched through the same gate that I'd used when infiltrating the Sect-controlled area, and I idly wondered whether the guards there had survived the assault.

I couldn't see any more reason to hang out in the command center, but I was stuck until Ismyna paid out on the bounty. When there was a lull in the activity around the map table, I waited until Ismyna looked my way and rubbed my thumb over my fingertips. I hoped the "pay me" gesture was universal.

The gnome nodded, and the notification appeared moments later. I mouthed a silent "Thank you" to Ismyna and then led Dayena out of the chamber. The dark elf walked beside me as we headed to meet with the others, lost in our thoughts along the way.

The cafeteria was eerily empty with all available forces out on the push to finish capturing the city, so it was easy to spot Lyrra and Creynora seated at one of the lengthy tables by themselves. Two place settings with full plates sat beside the pair.

Dayena glanced at me and grinned, launching herself into a sprint. My competitive nature kicked in and I hurried after the Truinnar, but the head start allowed the nimble dark elf to vault over the table and slip into the seat beside Lyrra. I slid in next to Creynora, who looked amused by her cousin's actions, but the dark elf placed a hand on the thigh plate of my armor beneath the table.

"Thanks for grabbing us food, though it looks like there isn't much of a rush right now," I said, nodding to the plate in front of me and gesturing to the empty room. Dayena just grunted and dug into her food.

The stack of small sandwiches on my plate consisted of homemade bread with slices of various deli meats, cheese, and veggies. I scooped up one and bit into it with a crunch as I tore through the layer of fresh lettuce. A hint of spicy mustard and horseradish complimented the meat and cheese perfectly. The sandwich disappeared in several bites and the rest of the stack quickly followed, leaving the plate empty within only a few minutes.

A contented sigh slipped out as I sat back, finding the others watching me with amusement. Despite Dayena's rush to the table, the dark elf had only finished two of the sandwiches from her stack and held a third in her hand, half-eaten.

I reached across the table and snagged an untouched sandwich from her plate. The Countess gasped and her free hand slapped down on the table as she reacted too slowly to stop the theft. I chomped down, tearing out a huge bite and chewing deliberately. Dayena pouted and pulled her plate closer to her side of the table before sullenly continuing her meal.

Creynora laughed at my heist and her cousin's exaggerated response. Her mirth held an airy, musical quality and I found myself wanting to hear her laugh more often.

Chewing on my ill-gotten gains, I brought up my pending notifications.

__Bounty Completed!__

You have successfully completed the bounty "Eliminate the Traitor" with the slaying of Olgec Crankblast. This bounty request does not require the return of the subject as proof of death.

200,000 Credits and 5,000 XP Awarded

Bonus Objective: Though Olgec relayed the news of the human military forces allying with the Pharyleri to a contact within the Binary Eclipse Sect, you eliminated Regional Manager Vynn Yimishi before the details could be passed on as actionable intelligence to the Sect forces.

1,000,000 Credits and 10,000 XP Awarded

The final line of the notification caught me by surprise, and I choked on a bite of the sandwich. A fit of coughing had the table looking at me with concern by the time I cleared my airway.

"Are you alright?" Creynora asked, sliding her hand up to my back.

I nodded and took a deep breath, then shared the notification with the trio of elves. "You'll all want to see this."

The astonishment on their faces as they read made it clear when they discovered the surprise payout.

"That is an incredible sum of Credits," Lyrra said, looking over at me with her eyes wide.

I nodded to the Movana as I split the total reward of 1.2 million Credits four ways, sending an even share of the funds to each of them. I made a mental note to find some way of thanking Emi out of my share, since she'd declined any Credit payout the last time I offered. "That's the largest single-target bounty I've completed so far, and it wouldn't have been possible without all of you."

Dayena looked at me suspiciously. "Are you trying to pay me off for stealing my dinner?"

Unable to tell if the Countess was serious, I just laughed and shook my head without bothering to address the accusation. A hint of a smile appeared on her face, and she sniffed with disdain. "I told you already that I have no need of your Credits."

The ping of my account balance updating showed that Dayena had returned her share.

Creynora glanced between Dayena and me. "Well, after my brother stole from me and emptied my accounts, I am rather short on funds. I will not turn down any Credits or the opportunity for further income."

"Thanks, Hal. I'm not giving anything back either," Lyrra added with a smirk.

I nodded to the Movana and looked around the table. "We make a good team. If things are settled with the Sect tomorrow, how about we see if there are any nearby Dungeons in need of clearing?"

The two Truinnar agreed, and Lyrra said, "I'll find us some locations and check how much traffic they see from the locals."

I stood from the table, scooping up my empty plate. "It's late, but make sure you all get some rest. I'm going to hit the Shop to resupply and then turn in for the night."

Taking the empty plates for Creynora and Lyrra, I dropped them in the cafeteria's return rack on my way out. When I transitioned to my instance of the Shop, Ryk greeted me with a smile. Or as close to a smile as his ram-like face could manage.

"Adventurer Mason! Welcome back, I hope that your journeys have been rewarding."

I returned his greeting, unable to resist smiling back. After I caught him up on some of my recent experiences, the shopkeeper brought us back to business and I transferred over my list of ammunition restocks.

I summoned my mangled bike to a clear space in the middle of the Shop floor. The shopkeeper looked over the wreckage and slowly shook his head.

"Maybe a specialist Mechanic or Engineer could do it, but the best I can do is a buy offer for any still-working components."

I sighed. "I was afraid of that. I'm guessing the same goes for similarly wrecked armor?"

I dropped Rhegnah's broken power armor beside the bike. Ryk looked from the distinctive indentation in the power armor's chest to the matching shape at the front of my ruined Outrider, then raised a brow as he looked at me. "I think I see what happened here, but you are correct. I can take the armor off your hands, at least."

I nodded, accepting the offer and we moved on to the bodies stashed in Meat Locker. I kept Rhegnah's head in the storage space but unloaded the rest of the Truinnar's corpse alongside the other dead. Ryk noticed the lack of a complete set of remains and chose not to comment. On the other hand, the dead Master Class warranted a sharply indrawn breath.

Ryk gazed at me with a critical expression and then nodded toward a recognizable display further down the museum-like hall. "You have come a long way since you first entered my Shop, wearing little more than rags and armed with weapons that would not even leave a scratch on your bare skin now."

I knew the display in question without needing to look. It was the Kevlar plate carrier and the other gear that survived my pre-System days as a bail bondsman.

"Two years," I said as I remembered those first hectic days.

The shopkeeper clapped a hand on my shoulder and resumed his earlier cheeriness. "Let us hope for many more to come!"

"I'll agree to that."

Ryk said nothing more about the bodies disgorged from Meat Locker, simply haggling out the prices. It was easily apparent that the Master Class corpse warranted more Credits than all of the others combined.

With that grisly task finished, Ryk prepared my munition order while I browsed through his vehicle terminal for a replacement bike. I had more experience now than I had on my first shopping trip for a System vehicle, so I felt confident in finding something new without needing the simulator room that I'd used two years prior.

By the time my ammo storage was refilled to the point that my Inventory was capable of serving as a resupply depot for a small army, I finished browsing and moved into customization options for my selected vehicle.

"An excellent choice, Adventurer Mason. Though I am slightly surprised by your selection."

I frowned at Ryk and brought up the stats for the vehicle. "What's wrong with it?"

Rudianos Class I Outrider

Core: Class I Hephaestus-II Mana Engine

CPU: Class B Xylik Core CPU

Armor Rating: Tier I

Hard Points: 6 (4 Used: Nano Garage Module, Anti-Grav Module, Forward-facing Twin-cannon Mount, Micro-missile Launcher)

Soft Points: 4 (2 Used: Neural Link, Comm-transmitter)

Optional: Neural Link for Remote Activation

Battery Capacity: 150/150

"There is absolutely nothing wrong. I just expected you to go with something new."

"If it ain't broke, don't fix it," I replied, finalizing the options for my new and improved bike.

Then I sighed. There was something broken after all. I was still going to get the new bike, but I looked up at Ryk and filled him in on my hijacked Krym'parke vehicle. "Do you have a way to replace the lock system permanently, so I don't have to keep hacking it?"

"In fact, I do. Very reasonably priced too."

"I'm sure. Let's see it," I said, and was pleasantly surprised when the nanotech control module actually turned out quite cheap—especially when compared to the cost of a new vehicle.

Closing out my transactions, I exchanged the final sum of Credits with Ryk. Despite the price tag on my new ride, the sale of Sect equipment and corpses nearly offset my total purchase cost.

"One of these days, I'll come out ahead," I said as I prepared to leave.

Ryk smiled. "Of course, Adventurer Mason. Of course."

We both knew that would never happen in the long run. Staying alive on a Dungeon World was an investment and things were only heating up as Galactic groups collided with each other.

I waved to the shopkeeper and departed, materializing back in the Pharyleri headquarters building an instant later.

Trudging through the halls, I realized that after five weeks out of touch, my room may not still be my room. A quick detour to the front desk ensured I still had the same assignment. Walking into the hotel room, I stripped down just inside the door and went straight for the shower.

With the hot water on full blast, I ducked under the rushing waterfall as steam quickly filled the tiny bathroom. I scrubbed down and luxuriated in the scalding water until the exhaustion from the long day hit me.

I climbed out of the shower and toweled myself dry, stepping out of the bathroom as I ran the fluffy cloth through my hair one final time.

"Yum."

I froze and pulled the towel away from my face, though I already recognized the voice. On the bed, Creynora lifted herself up on one elbow under the covers. The dark elf's pink tongue licked at her lips unconsciously while hunger filled her gaze roving over my body.

My fatigue disappeared as I found that I quite liked the expression on her face. My heart thundered in my chest as blood began rushing through me.

"Am I in the wrong room?" I asked, though I was certain this was my assigned place. I wanted there to be no confusion if things went as I thought they might.

Creynora shook her head without taking her eyes off me. "I certainly hope not, after the trouble I went through to get in here."

"I would hate to disappoint you then."

I tossed the damp towel toward the bathroom without looking. I doubted that I would find much sleep tonight and was not at all concerned.

Chapter 41

A week after the joint operation conquered the last of the Sect-held City Cores, the midnight skies over Denver burned. Streaks of flame poured down from orbit, washing across the translucent barrier of the settlement shield. Looking up at the blazing dome overhead, it was easy to imagine we stood inside some giant furnace.

A mixed-species crowd had gathered outside of the Union Station headquarters building that was now primarily staffed by civilian human administrators. The Pharyleri who remained were primarily logistics and trade staff responsible for ensuring the flow of raw materials continued through the trade hub.

The gnomes still made up a good portion of the crowd, along with a bunch of civilian and military humans. Clustered together along one wall, a couple squads of Hakarta were also present and everyone gave the heavily armed orcs a wide berth.

Nervous muttering in several languages ran through the gathering, audible amidst the blaring alarms responsible for waking everyone in the building. The strobe lights of the building's pre-System fire alarms also flashed in the dark plaza.

Those same sirens and lights had jolted me from a light sleep only a few minutes earlier. I had shot out of bed, throwing the covers across the room and pulling on my armor. On the far side of the room, the vision of a dark figure pulling on her own combat jumpsuit had certainly distracted me. Though I still enjoyed the sight of Creynora after nearly a week of spending the nights with the dark elf, I put it out of my mind as we followed the flow of traffic through the halls.

"Anyone know what's going on?" I asked over party chat as the rest of our group joined us to watch the fiery sky.

"Negative, I just woke," Dayena replied, wiping sleep from her eyes.

"Same here," Lyrra added.

Spotting Staff Sergeant Johnson through the crowd, standing with his squad and several other uniformed soldiers, I pushed through the throng to reach him. The Army NCO raised an eyebrow when he saw me, and I returned the look while pointing to the burning sky.

Johnson leaned over and kept his voice low. "A Binary Eclipse heavy freighter showed up less than an hour ago and assumed a geostationary orbit over the city."

"And now they're bombing the settlement?"

The Staff Sergeant shook his head. "They're just dropping rocks. Letting gravity do the work until the shield drops. Cheap, easy, effective."

"Then what?"

He sighed. "That's the sixty-four-thousand-dollar question, ain't it?"

"Where are your Samurai and Assassin friends?" I asked, glancing around and not seeing any sign of the deadly women who had accompanied Johnson's squad previously.

He shrugged. "Probably out of the city. They're not much for civilization and spend their free time clearing Dungeons with their party."

I grunted a thank you to the man and worked my way back to my party, filling them in on the little information I'd learned from the soldier.

Dayena shook her head when I finished. "I suspect that they will either launch an attack to retake the city or continue the bombardment to destroy it out of spite."

I frowned at the Truinnar's words. I had no problem with facing any threat I could fight, but a ship in orbit was entirely out of my reach. There was nothing I could do about it, and I clenched my fists as a sense of frustration built within me as I thought about how to possibly combat an enemy at that altitude.

Without a fleet or space-based defenses, planetary installations would always be vulnerable to orbital attack. Not even the Pittsburgh starport possessed the weaponry to reach a ship in orbit. I would need a starship of my own, along with someone who could pilot the craft.

The alarms cut off and the buzz of the surrounding crowd grew. A loudspeaker crackled and then Colonel Wier's voice echoed over the space. He summarized the information I'd gotten from Johnson and then commanded all troops to report to their units. With orders issued, the chaos lessened slightly as the majority of bystanders headed off to their rally points.

Through the reduced crowd, I spotted Eldri Giltwrench, the Repair Technician, hurrying between several smaller gatherings of other Pharyleri. He spoke briefly to the groups of three to four other gnomes and then each scurried off as Eldri moved on to another cluster.

Signaling for the elves to follow, I intercepted the gnome when he passed near us.

The Technician looked up when I called his name and detoured to meet us. "I'm glad I ran into you, Hal. We're prepping the Express for departure just in case things get ugly."

"The Alliance is pulling out?" After all the work the gnomes put in to kick the Sect out and form the agreement with the human military, it surprised me that they'd abandon the city without a fight.

Eldri shook his head. "That call is above my level, but we don't have anything that can deal with a ship in orbit."

"What about the Army?" I asked.

The gnome shrugged. "They aren't sharing right now."

I sighed, unsurprised.

"Check in with Ismyna," Dayena suggested through party chat.

I glanced at the Countess. "While you three make sure we have a ride out of here on the train?"

She nodded and I turned back to Eldri. "Where are you off to now?"

"I'm going straight to the Express, once I round up a few stragglers."

I gestured to the trio of elves with me. "They'll stick with you. I'll check in with command to see if there's anything else we can do."

The gnome agreed and I split off from the group to head back inside. When I reached the command center, one of the guards grabbed my shoulder as I approached the door. With the humans running the defenses now, the sentries posted here were both uniformed Army soldiers.

"You're not on the list of cleared personnel," explained the corporal.

I raised an eyebrow at the trooper and stepped forward, placing my hand on the palm scanner beside the door before they could react. The light on the scanner blinked green and the door slid open. I was only slightly surprised that the Army had not removed all the access levels for the Pharyleri forces.

"Would you look at that? I guess I am on the list of cleared personnel, Corporal Schmuckatelli."

The corporal released my shoulder, frowning at my insult, but he took no further action to stop me entering the busy control room.

Populated mostly by military humans now, the smaller desks and monitors used by the Pharyleri were sized up for their new owners. Army fatigues were in the majority, but I spotted Marine and Air Force uniforms throughout. A single Navy officer stood on the central command deck with Colonel Wier and the rest of his staff.

The main display showed a detailed holographic rendering of the vessel in orbit and my eyes narrowed as I recognized the craft. The freighter looked like the Washington Monument tipped on its side, a horizontal obelisk design that was the same as the ship that had dumped Borgym's clan off on Earth in the early days of the System's takeover. I had no way of knowing if the starship was actually the same one or if it was just the same model, but the appearance of the vessel threw me for a moment.

The central display was split to display the settlement shield and report on its status. A percentage indicator off to one side dropped lower with every impact that rained down from the sky.

Nesdyna leaned against the railing on the command dais off to one side. The older gnome beckoned, and I walked over to join her, but I saw no sign of her daughter or bodyguard nearby.

"Are you really planning on leaving?" I asked, keeping my voice low.

The gnome remained fixated on the display as she shook her head. "We've invested too heavily in the industries of this city to just give it up."

On the display, the shield counter dropped below thirty percent and the barrage from orbit seemed to slow by a faint amount. The attacks stepped down again at twenty and ten percent. Muttering ran around the room as the changes were observed by the human commanders.

"They're not planning on destroying the city. They know exactly how strong the shield is," I whispered, coming to the conclusion shared around the room.

"So it would seem," Nesdyna replied, tight lipped.

The fall of the meteorites narrowed from a storm that covered the entire shield to a tight stream of constantly dropping attacks against a single point, slowing the weakening of the shield to just more than its regeneration could handle.

Nesdyna and I shared a look. The only way that the Sect could manage that precision was if they knew the exact strength of the shield, information likely provided by the now-deceased traitor.

"And there goes the shield," one of the Army officers declared.

The translucent dome flickered and then disappeared as one single meteorite punched through and descended into the middle of the city in a streak of fire.

Smaller dots broke away from the Sect freighter and a signal officer turned away from his console. "Multiple craft launching from the freighter."

"Activate air defenses and tell our forces to prepare for an aerial assault," Colonel Wier ordered.

Dozens of indicators arced out from the starship and dropped straight for the city below. Tension escalated in the command center as voices called out intercepts and estimated landing plots with the forced calm of professionals relying on their training.

"Enemy craft are forming clusters with each group headed directly for a City Core. The landing craft have reached terminal velocity and show no signs of slowing. If they maintain that velocity, they'll only be within the firing window for a few seconds."

Weir slammed a hand down on the edge of the display. "They're using drop pods to punch through our anti-air defenses with minimal casualties."

On the display, lines of beam and cannon fire stretched upward for the descending indicators. A few lights winked out, but dozens remained to reach the ground.

Once again, we were in for a fight for the city. It seemed like Denver just couldn't get a break.

A part of me wondered just how much more the city, the people, and my allies could take.

Then, it got too busy for wondering any more.

Chapter 42

The command center shook, and the lights flickered as two of the drop pods targeting Union Station crashed into the building, disappearing from view in clouds of rubble and dust. Several other landing craft dropped just outside, and part of the display zoomed in close on the nearest.

The angular vessel looked vaguely pear-shaped, like a raindrop of sharp angles with a flat bottom that sat tilted slightly where the vessel cratered the street underneath. The walls of the craft shot outward, unfurling with explosive force as if the drop pod were some kind of deadly rosebud blooming to sprout ramps.

Fire blazed out from within the landing craft as soon as the ramps dropped clear and energy shields glimmered as a mass of Sect troops rushed out, revealing heavily armored infantry in burgundy-colored power armor. Spells and attacks from the defenders poured down from the walls around the compound and from defensive positions in Union Station itself. Smoke soon clouded the display, hiding the combatants from view as they closed the distance between each other.

"Enemy units are deploying jammers. We're losing the ability to track their ground forces that have breached the building," a technician called out.

More vibrations rippled through the command center as things exploded throughout the building. The din of combat grew gradually louder, the sounds of weapons fire and spell detonations growing closer.

Nesdyna still watched the display and the human commanders in the center of the room, all of them ignoring the conflict that seemed near to reaching the heart of the headquarters. Wier and the others remained focused on directing the troops across the city.

"We've lost contact with the command post at Aurora and the capture timer has started on the City Core," an officer reported to Wier.

The colonel grunted, leaning closer to the major and saying something I couldn't hear.

A burst of gunfire rattled outside the entrance to the command center, then went silent. I pulled on my helmet and stared at the door, casting Ice Armor on myself before slipping my pistols free from their holsters. If the Sect knew the strength of the settlement shield, it was just as likely they knew the location of the command center.

"If you're going to the Express, Nesdyna, you need to go now," I said, looking over at the older gnome.

Nesdyna raised a skeptical eyebrow, finally looking away from the central display. "Going to keep an eye on me?"

"I'm sure your daughter would kill me if I let anything happen to you."

Nesdyna snorted but didn't disagree.

More shots echoed outside, and a barrage of energy beams responded, overwhelming the gunfire that petered out. As the sounds beyond the door died out, a squad of soldiers formed up inside. The command escort unit deployed both physical and energy barriers in an arc, turning the entrance into a killzone.

I glanced at the defenders and frowned. Multiple Sect units were hitting the command center. If they had the blueprints, why would they only hit where the defenders expected them?

Pushing out with Greater Observation, I scanned beyond the perimeter of the room but found nothing. I took a deep breath and looked up, my gut screaming that a threat was approaching, even if I couldn't see it.

Up. The ceiling. Sweeping my Skill above, I snarled as I felt the ability slide around an area over the southwestern corner of the command center.

The sensation reminded me of when I failed to scan the Canadian Assassin, not quite the same but close enough to hint at the jammers deployed by the Sect.

"Wier, we've got incoming," I called out, my voice amplified by my helmet speaker as I raised my pistols to point at the location.

The Officer glanced over, saw where I was focused, and signaled several other troops. One of the soldiers deployed a tripod-mounted machine gun and aimed it upward as everyone throughout the room readied weapons or spellcraft. Motion from the corner of my eye showed that Nesdyna was also preparing, though I missed what she was doing while staying focused on that spot overhead.

The corner of the ceiling disappeared in a cloud as twin explosions thundered. Ignoring the breach at the main entrance, I opened fire on the hole overhead as the first burgundy figure dropped.

The massive figure of an armored Ceratophimi holding a tower shield slammed to the ground after barely squeezing through the breach, dropping the two-story height without any trouble and holding the shield steady. The barrier blocked the incoming fire and protected the landings of the next several troops, though I caught each of them with several rounds from my pistols.

"Hmmph," Nesdyna sneered, though the sound was muted.

Before I could start flanking the shield carrier, a surprise blast of cannon fire from directly beside me sent me reeling. I staggered to the side, my aim thrown off target momentarily as I regained my footing and looked at the source.

I found no sign of the elderly gray-and-green-haired gnome and a four-and-a-half foot tall mecha stood in her place, slowly lowering an arm-mounted cannon with a barrel diameter the size of my head. The weapon collapsed in on itself, folding back into a recessed housing that just looked like thicker plating on the arm of the suit.

Little remained of the initial quartet of Sect troops to drop through the ceiling. The giant shield had shattered from the cannon blast and turned into a hailstorm of shrapnel that had torn them apart. Several more figures jumped through the hole in the ceiling but were instantly cut down without the cover of the shield bearer as my fire joined back in with the Army machine-gunner.

More gunshots mingled with the sounds of blasting spells that included roaring flames, the crackling of electric bursts, and the shattering of icy hail from the killzone at the main entrance. Inhuman screams from outside the open doorway confirmed the defenders held, without any Sect forces even stepping inside the Command Center.

The forces dropping through the hole above trickled off and I spared a glance for the rest of the room. Bodies lay in the corridor outside, visible through the broken main entrance. On the central display, countdown timers ticked downward above every City Core on the map with the sole exception of Union Station.

While the military still controlled the core located in another part of the building, I suspected that was only due to the Sect splitting their first wave to hit both objectives here. The Binary Eclipse aerial assault had rapidly overwhelmed the defenders and seized the city.

Outside of Union Station, the fire from the compound walls trickled off as more enemy forces continued climbing out of the two drop pods and were slowly overwhelming the defenses with sheer numbers. The weight of attrition favored the Sect.

Two more burgundy-armored aliens dropped through the ceiling. Between the machine-gunner and I, by the time they hit the floor the pair were little more than bullet-riddled chunks of flesh leaking bodily fluids through their perforated armor.

"We just lost contact with the defenders in the Core room."

Weir's mouth turned to a tight line as he acknowledged the report. A few seconds later, a new timer appeared above Union Station.

"Signal all remaining forces to withdraw. Break contact and regroup at rally point Delta Echo. Otherwise, they are to retreat under fire until they are clear of the city and coordinate with our reserves to intercept any pursuit," Colonel Wier ordered, still standing beside the holographic display.

His aides moved off to coordinate the surviving forces as the technicians began packing up any portable gear. Left alone at the center of the command dais, Wier reached out with one hand and traced along the lip of the projector. The Officer gave the unit a little pat, as if saying goodbye for now, and then stepped away.

"That's our cue," Nesdyna said.

I glanced over at the gnome in her mech suit and gestured for her to lead the way. "I can see why you weren't worried."

The older gnome chuckled. "When you've been around for a while, you learn about the things worth investing in."

Nesdyna headed for the entrance, and I followed in her wake, but she stopped behind the squad holding the door and waited for the solitary minute it took for the soldiers to tear down their gear. Even that was surprisingly short, but having access to an Inventory generally made packing easy.

Once the technicians and command staff were lined up to depart, the soldiers watching the ceiling breach fell back to the door before leapfrogging past us to lead the way out of the command center. Nesdyna and I followed, joining the command staff in the middle of the group before the door squad brought up the tail end of the formation as a rearguard.

Everyone carried at least a pistol in hand, though trigger and muzzle discipline were observed rigorously despite the tension. A couple brief firefights broke out in the hallways ahead, but we kept a rapid pace.

Several intersections later, Weir nodded to Nesdyna and I.

"We're not done with Denver, so stay in touch," Nesdyna said as she split away from the group. I moved after her, nodding to the colonel and other officers.

"Don't worry, we're not going far."

The footsteps of the soldiers faded down the hall behind us as we headed for the rail platform and the Pistongrinder Express. Without the added firepower from the military forces, we slowed to a more cautious pace. At each corner, we split to either side and covered the cross passages in case there were any Sect troops lingering in the corridors, but we encountered no one until we reached the transit station.

The clash of melee weapons and the whine of beam fire greeted Nesdyna and me as we pushed out of the rear entrance. A drop pod cratered the terrace less than a dozen feet from the doorway, but the Sect troops pouring out of the craft were entirely focused on pushing their way across the platform to the parked train.

The deployed landing craft was little more than a series of A-frame scaffolds sticking up at the center of the lowered ramps that allowed the troops to debark. With the flower-like structure opened up, that metal framework was obscured by an energy shield surrounding the craft and protecting the Sect forces until they cleared the ramps.

Instead of joining the fray, I stuck one hand in front of Nesdyna and ducked behind one of the cement planters that lined the entryway. Something felt off here.

The drop pod was too small to account for the number of Sect forces now advancing toward the train, especially after tallying up the dead strewn around the craft where the gnomes defending the platform had cut them down.

"Teleporter or portal," Nesdyna hissed, identifying the source of the problem before I could voice my concerns.

"Can we take it out?"

"I'm damned well gonna try," she replied.

The armored gnome stepped out from the planter, raising her arm as her cannon deployed once again. This time, I was prepared for the thunder when she opened up on the drop pod.

Her shot splashed against the shield, which rippled from the force of the impact without giving way. Another crash of thunder echoed over the platform as she fired again. Seeing only the slightest give in the shield, I holstered my pistols and summoned my Banshee rifle.

Ignoring the Sect troops, I added the hybrid rifle's fire to the gnome's shots and our combined fire finally punched through the barrier. The shield failed in a cascade of flashing energy, revealing a glowing orange circle at the center of the drop pod that seemed to project from the top of the metallic framework.

Energy beams streaked all around me from the Binary Eclipse rearguard and the attacks caught the attention of more enemy troops. A mage in their midst turned back, sending a fireball washing over me and searing away most of my protective Ice Armor as the superheated air spiked the temperature within my armor.

Nesdyna fired again and the upper half of the A-frame disappeared in a hail of wreckage. The teleportation circle flashed so brightly that most of the Sect forces were blinded for an instant before it disappeared.

My helmet visor muted the blinding flare, and I shifted my fire to the mage, adjusting the weapon to feed anti-magic rounds. Several rifle shots silenced the source of my fireball problem.

As the Sect troops recovered from the flash of the destroyed teleporter, the energy and projectile fire picked up. I continued firing and dropped a portable shield from my Inventory, kneeling to take partial cover behind one of the planters.

Nesdyna blurred into motion, running evasively to dodge the incoming barrage, and leaving me to face the fire alone. The attacks overwhelmed the deployable shield, and my health ticked down despite the planter absorbing the brunt of the assault. I reapplied Ice Armor and returned fire with steady shots, fine with those troops focusing on me for a bit. With the teleporter down and their constant stream of reinforcements cut off, the attacks from the train tore through the front ranks of the Sect forces.

The end came suddenly. The last Sect trooper, a Scrofalori, jerked like a tangled marionette as my shot spun him around, just in time to take a blast from several of the train's mounted weapons.

Though distant weapons fire echoed from the opposite side of the building, the platform fell silent. I crawled out from behind the ruined planter and jogged over to the wreck of the drop pod.

The hexagonal central platform of the landing craft looked large enough to fit maybe twenty or thirty troops, supported by a frame that held the angular ramps closed until the vessel hit the ground, where it would open like a deadly blooming onion. The food analogy meant I was getting hungry again, but I doubted that there would be much quality snacking in the near future.

Nesdyna joined me as I left the broken landing craft, and we hurried across the platform toward the locomotive at the front of the train. The Pistongrinder Express now looked more like a train out of a World War 2 photo than a futuristic piece of technology. Cars at either end of the train sported forward and rear-facing tank turrets, each accompanied by an anti-air defense battery. Multiple cars were also equipped with multi-barrel turrets on their roofs, evidence that the Pharyleri had learned their lesson from the attacks on the transport following our initial return from Denver.

Those turrets largely held the Sect at bay, supported by individual defenders. One such defender, Lyrra, waved down from on top of a train car and I found that the rest of the party was also showing on my minimap now. Destroying the drop pod had also taken care of the jamming, at least in this area.

As soon as Nesdyna and I jumped onto the access platform at the rear of the engine, the train lurched into motion.

"I heard your stomach growling. Get something to eat, in case things heat back up, and we'll talk about our next steps," Nesdyna ordered before heading inside the control cabin for the locomotive.

I waved and headed for the dining car. By the time I reached it, the train was gaining speed and we were already near the edge of the settlement. Staring out the window, I ignored the posted menu as I took a last look out over the city.

Columns of smoke drifted skyward in the early light of dawn, reminding me of the earliest days of the System on Earth. So much had been lost then and I wondered what this latest loss would mean for the future of Denver.

Chapter 43

Six days after we fought our way out of the city, an armed camp spread out around the Pistongrinder Express with the train parked several miles north and east of Denver. Six days of frantic rescue missions, pulling personnel and equipment out from the ever-tightening control of the Sect as their forces massed in the city.

Arctic camouflage nets stretched between cars and the surrounding tent city. Beneath the cover of the netting, the anti-air turrets mounted on top of the train tracked in arcs as the gnomes who operated them scanned the sky for threats.

Though the Sect had left the gnomes alone once the train departed the city days ago, no one wanted to be caught off guard again. On top of that concern, the hazard of roaming monsters almost eclipsed any threat of a Binary Eclipse raid this far out from the borders of the settlement.

In the heart of the camp, a holographic display of the city floated above a portable projector that resembled an open suitcase. The makeshift setup lying out on the hard-packed snow was a significant downgrade from the Union Station headquarters building. It showed the Sect freighter hovering several feet above the city surface, though the altitude of the vessel was clearly not to scale.

Colonel Wier and a couple members of his staff knelt or stood around the display, their breath frosting with every exhale in the chill of the morning air. Staff Sergeant Johnson waited a short distance away with a squad that appeared to be a couple members short, showing more signs of the losses suffered by the Army in the hectic fighting of the Sect airborne assault and the subsequent evacuation of the human forces as the City Cores fell.

Nesdyna and several Pharyleri commanders were spread in a semicircle around the gathering, while Ismyna stood directly across the projector from the Army officer and pointed to the starship. "Sure, the drop pods are an issue, but the main problem is the teleporter on the ship. Anywhere they've got a beacon, they can pull forces up through the ship and then teleport them anywhere there is another beacon."

"Can we destroy the beacons?" Wier asked.

The gnome shrugged. "Sure, but then they'll just drop another one. Or send it in a drop pod, like the initial assault where they sent along an escort squad strong enough to hold until the beacon was online."

Weir's frustration was evident as he ran a hand over his face. Leaning on one knee, the exhausted man appeared to have aged a decade in the last week despite the System naturally restoring stamina and health.

The other gnome commanders and human officers debated strategy for dealing with the Sect, but no one offered a solid plan to deal with the threat in orbit. Until the ability to move their troops almost instantly was neutralized, the Binary Eclipse forces would continue to hold the upper hand in the city.

Staring down at the map, I looked between the city and the starship above as the beginnings of a bad idea blossomed into twelve percent of a plan.

I worked my way around the edge of the gathering until I got to Johnson. The NCO nodded to me before continuing a constant wary scan of the surroundings.

"Can you find me a pilot? One who flies starships," I asked, keeping my voice low.

"Why do you need a pilot?"

"Make sure your pilot has a vac suit."

452

The Staff Sergeant's eyes narrowed when I purposefully avoided his question, but after several seconds he nodded anyway, and I moved on without another word.

My next visit was the train parked on the other side of the planning meeting. Swinging up into the workshop car, I found the engineering staff repairing armor suits that sported varying amounts of damage.

Eldri glanced up from his workbench, distinctive neon blue mutton chops sticking out from the sides of the gnome's welding goggles. "Hal? Do you need something repaired?"

I shook my head. "No. I need to know if you still have those flamethrower mechas you used back when we first cleared the tracks into Denver."

"We haven't used those since, but we've got them boxed up in storage below deck." The gnome nodded, looking puzzled.

"Can you get them ready? Along with drivers and extra fuel for the flamers?"

The gnome looked distant for a moment and then he nodded again, tapping his foot on the floor of the workshop. "Sure, we'll have them pulled out and fueled in a few minutes."

"I've got one more thing to line up still," I said, then thanked the Technician before hopping out of the car and returning to the command meeting.

Ismyna saw my approach and stepped away from the holographic projection. "You've got that look on your face, Hal. What are you up to?"

"Hopefully, a way to do something about your teleporter problem. Do you have a survey of the Steamspanner starport?"

"What good would that do? Everything is frozen solid."

"I'm hoping for a sealed hangar, one that would have a ship inside."

Ismyna frowned. "Nobody has managed to get through that cursed ice."

"We got the Pistongrinder Express through," I countered, pointing to the train.

The gnome looked thoughtful and glanced around the command gathering. "I'll find Piklyn. If anyone has a manifest of what might be trapped there, it would be the acting head of the Steamspanner clan."

Wier was still staring at the map of the city, lost in thought. Ismyna gestured to Nesdyna that she was leaving and the clan elder nodded before signaling she would take care of things here. The Engineer grabbed the armor along the side of my thigh and tugged to pull me along after her, leading me deeper into the encampment and away from the Express.

An open-sided canopy covering multiple charging bays filled with suits of bronze power armor marked our entry into the Steamspanner section of the camp. Most of the suits sported signs of battle damage from the withdrawal from the city and teams of Pharyleri technicians clustered around the most damaged sets of armor. Sparks flew and lights flashed from the support cradles, filling the air with the scent of ozone as the techs welded armor panels and replaced destroyed components.

"Oi, Piklyn," Ismyna called out, her high-pitched voice carrying over the pounding of hammers on armor and the static crackling of the welding machines.

One of the welders turned away from the suit they were working on and raised his goggles before running a hand over the top of his disheveled neon blue mohawk. "Ismyna? What are you doing here?"

The Engineer gestured to me. "Hal needs some info on the ruins of the frozen starport."

"What do you want with that cursed place?" Piklyn asked, his face shifting into a scowl at the reminder of the monument to his clan's failure.

"I'm hoping there's a hangar that was sealed well enough to keep the ice out. One that might have a ship capable of making orbit stuck inside."

Piklyn grunted and glanced at Ismyna, clearly reluctant to even consider the request.

"It might help us deal with our unwanted neighbors upstairs," Ismyna said. She pointed up toward the Sect vessel over the city.

"Fine. Come with me."

The scowling gnome led us out of the repair center and along a path of hard-packed snow the cut between several other tents. He abruptly turned to the side of the path and threw open a flap to a small tent in the middle of a row of similar shelters, then he ducked inside without looking back.

Exchanging questioning glances with Ismyna, I followed the angry gnome through the narrow opening, and we found ourselves inside Piklyn's personal dwelling. I could barely stand up inside the tiny space, which contained a gnome-sized cot, a collapsible chair, and a small table.

Piklyn flopped on top of the cot and waved to the chair. "Have a seat."

I raised a skeptical eyebrow and gestured for Ismyna to take the offering that was clearly too small for any human to fit. As she settled into the chair, Piklyn slid the small table out to rest between them and activated the fist-sized projector in its center. Several menus flashed before a wireframe schematic of the Steamspanner starport project expanded from the device and slowly rotated in the air.

Piklyn waved a hand through the translucent image, and it rotated to follow his movements until he focused the image on a small rectangular structure on the southeast corner of the map. The Pharyleri tag on the building rated it as capable of housing up to four medium-sized vessels.

Piklyn finally looked up at me. "Hanger 032 is probably your best bet. It was built with extra reinforcement because we figured those corvette-class ships are popular with smugglers and those types have bad habits of crashing or damaging their landing spots. It's also why we stuck that hangar so far away from the primary passenger terminal, in the hopes that anyone there would stay out of trouble. Not that it helped."

The scowl returned to the gnome's face as he paused, and more text scrolled above the hangar. "There were two ships assigned to park in 032 on the day the starport was destroyed, *Fool's Folly* and *Starwhisper*. Both arrived the previous day and neither were slated to depart for another couple days."

The gnome sent me a datafile that contained the reported flight profiles of both craft. A quick glance showed both were tagged with warnings that the ships were suspected smugglers capable of significant deviation from the noted statistics in the files.

I returned to peering at the hangar display and took note of where the entrances were located. "Personnel access doors here and here?"

Piklyn looked where I was pointing and confirmed the spots. With the ice covering the structures and disguising the exteriors, ensuring we were at the actual entrances would be a priority. Once I copied the hangar data to my own map, I thanked the gnome for his help and ducked out of the tent. Ismyna followed me and we headed back to the command gathering.

"If you pull this off, my mother will throw Credits at you," Ismyna said as we retraced our steps back to the Pistongrinder Express.

"I'll hold you to that."

Johnson cut me off before we reached the circle of officers. "I found your pilot, but I want in on whatever you're doing."

"There's a good chance it'll be a one-way trip, but I won't turn down more guns."

The Staff Sergeant chuckled. "You don't strike me as the type to do anything without a chance you'll walk away."

I shook my head and sent him the files on the two ships. "Have your pilot get familiar with both. We won't know their condition until we get to them, so we'll take whichever is in better shape."

Johnson nodded. "When do we leave?"

"As soon as I figure out how we're going to move those," I replied, pointing to the two mechs that Eldri and his crew of engineers were pulling out from beneath the workshop car. A stack of fuel containers sat off to one side and continued to grow as several other gnomes added to the pile.

For the first time, I actually missed the hideous orange combat minivan I'd left behind when we pulled out of Denver. I could have at least crammed one of the mecha into the back if I didn't try to shut the rear door.

"The Army's got trucks. I'll talk to the S4 and get a few assigned to my squad."

The NCO left to track down the logistics officer and I took the time to offer a brief explanation of my plan over party chat.

Silence was the only response when I finished with the highlights. *"Any questions?"*

"If we do this, we get to sleep in real beds again instead of camping out, right?" Creynora asked. The dark elf winked at me when I glared in her direction.

"Are there any serious questions?"

When no one else responded, I nodded. *"Make sure you've got vacuum-rated gear and spares. Breaching charges and tools will be handy too."*

I followed my own advice and started one last check of my own gear. It took effort to push down the building anticipation and find my pre-mission focus.

If my plan worked out, I would be following through on a childhood dream.

I would be going to space.

Chapter 44

"Dayena, I'll tag the target spots through party chat so you can direct the fire. I probably won't have the focus to do much more than that."

The dark elf nodded, and I pulled off my gauntlet, feeling the icy wind of the abandoned starport scraping across my flesh. The tingling sensation of frostbite already pricked at my exposed hand. The cold only grew worse as I placed my hand on the ice that encased Hangar 032 and closed my eyes.

Reaching out into the frigid crystalline formation, I felt for the dragon's curse that caused the ice to constantly reform. Thanks to my Ice Affinity and previous interactions with the substance, I located the unnatural magic with ease. This time, I found that I could actually see the natural ice and the lingering curse as separate parts.

The curse was like a layer of oil that clung to the fractals within the ice, coating the rigid portions of the molecular structures and pulling the crystals all back together whenever anything disrupted the formation. Focusing on the magical film, I pushed at the clinging magical force and gradually scraped it away from the elegant angles of the ice crystals.

Molecule by molecule, I pushed that aberrant force from the ice and left only natural fractals behind. As I cleared away the curse, I projected the update to Dayena through party chat and she directed the flamethrowers to focus on the marked locations. The roar of the flamers barely registered on my conscious mind as I continued pushing back the curse bit by bit.

I lost all sense of time, focused only on holding back the curse as I cleared a channel to the door hidden beyond the layers of ice. Someone grabbed my shoulder and shook, pulling me back to myself and I realized I could barely breathe.

Coughing and choking from a congealing bloody mess that filled the inside of my helmet, I staggered back. The sudden motion tore off the outer layer of my frozen skin that stuck to the wall of ice and left behind a bloody handprint just beside the melted edges of the newly formed tunnel. I ripped off the helmet and fell to my hands and knees. Spitting the coppery mass of bloody phlegm from my mouth, I retched and coughed repeatedly before managing to catch my breath.

My head throbbed with a pounding headache and apparently my nose had been bleeding from the constant mental strain. I hadn't even noticed I was having trouble breathing. I shook my head to clear it as oxygen flowed once more. Now fully conscious, I realized dusk had fallen over the abandoned starport while we had tunneled to the hangar through over eighteen inches of cursed ice. It was now cleared to the edges of the door.

"We're in," Eldri reported from the mecha at the front as the hangar door opened for the first time in months, revealing only darkness beyond.

Johnson clapped my shoulder, looking impressed by the bloody mess strewn across the snow around me, most of it already frozen solid. "We've got it, you rest up for a minute."

The Staff Sergeant led his squad through the tunnel and beams of light flicked on, extending in front of the soldiers from tactical lights attached to the front of their combat armor and the barrels of their rifles.

The remaining Army troops from the logistics corps helped Eldri and the other mecha suit load back up into the deuce-and-a-half trucks that carried them here.

Creynora knelt beside me. "Are you alright?"

"I'll be fine," I replied.

Scooping up a handful of fresh snow, I rubbed it over my face and wiped away the worst of the congealed blood. Another few handfuls rubbed away the worst of what remained inside of my helmet. I added a Cleanse spell for good measure and accepted a hand from Creynora as I stood and slipped my helmet back on. I nodded my thanks to the dark elf and then paused as another Army truck drove up.

Two men jumped down from the cab, an Alchemist and a Technomancer. I didn't recognize either the skinny Hispanic or the man with salt-and-pepper hair in the leather coat, but their attire announced them as civilians. Then a third figure climbed from the vehicle—one I did recognize. The Samurai. A glance around the area showed no sign of the Assassin, but that wasn't surprising. I doubted she'd be careless enough to let me spot her again.

"Carlos, Sam, thanks for coming," Johnson called out as he returned from the hangar.

The man in the leather coat shook hands with the Staff Sergeant. "Took some time to get everything put together, but we've got the demo charges you wanted in the back, in containment. They'll be fine in Inventories, but once they're set..."

The Hispanic man grinned and mimed an explosion with both hands before heading around to the back of the truck.

"Perfect, let's get loaded up," Johnson said with a grim smile.

The Staff Sergeant beckoned for my team to follow as the rest of his guys returned from scouting the hangar. I nodded a greeting at the Samurai as I passed, and she nodded back.

Carlos had the containment unit opened and the giant, thick-walled safe filled the rear bed of the heavy-duty truck. The Alchemist gently pulled out the satchel charges one at a time, handing them out with extreme care as both the Army squad and my group filled our Inventories.

Sam stood at the back. "You'll want to deploy these at any hatches, against the outer hull, and you can leave them with any valuable equipment that's worth blowing. They've got both timers and trigger switches and will relay detonation commands via daisy-chain."

Once we were done, I followed the rest of the party through the tunnel.

The inside of the hangar was pitch dark, lit only by the lights of the Johnson's squad as they spread out across the cavernous interior. The building may only have been classified as a small hangar, but a football field would have fit inside the structure with room to spare.

I hated dark, enclosed spaces. Feeling glad that I still kept a stack of flares in my Inventory, I lit one and tossed it out to the side. A flickering red glow filled the chamber as I threw a second flare in the opposite direction, revealing the murky outline of the two vessels parked across the hangar.

The *Starwhisper* was a long, narrow-bodied craft with an aerodynamic fuselage and smooth curves that narrowed to a cone at the prow of the starship. *Fool's Folly*, on the other hand, had a blunt nose at the front of a wide body with stubby, angular wings studded with what appeared like weapon's ports.

"You're up, kid. Pick your poison," I said over my shoulder to the flight-suited pilot who entered the hangar behind us. The fresh-faced young man, one of the surviving Air Force Academy cadets, frowned when I called him a kid.

"My name is Cadet Second Class Bryce, thank you," he said, heading over to begin his inspection of the pair of starcraft.

The rest of us spread out, checking out the hangar and making sure there weren't any monster surprises hiding in the dark corners of the building. It didn't take long for the cadet to return with his report.

"Both ships are operational, but the *Folly* is the one we want. It's obvious once you set foot on board that it was designed with piracy in mind. There's a ventral docking clamp system with an airlock and hull cutters, along with a stealth package for covert approaches."

That was convenient. Almost too convenient. Johnson and I exchanged a glance, then I shrugged. None of us were going to look the gift horse in the mouth here.

My trio of elven companions followed after the soldiers as we traipsed up the boarding ramp into the *Fool's Folly*. The ramp rose behind us once everyone was inside the ship. I followed Bryce, Johnson, and one of the other soldiers to the bridge as the others found places to secure themselves for the launch.

With seats for a pilot and copilot forward of secondary crew positions, the control cabin's layout appeared similar to the cockpit of larger terrestrial transport planes. Johnson and I strapped into the rear jump seats while Bryce and the other soldier started figuring out how to fly the vessel. It turned out that Redford, the Humvee driver from Johnson's squad, had some vehicle-related Skills that would also apply to the starship, along with a shield-penetration ability that could prove useful once we reached orbit.

I observed the pair while they deciphered the controls and soon had the engines of the starship thrumming as the craft powered up. The vessel lifted a few feet from the ground and held position in a hover.

A targeting reticle appeared on the transparent canopy as Redford activated the ship's weapon systems.

"What does having sex and firing a cannon have in common?" the soldier asked the cabin at large without taking his eyes off the gunnery display. I just stared at the back of his balding head as Johnson rolled his eyes with a long-suffering sigh. Bryce looked over at his copilot in confusion.

"They're all about the bangs!" Redford exclaimed as he triggered the starship's cannons.

Beneath the pylons of the ship's stubby wings, heavy cannons roared out and traced converging lines of explosions onto the far wall of the hangar. A rotary energy gatling from under the cockpit joined the projectile fire and coherent light burned into the roiling firestorm.

"Are we worried about the Sect picking up any of this?" I asked, gesturing to the fireworks tracing across the hangar.

Johnson shook his head. "Nah, one of the trucks has a suppression field generator. The Sect would have to have someone literally watching us to pick this up. They've got orders to wait until they see us leave, at which point the show should be over and our own stealth active."

After several seconds of the barrage, the reinforced wall of the hangar collapsed away, and a cloud of steam filled that end of the structure as the attack dug into the ice entombing the building. The ice held up stronger than the wall, but it eventually gave way as well.

As Redford controlled the weapons, Bryce drifted the nose of the starship back and forth. The coordination gradually opened up a hole large enough to fit the vessel and Redford ceased fire as the pilot eased the craft forward. At the hole, we slowed to a crawl and the vessel inched through.

Then we were out and hovering in the open air. Snow from the frozen starport swirled around the craft, obscuring the view from the cockpit, but the sensors had no trouble picking out the surroundings.

"Engaging concealment, confirming all active sensors are offline. Stealth systems green across the board," Redford reported after flicking switches across the control console.

"I've got Shadow Cloak active now as well," Johnson added.

Bryce nodded. "Taking us up."

The canopy angled toward the nearly dark sky overhead with surprisingly little sensation of motion as the pilot increased the throttle. The ground on the sensor display fell away as the starship leapt upward. We broke out of the swirling snow and climbed away from the city, circling out to the north and west to get away from the populated settlement.

"Damn, I've never flown anything like this. This baby handles like a dream," Bryce muttered.

Redford glanced over at the younger man. "You fly much? You know, before."

The cadet nodded. "My dad had a little Cessna Citation and we'd go flying together every chance we got. Got my student license at sixteen and full pilot's license as soon as I turned eighteen. After the System came and all the planes stopped working, I was afraid of being grounded forever, but I took Pilot as my Class, anyway. Now I'm certainly glad I did."

I watched out the windows as the world dropped away below us, the starship climbing higher and faster than any commercial plane that I'd ever ridden. We shot through the clouds and soon reached the edges of the atmosphere. It felt a little surreal seeing the curve of the Earth so far beneath us, higher than anyone in the cockpit had ever been.

"There she is," Redford said, drawing our attention away from the planet below.

The dark obelisk of the Sect freighter appeared as a distant spec, at first. The vessel seemed to grow larger until it stretched across the entire canopy window. Bryce kept one hand on the throttle, slowing us further. The slower we moved, the better our stealth would work.

We hoped.

"That's no moon," Redford said, deadpan.

"Shut up, Redford," Johnson interrupted, before the soldier could finish the iconic line.

The copilot grinned, apparently quite pleased with himself, and the interaction eased some of the tension filling the cockpit.

Bryce looked over his shoulder at Johnson. "Still want me to aim for the middle of the ship?"

The Staff Sergeant nodded. "That's where the intel pukes pegged the highest Mana spikes during times we know the teleporter was active."

I waited until the pilot settled on a course that brought us over the Sect vessel. "Your team is still going for the teleportation platform then?"

"Disrupting that means they can't reinforce, so that's the priority target."

The logic made sense, but I thought we could take down the entire ship.

"You're set on taking engineering?" Johnson asked and I nodded.

We already had this argument with Wier and the other ground force commanders. I got the feeling they weren't telling the whole story, not that it came as any surprise. We planned to split once we breached the hull, the Army squad going one way and mine the other. Our comm links would allow us to keep each other updated on our progress.

"Coming up on the target position and matching velocity," Bryce reported.

The hull of the freighter stretched out of sight as far as I could see through the cockpit canopy. The pilot focused entirely on his instruments for the last short distance as our vessel dropped onto the upper hull of the freighter. "I've got what looks like a maintenance hatch almost where we were planning to latch on. Want me to go for a hard dock there?"

"Do it. I'll let my team know of the change in plans," Johnson commanded, while I updated the elves in my team through party chat.

The sensor display showed the hatch set in the hull as we slowly lowered over it. A clang echoed through the *Folly* as we set down and Bryce engaged the pirate docking clamps. "We're down."

Despite the tension of the approach and the relief at making it to the capital ship, now came the hard part.

I threw off the safety harness and checked my helmet seal, following Johnson as we rushed to the boarding airlock in the center of the ship. By the time we reached them, our teams already had the freighter's outer airlock doors open and were helping each other down through the access portal.

The cramped maintenance airlock only fit two of the Army soldiers, but Dayena slipped down between them before we cycled them through. Creynora and Lyrra went next with Johnson. By the time we were ready for a third group, Redford joined me from the cockpit as the last wave through.

Redford signaled Bryce that we were all out as I sealed the *Fool's Folly* airlock one last time, from the outside. I hoped that we would go home after a successful mission, but the odds that we would all make it back to Earth were slim. As the airlock cycled and the doors into the freighter slid open, the sound of suppressed gunshots rang out down the corridor.

The first orbital combat over the planet Earth had just begun.

Chapter 45

Chuffing echoes from the lone burst reverberated through the air and trailed off into silence as the hatch slid open. The Army silencers lacked the quality of mine, so it seemed the government still sourced contracts from the lowest bidder. Even in the apocalypse, bureaucracy never changed.

I stepped into the corridor with silenced pistols in hand, finding the Army squad posted up at an intersection in the direction of the shots, but facing no immediate threat.

The wear-resistant decking of passageways could have passed for nearly any naval vessel of the last century that had seen too many years and too little preventative maintenance, but for the coppery metallic alloys, alien sigils stenciled on the bulkheads, and the greater height to accommodate larger Galactic species. The air possessed a stale quality that highlighted the chemical scents of lubricants and machinery.

"Are we clear, Malik?" Johnson asked the scout at the front of the squad.

The man kept his eyes on the scope of his rifle. "Target down, no sign of response. Yet."

Redford slipped past me and hurried to catch up to the squad. The Staff Sergeant turned back as the soldier reached them. "Good luck, Marine."

"Catch you on the flipside, Army." I nodded to Johnson in farewell.

The squad disappeared around the corner, and I signaled for Creynora to lead us off. The dark elf deployed her shield as she headed off down the corridor toward the aft end of the ship. I followed, casting Ice Armor to bolster my defenses. Dayena trailed along behind me and Lyrra watched our rear.

Jogging through the passageways, we kept to the outer areas of the ship in order to avoid the majority of the crew. The ship seemed to stretch on forever. We navigated the passages, pausing frequently to place the explosive charges at the damage control hatchways. We also left a charge anytime we found a main power conduit or life support component. Dayena performed most of the work as her Class provided bonuses to sabotage activities, but we took turns supplying the detonator from Inventory.

Stacks of crates and other storage containers were stuffed in many of the corners beside long unused hatches and ladders. Some were left torn open, with scraps of packing materials littering the surrounding deck. The whole place felt poorly maintained and in need of a good cleaning, growing worse the farther aft we traveled toward the engineering spaces.

When a Sect technician suddenly stepped out of a crossway in front of us, Creynora sped up and her charge ability delivered a shield bash that threw the blue-skinned humanoid into the bulkhead. The stunned alien bounced off the wall and I opened fire with the silenced pistols. I squeezed off a half dozen shots before the dark elf eclipsed my view of the target, but she knocked the crew member from their feet before they could take any action.

Dayena slipped past me and pounced on the fallen alien, driving her short swords into the technician's neck and stomach. The crew member was dead in moments, and I stashed the corpse in Meat Locker. We continued on, leaving behind only a few spatters of purple blood on the deck to mark our passage.

We encountered a handful more lone crewmembers who were quickly dispatched, but twice we were forced to backtrack and find alternate routes when we detected larger groups. The alarms would get triggered eventually, but our chances were higher the closer we got to the bridge before that occurred.

A low beep preceded a burst of static crackling in my helmet as Johnson's comm signal punched through the mass of the freighter between us. "Friendly warning, we're about to go loud. We've gotten as close to the teleporter as we're going to get."

"Copy," I acknowledged before the soldier cut the transmission.

"Let's pick up the pace. The Army boys are about to get stuck in," I signaled through party chat.

No longer concerned with staying unnoticed, our footsteps pounded the decking as we rushed on.

"My translator has finished decoding the Sect compartment numbering. We need to go aft two more frames and down six decks, based on a damage control schematic we passed a couple intersections back," Lyrra said.

"Wait, they actually have the engineering near the exterior hull?" Dayena asked.

Creynora scoffed. *"This is a freighter, not a true warship. It is easier for maintenance work if they can just open up the hull and swap the larger components."*

"Then we'll have to make sure there's too much damage to fix," I said with a dark chuckle.

The passage lights flickered and turned red as a horn sounded in alarm, drowning out the sound of our footsteps. A harsh alien voice barked garbled words over a loudspeaker, but the steady drone of the alarm covered most of the transmission.

"In case it wasn't obvious, they just figured out they have boarders," Lyrra translated.

Creynora swung around a corner and launched herself through a hatch that led down an almost vertical stairway. Her boots caught a climbing Scrofalori crewmember. The blow to the snout tumbled him from the top steps of the ladder.

The dark elf grabbed hold of the hatch as she dropped, then swung herself over the prone crewmember. With the ladder clear, I jumped after her. My armored greaves drove into the alien's stomach, crushing the lower torso and sending bile spewing from the alien's mouth.

Creynora's shield slammed down on the boar-like alien's snout and crushed his head before he could recover. I quickly pulled the dead crewmember into Meat Locker, clearing the bottom of the ladder for Dayena and Lyrra to descend.

"One frame aft, five decks down," Lyrra called out and we took off once again.

More crew appeared the deeper we descended. The exclusively alien crew startled after spotting us and sealed the hatches behind them as they ran. We let them go, since none were armed and chasing after them would only slow us from reaching our target. With the boarding alarm still blaring, it wasn't like more alarms could trigger, but we dropped any crew that failed to clear our direct approach to engineering.

The passageway remained empty when we dropped down to the final deck and rushed the last stretch of the corridor, only to find that the double-wide hatch leading into the main engineering space was shut. Sealing the hatch showed that the crew here at least followed best practice for any potential hull breaches.

Dayena crouched at the hatch as the rest of us covered her from behind.

"The hatch is not locked down," the Countess reported.

The dark elf shook her head and reached up, placing another explosive above the point where the twin doors joined together. Then she allowed Creynora to replace her and the Darkheart Guardian deployed her shield before easing open the hatch.

Alien voices barked out within the compartment ahead, but our initial entry remained unnoticed as I joined Creynora.

The freighter's engine control room was a large compartment that stretched a dozen yards wide with two rows of terminals and sensor stations. Tall windows ran across the opposite side of the control center, offering a view out over the three decks of the engineering spaces.

Another Scrofalori stood at the rear of the compartment, this one with a bulging potbelly protruding from a poor-fitting burgundy jumpsuit. The alien's brown hair stuck out from beneath the fabric, obscuring most of the excessive amounts of gold braid that trimmed the collar and sleeves. The portly alien harangued the half dozen crew members in the engine control room, all of whom remained bent over their workstations as they focused on their duties in an attempt to avoid the ire of their commander.

Megevabat (Merchant Journeyman Engineer Level 21) (A)

[Binary Eclipse Sect]

HP: 330/330

MP: 3860/3860

Status: Replacement Parts, Efficient Engines, Well-oiled Machine

Nothing in the Merchant Engineer's status offered a hint of danger, but he still represented a threat while he remained in engineering. I opened fire on the Scrofalori as we advanced. My barrage shredded the alien's health pool, cutting off his shouts as the rest of my team fanned out around me.

Some of the crew spun at the abrupt interruption of the shouting, but it was too late. We couldn't risk leaving them alive any more than we could the Engineer.

Creynora and Dayena charged the nearest aliens as Lyrra and I raked precision fire over the crew farthest from the entrance. Screams of terror and pain cut off abruptly as they were silenced one by one, leaving us in control of the compartment.

I keyed my comm to signal Johnson. "We've got the engine control room. What is your status?"

"Under fire. Pinned by a security team, but we've shut down the teleporter. Setting charges."

The Staff Sergeant's breathless voice was filled with pain.

"Don't quit on me, Staff Sergeant. Can you hold?"

His silence told me the answer Johnson refused to put into words.

I shook my head. "Extract, if you can. We can do real damage from here."

"No promises. Starting the timers. You've got ten minutes," Johnson grunted, killing the signal.

Shit.

"Lyrra, find us an exit. The Army squad is starting the countdown on their detonators," I said, stepping over bodies as I looked over the terminals for the freighter's helm controls.

"Escape pod, right there." The elf pointed to the rear of the control room where faded red and yellow hazard stripes bordered a hatch. Hopefully, the maintenance on that was a little better than the rest of the ship.

"Now what?" Dayena asked.

I pointed to an engraved damage control schematic that highlighted the engineering spaces mounted on one wall. I couldn't read the labels, but I didn't need to when the colored images illustrated the components, and I indicated each in turn. *"Engines. Mana scoop. Mana batteries. Life support. Four targets, we destroy those and this ship is just a dead hunk of metal floating in space."*

Dayena headed for the door that led beyond the control room. *"No time to waste then. I have the engines."*

"Can we not just shut them all down from here?" Creynora asked as she and Lyrra followed her cousin.

I brought up the rear. *"No guarantee they couldn't make repairs. Set your charges and meet back here in no more than five minutes."*

The noise of working machinery and roaring engines flooded the control room when Dayena opened the hatch to the main engines, where we split up. The Countess jumped over the railing that lined the multi-level opening with the engines three levels below. The rest of us hurried to the stairs.

Down one level, Creynora headed into the life support section that ran forward from beneath the engineering control room. Lyrra and I descended to the second level before heading opposite ways. While the Movana targeted the scoop that aided the ship in collecting ambient Mana while traveling between the stars, I headed into the compartment holding the capacitors and batteries that stored the accumulated energy.

The power banks were massive boxy rectangles with rounded edges that bore faint resemblance to the batteries used by beam weaponry and vehicles. Just much, much larger. Dozens of the batteries ran in a row along the outside edge of the compartment, easily extending the length of a football field or more. Each battery stood taller than I did, even standing on the raised walkway that ran along the front of the mounted power cells. Cabling the thickness of my arm ran between each unit and into connectors in the overhead. Brightly colored warning labels across the power banks and the cables urged caution in an unknown language.

With the number of batteries and the size of the compartment, I wasn't sure I carried enough explosives. I wedged myself between the first pair of

Mana batteries. Squeezing my way to the cable connecting the units, I reached behind the obstruction and activated a breaching charge. The explosive sat squarely on the side of the first battery.

My hope was that the narrow space would lead the explosive to damage the second unit.

There wasn't much time, so I repeated my placement between the third and fourth batteries. The pattern continued as I raced down the line of power banks.

After placing a half dozen charges, two Sect crewmembers intercepted me on the walkway. One carried a wrench longer than my leg on his shoulder. The other pointed a beam pistol my way.

"Who are you? What are you doing here?" Three eyes protruded from on top of the alien's head, each extending from a short eyestalk that curved above a bucktoothed snout that resembled a beaver. The beam pistol it held in one hand tremored, the motion giving away the engineer's nerves.

I ignored the pistol. "Setting demolition charges. Run and you get to live for a few more minutes."

The two Sect crew members glanced at each other. Then the one carrying the wrench swung it at my face like a baseball bat.

I stepped away, drawing Last Word and Ace. No time remained for subtlety and the handcannons roared, the deafening sound almost a sonic attack in the enclosed compartment. Poorly aimed energy beams lanced around me as the wrench carrier's torso jerked. The alien dropped a few shots later and I turned my fire on the three-eyed wielder of the beam pistol. My mental clock continued to tick down as the second alien collapsed to the walkway, leaking green blood that dripped through the grating.

I no longer had enough time to hide the explosives. Instead, I dashed down the walkway. At Olympic sprinter pace, I activated a detonator and slapped the pack to the side of a power cell. Continuing to the next cell without breaking stride, I repeated the process the length of the compartment.

"Where are you, Hal? Your five minutes were up well over a minute ago," Dayena asked.

"On my way. Get the escape pod ready."

"We'll wreak a little havoc on the controls first," Lyrra added.

At the end of the batteries, I stuck one last det pack on the large bore conduit that extended into the bulkhead. Only two charges remained in my Inventory as I turned on my heel and sprinted back the way I'd come.

It took less than a minute to clear the distance back to the control room. Bursting through the door from the main engineering spaces, the hatch swung closed behind me. Weaving around the terminals toward the rear of the compartment, I only stopped long enough to loot the Merchant Engineer.

Stepping into the hatchway, I paused as a yell echoed through the compartment.

"Get the controls!"

The shout in Galactic started a clamor as the Sect naval security team rushed into the engine control room. With their attention focused on the carnage spread around the control terminals, the Sect crewmembers completely missed my presence at the rear of the compartment.

Two stocky Ceratophimi bounced off each other and the rear row of consoles as they lunged for the controls in the middle of the forward terminals and an instant calculation flashed through my mind. I considered the eight members of the security squad, my three elven companions already in the escape pod, how long a fight would take, and the rapidly depleting timer in my head.

Nearly eight minutes had already elapsed since Johnson started the countdown. I didn't think that the security team could disable enough charges to matter, but I couldn't take the chance.

Smacking the launch button for the escape pod, I jerked my arm clear of the hatch just before it snapped shut.

"Sorry," I sent through party chat, ignoring the responding shouts as the pod launched. The whoosh was the last cry of a dying animal, taking my friends and my escape with it.

Chapter 46

Alien heads jerked toward the sound as I stepped back onto the bridge with both arms in motion. Each flick of my wrist launched a plasma grenade, sowing the seeds of death amongst the Sect crewmembers as fast as I could pull them from my Inventory. My initial throw caught the leading rhino-like security trooper in the kidney and the alien crumpled around the surprise impact, staggering into the consoles.

The explosive detonated, lifting the alien from the controls and bathing the engineering stations in burning plasma. The subsequent grenades extended the arc of blue fire and spread the damage across the screaming security troopers.

The last pair of troopers evaded the worst of the blasts and charged at me across the rear of the engine control room. Tentacles waved from the mouth of the beige-skinned humanoid in the lead as the alien swung for me with a coppery two-handed boarding axe. I activated Hinder and dodged away in a spray of sparks that shot up as the weapon crashed into the deck.

Standing well back, the bronze-haired Movana pulled up and fired around his companion with a pair of wrist-mounted dart launchers. The barrage of toothpick-sized projectiles glanced off my Ice Armor before exploding, buffeting me with their detonations as I vaulted over the rear consoles.

Tentacle-face circled the row of terminals at a run, intending to flank me from the far side of the compartment instead of climbing over to follow me immediately. I took the opportunity to throw another pair of grenades toward the rest of the still-burning squad before drawing my pistols.

The roar of my handcannons drowned out the explosive hailstorm of the Movana's dart attack. The force of my own attacks drove the elf to retreat behind the double doors at the entrance rather than face the fusillade. The dart-launching elf took cover out of sight behind the hatch combing, and I spun to focus on the axe wielder.

Whilg Dod (Mad Harrier Level 19) (A)

HP: 324/680

MP: 356/440

Status: Steady Footing, Swirling Blade, Burning

The Harrier's first ability explained why Hinder hadn't slowed the alien much, but at least the plasma kept burning. The health ticking down from the burning effect plummeted faster as I opened up with my pistols. The tentacle-faced alien's torso jerked with each shot, but the Harrier still advanced despite the attacks.

My jump over the consoles to avoid the incoming fire put me in reach of my initial targets. With a roar, arms wreathed in blue flames extended from behind me and attempted to wrap me in a bear hug. I slipped from the clenching arms of one of the Ceratophimi and ducked around the burning alien, into a new barrage of exploding darts. My armor held, but the detonations sent me stumbling into the row of consoles.

Regaining my balance, I fired off a few shots at the entrance without looking and snapped a kick to the side of the rhino's knee. Bone cracked and the Ceratophimi collapsed, reducing that threat as I kept moving away. The bulky alien's fall obstructed tentacle-face's path and I continued firing Last Word at the Harrier.

A low rumble traveled through the ship and vibrated the deck plates underfoot, subtle at first but growing. I knew what was coming. I was out of time.

Ducking under a console and securing my weapons, I recast Ice Armor to bolster my defenses. An instant after I wedged myself in place, an eruption of fire caved in the engineering hatch. The roar of the explosion drowned out the brief scream from the Movana in the passageway.

Though I expected the explosion and braced, the heaving deck slammed me against the console above before tossing me out of my cover and into the maelstrom roaring through the engine control room. The flames stripped away the short-lived protection of Ice Armor and the temperature within my armor spiked.

Further explosions rumbled as the charges set throughout the engineering spaces detonated in sequence. One must have torn a hull breach, as the flames were sucked out of the control room in a rush of wind that flowed deeper into engineering.

Dust, debris, and charred body parts whirled around for several moments, but I just celebrated the lack of continued fire damage until the disturbances settled. An icon blinked on my helmet's visor, indicating the presence of a vacuum and the automated activation of stored oxygen.

I stood and a motion caught my eye. Crawling over the deck with hate-filled eyes locked onto me, the Harrier clung to life. The alien's mouth worked, unable to breathe. Only a few points of its health remained and blistered flesh sloughed off the alien's face, so a single shot from Ace finished the Harrier.

Before I could loot the dead alien, the overhead lights flickered and went out. Emergency lighting clicked on, much dimmer than the normal lighting. Then the emergency lights flickered too.

Right, we'd blown up the power systems. And life support.

Mission successful on turning the ship into a dying hunk of metal floating in space. Now I needed off of this ride without joining in the dying myself.

While my companions had taken the nearest escape pod, there should have been others. I would just have to find them.

Summoning a tactical light from my Inventory, I attached the finger-sized cylinder beneath the barrel of Ace. I left the light off for now, but I wanted it ready if needed. Instead, I activated the low-light vision feature of my helmet.

The flickering emergency lights offered more than enough illumination now and I looked around for any useful information. My gaze rested on the damage control layout engraved on the wall and I moved over for a better look.

A symbol in the engine control room clearly marked the location of the escape pod location, but there were no similar markers anywhere else in the engineering space. The damage control layout stretched farther than just the engineering areas, and I traced my finger along the passageway where we'd entered. I found the ladder where we dropped down to the engineering level and continued beyond.

After several hatches, I discovered another escape pod symbol at the edge of another large compartment. I nearly stopped there but knew better than to count on that pod still waiting there untouched. Surviving crew could have already reached it and departed.

The space just past the pod location appeared larger than engineering and showed several circular chutes that extended out the bottom of the ship. Launch tubes. The compartment was where the Sect drop pods launched. If I couldn't find an escape pod, riding one of the assault craft down to the surface seemed like a solid alternative.

I turned away from the diagram and found myself floating up from the deck. I drifted upward and realized that the failing power also meant the ship's artificial gravity was dying. A few seconds of drifting brought me to the overhead, and I pushed myself back down to the deck where I engaged the magnetic clamp feature on my boots.

Walking in zero gravity was certainly easier than fighting on the roof of a moving high-speed train.

I paused to loot the dead Harrier, then again to loot the corpse of the Movana in the dark passageway outside the compartment as I left the engine control room behind. With the hatches nearly ripped from their hinges, the cracked and twisted walls of the airless corridor showed off the damage from the demolition pack.

Standing in the hatchway, the emergency lights turned my outline into a lengthy shadow that stretched out in the passageway's only illumination. The lack of light somehow seemed to shrink the corridor and a shiver traveled down my spine at the idea of being trapped alone in the dark. I hated dark, enclosed spaces. They served as uncomfortable reminders of past failures. My heartbeat raced and my breath quickened.

I couldn't stay here. If my fear paralyzed me, I was as dead as the ship. Forcing myself into action, I took a step into the dark passage.

No sound traveled in a vacuum, so my footsteps were eerily silent as I traversed the corridor. The surreal feeling of hearing my breath within the helmet and yet nothing through my external helmet pickups left me unsettled. The farther I went, the fewer emergency lights remained on.

Flicking on the tac light affixed to Ace, I gave up on my helmet's low-light mode. The beam of light blazed through the corridor and helped me avoid the worst spots of damage. Broken pipes and bent conduits lay across the deck or hung tangled up in wiring torn from the overhead. I avoided the jagged bits of ductwork, carefully working around the obstructions in the passageway to avoid tearing my sealed jumpsuit. Any breach at this point would expose me to the vacuum that filled this section of the Sect freighter.

If that happened, I wouldn't have to worry about getting off the ship for long.

The indicator on my helmet display still showed my stored oxygen in the green, but the percentage ticked downward the farther I delved into the dead ship. I had no choice but to continue forward.

The destruction eased after I passed the ladder where my companions and I had reached this level earlier. The lack of debris allowed me to move faster, but my vigilance increased. Without the damage from the breaching charges, the likelihood grew that I would encounter Sect survivors. Just in case, I cast Ice Armor for extra protection.

Several times, I almost fired on floating shapes that appeared suddenly in the beam of my tac light from gloomy cross corridors or open hatches. The dead crew members hadn't equipped their vacuum gear in time. The near misses only served to remind me how much my nerves were affecting me.

I traveled the corridor between several frames, the evenly spaced ribs that supported the ship's hull, and discovered that the automatic hatches had failed to close in several areas. In a couple cases, random debris prevented the hatch from closing, but more often it seemed that the mechanism just failed to engage. I wasn't going to complain, not when each unsecured hatch brought me closer to the launch bay.

My oxygen indicator dipped lower, and I consciously suppressed my concern when it shifted to yellow just before I reached the location of the escape pod. Unsurprisingly, only an empty launch chute remained. The pod itself was long gone. Glad that I'd considered the possibility and still had options, I continued toward the launch bay.

It took prying my way through two more partially open hatches and bypassing a half dozen floating corpses before I reached the bay, where I discovered the first signs of living crew.

The clear plastic tent of a temporary airlock attached to the outside of the hatch led into the bay. A little trial and error got me into the tent, where I sealed the flap back up from the inside. A bottle of compressed air lay on the plastic-covered deck, and I triggered the cannister to replenish the atmosphere inside the airlock.

The hatch indicator turned green, presumably indicating that the hatch was safe to open. I stopped the air releasing from the cannister before returning the bottle to the deck. Not wanting to alert whoever might be on the other side to my presence, I switched off the tac light before cautiously opening the hatch.

Darkness loomed beyond as the door swung open, indicating that the power remained out here. Even if this section of the ship retained air for now, the fact that life support was out meant that the supply was limited. I closed the hatch gently, and the yellow oxygen symbol blinked out as my armor let me breathe from the ship's air.

Without my light, the launch bay appeared as a dark cavernous space. A hundred or so yards distant, a pair of yellow lights bobbed as they swept over the blocky teardrop shape of a drop pod. Whoever those remote figures were, I hoped they hadn't noticed my arrival.

I stalked across the otherwise pitch-black expanse of the launch bay, both pistols drawn and trained on the lights. The solid deckplates consisted of thick armor, and my boots weren't impacting hard enough to transmit any vibration. When I could make out the humanoid shapes of the two figures, I triggered Greater Observation to measure their threat.

Nexi Shivshift (Repair Technician Level 44) (B)
[Binary Eclipse Sect]
_HP: 510/510_
_MP: 229/760_
Status: Quick Wrench, Solid Weld

Uran Surrymer (Tech Foreman Level 26) (A)
[Binary Eclipse Sect]
_HP: 660/660_
_MP: 425/820_
Status: Overtime, Precise Calibration

Neither sported any combat gear, and their low Mana pools showed just how caught up they were in their work. They both wore magboots and complete vacuum suits that were sealed to their helmets. Whether they always did so or were just taking precautions, it seemed wise in a ship with failing life support.

"Let me finish one more weld sequence before you test hull integrity. This plate is almost done, but I'll still have the stabilizer fin to finish," Nexi, the shorter figure, spoke without looking up from a handheld device that traced a line of sparks across the surface of the battered drop pod. The nasal tones of the voice reminded me of the Gribbari goblins from Pittsburgh.

"That ssstabilizer is the last piece of the guidance sssystem. I wouldn't trust a combat drop with thisss thing, but it should get usss to the ground intact." Though humanoid, the taller figure of the Foreman talked like an animated snake from any number of cartoons.

"Can we still launch it?" Nexi asked.

"Isssolated sssystem. Enough power for one launch."

Now that I was closer, I could see that the parts of several damaged landing craft were strewn over the bay. The one where the two techs worked was being reassembled in a launch cradle over a circular hatch in the deck below. Seeing the display made sense of the Sect's tactics. Their forces had recovered broken pods in pieces and teleported them back up to the freighter in orbit to be repaired.

Without power to the ship or the teleporter, the Sect could no longer use that tactic. The ground battle would shift to a conventional fight. Or at least as conventional as things got under the System with magic and Skills involved.

That still left me stuck in orbit, but it seemed like the two techs here were almost finished with the repairs to the last available drop pod. The craft appeared whole but sported dents, charring, and melted streaks.

I slowed my approach and kept my distance beyond the dim radius of the work lights attached to the front of the tool harnesses worn by both techs. There was no advantage to making my presence known, at least until they were finished with the repairs, so I was content to wait.

"All done. Will it hold?" Nexi asked a few short minutes later.

Uran reached out to touch the side of the armored panel and the alien's head bobbed. "Yesss."

"Then let's get off this deathtrap. Taking my chances on a Dungeon World is better than waiting to suffocate." Nexi activated a recessed control and one of the panels lowered to form a ramp.

The two walked up the ramp. Neither noticed as I slipped up behind them, keeping a pistol pointed at each until I stepped into the pod. Both techs were already prepping harness rigs and strapping in for the drop when I figured it was time for introductions.

"If you don't mind, I'll be joining you for the trip planetside."

The two aliens turned toward me in shock, and I got a good look at the pair through the clear faceplates of their helmets. The shorter one was a green-skinned Gribbari, but I had no clue about the taller alien's species. Golden, slit-pupiled eyes stared at me from a face covered in tiny bronze scales.

Uran hissed from a mouth filled with far too many sharp teeth. "You. You are one of the sssaboteursss."

I nodded and waited to see what they would do. The pair exchanged glances after a long silence. Nexi shrugged and returned to fastening the drop harness. Uran looked back at me for another moment.

"Fine." The alien's arm shot out and smacked a button on the wall. The open ramp behind me shot up and slammed into place, sealing the drop pod. An instant later, the floor seemed to give way with a whoosh as the craft shot downward.

My magboots held me in place despite the sudden acceleration and I stared at Uran. The Foreman seemed surprised to see me still standing and I grinned at the snake-like alien.

The drop pod shook as it hit atmospheric turbulence. A display on the side of the pod listed altitude and external temperature. The temperature climbed as the altitude decreased, the effect of friction at orbital reentry. Physics still held some sway.

Thinking I had cowed the two non-combatants, I holstered my pistols and grabbed hold of a harness opposite the two aliens. I wasn't going to try to figure out the straps in free-fall, but I wanted more support than just my magboots.

"You killed far too many of my friendsss to let you live, human," Uran shouted over the turbulence that shook the drop pod.

"Uran, please don't do this. Let's just get to the surface," Nexi begged.

The serpentine alien ignored the goblin's pleas and its golden eyes remained fixated on me. "You killed my mate."

Instincts screaming, I released the harness and threw myself to the side as a shotgun appeared in the alien's hands. The weapon roared in the enclosed pod and the blast traveled over my diving body. The round pinged into the side of the pod, the sound of a bullet hitting a steel plate at a firing range. A very large bullet.

I rolled to my feet with pistols in hand and fired back at the alien. My shots tore through the thin material of its unarmored vacuum suit, stacking Rend as I applied Hinder for good measure.

Still strapped into the harness, Uran was a stationary target who struggled to keep the shotgun pointed at me. Between the restraints, the turbulence, and my own movements, the alien's next shot also missed. The tone of the impact was different, and a high-pitched whistling filled the inside of the landing craft. The round had punched through a weak point in the hull.

I needed to end this before we destroyed the pod from the inside. I triggered Kill Shot and fired again, obliterating the alien's chest and punching my own fist-sized hole in the opposite wall of the pod.

Oops.

The pod's shaking increased and unseen bits of metal began rattling. Several warnings on the altitude display flashed in red text, but any audible alarms were drowned out by the sound of tearing metal. One of the ramp panels shook loose, banging against the hull before giving way in a scream even louder than the goblin's shriek of terror.

The pod began to spin, slowly at first and then speeding up. The automated systems weren't correcting and I lost any faith that the craft could land in one piece now. Maybe a trained pilot could have manually recovered, but the goblin helplessly clutching the harness straps in terror wasn't making any moves.

Straining against the forces of the increasing spin, I crawled to the opening. It was large enough that I had no problem fitting through, though the real challenge was avoiding the worst of the jagged metal that could catch on my armor. Easing myself to the edge, I kicked hard to launch myself out into the open air.

The separation sent me twisting out of control. Pulling myself tight into a ball, I let gravity orient me in free fall. Then I popped out and pointed my belly toward the ground as I arched my back. The maneuver worked to stabilize my flight, eliminating the spin.

I found myself thousands of feet in the air, falling toward a body of water and a distant coastline below. I had no idea where exactly I was anymore but figuring that out was a problem for future Hal. Current Hal needed to survive the landing.

Deploying the energy barriers of my drop harness turned my fall into a wingsuit flight. Now that I had more control, I tracked toward the shoreline. Landing in water instead of on land offered a better chance at survival.

Faster than expected, the water grew closer. I steered myself a little further from shore and pulled up, attempting to stall out as I flared the wingsuit. It didn't work as well as my landing after my assassination mission.

I hit the white-crested waves feet first and the jarring impact knocked me from consciousness.

Chapter 47

"Warning. Oxygen level critical."

The drone of my armor's automated alarm dragged me back to consciousness and I jerked awake. I expected more pain but instead the stale air inside my helmet competed with the sluggish and heavy feeling of my arms for my immediate notice. My legs ached in the dull way that told me the bones were still healing from the damage of the landing.

"Warning. Oxygen level critical."

Opening my eyes, I saw light dancing across waves a few feet above my head. Being underwater explained the dragging as I moved my arms and the fact that the oxygen readout on my heads-up display flashed red. At least the armor held integrity and I hadn't drowned while unconscious.

"Warning. Oxygen level critical."

I growled, silencing the annoying alarm before attempting to push for the surface. Instead, I almost toppled over, finding both of my legs embedded to mid-calf in the sandy seafloor and confirming that I must have hit the water pretty damn hard.

The suit display flashed more urgently as I spent precious moments digging myself free of the silt that trapped me in place. Pushing off the seafloor, I dragged myself to the surface despite the weight of the armor threatening to pull me back down. Thank you, System, for the enhanced attributes.

After breaching the surface long enough to spot the shore, I sank down to the bottom and pushed off once more to launch myself in the right direction. I couldn't stay above the surface long enough for my armor to cycle in fresh air, but I managed to reach a sandbar where the water was only chest high and tugged off my helmet.

The salty ocean air flooded in as soon as I broke the seal, then the breeze washed over my face as the helmet lifted clear. I gasped for breath, inhaling deeply and luxuriating in the sensation of fresh air filling my lungs. The waves splashed and smacked against the lower part of my face, but I didn't care as I gulped down more precious oxygen.

I stood on the sandbar for several minutes while my breathing stabilized and then lingered while my suit replenished its oxygen reserves. When the armor reported full capacity once more, I replaced my helmet before plunging back into the deeper water for the trek to the sandy shore that remained dozens of yards distant.

After battling a riptide and a crab that erupted out of the seafloor, I finally reached the shore and crawled out onto the beach. I dragged myself clear of the waterline and then sprawled onto my back.

Closing my eyes, I rested for a moment and just listened to the crash of the waves. Several notifications pinged incessantly at the corner of my vision and I finally acknowledged them.

Bounty Completed!

Nesdyna Pistongrinder has terminated the bounty "Bring them in Cold" after the slaying of 63 Basic Class, 8 Advanced Class, and 2 Master Class members of the Binary Eclipse Sect by Hal Mason and party.
2,490,000 Credits and 5,000 XP Awarded
Bonus Objective: Disabling the Sect-owned heavy freighter "Ever Antumbra" and removing the Binary Eclipse Sect ability to teleport their forces around Denver.
1,000,000 Credits and 10,000 XP Awarded

My eyebrows shot up as I read the bounty completion. Ismyna certainly hadn't been joking when she said Nesdyna would pay well for that ship.

Now I just had to figure out how to split out the Credits to the rest of my party, but I could do that later. For now, I had one more notification waiting.

Level Up!

You have reached Level 47 as a Relentless Huntsman. Stat Points automatically distributed. You have 2 Free Attributes and 1 Class Skill Point to distribute.

That notification brought a smile since it had been a bit since my last Level. While tracking down and rescuing Dayena, I had been inching closer, but the retreat from Denver put a damper on any chance for quick advancement. The completed bounty finally pushed my experience the rest of the way there.

On the other hand, my party chat link seemed broken again. I suspected that I was the problem this time, rather than anything happening to the Countess. Dayena and the others went dark when they left the starship. Or rather, when I ejected their escape pod. I hoped that the issue was just me being beyond the range of her Skill, though the elves being upset with me felt like another distinct option.

I sat up and glanced around, spotting nothing but waves and sand along the beach in either direction. The lack of contact with my companions was concerning, but I had a bigger problem.

The firefight on the drop pod and falling without a parachute from the edges of the atmosphere had kept me preoccupied as I returned to Earth. I hadn't spared much attention for the surface below or landmarks beyond avoiding splattering onto the ground like a bug on a windshield. That left me with one question about my situation.

Where the hell had I ended up?

Epilogue

Footsteps echoed on the Miraxian marble floor as a dark elf entered an expansive office. A single panel of clear Ithicani shieldglass took up the entire exterior wall of the long room, providing a magnificent panorama over the beaches and docks of the seaside metropolis many stories below the tower. Even with rain pounding silently against the giant window as an unusually large storm swept across the bay, the vista remained remarkable. The view further complimented the splendor of the elegant furnishings throughout the office.

Each section of the room served a purpose, from the comfortable auto-conforming lounges and couches along the walls that were reserved for casual audiences, to the elegant desks and office fixtures dedicated to formal matters of state.

Like the polished marble floor and the expense of the massive window, almost every piece of furniture in the room could individually outfit an entire Advanced Class adventuring party. With Credits to spare.

As the duchy's adjutant, Dimintri Gaunis knew the enchantment causing his footsteps to echo throughout the room was just one of the more subtle defenses that protected his employer from the constant threat of assassination. The duke's oathsworn bodyguards monitored their liege and could appear inside the room in a moment, should any threat arise.

Not that the obsidian-skinned Truinnar sitting behind the desk at the end of the room needed to rely on others for his own protection. Lord Achyr Wesen, Duke of the Sun Jeweled Ocean, Hunter of Djevels, and Slayer of far too many species to summarize in any brevity, sat with his elbows on the armrests of a Sinythran velvet chair and his hands steepled beneath his chin. His gray eyes stormed like the clouds outside the office and observed Dimintri as the adjutant approached.

Beneath the shadow of that gaze, Dimintri unconsciously straightened his burgundy and white uniform as he reached the desk and then stood at attention before his liege.

"Report."

The single word came out in a clipped tone, bearing the authority of an elf used to commanding others and having those instructions followed instantly.

"The duchy is secure. All posts report that the weather seals are in place and will hold against the projected force of the hurricane. Supplies are distributed through the populace and shelters are provisioned throughout the city districts, should a breach occur. Response squads are prepared and on station, should any monster spawns breach during the storm surge."

Wesen nodded, expecting the response. "And what of the Baluisa matter?"

Dimintri shifted uncomfortably at the question but there was no point in hiding the answer. "They are still delaying the ceremony from moving forward."

The duke appeared unphased by the news and gestured for his aide to continue with the report.

"The family has provided numerous excuses but they're still avoiding any official acknowledgement that the girl has become a runaway. Despite the lack of official information from the Baluisas, our agents on the Dungeon World have provided a significant update in their latest report. It seems that the Countess has continued to resist the efforts to return her home, and the last skirmish resulted in the death of a Deputy Adjudicator at the hands of the girl's pet mercenary. The family has cut off her funds in response and posted a bounty for the death of her retainer."

Wesen sat up, his eyes flashing like the lightning in the storm raging outside the office and the duke grinned. "Excellent."

Dimintri failed to comprehend the sudden delight shown by his liege. "Your Grace?"

"The Countess is living up to the potential I saw in her all those years ago. Her efforts to increase her personal strength by braving a Dungeon World only show her worthiness. That she has inspired such loyalty in a retainer capable of spilling blood on her behalf is yet another mark in her favor. The pressure being applied by her family will only serve to continue her forging into a dangerous weapon, should she survive."

"That's why you arranged the match, your Grace?" Dimintri blinked in surprise. All of the quiet gossip between the Duke's staff shared the belief that the arrangement with the Baluisa family primarily involved finding a suitable beauty to adorn the arm of their liege with the added bonus of tying the two houses together with bonds of blood.

Wesen sighed, disappointed but clearly expecting the unspoken reasons for Dimintri's response. "Of course. I seek a worthy partner, one able to stand strong at my side, and not a trophy or a toy."

"I apologize for any assumptions, Your Grace." Dimintri bowed low.

"Come, my friend. There is no need for you to repent. Many in the courts have made the same erroneous assumption. Their lack of insight will only serve to benefit our future plans as they continue to underestimate the potential of my future partner in the Great Dance."

Dimintri nodded, finally seeing how far-reaching the threads of this particular plan had been spun out by the duke. "Do you believe that you can win the girl's favor and her good will to support your plans? She may resent you in addition to the hostilities she has displayed to her own family."

Wesen smiled and then stood, smoothing the elegant aracahni silk of his tunic. "I think the time has come to take matters into my own hands. Notify the flagship to prepare for departure. I shall see to the matter of my future bride myself."

#

**The adventures of Hal will continue in book 4
The Outlaw Harold Mason**

**www.starlitpublishing.com/products/
the-outlaw-harold-mason**

Glossary

Relentless Huntsman Skill Tree

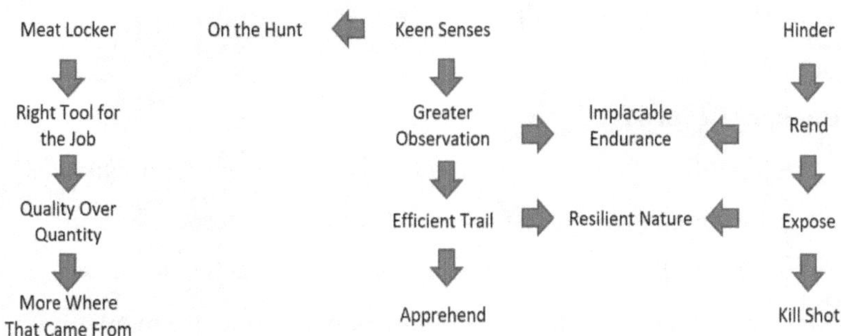

Hal's Relentless Huntsman Skills

Hinder (Level 2)

Effect: All physical movement by a designated target within 15 feet is significantly impaired for 1 minute.

Cost: 40 Stamina + 20 Mana.

Keen Senses (Level 1)

The user is more in tune with their body and more accurately interprets information gained from their surroundings. This manifests in the user as increases to vision, audition, gustation, olfaction, tactition, and proprioception. Mana regeneration reduced by 5 Mana per minute permanently.

On the Hunt (Level 5)

The Relentless Huntsman has a reduced System presence and increased ability to disguise their visible titles, class, level, and stats. Effectiveness is based on the user's Skill level and Charisma. Mana regeneration reduced by 25 Mana per minute permanently.

Meat Locker (Level 3)

Effect: The Relentless Huntsman now has access to an extra-dimensional storage location of 60 cubic feet. Only deceased bounty targets or slain creatures may be added to this location and must be touched to be willed inside. Mana regeneration reduced by 15 Mana per minute permanently.

Right Tool for the Job (Level 2)

Effect: The Relentless Huntsman now has access to an extra-dimensional storage location of 10 cubic feet. Items stored must be touched to be willed in and may only include weapons, armor, equipment, or supplies owned by the Relentless Huntsman. Any qualifying System-recognized item can be placed or removed from this inventory location if space allows. Cost: 5 Mana per item.

Greater Observation (Level 3)

Effect: User may now detect System creatures up to 100 meters away and is provided an analysis of the subject upon detection. Increased Skill levels may reveal additional System information not normally available. Depending on comparative overall level and Skills in effect, the target of focused Observation may know that the user has gained some level of information. Mana regeneration reduced by 15 Mana per minute permanently.

Rend (Level 1)

Effect: Physical weapon attacks that cause health damage apply a bleed effect, causing the target to bleed for 15 damage over 15 seconds. This effect can be stacked if the health damage occurs at a different location on the target.

Cost: 10 Stamina.

Implacable Endurance (Level 1)

Effect: Reduces Stamina cost for physical exertion and activated physical abilities by 25%. Does not stack with other Stamina reduction skills. Mana regeneration reduced by 5 Mana per minute permanently.

Expose (Level 1)

The Relentless Huntsman's consistent and methodical attacks continually weakens their target's defenses.

Effect: Damage applied to shields, armor, or defensive abilities applies an additional 2% damage to those defenses. This effect is cumulative and remains for one minute, with repetitive damage refreshing the cooldown. Should all defenses fail with this effect active, the damage bonus is reset but can be reapplied with continued attacks to the target and will then stack again until combat ends. Mana regeneration reduced by 5 Mana per minute permanently.

Efficient Trail (Level 1)

Effect: Environmental and terrain features present reduced difficulty to the user, allowing the user to cover distance more rapidly. Mana regeneration reduced by 5 Mana per minute permanently.

Resilient Nature (Level 2)

Effect: Increase natural health regeneration and reduce on-going health status effects by 10% respectively. Poison and disease resistance increased by 12%. Relentless Huntsman may now regenerate lost limbs. Mana regeneration reduced by 10 Mana per minute permanently.

Quality Over Quantity (Level 2)

Effect: Equipped gear is resistant to environmental and passive aura effects. Only direct damage to the item will cause durability loss so long as it remains equipped and may have durability loss repaired directly by the user actively channeling Mana. The user may also designate a soulbound Personal Weapon. Personal Weapons cause an additional 6% damage. Mana regeneration reduced by 10 Mana per minute permanently.

More Where That Came From (Level 1)

The Relentless Huntsman is now more efficient with their use of weapons, ammunition, and supplies, drawing directly from their stockpiled equipment in the heat of battle.

Effect: When a Relentless Huntsman fires a charge-based or ammunition-based weapon, the weapon magazine will automatically replenish itself from Inventory storage so long as that type of reload is available. Single use items summoned from storage (such as grenades, mines, and rockets) will be 25% more effective in strength. Designated Personal Weapons double the effect of this Skill. Mana regeneration reduced by 5 Mana per minute permanently.

Apprehend (Level 1)

On rare occasions, the Relentless Huntsman is assigned to bring in their prey warm instead of cold. This Skill ensures the target remains alive until they are brought to face their fate.

Effect: Creates Mana shackles on a target within line of sight from the user. Shackles restrict the target's movement, spell, and Skill usage. The user must specify how the shackles take form to restrain the target as part of Skill activation. Strength and durability of Mana shackles increases for each negative status effect on target at the time of casting. If the target is incapacitated at the time of casting, the strength and durability of the bonds are doubled. Shackles last for 4 hours.

Cost: 100 Mana.

Kill Shot (Level 9)

Sometimes, bringing the target in cold is the only way.

Effect: The Relentless Huntsman's next attack hits the target for 360% damage. This damage is increased by 5% for each debilitating effect or negative status on the target when the attack lands. This damage increases an additional three percent for each effect applied by the Relentless Huntsman.

Cost: 260 stamina + 130 Mana.

Other Class Skills

Blood Scent (Level 1)

Effect: Select a scent present in the current environment and follow any object or individual to which that scent clings.

Cost: 30 Mana per minute

Silver Fox Mimesis (Level 1)

Named for the pinnacle deity of the Ruidian kitsune pantheon, this Class Skill allows the user to alter their appearance nearly at will. While the outward characteristics of the user are mutable under the effect of this Skill, Attributes remain unchanged. At higher Levels, this Skill may even allow the user to mimic an entirely different species.

Effect: User may alter their physical form to change their outward appearance. This includes height, weight, bone structure, and muscle mass within 10% of their base form.

Cost: 100 Mana + Variable rate dependent on changes made.

Spells

Minor Healing (IV)

Effect: Heals 40 Health per casting.

Target must be in contact during healing. Cooldown 60 seconds.

Cost: 20 Mana.

Frostbolt (VI)

Effect: Creates a Frost bolt from the user's Mana, which can be directed to damage a target. The dart does 60 Ice damage and slows the target by 3%. Slow effect stacks up to three times (9%).

Cooldown 10 seconds.

Cost: 25 Mana.

Frostnova (IV)

Effect: Creates a ring of Frost from the user's Mana which blasts outward in a 5-meter radius centered on the user. The ring does 20 Ice damage and may affect enemies with a Freeze effect, rooting them in place for up to 8 seconds. Cooldown 30 seconds.

Cost: 50 Mana.

Lesser Disguise (VI)

Effect: Creates an illusory visage over the target of the spell that changes the target's appearance. The caster's familiarity with the desired form of the disguise increases effectiveness. The spell does not provide any abilities or mannerisms of the desire form, nor does it alter the perceived audible or tactile features of the target.

Cost: 115 Mana plus 10 Mana per minute to maintain the illusion.

Earth Spike (II)

Effect: A jagged spike of rock erupts from the ground beneath the target, causing 70 earth damage if it impacts the target. Cooldown 25 seconds.

Cost: 50 Mana.

Firespray (II)

Effect: Sprays a rushing stream of fire at the direction of the caster. Does 50 points of fire damage. Cooldown 60 seconds.

Cost: 60 Mana.

Continuous cast cost: 5 Mana / sec

Greater Healing (I)

Effect: Heals 75 Health per casting. Target does not require contact during healing. Cooldown 60 seconds per target

Cost: 50 Mana.

Greater Regeneration (I)

Effect: Increases natural health regeneration of target by 5%. Only a single use of this spell may affect a target at a time. Cooldown 120 seconds.

Duration: 10 minutes

Cost: 100 Mana.

Minor Renew (II)

Effect: Heals 1 Health per second for 30 seconds. Only single use of spell effective on a target at a time. Target must be in contact during healing. Cooldown 80 seconds.

Cost: 15 Mana.

Ice Armor (I)

Effect: Creates a suit of armor made of ice. While cold to the touch, it does not harm the wearer, especially if applied over clothing or armor. Armor has 500 Hit Points.

Cost: 125 Mana.

Ice Armor may be enhanced by using the Elemental Affinity of Ice. Armor durability increased by 10% per level of affinity.

Whiteout (I)

Effect: Covers a 10-meter radius area with chilling frost and fills the affected zone with frozen fog, dealing 5 cold damage per second to hostile targets within the spell's area of effect and decreasing visibility for affected targets.

Duration: 1 minute.

Cost: 50 Mana.

Whiteout may be enhanced by using the Elemental Affinity of Ice. Duration and coverage area increased by 20% per level of affinity.

Howling Blast (I)

Effect: Effect: Blasts out a cone of frigid wind from the caster, dealing 100 cold damage to all enemies within the cone out to a range of 10 meters. Targets taking damage from this spell are knocked back 1 meter from the force of the gust. Cooldown: 60 seconds.

Cost: 75 Mana.

Howling Blast may be enhanced by using the Elemental Affinity of Ice. Damage and knockback distance increased by 20% per level of affinity.

Greater Disguise (I)

Effect: Creates an illusory visage over the target of the spell that changes the target's appearance. The caster's familiarity with the desired form of the disguise increases effectiveness. While the spell does not provide any abilities or mannerisms of the desire form, the spell visage provides corresponding audible and tactile features of the target.

Cost: 250 Mana plus 20 Mana per minute to maintain the illusion.

Equipment

Silversmith Mark II Beam Pistol (Upgradeable)

Base Damage: 18

Battery Capacity: 24/24

Recharge Rate: 2 per hour per GMU

Luxor Series III Projectile Pistol

Base Damage: N/A (Dependent Upon Ammunition)

Ammo Capacity: 12/12

Ammunition Types: Standard, Armor Piercing, High Explosive, Tracer, Hollow Point

Tier II Knife (Soulbound Personal Weapon of a Relentless Huntsman)

Base Damage: 40

Durability: NA (Personal Weapon)

Special Abilities: Recall

Tier III Hand-axe

Base Damage: 25

Durability: 200/200

Special Abilities: None

Banshee II Gauss Hybrid Rifle

Base Damage: N/A (Dependent Upon Ammunition)

Ammo Capacity: 18/18

Battery Capacity: 40/40

Recharge Rate: 4 per hour per GMU

Cost: 5,400 Credits

Rudianos Class I Outrider

Core: Class I Hephaestus-II Mana Engine

CPU: Class B Xylik Core CPU

Armor Rating: Tier I

Hard Points: 6 (4 Used: Nano Garage Module, Anti-Grav Module, Forward-facing Twin-cannon Mount, Micro-missile Launcher)

Soft Points: 4 (2 Used: Neural Link, Comm-transmitter)

Optional: Neural Link for Remote Activation

Battery Capacity: 150/150

Tier V Neural Link

Neural link may support up to 4 connections.

Current connections: Rudianos Class IV Outrider

Software Installed: Rich'lki Fire-wall Class IV, Rudianos Class V Controller

Ace (Tier I Projectile Pistol)

The twin enchantments worked into the frame of this hand cannon by Maestro Gunsmith Syx Cayde provide a minor enhancement to the wielder's reload speed and additional shield penetration to any ammunition fired through this weapon.

Base Damage: N/A (Dependent Upon Ammunition)

Ammo Capacity: 12/12 (Standard cylinder-style magazine)

Effect: +12% Energy Shield Penetration, +10% Reload Speed

Last Word (Tier I Projectile Pistol)

Customized by Master Armscrafter Malphyr, the enchantments engraved into the body of this hand cannon are guaranteed to deliver the final statement in any firefight with increased armor penetration added to any ammunition fired through this weapon.

Base Damage: N/A (Dependent Upon Ammunition)

Ammo Capacity: 12/12 (Standard cylinder-style magazine)

Effect: +15% Armor Penetration

Elysian Drop Harness Mk. IV (Modified)

This shoulder rig began life as a standard grav-chute issued to a member of the Elysian Home Guard. The air-mobile troopers of the Guard are known for lightning-fast deployments and guerilla attacks behind enemy lines. This particular harness was customized by a Guard trooper to carry twin pistols into battle and was promptly disposed of as surplus after the non-regulation modifications were discovered by a superior officer.

Hastati-VI Launcher Control System

This reusable launcher control system is the targeting and trigger unit for the two-part Hastati-VI Modular Missile System. When paired with the single-use MMS disposable firing tubes, the launcher control system allows the user to designate the appropriate target for the type of missile indicated by the color code on the MMS housing:

Red - Anti-monster Plasma Ignitor

Yellow - Anti-vehicle Armor Penetrator

Blue- Anti-shield Disruptor

Green - Anti-personnel Cluster Munitions

Brumwell Necklace of Anonymity

While the Brumwell Necklace of Shadow Intent is the hallmark item of the Brumwell Clan, this lesser trinket is still the work of a high-tier Journeyman. Constructed as part of the Journeyman transition to a Master Crafter, the Clan's signature enchantments work to layer the wearer with a shroud of anonymity. This shroud prevents any Titles or Class Features from being identifiable on casual examination. Often used by nobles out for a night on the town, this trinket is perfect for illicit affairs and back-alley dealing.

Effect: Persistent effect of Anonymity (Level 3) results in the shrouding of any titles displayed by the wearer, but also disables any status effects provided by shrouded titles. Effect is persistent in hiding all titles while necklace is worn.

Tyrfing Semi-Powered Assault Armor

Designed for surviving the rigors of a Dungeon World by a team of human game-designers-turned-engineers and crafted by a Gimsar Master Armorsmith of the Ares Corporation, this exoskeleton is the perfect fit for human combatants seeking to increase durability without sacrificing mobility. The suit is specially augmented to take advantage of the high Mana density on Earth, allowing the Core to combine ambient Mana collection with the movements of the wearer to power the battlesuit's motion and provide limited shield regeneration. When used in conjunction with most standard adventurer coveralls, the battlesuit is able to seal for use in toxic environments or extra-vehicular activity in a vacuum.

Core: Class III Blam Physics Mana Engine

CPU: Class D Roland Core CPU

Armor Rating: Tier III

Hard Points: 6 (5 Used - ProTek Grappler G4, Promethium II Wrist Flame-Projector, Modified Elysian Drop Harness, CMN, Ares Type IV Shield Generator)

Soft Points: 3 (1 Used - Neural Link)

Battery Capacity: 180/180

Authors' Note

I hope that you've enjoyed this continuation of Hal's adventure through the System Apocalypse universe.

I also want to thank Tao again for letting me play in his sandbox and explore the world that John Lee left behind here on Earth.

If you enjoyed your time with Hal, or even if you didn't, please leave a review or rating to let Amazon know what you think!

~Craig

About the Authors

Craig Hamilton spends most of his day as a technical sales engineer, translating specifications and talking about IT infrastructure. While writing has been taking up most of his free time lately, Craig also appreciates playing tabletop RPGs or board games with friends. When his inner introvert demands a break from polite company, Craig can be found sprawled on a couch with a book or e-reader.

Want to know more on what Craig is doing, follow him on his Author Page: www.facebook.com/AuthorCraigHamilton

Tao Wong is a Canadian author based in Toronto who is best known for his System Apocalypse post-apocalyptic LitRPG series and A Thousand Li, a Chinese xianxia fantasy series. His work has been released in audio, paperback, hardcover and ebook formats and translated into German, Spanish, Portuguese, Russian and other languages. He was shortlisted for the UK Kindle Storyteller award in 2021 for his work, A Thousand Li: the Second Sect. When he's not writing and working, he's practicing martial arts, reading and dreaming up new worlds.

Tao became a full-time author in 2019 and is a member of the Science Fiction and Fantasy Writers of America (SFWA) and Novelists Inc.

If you'd like to support Tao directly, he has a Patreon page - benefits include previews of all his new books, full access to series short stories, and other exclusive perks. www.patreon.com/taowong

Want updates on upcoming deluxe editions and exclusive merch? Follow Tao on Kickstarter to get notifications on all projects. www.kickstarter.com/profile/starlitpublishing

For updates on the series and his other books (and special one-shot stories), please visit his website. www.mylifemytao.com

Subscribers to Tao's mailing list to receive exclusive access to short stories in the Thousand Li and System Apocalypse universes.

About the Publisher

Starlit Publishing is wholly owned and operated by Tao Wong. It is a science fiction and fantasy publisher focused on the LitRPG & cultivation genres. Their focus is on promoting new, upcoming authors in the genre whose writing challenges the existing stereotypes while giving a rip-roaring good read.

For more information on Starlit Publishing, early access to books and exclusive stories visit our webshop! www.starlitpublishing.com

You can also join Starlit Publishing's mailing list to learn about new, exciting authors and book releases.

www.starlitpublishing.com/newsletter-signup

For more great information about LitRPG series, check out these Facebook groups:

- GameLit Society

    www.facebook.com/groups/LitRPGsociety

- LitRPG Books

    www.facebook.com/groups/LitRPG.books

- Fantasy Nation

    www.facebook.com/groups/TheFantasyNation

- LitRPG Legion

    www.facebook.com/groups/litrpglegion

A Thousand Li: the First Step

Deluxe Edition

Mark your calendars for April 2024 as *A Thousand Li: the First Step* is getting a deluxe edition to celebrate the series' five-year anniversary!

Don't want to miss the launch of this one-of-a-kind edition?

Sign up for notifications on Starlit Publishing.

www.starlitpublishing.com/products/the-first-step-deluxe-edition

System Apocalypse: Kismet

Not everyone falls during an apocalypse. Some rise to the occasion.

For Fool and Jackal, the System Apocalypse was a chance to start again. A chance to rise, and be who they were meant to be.

Now, they're trying to offer others the same opportunities as part of a secret organization helping humanity survive the System.

Today's mission? Nothing big, just your typical save-the-princess quest.

But when you're the Acolyte of a Trickster god, typical is the last thing you should expect.

Just ask Fool's cat.

Fool's Play is the first book in a new series in the System Apocalypse universe. Written by David R. Packer in Tao Wong's bestselling post-apocalyptic LitRPG universe, *System Apocalypse: Kismet* follows a different path through a post-apocalyptic world, one of hope, redemption, and second chances.

Check out this new spinoff series Fool's Play.

www.starlitpublishing.com/products/fools-play

To learn more about LitRPG, talk to authors including myself, and just have an awesome time, please join the LitRPG Group!

www.facebook.com/groups/LitRPGGroup